The door gave way under her hand and Pauline was caught in the
arms of De Blenau.   Page 239.

Frontispiece.   *Richelieu.*

❧ RICHELIEU ❧

A Tale of France in the Reign of King Louis XIII

By G. P. R. JAMES

Author of "Darnley," "Ticonderoga,"
"Mary of Burgundy," etc.

"I advise you that you read
The Cardinal's malice and his potency
Together ; to consider further, that
What his high hatred would effect, wants not
A minister in his power."

SHAKESPEARE.

WITH FOUR PAGE ILLUSTRATIONS
By J. WATSON DAVIS

H. L. Burt Company, ❧ ❧ ❧
❧ ❧ ❧ Publishers, New York

RICHELIEU.

CHAPTER I.

Which shows what a French forest was in the year of our Lord 1642, and by whom it was inhabited.

THE vast Sylva Lida which, in the days of Charlemagne stretched far along the banks of the Seine, and formed a woody screen round the infant city of Paris, has now dwindled to a few thousand acres in the neighborhood of St. Germain-en-Laye. Not so in the time of Louis the Thirteenth. It was then one of the most magnificent forests of France, and extending as far as the town of Mantes, took indifferently the name of the Wood of Mantes, or the Forest of Laye. That portion to the north of St. Germain has been long cut down: yet there were persons living, not many years since, who remembered some of the old trees still standing, bare, desolate, and alone, like parents who had seen the children of their hopes die around them in their prime.

In the heart of the wood, at that point where two roads divaricated from each other, stood the hut of a woodman, and the *abreuvoir* where many a gay lord of the court would stop when his hunting was over, and give his horse time to drink. There, too, many a traveller would pause to ask his way through the forest; so that Philip, the woodman, and his young family, were known to almost all whom business or pleasure brought through the wood of Mantes.

It was at that season of the year when the first leaves

1

of summer begin to leave the branches from which they sprang, like the bright and tender hopes of early years, that fade and fall before the autumn of life has fully commenced. The sun had abated but little of his force, and the days scarcely seemed to have contracted their span.

Philip, the woodman, humming the air of *Le bon roi Dagobert,* advanced slowly along the road, with his brow knit in such a manner as to evince that his light song had no part in his thoughts. He was a man perhaps nearly fifty, still hale and athletic, though a life of labor had changed the once dark locks of his hair to gray. His occupation was at once denoted by his dress, which consisted simply of a long-bodied blue coat of coarse cloth, covered over, except the arms, with what it is called in Brittany, a *Peau de bicque,* or goat-skin: a pair of leather breeches, cut off above the knee, with thick gaiters to defend his legs from the thorns, completed his dress below; and a round broad-brimmed hat was brought far over his eyes, to keep them from the glare of the declining sun. His apparel was girded round him by a broad buff belt, in the left of which hung his woodman's knife; in the right he had placed the huge ax, which he had been using in his morning's occupation: and thus accoutred, Philip would have been no insignificant opponent, had he met with any of those lawless rovers who occasionally frequented the forest.

As he approached his dwelling, he suddenly stopped, broke off his song, and turning round, listened for a moment attentively; but the only noise to be heard was the discordant cry of the jay in the trees round about.

Philip proceeded, but he sang no more; and opening the cottage door, he spoke without entering. " Charles," demanded he, " has the young gentleman returned, who passed by this morning to hunt? "

" No, father," answered the boy coming forward; " nobody has passed since you went—I am sure no one has, for I sat on the old tree all the morning, carving you a sun-

dial out of the willow branch you brought home yesterday;" and he drew forth one of those ingenious little
machines, by means of which the French shepherds tell
the time.

"Thou art a good boy," said his father, laying his hand
on his head, "thou art a good boy." But still, as the
woodman spoke, his mind seemed occupied by some
anxiety, for again he looked up the road and listened.
"There are strange faces in the forest," said Philip, not
exactly soliloquizing, for his son was present, but certainly
speaking more to himself than to the boy. "There are
strange faces in the forest, and I fear me some ill deed is
to be done. But, here they come, thank God!—No! what
is this?"

As he spoke, there appeared, just where the road
turned into the wood, a sort of procession, which would
have puzzled any one of later days, more than it did
the woodman. It consisted of four men on horseback,
and four on foot, escorting a vehicle, the most elegant and
tasteful that the age produced. It was more like a
state carriage than any other; broad at the top, low in
the axle, all covered over with painting and gilding, with
long wooden shafts for the horses, and green taffeta curtains to the windows.

When the carriage arrived at the *abreuvoir,* by the side
of which Philip had placed himself, the footman took the
bridles from the horses' mouths to give them drink, and
a small white hand, from within, drew back the taffeta
curtain, displaying to the woodman one of the loveliest
faces he had ever beheld. The lady looked round for a
moment at the forest scene, in the midst of whose wild
ruggedness they stood, and then raised her eyes towards
the sky, letting them roam over the clear deepening ex-
panse of blue, as if to satisfy herself how much daylight
still remained for their journey.

"How far is it to St. Germain, good friend?" said she,
addressing the woodman, as she finished her contempla-

tions; and her voice sounded to Philip like the warble of a bird, notwithstanding a slight peculiarity of intonation, which more refined ears would instantly have decided as the accent of Roussillon, or some adjacent province.

"I wish, Pauline, that you would get over that bad habit of softening all your syllables," said an old lady who sat beside her in the carriage. "Your French is scarcely comprehensible."

"Dear mamma!" replied the young lady playfully, "am not I descended lineally from Clemence Isaure, the patroness of song and chivalry? And I should be sorry to speak aught but my own *langue d'oc*—the tongue of the first knights and first poets of France.——But hark! what is that noise in the wood?"

"Now help, for the love of God!" cried the woodman, snatching forth his axe, and turning to the horsemen who accompanied the carriage; "murder is doing in the forest. Help, for the love of God!"

But as he spoke, the trampling of a horse's feet was heard, and in a moment after, a stout black charger came down the road like lightning; the dust springing up under his feet, and the foam dropping from his bit.

Half falling from the saddle, half supported by the reins, appeared the form of a gallant young cavalier; his naked sword still clasped in his hand, but now fallen powerless, and dragging by the side of the horse; his head uncovered and thrown back, as if consciousness had almost left him, and the blood flowing from a deep wound in his forehead, and dripping amongst the thick curls of his dark brown hair.

The charger rushed furiously on; but the woodman caught the bridle as he passed, and with some difficulty reined him in; while one of the footmen lifted the young gentleman to the ground, and placed him at the foot of a tree.

The two ladies had not beheld this scene unconcerned: and were descending from the carriage, when four or five servants in hunting livery were seen issuing from the wood at the turn of the road, contending with a very superior party of horsemen, whose rusty equipments and wild anomalous sort of apparel, bespoke them free of the forest by not the most honorable franchise.

"Ride on, ride on!" cried the young lady to those who had come with her: "Ride on and help them;" and she herself advanced to give aid to the wounded cavalier, whose eyes seemed now closed forever.

He was as handsome a youth as one might look upon: one of those forms which we are fond to bestow upon the knights and heroes that we read of in our early days. The young lady, whose heart•had never been taught to regulate its beatings by the frigid rules of society, or the sharp scourge of disappointment, now took the wounded man's head upon her knee, and gazed for an instant upon his countenance, the deadly paleness of which appeared still more ghastly from the red streams that trickled over it from the wound in his forehead. She then attempted to stanch the blood, but the trembling of her hands defeated her purpose, and rendered her assistance but of little avail.

The elder lady had hitherto been giving her directions to the footmen, who remained with the carriage, while those on horseback rode on towards the fray. "Stand to your arms, Michel!" cried she. "You take heed to the coach. You three, draw up across the road, each with his arquebuse ready to fire. Let none but the true men pass.—Fie! Pauline; I thought you had a firmer heart," she continued, approaching the young lady, "give me the handkerchief.—That is a bad cut in his head, truly: but here is a worse stab in his side." And she proceeded to unloose the gold loops of his hunting-coat, that she might reach the wound. But that action seemed to recall, in a degree, the senses of the wounded cavalier.

"Never! never!" he exclaimed, clasping his hand upon his side, and thrusting her fingers away from him, with

no very ceremonious courtesy,—"never, while I have
life."

"I wish to do you no harm, young sir, but good," replied the old lady;—"I seek but to stop the bleeding of
your side, which is draining your heart dry."

The wounded man looked faintly round, his senses still
bewildered, either by weakness from loss of blood, or
from the stunning effects of the blow on his forehead.
He seemed, however, to have caught and comprehended
some of the words which the old lady addressed to him,
and answered them by a slight inclination of the head,
but still kept his hand upon the breast of his coat, as if
he had some cause for wishing it not to be opened.

The time which had thus elapsed more than sufficed
to bring the horsemen who had accompanied the carriage
(and who, as before stated, had ridden on before) to the
spot where the servants of the cavalier appeared contending with a party, not only greater in number, but superior
in arms.

The reinforcement which thus arrived, gave a degree
of equality to the two parties, though the freebooters
might still have retained the advantage, had not one of
their companions commanded them, in rather a peremptory manner, to quit the conflict. This personage, we
must remark, was very different, in point of costume,
from the forest gentry with whom he herded for the time.
His dress was a rich livery suit of * Isabel and silver; and
indeed he might have been confounded with the other
party, had not his active co-operation with the banditti
(or whatever they might be) placed the matter beyond
a doubt.

Their obedience, also, to his commands showed, that if
he were not the instigator of the violence we have described, at least his influence over his lawless companions
was singularly powerful; for at a word from him they
drew off from a combat in which they were before en-

* A yellowish-gray, or grayish-buff color; a certain shade of drab.—(*Ed.*)

gaged with all the hungry fury of wolves eager for their
prey; and retreated in good order up the road, till its
windings concealed them from the view of the servants
to whom they had been opposed.

These last did not attempt to follow, but turning their
horses, together with those who had brought them such
timely aid, galloped up to the spot where their master lay.
When they arrived, he had again fallen into a state of
apparent insensibility, and they all flocked round him with
looks of eager anxiety, which seemed to speak more
heartfelt interest than generally existed between the murmuring vassal and his feudal lord.

One sprightly boy, who appeared to be his page, sprang
like lightning from the saddle, and kneeling by his side,
gazed intently on his face, as if to seek some trace of
animation. "They have killed him!" he cried at length,
"I fear me they have killed him!"

"No, he is not dead," answered the old lady; "but I
wish, Sir Page, that you would prevail on your master to
open his coat, that we may stanch that deep wound in
his side."

"No, no! that must not be," cried the boy quickly;
"but I will tie my scarf round the wound." So saying,
he loosed the rich scarf of blue and gold, that passing
over his right shoulder crossed his bosom till it nearly
reached the hilt of his sword, where, forming a large knot,
it covered the bucklings of his belt. This he bound tightly
over the spot in his master's side from whence the blood
flowed; and then asked thoughtfully, without raising his
eyes, "But how shall we carry him to St. Germain?"

"In our carriage," said the young lady; "we are on
our way thither, even now."

The sound of her voice made the page start, for since
his arrival on the spot he had scarcely noticed any one but
his master, whose dangerous situation seemed to occupy
all his thoughts: but now there was something in that
sweet voice, with its soft Languedocian accent, which

awakened other ideas, and he turned his full sunny face towards the lady who spoke.

"Good heavens!" exclaimed she, as that glance showed her a countenance not at all unfamiliar to her memory: "is not this Henry de La Mothe, son of our old farmer Louis?"

"No other, indeed, Mademoiselle Pauline," replied the boy; "though, truly, I neither hoped nor expected to see you at such a moment as this."

"Then who"—demanded the young lady, clasping her hands with a look of impatient anxiety—"in the name of heaven, tell me who is this?"

For an instant, and but for an instant, a look of arch meaning played over the boy's countenance; but it was like a flash of lightning on a dark cloud, lost as quickly as it appeared, leaving a deep gloom behind it, as his eye fell upon the inanimate form of his master. "That, madam," said he, while something glistened brightly, but sadly, in his eye, "that is Claude, Count de Blenau."

Pauline spoke not, but there was a deadly paleness come upon her face, which very plainly showed how secondary a feeling is general benevolence, compared with personal interest.

"Is it possible?" exclaimed the elder lady, her brow darkening thoughtfully. "Well, something must be done for him."

The page did not seem particularly well pleased with the tone in which the lady spoke, and, in truth, it had betrayed more pride than compassion.

"The best thing that can be done for him, Madame la Marquise," answered he, "is to put him in the carriage and convey him to St. Germain as soon as possible, if you should not consider it too much trouble."

"Trouble!" exclaimed Pauline; "trouble! Henry de La Mothe, do you think that my mother or myself would find anything a trouble that could serve Claude de Blenau in such a situation?"

"Hush, Pauline!" said her mother. "Of course we shall be glad to serve the count—Henry, help Michel and Regnard to place your master in the carriage. Michel, give me your arquebuse; I will hold it till you have done. Henry, support your master's head."

But Pauline took that post upon herself, notwithstanding a look from the marchioness, if not intended to forbid, at least to disapprove. The young lady, however, was too much agitated with all that had occurred to remark her mother's looks, and following the first impulse of her feelings, while the servants carried him slowly to the carriage, she supported the head of the wounded cavalier on her arm, though the blood continued to flow from the wound in his forehead, and dripped amidst the rich slashings of her Spanish sleeves, dabbling the satin with which it was lined.

"Oh, mademoiselle!" said the page, when their task was accomplished, "this has been a sad day's hunting. "But if I might advise," he continued, turning to the marchioness, "the drivers must be told to go with all speed."

"Saucy as a page!" said the old lady, "is a proverb, and a good one. Now, Monsieur La Mothe, I do not think the drivers must go with all speed; for, humbly deferring to your better opinion, it would shake your master to death."

The page bit his lip, and his cheek grew somewhat red, in answer to the high dame's rebuke, but he replied calmly, "You have seen, madam, what has happened to-day, and depend on it, if we be not speedy in getting out of this accursed forest, we shall have the same good gentry upon us again, and perhaps in greater numbers. Though they have wounded the count, they have not succeeded in their object; for he has still about him that which they would hazard all to gain."

"You are in the right, boy," answered the lady; "I was over hasty. Go in, Pauline. Henry, your master's horse must carry one of my footmen, of whom the other three can mount behind the carriage—thus we shall go quicker. You, with the count's servants, mix with my horsemen, and keep close round the coach; and now bid them on, with all speed." Thus saying, she entered the vehicle; and the rest having disposed themselves according to her orders, the whole cavalcade was soon in motion on the road to St. Germain.

CHAPTER II.

In which new characters are brought upon the stage, and some dark hints given respecting them.

Two grand objects fully occupied the mind of that famous minister, the Cardinal de Richelieu (who then governed the kingdom with almost despotic sway) : the prosecution of those mighty schemes of foreign policy which at the time shook many a throne, and in after-years changed more than one dynasty; and the establishment of his own power at home, which, threatened by factions, and attacked by continual conspiracies, was supported alone by the terror of his name, and the favor of a weak and irresolute monarch. These more immediate calls upon his attention gave him but little time to regulate the long-neglected police of the country; and, indeed, it was whispered that Richelieu not only neglected, but knowingly tolerated many of the excesses of the times, the perpetrators of which were often called upon to do some of those good services which statesmen occasionally require of their less circumspect servants. It was said, too, that scarce a forest in France but sheltered a band of these free rovers, who held themselves in readiness to merit pardon for their other offences, by offending in the State's behalf whenever it should be demanded, and in the meantime took very sufficient care to do those things on their own account for which they might be pardoned hereafter.

We may suppose then, it rarely happened that travellers chose that hour for passing through the wood of Mantes, and that those who did so were seldom of the best description. But on the night I speak of, two horsemen wound slowly along the road towards the cottage of the woodman, with a sort of sauntering, idle pace, as if thoughtless of danger, and entirely occupied in their own conversation.

They were totally unattended also, although their dress bespoke a high station in society, and by its richness might have tempted a robber to inquire farther into their circumstances. Both were well armed with pistol, sword, and dagger, and appeared as stout cavaliers as ever mounted horse, having, withal, that air of easy confidence, which is generally the result of long familiarity with urgent and perilous circumstances.

Having come near the *abreuvoir*, one of the two gave his horse to drink without dismounting, while the other alighted, and taking out the bit, let his beast satisfy its thirst at liberty. As he did so, his eye naturally glanced over the ground at the foot of the tree. Something caught his attention; and stooping down to examine more closely, " Here is blood, Chavigni ! " he exclaimed; " surely, they have never been stupid enough to do it here, within sight of this cottage."

" I hope they have not done it at all, Lafemas," replied the other. " I only told them to tie him, and search him thoroughly; but not to give him a scratch, if they could avoid it."

" Methinks thou hast grown mighty ceremonious of late, and somewhat merciful, Master Chavigni," replied his companion. " I remember the time when you were not so scrupulous. Would it not have been the wiser way to have quieted this young plotter at once, when your men had him in their hands? "

" Thou wert born in the Faubourg St. Antoine, I would swear, and served apprenticeship to a butcher," replied Chavigni. " Why, thou art as fond of blood, Lafemas, as if thou hadst sucked it in thy cradle ! Tell me, when thou wert an infant Hercules, didst thou not stick sheep, instead of strangling serpents? "

" Not more than yourself, lying villain ! " answered the other in a quick deep voice, making his hand sound upon the hilt of his sword. "Chavigni, you have taunted me all along the road; you have cast in my teeth things that you yourself caused me to do. Beware of yourself! Urge me not too far, lest you leave your bones in the forest!"

"Pshaw, man! pshaw!" cried Chavigni, laughing. "Here's a cool-headed judge! Here's the calm, placid Lafemas! Here's the cardinal's gentle hangman, who can condemn his dearest friends to the torture with the same meek look that he puts on to say grace over a Beccafico, suddenly metamorphosed into a bully and a bravo in the wood of Mantes.—But hark ye, Sir Judge!" he added, in a prouder tone, tossing back the plumes of his hat, which before hung partly over his face, and fixing his full dark eye upon his companion, who still stood scowling upon him with ill-repressed passion—"hark ye, Sir Judge! Use no such language towards me, if you seek not to try that same sharp axe you have so often ordered for others. Suffice it for you to know, in the present instance, that it was not the Cardinal's wish that the young man should be injured. *We* do not desire blood, but when the necessity of the State requires it to be shed. Besides, man," and he gradually fell into his former jeering tone—"besides, in future, under your gentle guidance, and a touch or two of the *peine forte et dure,* this young nightingale may be taught to sing, and, in short, be forced to tell us all he knows. Now do you understand?"

"I do, I do," replied Lafemas. "I thought that there was some deep, damnable wile that made you spare him; and as to the rest, I did not mean to offend you. But when a man condemns his own soul to serve you, you should not taunt him, for it is hard to bear."

"Peace! peace!" cried Chavigni, in a sharp tone; "let me hear no more in this strain. Who raised you to what you are? We use you as you deserve; we pay you for your services; we despise you for your meanness; and as to your soul," he added with a sneer, "if you have any fears on that head—why, you shall have absolution. Are you not our dog, who worries the game for us? We house and feed you, and you must take the lashes when it suits us to give them. Remember, sir, that your life is in my hand! One word respecting the affair of Chalais, mentioned to the Cardinal, brings your head to the block! And now let us see what is this blood you speak of?"

So saying, he sprang from his horse, while Lafemas, as he had been depicted by his companion, hung his head like a cowed hound, and in sullen silence pointed out the blood, which had formed a little pool at the foot of the tree, and stained the ground in several places round about.

Chavigni gazed at it with evident symptoms of displeasure and uneasiness; for although, when he imagined that the necessities of the State required the severest infliction on any offender, no one was more ruthless than himself as to the punishment, no one more unhesitating as to the means—although, at those times, no bond of amity, no tie of kindred, would have stayed his hand, or restrained him in what he erroneously considered his political duty; yet Chavigni was far from naturally cruel; and, as his after-life showed, even too susceptible of the strongest and deepest affections of human nature.

Between Chavigni and the Judge Lafemas, who was the Jeffreys of his country, and had received the name of *Le Bourreau du Cardinal,* existed a sort of original antipathy; so that the statesman, though often obliged to make use of the less scrupulous talents of the judge, and even occasionally to associate with him, could never refrain for any length of time from breaking forth into those bitter taunts which often irritated Lafemas almost to frenzy. The hatred of the judge, on his part, was not less strong, even at the times it did not show itself; and he still brooded over the hope of exercising his ungentle functions upon him who was at present, in a degree, his master.

But to return. Chavigni gazed intently on the spot to
which Lafemas pointed. " I believe it is blood, indeed,"
said he, after a moment's hesitation, as if the uncertainty
of the light had made him doubt it at first; "they shall
rue the day that they shed it contrary to my command.
It is blood surely, Lafemas: is it not?"

" Without a doubt," said Lafemas; " and it has been
shed since mid-day."

" You are critical in these things, I know," replied the
other with a cool sneer: " but we must hear more of this,
Sir Judge, and ascertain what news is stirring, before
we go farther. Things might chance which would render
it necessary that one or both of us should return to the
Cardinal. We will knock at this cottage and inquire.
Our story must run, that we have lost our way in the
wood, and need both rest and direction."

So saying, he struck several sharp blows with the hilt
of his sword against the door, whose rickety and unso-
norous nature returned a grumbling, indistinct sound, as
if it too had shared the sleep of the peaceable inhabitants
of the cottage, and loved not to be disturbed by such
nocturnal visitations. " So ho!" cried Chavigni; " will
no one hear us poor travellers who have lost our way in
this forest!"

In a moment after the head of Philip, the woodman,
appeared at the little casement by the side of the door,
examining the strangers, on whose figures fell the full
beams of the moon, with quite sufficient light to display
the courtly form and garnishing of their apparel, and to
show that they were no dangerous guests. " What would
ye, messieurs?" demanded he, through the open window;
" it is late for travellers."

" We have lost our way in your wood," replied
Chavigni, " and would fain have a little rest, and some
direction for our further progress. We will pay thee
well, good man, for thy hospitality."

" There is no need of payment, sir," said the woodman,

opening the door. " Come in, I pray, messieurs.
Charles," he added, calling to his son, " get up and tend
these gentlemen's horses. Get up, I say, Sir Sluggard!"

The boy crept sleepily out of the room beyond, and
went to give some of the forest hay to the beasts which
had borne the strangers thither, and which gave but
little signs of needing either rest or refreshment. In the
meanwhile his father drew two large yew-tree seats to
the fireside, soon blew the white ashes on the hearth into
a flame, and having invited his guests to sit, and lighted
the old brazen lamp that hung above the chimney, he
bowed low, asking how he could serve them further; but,
as he did so, his eye ran over their persons with a half-
satisfied and inquiring glance, which made Lafemas turn
away his head. But Chavigni answered promptly to his
offer of service: " Why, now, good friend, if thou couldst
give us a jug of wine, 'twould be well and kindly come,
for we have ridden far."

" This is no inn, sir," replied Philip, " and you would
find my wine but thin; nevertheless, such as it is, most
welcomely shall you taste."

From whatever motive it proceeded, Philip's hospitality
was but lukewarm towards the strangers; and the manner in which he rinsed out the tankard, drew the wine
from a *barrique* standing in one corner of the room,
half covered with a wolf-skin, and placed it on a table by
the side of Chavigni, bespoke more churlish rudeness
than good-will. But the statesman heeded little either the
quality of his reception or of his wine, provided he could
obtain the information he desired; so, carrying the tankard to his lips, he drank, or seemed to drink, as deep a
draught as if its contents had been the produce of the best
vineyard in Medoc. " It is excellent," said he, handing
it to Lafemas, " or my thirst does wonders. Now, good
friend, if we had some venison-steaks to broil on your
clear ashes, our supper were complete."

"Such I have not to offer, sir," replied Philip, "or to that you should be welcome too."

"Why, I should have thought," said Chavigni, "the hunters who ran down a stag at your door to-day should have left you a part, as the woodman's fee."

"Do you know those hunters, sir?" demanded Philip, with some degree of emphasis.

"Not I, in truth," replied Chavigni; though the color rose in his cheek, notwithstanding his long training to courtly wile and political intrigue, and he thanked his stars that the lamp gave but a faint and glimmering light: "Not I, in truth; but whoever ran him down got a good beast, for he bled like a stag of ten. I suppose they made the *curée* at your door?"

"Those hunters, sir," replied Philip, "give no woodman's fees; and as to the stag, he is as fine a one as ever brushed the forest dew, but he has escaped them this time."

"How! did he get off with his throat cut?" demanded Chavigni, "for there is blood enough at the foot of yon old tree, to have drained the stoutest stag that ever was brought to bay."

"Oh! but that is not a stag's blood!" interrupted Charles, the woodman's son, who had by this time not only tended the strangers' horses, but examined every point of the quaint furniture with which it was the fashion of the day to adorn them. "That is not stag's blood; that is the blood of the young cavalier, who was hurt by the robbers, and taken away by——"

At this moment the boy's eye caught the impatient expression of his father's countenance.

"The truth is, messieurs," said Philip, taking up the discourse, "there was a gentleman wounded in the forest this morning. I never saw him before, and he was taken away in a carriage by some ladies, whose faces were equally strange to me."

"You have been somewhat mysterious upon this busi-

2

ness, Sir Woodman," said Chavigni, his brow darkening as he spoke; " why were you so tardy in giving us this forest news, which imports all strangers travelling through the wood to know? "

" I hold it as a rule," replied Philip, boldly, " to mind my own business, and never to mention anything I see; which in this affair I shall do more especially, as one of the robbers had furniture of Isabel and silver;" and as he spoke he glanced his eye to the scarf of Chavigni, which was of that peculiar mixture of colors then called Isabel, bordered by a rich silver fringe.

" Fool! " muttered Chavigni between his teeth; " fool! what need had he to show himself? "

Lafemas, who had hitherto been silent, now came to the relief of his companion, taking up the conversation in a mild and easy tone. " Have you many of these robbing fraternity in your wood? " said he; " if so, I suppose we peril ourselves in crossing it alone." And, without waiting for any answer, he proceeded, " Pray, who was the cavalier they attacked? "

" He was a stranger from St. Germain," answered the woodman; " and as to the robbers, I doubt that they will show themselves again, for fear of being taken."

" They did not rob him, then? " said the judge. Now nothing that Philip had said bore out this inference; but Lafemas possessed in a high degree the talent of cross-examination, and was deeply versed in all the thousand arts of entangling a witness, or leading a prisoner to condemn himself. But there was a stern reserve about the woodman which baffled the judge's cunning: " I only saw the last part of the fray," replied Philip, " and therefore know not what went before."

" Where was he hurt? " asked Lafemas; " for he lost much blood."

" On the head and in the side," answered the woodman.

" Poor youth! " cried the judge in a pitiful tone.

"And when you opened his coat, was the wound a deep one?"

"I cannot judge," replied Philip, "being no surgeon."

It was in vain that Lafemas tried all his wiles on the woodman, and that Chavigni, who soon joined in the conversation, questioned him more boldly. Philip was in no communicative mood, and yielded them but little information respecting the events of the morning.

At length, weary of this fruitless interrogation, Chavigni started up—"Well, friend!" said he, "had there been danger in crossing the forest, we might have stayed with thee till daybreak; but, as thou sayest there is none, we will hence upon our way." So saying he strode towards the door, the flame-shaped mullets of his gilded spurs jingling over the brick-floor of Philip's dwelling, and calling the woodman's attention to the knightly rank of his departing guest. In a few minutes all was prepared for their departure, and having mounted their horses, the statesman drew forth a small silk purse tied with a loop of gold, and holding it forth to Philip, bade him accept it for his services. The woodman bowed, repeating that he required no payment.

"I am not accustomed to have my bounty refused," said Chavigni, proudly; and dropping the purse to the ground, he spurred forward his horse.

"Now, Lafemas," said he, when they had proceeded so far as to be beyond the reach of Philip's ears, "what think you of this?"

"Why, truly," replied the judge, "I deem that we are mighty near as wise as we were before."

"Not so," said Chavigni. "It is clear enough these fellows have failed, and De Blenau has preserved the packet: I understand it all. His eminence of Richelieu, against my advice, has permitted Madame de Beaumont and her daughter Pauline to return to the queen, after an absence of ten years. The fact is, that when the cardinal banished them the court, and ordered the marchioness to retire to Languedoc, his views were not so extended as they are now, and he had laid out in his own mind a match between one of his nieces and this rich young Count de Blenau; which, out of the royal family, was one of the best alliances in France. The boy, however, had been promised, and even, I believe, affianced by his father to this Pauline de Beaumont; and accordingly his eminence sent away the girl and her mother with the same *sang-froid* that a man drives a strange dog out of his court-yard; at the same time he kept the youth at court, forbidding all communication with Languedoc: but now that the cardinal can match his niece to the Duke d'Enghien, De Blenau may look for a bride where he lists, and the marquise and her daughter have been suffered to return. To my knowledge, they passed through Chartres yesterday morning on their way to St. Germain."

"But what have these to do with the present affair?" demanded Lafemas.

"Why, thus has it happened," continued Chavigni. "The youth has been attacked. He has resisted, and been wounded. Just then, up come these women, travelling through the forest with a troop of servants, who join with the count and drive our poor friends to cover. This is what I have drawn from the discourse of yon surly woodman."

"You mean from your own knowledge of the business," replied Lafemas, "for he would confess nothing."

"Confess, man!" exclaimed Chavigni. "Why he did not know that he was before a confessor, and still less before a judge, though thou wouldest fain have put him to the question. I saw your lip quivering with anxiety to order him the torture—rack and thumb-screw and *oubliette* were in your eye, every sullen answer he gave."

"Were it not as well to get him out of the way?" demanded Lafemas. "He remarked your livery, Chavigni, and may blab."

"Short-sighted mole!" replied his companion. "The

very sulkiness of humor which has called down on him thy rage, will shield him from my fears—which might be quite as dangerous. He that is so close in one thing, depend upon it, will be close in another. Besides, unless he tells it to the trees, or the jays, or the wild boars, whom should he tell it to? I would bet a thousand crowns against the Prince de Conti's brains, or the Archbishop Coadjutor's religion, or Madame de Chevreuse's reputation, or against anything else that is worth nothing, that this good woodman sees no human shape for the next ten years, and then all that passes between them will be, ' Good-day, woodman!'—' Good-day, sir!'"—and he mimicked the deep voice of him of whom they spoke. But, notwithstanding this appearance of gaiety, Chavigni was not easy; and even while he spoke, he rode on with no small precipitation till, turning into a narrow forest path, the light of the moon, which had illumined the greater part of the high-road, was cut off entirely by the trees, and the deep gloom obliged them to be more cautious in proceeding. At length, however, they came to a little savanna, surrounded by high oaks, where Chavigni entirely reined in his horse, and blew a single note on his horn, which was soon answered by a similar sound at some distance.

CHAPTER III.

Which shows what a French forest was at night, and who inhabited it.

IN the heart of the forest of St. Germain, at a considerable distance from any of the roads, or even by-paths of
the wood, lay a deep dingle or dell. At the time I speak
of, a considerable part of the dell itself was filled up with
tangled brushwood, which a long hot season had stripped
and withered; and over the edge hung a quantity of dry
shrubs and stunted trees, forming a thick screen over the
wild recess below.

One side, and one side only, was free of access, and
this was by means of a small sandy path winding down
into the bottom of the dell, between two deep banks,
which assumed almost the appearance of cliffs as the road
descended. This little footway conducted, it is true, into
the most profound part of the hollow, but then immediately lost itself in the thick underwood, through which
none but a very practised eye would have discovered the
means of entering a deep lair of ground, sheltered by the
steep bank and its superincumbent trees on one side, and
concealed by a screen of wood on every other.

On the night I have mentioned, this well-concealed retreat was tenanted by a group of men, whose wild attire
harmonized perfectly with the rudeness of the scene
around. The accoutrements of these denizens of the
forest were kept in countenance by every other accessory
circumstance of appearance; and a torch stuck in the
sand in the midst glared upon features which Salvator
might have loved to trace. It was not alone the negligence of personal appearance, shown in their long dis-
hevelled hair and untrimmed beards, which rendered
them savagely picturesque, but many a furious passion

had there written deep traces of its unbounded sway, and marked them with that wild undefinable expression which habitual vice and lawless licence are sure to leave behind in their course.

At the moment I speak of, wine had been circulating very freely amongst the robbers; for such indeed they were. Some were sleeping, either with their hands clasped over their knees and their heads drooping down to meet them, or stretched more at their ease under the trees, snoring loud in answer to the wind, that whistled through the branches. Some sat gazing with a wise sententious look on the empty gourds, many of which, fashioned into bottles, lay scattered about upon the ground: and two or three, who had either drunk less of the potent liquor, or whose heads were better calculated to resist its effects than the rest, sat clustered together singing and chatting by turns, arrived exactly at that point of ebriety where a man's real character shows itself, notwithstanding all his efforts to conceal it.

One of the freebooters stood conspicuous amongst the others, from the Herculean proportion of his limbs; but he had, in addition, other qualities to distinguish him from the rest. His brow was broad, and of that peculiar form to which physiognomists have attached the idea of a strong determined spirit; at the same time, the clear sparkle of his blue Norman eye bespoke an impetuous, but not a depraved mind.

A deep scar was apparent on his left cheek; and the wound which had been its progenitor, was most probably the cause of a sneering turn in the corner of his mouth, which, with a bold expression of daring confidence, completed the mute history that his face afforded, of a life spent in arms, or well, or ill, as circumstances prompted, —an unshrinking heart, which dared every personal evil, and a bright but unprincipled mind, which followed no dictates but the passions of the moment.

He was now in his gayest mood, and holding a horn in

his hand, trolled forth an old French ditty, seeming confident of pleasing, or perhaps careless whether he pleased or not.

> "Thou'rt an ass, Robin, thou'rt an ass,
>   To think that great men be
> More gay than I that lie on the grass
>   Under the greenwood tree.
> To tell thee no, I tell thee no,
> The Great are slaves to their gilded show.

So sang he who wore a buff jerkin, and his song met with more or less applause from his companions, according to the particular humor of each. One only amongst the freebooters seemed scarcely to participate in the merriment. He had drunk as deeply as the rest, but he appeared neither gay, nor stupid, nor sleepy; and while the tall Norman sang, he cast, from time to time, a calm sneering glance upon the singer, which showed no especial love either for the music or musician.

"You can sing," said he, as the other concluded his ditty, "and yet you can show no other accomplishment, after all, if we may judge from to-day."

"And why not, Monsieur Pierrepont Le Blanc?" demanded the Norman, without displaying aught of ill-humor in his countenance: "though they ought to have called you Monsieur Le Noir—Mr. Black, not Mr. White. —Nay, do not frown, good comrade; I speak but of your beard, not of your heart. What, art thou still grumbling because we did not cut the young count's throat outright?"

"Nay, not for that," answered the other, "but because we have lost the best man amongst us, for want of his being well seconded."

"You lie, parbleu!" cried the Norman, drawing his sword, and fixing his thumb upon a stain, about three inches from the point. "Did not I lend the youth so much of my iron toothpick? and would have sent it through him, if his horse had not carried him away. But I know you, Master Buccaneer—you would have had me stab him behind, while Mortagne slashed his head before. That would have been a fit task for a Norman gentleman, and a soldier! I whose life he saved too!"

"Did you not swear, when you joined our troop," demanded the other, "to forget everything that went before?"

The Norman hesitated; he well remembered his oath, against which the better feelings of his heart were perhaps sometimes rebellious. He felt, too, confused at the direct appeal the other had made to it; and to pass it by, he caught at the word forget, answering with a stave of the song—

> "Forget! forget! let slaves forget
> The pangs and chains they bear;
> The brave remember every debt
> To honor, and the fair.
> For these are bonds that bind us more,
> Yet leave us freer than before.

"Yes, let those that can do so, forget: but I very well remember, at the battle at Perpignan, I had charged with the advance guard, when the fire of the enemy's musketeers, and a masked battery which began to enfilade our line, soon threw our left flank into disorder, and a charge of cavalry drove back De Coucy's troop. Mielleraye's standard was in the hands of the enemy, when I and five others rallied to rescue it. A gloomy old Spaniard fired his petronel and disabled my left arm, but still I held the standard-pole with my right, keeping the standard before me; but my Don drew his long Toledo, and had got the point to my breast, just going to run it through me and standard and all, as I've often spitted a duck's liver and a piece of bacon on a skewer; when, turning round my head, to see if no help was near, I perceived this young Count de Blenau's banderol, coming like lightning over the field, and driving all before it; and blue and gold were then the best colors that ever I saw, for they gave me new heart, and wrenching the standard-pole round—but hark, there is the horn!"

As he spoke, the clear full note of a hunting-horn came swelling from the southwest; and in a moment after, another, much nearer to them, seemed to answer the first. Each, after giving breath to one solitary note, relapsed into silence; and such of the robbers as were awake, having listened till the signal met with the reply, bestirred themselves to rouse their sleeping companions, and to put some face of order upon the disarray which their revels had left behind.

"Now, Sir Norman," cried he that they distinguished by the name of Le Blanc; "we shall see how monseigneur rates your slackness in his cause. Will you tell him your long story of the siege of Perpignan?"

"Pardie!" cried the other, "I care no more for him, than I do for you. Every man that stands before me on forest ground is but a man, and I will treat him as such."

"Ha! ha! ha!" exclaimed his companion; "it were good to see thee bully a privy counsellor; why, thou darest as soon take a lion by the beard."

"I dare pass my sword through his heart, were there need," answered the Norman; "but here they come,— stand you aside and let me deal with him."

Approaching steps, and a rustling sound in the thick screen of wood already mentioned, as the long boughs were forced back by the passage of some person along the narrow pathway, announced the arrival of those for whom the robbers had been waiting.

"Why, it is as dark as the pit of Acheron!" cried a deep voice amongst the trees. "Are we never to reach the light I saw from above? Oh, here it is. Chauvelin, hold back that bough; it has caught my cloak." As the speaker uttered the last words, an armed servant, in Isabel and silver, appeared at the entrance of the path, holding back the stray branches, while Chavigni himself advanced into the circle of robbers, who stood grouped around in strange picturesque attitudes.

The statesman himself advanced in silence; and, with

something of a frown upon his brow, glanced his eye firmly over every face around, nor was there an eye amongst them that did not sink before the stern commanding fire of his, as it rested for a moment upon the countenance of each.

"Well, sirs," said he at length, "my knave tells me that ye have failed in executing my commands."

The Norman we have somewhat minutely described heretofore now began to excuse himself and his fellows; and was proceeding to set forth that they had done all which came within their power and province to do, and was also engaged in stating that no man could do more, when Chavigni interrupted him. "Silence!" cried he, with but little apparent respect for these lords of the forest; "I blame ye not for not doing more than ye could do; but how dare ye, mongrel bloodhounds, to disobey my strict commands? and when I bade ye abstain from injuring the youth, how is it ye have mangled him like a stag torn by the wolves?"

The Norman turned with a look of subdued triumph towards him who had previously censured his forbearance. "Speak, speak, Le Blanc!" cried he; "answer monseigneur. Well," continued he, as the other drew back, "the truth is this, Sir Count: we were divided in opinion with respect to the best method of fulfilling your commands, so we called a council of war——"

"A council of war!" repeated Chavigni, his lip curling into an ineffable sneer. "Well, proceed, proceed! You are a Norman, I presume—and braggart, I perceive. Proceed, sir, proceed!"

Be it remarked, that by this time the influence of Chavigni's first appearance had greatly worn away from the mind of the Norman. The commanding dignity of the statesman, though it still, in a degree, overawed, had lost the effect of novelty; and the bold heart of the freebooter began to reproach him for truckling to a being who was inferior to himself, according to his estimate of human dignities—an estimate formed not alone on personal courage, but also on personal strength.

However, as we have said, he was, in some measure, overawed; and though he would have done much to prove his daring in the sight of his companions, his mind was not yet sufficiently wrought up to shake off all respect, and he answered boldly, but calmly, " Well, Sir Count, give me your patience and you shall hear. But my story must be told my own way, or not at all. We called a council of war, then, where every man gave his opinion; and my voice was for shooting Monsieur de Blenau's horse as he rode by, and then taking advantage of the confusion among his lackeys to seize upon his person, and carrying him into St. Herman's brake, which lies between Le Croix de bois and the river—you know where I mean, monsigneur?"

" No, truly," answered the statesman; " but, as I guess, some deep part of the forest, where you could have searched him at your ease—the plan was a good one. Why went it not forward?"

" You shall hear in good time," answered the freebooter, growing somewhat more familiar in his tone. " As you say, St. Herman's brake is deep enough in the forest—and if we had once housed him there, we might have searched from top to toe for the packet—ay, and looked in his mouth, if we found it nowhere else. But the first objection was, that an arquebuse, though a very pretty weapon, and pleasant serviceable companion in broad brawl and battle, talks too loud for secret service, and the noise thereof might put the count's people on their guard before we secured his person. However, they say a ' *Norman cow can always get over a stile,*' so I offered to do the business with yon arbalete; " and he pointed to a steel cross-bow lying near, of that peculiar shape which seems to unite the properties of the crossbow and gun, propelling the ball or bolt by means of the stiff arched spring and cord, by which little noise is made, while the aim is rendered more certain by a long tube similar to the barrel of a musket, through which the shot passes.

" When was I ever known to miss my aim? " continued the Norman. " Why, I always shoot my stags in the eye, for fear of hurting the skin. However, Mortagne— your old friend, Monsieur de Chavigni—who was a sort of band captain amongst us, loved blood, as you know, like an unreclaimed falcon; besides, he had some old grudge against the count, who turned him out of the queen's ante-room, when he was ancient in the cardinal's guard. He it was who overruled my proposal. He would have shot him willingly enough, but your gentle- man would not hear of that; so we attacked the count's train at the turn of the road—boldly, and in the face. Mortagne was lucky enough to get a fair cut at his head, which slashed through his beaver, and laid his skull bare, but went no farther, only serving to make the youth as savage as a hurt boar; for I had only time to see his hand laid upon his sword, when its cross was knocking against Mortagne's ribs before, and the point shining out between his blade-bones behind. It was done in the twinkling of an eye."

" He is a gallant youth," said Chavigni; " he always was from a boy; but where is your wounded com- panion? "

" Wounded! " cried the Norman. " Odds life! he's dead. It was enough to have killed the devil. There he lies, poor fellow, wrapped in his cloak. Will you please to look upon him, Sir Counsellor? " and snatching up one of the torches, he approached the spot where the dead man lay, under a bank covered with withered brushwood and stunted trees.

Chavigni followed with a slow step and gloomy brow, the robbers drawing back at his approach; for though they held high birth in but little respect, the redoubted name and fearless bearing of the statesman had power over even their ungoverned spirits. He, however, who

had been called Pierrepont Le Blanc by the tall Norman,
twitched his companion by the sleeve as he lighted
Chavigni on. "A cowed hound, Norman!" whispered
he—"thou hast felt the lash—a cowed hound!"

The Norman glanced on him a look of fire, but passing
on in silence, he disengaged the mantle from the corpse,
and displayed the face of his dead companion, whose
calm closed eyes and unruffled features might have been
supposed to picture quiet sleep, had not the ashy paleness
of his cheek, and the drop of the under-jaw, told that the
soul no longer tenanted its earthly dwelling.

Chavigni gazed upon him, with his arms crossed upon
his breast, and for a moment his mind wandered far into
those paths to which such a sight naturally directs the
course of our ideas, till, his thoughts losing themselves
in the uncertainty of the void before them, by a sudden
effort he recalled them to the business in which he was
immediately engaged.

"Well, he has bitterly expiated the disobedience of my
commands; but tell me," he said, turning to the Norman,
who still continued to hold the torch over the dead man,
"how is it ye have dared to force my servant to show
himself, and my liveries, in this attack, contrary to my
special order?"

"That is easily told," answered the Norman, assuming
a tone equally bold and peremptory with that of the statesman. "Thus it stands, Sir Count: you men of quality
often employ us nobility of the forest to do what you
either cannot or dare not do for yourselves; then, if
all goes well, you pay us scantily for our pains; if it goes
ill, you hang us for your own doings. But we will have
none of that. If we are to be falcons for your game, we
will risk the stroke of the heron's bill, but we will not
have our necks wrung after we have struck the prey.
When your lackey was present, it was your deed. Mark
ye that, Sir Counsellor?"

"Villain, thou art insolent!" cried Chavigni, forgetting, in the height of passion, the fearful odds against him, in case of quarrel at such a moment. "How dare you, slave, to——"

"Villain! and slave!" cried the Norman, interrupting him, and laying his hand on his sword. "Know, proud sir, that I dare anything. You are now in the green forest, not at council-board, to prate of daring."

Chavigni's dignity, like his prudence, became lost in his anger. "Boasting Norman coward!" cried he, "who had not even courage, when he saw his leader slain before his face——"

The Norman threw the torch from his hand, and drew his weapon; but Chavigni's sword sprang in a moment from the scabbard. He was, perhaps, the best swordsman of his day; and before his servant (who advanced, calling loudly to Lafemas to come forth from the wood where he had remained from the first) could approach, or the robbers could show any signs of taking part in the fray, the blades of the statesman and the freebooter had crossed, and, maugre the Norman's vast strength, his weapon was instantly wrenched from his hand, and, flying over the heads of his companions, struck against the bank above.

Chavigni drew back, as if to pass his sword through the body of his opponent; but the one moment he had been thus engaged, gave time for reflection on the imprudence of his conduct, and calmly returning his sword to its sheath, "Thou art no coward after all," said he, addressing the Norman in a softened tone of voice; "but trust me, friend, that boasting graces but little a brave man. As for the rest, it is no disgrace to have measured swords with Chavigni."

The Norman was one of those men so totally unaccustomed to command their passions, that like slaves who have thrown off their chains, each struggles for the mastery, obtains it for a moment, and is again deprived of power by some one more violent still.

The dignity of the statesman's manner, the apparent generosity of his conduct, and the degree of gentleness with which he spoke, acted upon the feelings of the Norman, like the waves of the sea when they meet the waters of the Dordogne, driving them back even to their very source with irresistible violence. An unwonted tear trembled in his eye. "Monseigneur, I have done foul wrong, said he, "in thus urging you, when you trusted yourself amongst us. But you have punished me more by your forbearance, than if you had passed your sword through my body."

"Ha! such thoughts in a freebooter!" cried Chavigni. "Friend, this is not thy right trade. But what means all this smoke that gathers round us?—Surely those bushes are on fire;—see the sparks how they rise!"

His remark called the eyes of all upon that part of the dingle into which the Norman had incautiously thrown his torch, on drawing his sword upon the statesman. Continued sparks, mingled with a thick cloud of smoke, were rising quickly from it, showing plainly that the fire had caught some of the dry bushes thereabout; and in a moment after a bright flame burst forth, speedily communicating itself to the old withered oaks round the spot, and threatening to spread destruction into the heart of the forest.

In an instant all the robbers were engaged in the most strenuous endeavors to extinguish the fire; but the distance to which the vast strength of the Norman had hurled the torch among the bushes, rendered all access extremely difficult. No water was to be procured, and the means they employed, that of cutting down the smaller trees and bushes with their swords and axes, instead of opposing any obstacle to the flames, seemed rather to accelerate their progress. From bush to bush, from tree to tree, the impetuous element spread on, till, finding themselves almost girt in by the fire, the heat and smoke of which were becoming too intense for endurance, the robbers abandoned their useless efforts to extinguish it, and hurried to gather up their scattered arms and garments before the flames reached the spot of their late revels.

The Norman, however, together with Chavigni and his servant, still continued their exertions; and even Lafemas, who had come forth from his hiding-place, gave some awkward assistance; when suddenly the Norman stopped, put his hand to his ear, to aid his hearing amidst the cracking of the wood and the roaring of the flames, and exclaimed, " I hear horse upon the hill—follow me, monseigneur. St. Patrice guide us! this is a bad business :—follow me ! " So saying, three steps brought him to the flat below, where his companions were still engaged in gathering together all they had left on the ground.

" Messieurs ! " he cried to the robbers, " leave all useless lumber; I hear horses coming down the hill. It must be a lieutenant of the forest, and the *gardes champêtres,* alarmed by the fire—seek your horses, quick !— each his own way. We meet at St. Herman's brake— you, monseigneur, follow me, I will be your guide; but dally not, sir, if, as I guess, you would rather be judged in the Rue St. Honoré than in the Forest of St. Germain."

So saying, he drew aside the boughs, disclosing a path somewhat to the right of that by which Chavigni had entered their retreat, and which apparently led to the high sand-cliff which flanked it on the north. The statesman, with his servant and Lafemas, followed quickly upon his steps, only lighted by the occasional gleam of the flames, as they flashed and flickered through the foliage of the trees.

Having to struggle every moment with the low branches of the hazel and the tangled briars that shot across the path, it was some time ere they reached the bank, and there the footway they had hitherto followed seemed to end. " Here are steps," said the Norman, in

3

a low voice; " hold by the boughs, monseigneur, lest your
footing fail. Here is the first step."

The ascent was not difficult, and in a few minutes they
had lost sight of the dingle and the flames by which it
was surrounded; only every now and then, where the
branches opened, a broad red light fell upon their path,
telling that the fire still raged with unabated fury. A
moment or two after they could perceive that the track
entered upon a small savanna, on which the moon was still
shining, her beams showing with a strange sickly light,
mingled as they were with the fitful gleams of the flames
and the red reflection of the sky. The whole of this
small plain, however, was quite sufficiently illuminated to
allow Chavigni and his companion to distinguish two
horses fastened by their bridles to a tree hard by; and a
momentary glance convinced the statesman that the spot
where he and Lafemas had left their beasts was again before him, although he had arrived there by another and
much shorter path than that by which he had been conducted to the rendezvous.

" We have left all danger behind us, monseigneur," said
the robber, after having carefully examined the savanna,
to ascertain that no spy lurked amongst the trees around.
" The flies are all swarming round the flames. There
stand your horses—mount, and good speed attend you.
Your servant must go with me, for our beasts are not so
nigh."

Chavigni whispered a word in the robber's ear, who
in return bowed low, with an air of profound respect.
" I will attend your lordship," replied he, " and without
fear."

" You may do so in safety," said the statesman, and
mounting his horse, after waiting a moment for the judge,
he took his way once more towards the high-road to St.
Germain.

CHAPTER IV.

In which the learned reader will discover that it is easy to raise suspicions without any cause, and that royalty is not patent against superstition.

WE must now return to the principal personage of our
history, and accompany him on his way towards St. Germain, whither he was wending when last we left him.

The distance to St. Germain was considerable, and
naturally appeared still longer than it really was, to persons unacquainted with one step of the road before them,
and apprehensive of a thousand occurrences both likely
and unlikely. Nothing, however, happened to interrupt
them on the way, and their journey passed over, not only
in peace, but pretty much in silence also. Both the ladies
who occupied the inside of the carriage seemed to be very
sufficiently taken up with their own thoughts, and no
way disposed to loquacity, so that the only break to the
melancholy stillness which hung over them was now and
then a half-formed sentence, proceeding from what was
rapidly passing in the mind of each, or the complaining
creak of the heavy wheels as they ground their unwilling
way through the less practical parts of the forest road.

At times, too, a groan from the lips of their wounded
companion interrupted the silence, as the roughness of
the way jolted the ponderous vehicle in which he was
carried, and re-awakened him to a sense of pain.

Long ere they had reached St. Germain night had
fallen over their road, and nothing could be distinguished
by those within the carriage but the figures of the two
horsemen who kept close to the windows. The interior
was still darker, and it was only a kind of inarticulate
sob from the other side which made the marchioness inquire, " Pauline! you are not weeping?"

The young lady did not positively say whether she was so or not, but replied in a voice which showed her mother's conjecture to be well founded.

" It was not thus, mamma," she said, " that I had hoped to arrive at St. Germain."

" Fie, fie! Pauline," replied the old lady; " I have long tried to make you feel like a woman, and you are still a child, a weak child. These accidents, and worse than these, occur to every one in the course of life, and they must be met with fortitude. Have you flattered yourself that *you* would be exempt from the common sorrows of humanity? "

" But if he should die? " said Pauline, with the tone of one who longs to be soothed out of her fears. The old lady, however, applied no such unction to the wound in her daughter's heart. Madame de Beaumont had herself been reared in the school of adversity, and while her mind and principles had been thus strengthened and confirmed, her feelings had not been rendered more acute. In the present instance, whether she spoke it heedlessly, or, whether she intended to destroy one passion by exciting another to cure Pauline's grief by rousing her anger, her answer afforded but little consolation. " If he dies," said she dryly, " why, I suppose the fair lady whose picture he has in his bosom would weep, and you——"

A deep groan from their wounded companion broke in upon her speech, and suggested to the marchioness that he might not be quite so insensible as he seemed. Such an answer, too, was not so palatable to Pauline as to induce her to urge the conversation any farther; so that silence again resumed her empire over the party, remaining undisturbed till the old lady, drawing back the curtain, announced that they were entering St. Germain.

A few minutes more brought them to the lodging of the Count de Blenau; and here the marchioness, descending, gave all the necessary directions in order that the young gentleman might be carried to his sleeping-cham-

ber in the easiest and most convenient method, while
Pauline, without proffering any aid, sat back in a dark
corner of the carriage. Nor would anything have shown
that she was interested in what passed around her, but
when the light of a torch glared into the vehicle, discovering a handkerchief pressed over her eyes to hide the
tears she could not restrain.

As soon as the count was safely lodged in his own
dwelling, the carriage proceeded towards the palace,
which showed but little appearance of regal state. However, the mind of Pauline might have been accustomed to
picture a court in all the gay and splendid coloring which
youthful imagination lends to anticipated pleasure, her
thoughts were now far too fully occupied to admit of her
noticing the lonely and deserted appearance of the scene.
But to Madame de Beaumont it was different. She, who
remembered St. Germain in other days, looked in vain
for the lights flashing from every window of the palace;
for the servants hurrying along the different avenues, the
sentinels parading before every entrance, and the gay
groups of courtiers and ladies, in all the brilliant costume
of the time, which used to crowd the terrace and gardens
to enjoy the cool of the evening after the sun had gone
down.

All that she remembered had had its day; and nothing
remained but silence and solitude. A single sentry at
the principal gate was all that indicated the dwelling of
a king; and it was not till the carriage had passed under
the archway that even an attendant presented himself to
inquire who were the comers at that late hour.

The principal domestic of Madame de Beaumont, who
had already descended from his horse, gave the name of
his lady with all ceremony, and also tendered a card (as
he had been instructed by the marchioness) on which her
style and title were fully displayed. The royal servant
bowed low, saying that the queen, his mistress, had expected the marchioness before; and seizing the rope of a

great bell, which hung above the staircase, he rang such
a peal that the empty galleries of the palace returned a
kind of groaning echo to the rude clang which seemed to
mock their loneliness.

Two or three more servants appeared, in answer to
the bell's noisy summons; yet such was still the paucity
of attendants, that Madame de Beaumont, even while she
descended from her carriage, and began to ascend the
" grand escalier," had need to look, from time to time,
at the splendid fresco paintings which decorated the walls,
and the crowns and fleur-de-lis with which all the cornices
were ornamented, before she could satisfy herself that she
really was in the royal château of St. Germain.

There were a thousand reasons why Mademoiselle de
Beaumont, as she followed the attendant through the
long empty galleries and vacant chambers of the palace,
towards the apartments prepared for her mother and herself, felt none of those happy sensations which she had
anticipated from her arrival at court; nor was it till, on
entering the ante-chamber of their suite of rooms, she beheld the gay smiling face of her Lyonnaise waiting-maid,
that she felt there was anything akin to old recollections
within those cold and pompous walls, which seemed to
look upon her as a stranger.

The soubrette had been sent forward the day before
with a part of the Marchioness de Beaumont's equipage;
and now, having endured a whole day's comparative
silence with the patience and fortitude of a martyr, she
advanced to the two ladies with loquacity in her countenance, as if resolved to make up, as speedily as possible,
for the restraint under which her tongue had labored
during her short sojourn in the palace; but the deep
gravity of Madame de Beaumont, and the melancholy
air of her daughter, checked Louise in full career; so that,
having kissed her mistress on both cheeks, she paused,
while her lip, like an overfilled reservoir whose waters are

trembling on the very brink, seemed ready to pour forth the torrent of words which she had so long suppressed.

Pauline, as she passed through the ante-room, wiped the last tears from her eyes, and on entering the saloon, advanced towards a mirror which hung between the windows, as if to ascertain what traces they had left behind. The soubrette did not fail to advance, in order to adjust her young lady's dress, and finding herself once more in the exercise of her functions, the right of chattering seemed equally restored; for she commenced immediately, beginning in a low and respectful voice, but gradually increasing as the thought of her mistress was swallowed up in the more comprehensive idea of herself.

"Oh, dear mademoiselle," said she, "I am so glad you are come at last. This place is so sad and so dull! Who would think it was a court? Why, I expected to see it all filled with lords and ladies, and instead of that, I have seen nothing but dismal-looking men, who go gliding about in silence, seeming afraid to open their lips, as if that cruel old cardinal, whom they all tremble at, could hear every word they say. I did see one fine-looking gentleman this morning to be sure, with his servants all in beautiful liveries of blue and gold, and horses as if there were fire coming out of their very eyes; but he rode away to hunt, after he had been half an hour with the queen and Mademoiselle de Hauteford, as they call her."

"Mademoiselle who?" exclaimed Pauline, quickly, as if startled from her reverie by something curious in the name. "Who did you say, Louise?"

"Oh, such a pretty young lady!" replied the waiting-woman. "Mademoiselle de Hauteford is her name. I saw her this morning as she went to the queen's levée. She has eyes as blue as the sky, and teeth like pearls themselves; but withal she looks as cold and as proud as if she were the queen's own self."

While the soubrette spoke, Pauline raised her large dark eyes to the tall Venetian mirror which stood before her, and which had never reflected anything lovelier than herself, as hastily she passed her fair small hand across her brow, brushing back the glossy ringlets that hung clustering over her forehead. But she was tired and pale with fatigue and anxiety; her eyes, too, bore the traces of tears, and with a sigh and look of dissatisfaction, she turned away from the mirror.

Madame de Beaumont's eyes had been fixed upon Pauline; and translating her daughter's looks with the instinctive acuteness of a mother, she approached with more gentleness than was her wont. "You are beautiful enough, my Pauline," said she, pressing a kiss upon her cheek; "you are beautiful enough. Do not fear."

"Nay, mamma," replied Pauline, "I have nothing to fear, either from possessing or from wanting beauty."

"Thou art a silly girl, Pauline," continued her mother, "and take these trifles far too much to heart. Perhaps I was wrong concerning this same picture. It was but a random guess. Besides, even were it true, where were the mighty harm? These men are all alike, Pauline. Like butterflies, they rest on a thousand flowers before they settle on any one. We all fancy that our own lover is different from his fellows; but, believe me, my child, the best happiness a woman can boast is that of being most carefully deceived."

"Then no such butterfly love for me, mamma," replied Pauline, her cheek slightly coloring as she spoke. "I would rather not know this sweet poison—love. My heart is still free, though my fancy may have—have—"

"May have what, Pauline?" demanded her mother, with a doubtful smile. "My dear child, thy heart, and thy fancy, I trow, have not been so separate as thou thinkest."

"Nay, mamma," answered Pauline, "my fancy, like an insect, may have been caught in the web of a spider; but the enemy has not yet seized me, and I will break through while I can."

"But, first, let us be sure that we are right," said Madame de Beaumont. "For as every rule has its exception, there be some men whose hearts are even worthy the acceptance of a squeamish girl, who, knowing nothing of the world, expects to meet with purity like her own. At all events, love, de Blenau is the soul of honor, and will not stoop to deceit. In justice, you must not judge without hearing him."

"But," said Pauline, not at all displeased with the refutation of her own ideas, and even wishing, perhaps, to afford her mother occasion to combat them anew— "but——"

The sentence, however, was never destined to be concluded; for, as she spoke, the door of the apartment opened, and a form glided in, the appearance of which instantly arrested the words on Pauline's lips, and made her draw back with an instinctive feeling of respect.

The lady who entered had passed that earlier period of existence when beauties and graces succeed each other without pause, like the flowers of spring that go blooming on from the violet to the rose. Her brown hair fell in a profusion of large curls round a face which, if not strictly handsome, was highly pleasing; and even many sorrows and reverses, by mingling an expression of patient melancholy with the gentle majesty of her countenance, produced a greater degree of interest than the features could have originally excited.

Those even who sought for mere beauty of feature would have perceived that her eyes were quick and fine; that her skin was of the most delicate whiteness, except where it was disfigured by the use of rouge; and that her small mouth might have served as a model to a statuary, especially while her lips arched with a warm smile of pleasure and affection, as advancing into the apartment, she pressed Madame de Beaumont to her bosom, who on her part, bending low, received the embrace of Anne of

Austria with the humble deference of a respectful subject
towards the condescension of her sovereign.

"Once more restored to me, my dear Madame de Beaumont!" said the queen. "His eminence of Richelieu does
indeed give me back one of the best of my friends. And
this is your Pauline," she added, turning to Mademoiselle
de Beaumont. "You were but young, my fair demoiselle,
when last I saw you. You have grown up a lovely flower
from a noble root; but truly you will never be spoiled by
splendor at our court."

As she spoke, her mind seemed naturally to return to
other days, and her eye fixed intently on the ground, as if
engaged in tracing out the plan of her past existence,
running over all the lines of sorrow, danger, and disappointed hope, till the task became too bitter, and she
turned to the marchioness with one of those long deep
sighs that almost always follow a review of the days gone
by, forming a sort of epitaph to the dreams, the wishes,
and the joys that once were dear, and are now no more.

"When you met me, De Beaumont," said the queen,
"with the proud Duke of Guise, on the banks of the
Bidasoa—quitting the kingdom of my father and entering the kingdom of my husband, with an army for my
escort, and princes kneeling at my feet—little, little did
ever you or I think that Anne of Austria, the wife of a
great king, and daughter of a long line of monarchs,
would, in after-years, be forced to dwell at St. Germain,
without guards, without court, without attendants but
such as the Cardinal de Richelieu chooses to allow her.
The Cardinal de Richelieu!" she proceeded thoughtfully;
"the servant of my husband! but no less the master of
his master, and the king of his king."

"I can assure your majesty," replied Madame de Beaumont, with a deep tone of feeling which had no hypocrisy
in it, for her whole heart was bound by habit, principle,
and inclination to her royal mistress—"I can assure your
majesty that many a tear have I shed over the sorrows

of my queen; and when his eminence drove me from the court, I regretted not the splendor of a palace, I regretted not the honor of serving my sovereign, I regretted not the friends I left behind or the hopes I lost, but I regretted that I could not be the sharer of my mistress's misfortunes. But your majesty has now received a blessing from Heaven," she continued, willing to turn the conversation from the troubled course of memory to the more agreeable channels of hope—"a blessing which we scarcely dreamed of, a consolation under all present sorrows, and a bright prospect for the years to come."

"Oh, yes, my little Louis, you would say," replied the queen, her face lightening with all a mother's joy as she spoke of her son. "He is indeed a cherub; and sure am I, that if God sends him years, he will redress his mother's wrongs by proving the greatest of his race."

She spoke of the famous Louis the Fourteenth, and some might have thought she prophesied. But it was only the fervor of a mother's hope, an ebullition of that pure feeling which alone, of all the affections of the heart, the most sordid poverty cannot destroy, and the proudest rank can hardly check.

"He is indeed a cherub," continued the queen; "and such was your Pauline to you, De Beaumont, when the cardinal drove you from my side—a consolation, not only in your exile, but also in your mourning for your noble lord. Come near, young lady; let me see if thou art like thy father."

Pauline approached; and the queen, laying her hand gently upon her arm, ran her eye rapidly over her face and figure, every now and then pausing for a moment, and seeming to call memory to her aid in the comparison she was making between the dead and the living. But suddenly she started back: "*Sainte Vierge!*" cried she, crossing herself, "your dress is all dabbled with blood. What bad omen is this?"

"May it please your majesty," said the marchioness,

half smiling at the queen's superstition, for her own strong mind rejected many of the errors of the day, "that blood is only an omen of Pauline's charitable disposition; for in the forest hard by, we came up with a wounded cavalier, and, like a true *demoiselle errante*, Pauline rendered him personal aid, even at the expense of her robe."

"Nay, nay, De Beaumont," said the queen; "it matters not how it came; it is a bad omen; some misfortune is about to happen. I remember the day before my father died, the Conde de Saldana came to court with a spot of blood upon the lace of his cardinal; and on that fatal day which——"

The door of the apartment at this moment opened, and Anne of Austria, filled with her own peculiar superstition, stopped in the midst of her speech and turned her eye enxiously towards it, as if she expected the coming of some ghastly apparition. The figure that entered, however, though it possessed a dignity scarcely earthly, and a still calm grace—an almost inanimate composure, rarely seen in beings agitated by human passions, was, nevertheless, no form calculated to inspire alarm.

"Oh, Mademoiselle de Hauteford!" cried the queen, her face brightening as she spoke; "De Beaumont, you will love her, for that she is one of my firmest friends."

At the name of De Hauteford, Pauline drew up her slight elegant figure to its full height, with a wild start, like a deer suddenly frightened by some distant sound, and drawing her hand across her forehead, brushed back the two or three dark curls which had again fallen over her clear fair brow.

"De Hauteford!" cried Anne of Austria as the young lady advanced, "what has happened? You look pale—some evil is abroad."

"I would not have intruded on your majesty or on these ladies," said Mademoiselle de Hauteford, with a graceful but cold inclination of the head towards the strangers, "had it not been that Monsieur Seguin, your majesty's surgeon, requests the favor of an audience immediately. Nor does he wish to be seen by the common attendants; in truth, he has followed me to the antechamber, where he waits your majesty's pleasure."

"Admit him, admit him!" cried the queen. "What can he want at this hour?"

The surgeon was instantly brought into the presence of the queen by Mademoiselle de Hauteford; but, after approaching his royal mistress with a profound bow, he remained in silence, glancing his eye towards the strangers who stood in the apartment, in such a manner as to intimate that his communication required to be made in private.

"Speak, speak, Seguin!" cried the queen, translating his look and answering it at once; "these are all friends, old and dear friends."

"If such be your majesty's pleasure," replied the surgeon, with that sort of short dry voice which generally denotes a man of few words, "I must inform you at once, that young Count de Blenau has been this morning attacked by robbers, while hunting in the forest, and is severely hurt."

While Seguin communicated this intelligence, Pauline (she scarce knew why) fixed her eye upon Mademoiselle de Hauteford, whose clear pale cheek, ever almost of the hue of alabaster, showed that it could become still paler. The queen too, though the rouge she wore concealed any change of complexion, appeared manifestly agitated. "I told you so, De Beaumont," she exclaimed —"that blood foreboded evil: I never knew the sign to fail. This is bad news truly, Seguin," she continued. "Poor De Blenau! Surely he will not die?"

"I hope not, madam," replied the surgeon; "I see every chance of his recovery."

"But speak more freely," said the queen. "Have you

learnt anything from him? These are all friends, I tell you."

"The count is very weak, madam," answered Seguin, both from loss of blood and a stunning blow on the head; but he desired me to tell your majesty, that though the wound is in his side, his heart is uninjured!"

"Oh, I understand, I understand," exclaimed the queen. "De Blenau is one out of a thousand; I must write him a note; follow me, Seguin. Good-night, dear Madame de Beaumont. Farewell, Pauline!—Come to my levée to-morrow, and we will talk over old stories and new hopes.—But have a care, Pauline—no more blood upon your robe. It is a bad sign in the house of Austria."

The moment the queen was gone, Pauline pleaded fatigue, and retired to her chamber, followed by her maid Louise, who, be it remarked, had remained in the room during the royal visit.

"This is a strange place, this St. Germain," said the waiting-woman, as she undressed her mistress.

"It is indeed!" replied Pauline. "I wish I had never seen it. But of one thing let me warn you, Louise, before it is too late. Never repeat anything you may see or hear, while you are at the court; for if you do, your life may answer for it."

"My life! Mademoiselle Pauline," exclaimed the soubrette, as if she doubted her ears.

"Yes, indeed, your life!" replied the young lady. "So beware."

"Then I wish I had never seen the place either," rejoined the maid; "for what is the use of seeing and hearing things, if one may not talk about them?—and who can be always watching one's tongue?"

With the happy irregularity of all true stories, we must return, for a moment, to a very significant person,—the woodman of Mantes.

Chavigni, as we have seen, cast his purse upon the ground, and rode away from the cottage of the wood-

man, little heeding what so insignificant an agent might
do or say. Yet Philip's first thought was one which
would have procured him speedy admission to the Bastile, had Chavigni been able to divine its nature. "The
young count shall know all about it," said Philip to himself. "That's a great rogue in Isabel and silver, for all
his fine clothes, or I'm much mistaken."

His next object of attention was the purse; and after
various *pros* and *cons,* inclination, the best logician in
the world, reasoned him into taking it. "For," said
Philip, "dirty fingers soil no gold;" and having carefully put it into his pouch, the woodman laid his finger
upon the side of his nose, and plunged headlong into a
deep meditation concerning the best and least suspicious
method of informing the young Count de Blenau of all
he had seen, heard, or suspected.

In the first place, he commanded his son Charles to
load the mule with wood, notwithstanding the boy's observation, that no one would buy wood at that time of
the morning, or rather the night. Philip then contrived
to awaken Joan, his wife, to a sense of external things;
and perceiving that, after various yawns and stretches,
her mind had arrived at the point of comprehending a
simple proposition, "Get up, Joan, get up!" cried he.
"I want you to write a letter for me; writing being a
gift that, by the blessing of God, I do not possess."

The wife readily obeyed; for Philip, though as kind as
the air of spring, had a high notion of marital privileges,
and did not often suffer his commands to be disputed
within his little sphere of dominion. However, it seemed
a sort of tenure by which his sway was held, that Joan,
his wife, should share in all his secrets; and accordingly,
in the present instance, the good woodman related in
somewhat prolix style, not only all that had passed between Chavigni and Lafemas in the house, but much of
what they had said before they even knocked at his door.

"For you must know, Joan," said he, "that I could

not sleep for thinking of all this day's bad work; and, as I lay awake, I heard horses stop at the water, and people speaking, and very soon what they said made me wish to hear more, which I did, as I have told you. And now, Joan, I think it right, as a Christian and a man, to let this young cavalier know what they are plotting against him. So sit thee down; here is a pen and ink, and a plain sheet out of the boy's holy catechism,— God forgive me! But it could not go to a better use."

It matters not much to tell all the various considerations which were weighed and discussed by Philip and his wife in the construction of this epistle. Suffice it to say that it was calculated to convey to the Count de Blenau all the information which the woodcutter possessed, although that information might be clothed in homely language, without much perfection, either in writing or orthography.

When it had been read, and re-read, and twisted up according to the best conceit of the good couple, it was entrusted to Charles, the woodman's boy, with many a charge and direction concerning its delivery. For his part, glad of a day's sport, he readily undertook the task, and driving the laden mule before him, set out, whistling, on his way to St. Germain. He had not, however, proceeded far, when he was overtaken by Philip with new directions; the principal one being to say, if any one should actually see him deliver the note, and make inquiries, that it came from a lady. " For," said Philip,— and he thought the observation was a shrewd one,— " so handsome a youth as the young count must have many ladies who write to him."

Charles did not very well comprehend what it was all about, but he was well enough contented to serve the young count, who had given him many a kind word and a piece of silver when the hunting-parties of the court had stopped to water their horses at the *abreuvoir*. The boy was diligent and active, and soon reached St. Germain.

His next task was to find out the lodging of the Count de Blenau: and, after looking about for some time, he addressed himself for information, to a stout, jovial-looking servant, who was sauntering down the street, gazing about at the various hotels, with a look of easy *nonchalance*, as if idleness was his employment.

"Why do you ask, my boy?" demanded the man, without answering his question.

"I want to sell my wood," replied the woodman's son, remembering that his errand was to be private. "Where does he lodge, good sir?"

"Why, the count does not buy wood in this hot weather," rejoined the other.

"I should suppose the count does not buy wood himself, at all," replied the boy, putting the question aside with all the shrewdness of a French peasant; "but, perhaps, his cook will."

"Suppose I buy your wood, my man," said the servant.

"Why, you are very welcome, sir," answered Charles; "but if you do not want it, I pray you in honesty show me which is the Count de Blenau's hotel."

"Well, I will show thee," said the servant; "I am e'en going thither myself, on the part of the Marquise de Beaumont, to ask after the young count's health."

"Oh, then, you are one of those who were with the carriage yesterday, when he was wounded in the wood," exclaimed the boy. "Now I remember your colors. Were you not one of those on horseback?"

"Even so," answered the man; "and if I forget not, thou art the woodman's boy. But come, prithee, tell us what is thy real errand with the count. We are all his friends, you know, and selling him the wood is all a tale."

Charles thought for a moment, to determine whether he should tell the man all he knew or not; but remembering the answer his father had furnished him with, he replied, "The truth then is, I carry him a note from a lady."

4

"Oh, ho! my little Mercury!" cried the servant; "so you are as close with your secrets as if you were an older politician. This is the way you sel¹ wood, is it?"

"I do not know what you mean by Mercury," rejoined the boy.

"Why he was a great man in his day," replied the servant, "and, as I take it, used to come and go between the gods and goddesses; notwithstanding which, Monsieur Rubens, who is the greatest painter that ever lived, has painted this same Mercury as one of the late queen's * council, but nevertheless he was a carrier of messages, and so forth."

"Why, then, thou art more Mercury than I, for thou carriest a message, and I a letter," answered Charles, as they approached the hotel of the count, towards which they had been bending their steps during this conversation. Their proximity to his dwelling, in all probability, saved Charles from an angry answer; for his companion did not seem at all pleased with having the name of Mercury retorted upon himself; and intending strongly to impress upon the woodman's boy that he was a person of far too great consequence to be jested with, he assumed a tone of double pomposity towards the servant who appeared on the steps of the hotel. "Tell Henry de La Mothe, the count's page," said the servant, "that the Marquise de Beaumont has sent to inquire after his master's health."

The servant retired with the message, and in a moment after Henry de La Mothe himself appeared, and informed the messenger that his master was greatly better. He had slept well, he said, during the night; and his surgeons assured him that the wounds which he had received were likely to produce no further harm than the weakness naturally consequent upon so great a loss of blood as

* Alluding, no doubt, to the picture of the reconciliation of Mary de Medicis and her son Louis XIII. in which Mercury seems hand in glove with the cardinals and statesmen of the day.

that which he had sustained. Having given this message on his master's account, Henry, on his own, began to question the servant concerning many little particulars of his own family; his father being, as already said, *fermier* to Madame de Beaumont.

Charles, the woodman's son, perceiving that the conversation had turned to a subject too interesting soon to be discussed, glided past the marchioness's servant, placed the note he carried in the hand of the count's page, pressed his finger on his lip, in sign that it was to be given privately, and detaching himself from them, without waiting to be questioned, drove back his mule through the least known parts of the forest, and rendered an account to his father of the success of his expedition.

" Who can that note be from? " said the Marchioness de Beaumont's servant to Henry de La Mothe. " The boy told me it came from a lady."

" From Mademoiselle de Hauteford, probably," replied the page, thoughtfully. " I must give it to my master without delay, if he be strong enough to read it. We will talk more another day, good friend; "—and he left him.

" From Mademoiselle de Hauteford! " said the man. " Oh, ho! " and he went home to tell all he knew to Louise, the soubrette.

CHAPTER V.

The Marquis de Cinq Mars, the Count de Fontrailles, and King Louis XIII. all making fools of themselves in their own way.

At the time of my tale the brighter part of life had passed away from King Louis; and now that it had fallen into the sear, he seemed to have given it up as unworthy a further effort. He struggled not even for that appearance of royal state which his proud minister was unwilling to allow him, and, retired at Chantilly, passed his time in a thousand weak amusements, which but served to hurry by the moments of a void and weary existence.

It was at this time that the first news of the Cardinal de Richelieu's illness began to be noised abroad. His health had long been declining; but so feared was that redoubtable minister, that though many remarked the increased hollowness of his dark eye, and the deepening lines upon his pale cheek, no one dared to whisper what many hoped—that the tyrant of both king and people was falling under the sway of a still stronger hand.

The morning was yet in its prime. The gray mist had hardly rolled away from the old towers and battlements of the Château of Chantilly, which, unlike the elegant building afterwards erected on the same spot, offered then little but strong fortified walls and turrets. The heavy night-dew lay still sparkling upon the long grass in the avenues of the park, when two gentlemen were observed walking near the palace, turning up and down the alley, then called the Avenue de Luzarches, with that kind of sauntering pace which indicated their conversation to be of no very interesting description.

Perhaps in all that vast variety of shapes which Nature has bestowed upon mankind, and in all those innate differences by which she has distinguished man's soul, no two figures or two minds could have been found more opposite than those of the two men thus keeping a willing companionship—the Count de Fontrailles and the Marquis de Cinq Mars, Grand Ecuyer, or, as it may be best translated, Master of the Horse.

Cinq Mars, though considerably above the common height of men, was formed in the most finished and elegant proportion, and possessed a native dignity of demeanor, which characterized even those wild gesticulations in which the excess of a bright and enthusiastic mind often led him to indulge.

On the other hand, Fontrailles, short in stature and mean in appearance, was in countenance equally unprepossessing. He had but one redeeming feature, in the quick gray eye, that, with the clear keenness of its light, seemed to penetrate the deepest thoughts of those upon whom it was turned.

And yet, though not friends, they were often (as I have said) companions; for Cinq Mars was too noble to suspect, and Fontrailles too wary to be known—besides, in the present instance, he had a point to carry, and therefore was doubly disguised.

"You have heard the news, doubtless, Cinq Mars," said Fontrailles, leading the way from the great Avenue de Luzarches into one of the smaller alleys, where they were less liable to be watched; for he well knew that the conversation he thus broached would lead to those wild starts and gestures in his companion which might call upon them some suspicion, if observed. Cinq Mars made no reply, and he proceeded. "The cardinal is ill!" and he fixed his eye upon the Master of the Horse as if he would search his soul. But Cinq Mars still was silent, and, apparently deeply busied with other thoughts, continued beating the shrubs on each side of the path with his sheathed sword, without even a glance towards his companion. After a moment or two, however, he raised his head with an air of careless abstraction: "What a desert this place has become!" said he; "look how all these have grown up between the trees. One might really be as well in a forest as a royal park nowadays."

"But you have made me no answer," rejoined Fontrailles, returning perseveringly to the point on which his companion seemed unwilling to touch: "I said the cardinal is ill."

"Well, well! I hear," answered Cinq Mars with a peevish start, like a restive horse forced forward on a road he is unwilling to take. "What is it you would have me say?—That I am sorry? Well, be it so—I am sorry for it—sorry that a trifling sickness, which will pass away in a moon, should give France hopes of that liberation which is yet far off."

"But, nevertheless, you would be sorry were this great man to die," said Fontrailles, putting it half as a question, half as an undoubted proposition, and looking in the face of the marquis, with an appearance of hesitating uncertainty.

Cinq Mars could contain himself no more. "What!" cried he vehemently, "sorry for the peace of the world! —sorry for the weal of my country!—sorry for the liberty of my king! Why, I tell thee, Fontrailles, should the Cardinal de Richelieu die, the people of France would join in pulling down the scaffolds and the gibbets to make bonfires of them!"

"Who ever dreamed of hearing *you* say so?" said his companion. "All France agrees with you, no doubt: but we all thought that the Marquis de Cinq Mars either loved the cardinal, or feared him, too much to see his crimes."

"Fear him?" exclaimed Cinq Mars, the blood mounting to his cheek as if the very name of fear wounded his sense of honor. He then paused, looked into his real feelings, shook his head mournfully, and after a moment's interval of bitter silence, added, "True! true! Who is there that does not fear him? Nevertheless, it is impossible to see one's country bleeding for the merciless cruelty of one man, the prisons filled with the best and bravest of the land to quiet his suspicions, and the king held in worst bondage than a slave to gratify the daring ambition of this insatiate churchman, and not to wish that Heaven had sent it otherwise."

" It is not Heaven's fault, sir," replied Fontrailles; " it is our own, that we do suffer it. Had we one man in France who, with sufficient courage, talent, and influence, had the true spirit of a patriot, our unhappy country might soon be freed from the bondage under which she groans."

" But where shall we find such a man?" asked the Master of the Horse, either really not understanding the aim of Fontrailles, or wishing to force him to a clearer explanation of his purpose. " Such an undertaking as you hint at," he continued, " must be well considered, and well supported, to have any effect. It must be strengthened by wit—by courage—and by illustrious names.—It must have the power of wealth and the power of reputation.—It must be the rousing of the lion with all his force, to shake off the toils by which he is encompassed."

" But still there must be some one to rouse him," said Fontrailles, fixing his eyes on Cinq Mars with a peculiar expression, as if to denote that he was the man alluded to. " Suppose this were France," he proceeded, unbuckling his sword from the belt, and drawing a few lines on the ground with the point of the sheath: " show me a province or a circle that will not rise at an hour's notice to cast off the yoke of this hated cardinal. Here is Normandy, almost in a state of revolt;—here is Guienne, little better;—here is Sedan, our own;—here are the mountains of Auvergne, filled with those whom his tyranny has driven into their solitude for protection;—

and here is Paris and its insulted parliament, waiting but for opportunity."

"And here," said Cinq Mars, with a melancholy smile, following the example of his companion, and pointing out with his sword, as if on a map, the supposed situations of the various places to which he referred—"and here is Peronne, and Rouen, and Havre, and Lyons, and Tours, and Brest, and Bordeaux, and every town or fortress in France filled with his troops and governed by his creatures; and here is Flanders, with Chaunes and Mielleray, and fifteen thousand men at his disposal; and here is Italy, with Bouillon, and as many more, ready to march at his command!"

"But suppose I could show," said Fontrailles, laying his hand on his companion's arm, and detaining him as he was about to walk on—"but suppose I could show that Mielleray would not march,—that Bouillon would declare for us,—that England would aid us with money, and Spain would put five thousand men at our command, —that the king's own brother——"

Cinq Mars waved his hand: "No! no! no!" said he, in a firm, bitter tone; "Gaston of Orleans has led too many to the scaffold already. The weak, wavering duke is ever the executioner of his friends. Remember poor Montmorency!"

"Let me proceed," said Fontrailles; "hear me to an end, and then judge. I say, suppose that the king's own brother should give us his name and influence, and the king himself should yield us his consent."

"Ha!" exclaimed Cinq Mars, pausing abruptly. The idea of gaining the king had never occurred to him; and now it came like a ray of sunshine through a cloud, brightening the prospect which had been before in shadow. "Think you the king would consent?"

"Assuredly!" replied his companion. "Does he not hate the cardinal as much as any one? Does not his blood boil under the bonds he cannot break? And would

he not bless the man who gave him freedom? Think,
Cinq Mars!" he continued, endeavoring to throw much
energy in his manner, for he knew that the ardent mind
of his companion wanted but the spark of enthusiasm to
inflame—" think, what a glorious object! to free alike the
people and their sovereign, and to rescue the many victims even now destined to prove the tyrant's cruelty!
Think, think of the glorious reward, the thanks of a
king, the gratitude of a nation, and the blessings of thousands saved from dungeons and from death!"

It worked as he could have wished. The enthusiasm
of his words had their full effect on the mind of his companion. As the other went on, the eye of Cinq Mars
lightened with all the wild ardor of his nature, and striking his hand upon the hilt of his sword, as if longing to
draw it in the inspiring cause of his country's liberty,
" Glorious indeed!" he exclaimed; " glorious indeed!"

But immediately after, fixing his glance upon the
ground, he fell into meditation of the many circumstances
of the times; and as his mind's eye ran over the difficulties and dangers which surrounded the enterprise, the
enthusiasm which had beamed in his eye, like the last
flash of an expiring fire, died away, and he replied with
a sigh, " What you have described, sir, is indeed a glorious form; but it is dead—it wants a soul. The king,
though everything great and noble, has been too long
governed now to act for himself. The Duke of Orleans
is weak and undecided as a child. Bouillon is far
away——"

" And where is Cinq Mars?" demanded Fontrailles;
" where is the man whom the king really loves? If Cinq
Mars has forgot his own powers, so has not France; and
she now tells him—though by so weak a voice as mine—
that he is destined to be the soul of this great body, to
animate this goodly frame, to lead this conspiracy, if
that can be so called which has a king at its head, and
princes for its support."

What Fontrailles proposed to him bore a plausible aspect. It appeared likely to succeed; and, if it did so, offered him that reward for which, of all others, his heart beat—glory! But there was one point on which he paused: "You forget," said he,—"you forget that I owe all to Richelieu,—you forget that, however he may have wronged this country, he has not wronged me; and though I may wish that such a being did not exist, it is not for me to injure him."

"True, most true!" replied his wily companion, who knew that the appearance of frank sincerity would win more from Cinq Mars than aught else: "if he has done as you say, be still his friend. Forget your country in your gratitude; though in the days of ancient virtue patriotism was held paramount. We must not hope for such things now—so no more of that. But if I can show that this proud minister has never served you; if I can prove that every honor which of late has fallen upon you, far from being a bounty of the cardinal, has proceeded solely from the favor of the king, and has been wrung from the hard churchman as a mere concession to the monarch's whim; if it can be made clear that the Marquis de Cinq Mars would now have been a duke and Constable of France, had not his kind friend the cardinal whispered he was unfit for such an office: then will you have no longer the excuse of friendship, and your country's call must and shall be heard."

"I can scarce credit your words, Fontrailles," replied Cinq Mars. "You speak boldly, but do you speak truly?"

"Most truly, on my life!" replied Fontrailles. "Think you, Cinq Mars, if I did not well know that I could prove each word I have said, that thus I would have placed my most hidden thoughts in the power of a man who avows himself the friend of Richelieu?"

"Prove to me,—but prove to me, that I am not bound to him in gratitude," cried Cinq Mars vehemently; "take from me the bonds by which he has chained my honor, and I will hurl him from his height of power, or die in the attempt."

"Hush!" exclaimed Fontrailles, laying his finger on his lip as they turned into another alley, "we are no longer alone. Govern yourself, Cinq Mars, and I will prove every title of what I have advanced ere we be two hours older."

This was uttered in a low tone of voice; for there was indeed another group in the same avenue with themselves. The party, which was rapidly approaching, consisted of three persons, of whom one was a step in advance, and, though in no degree superior to the others in point of dress, was distinguished from them by that indescribable something which constitutes the idea of dignity. He was habited in a plain suit of black silk, with buttons of jet, and every part of his dress, even to the sheath and hilt of his *couteau de chasse*, corresponding. On his right hand he wore a thick glove, of the particular kind generally used by the sportsmen of the period, but more particularly by those who employed themselves in the then fashionable sport of bird-catching; and the nets and snares of various kinds carried by the other two seemed to evince that such had been the morning's amusement of the whole party.

The king, for such was the person who approached, was rather above the middle height, and of a spare habit. His complexion was very pale; and his hair, which had one time been of the richest brown, was now mingled throughout with gray. But still there was much to interest, both in his figure and countenance. There was a certain air of easy self-possession in all his movements; and even when occupied with the most trivial employment, which was often the case, there was still a degree of dignity in his manner that seemed to show his innate feeling of their emptiness, and his own consciousness of how inferior they were both to his situation and his talents. His features at all times appeared handsome, but more especially when any sudden excitement called up the latent animation of his dark-brown eye, recalling to the mind of those who remembered the days gone before, that young and fiery prince who could not brook the usurped sway even of his own highly-talented mother, but who had now become the slave of her slave. The consciousness of his fallen situation, and of his inability to call up sufficient energy of mind to disengage himself, generally cast upon him an appearance of profound sadness: occasionally, however, flashes of angry irritability would break across the cloud of melancholy which hung over him, and show the full expression of his countenance, which at other times displayed nothing but the traces of deep and bitter thought, or a momentary sparkle of weak, unthinking merriment. So frequent, however, were the changes to be observed in the depressed monarch, that some persons even doubted whether they were not assumed to cover deeper intentions.

The rapid pace with which he always proceeded, soon brought the king close to Cinq Mars and Fontrailles. "Good-morrow, Monsieur de Fontrailles," said he, as the count bowed low at his approach. "Do not remain uncovered. 'Tis a fine day for forest sports, but not for bare heads; though I have heard say, that if you were in the thickest mist of all Holland you would see your way through it. What! *mon grand ecuyer*," he continued, turning to Cinq Mars; "as sad as if thou hadst been plotting, and wert dreaming even now of the block and axe?" And with a kind and familiar air he laid his hand upon his favorite's arm: who on his part started, as if the monarch had read his thoughts and foretold his doom.

Fontrailles fixed his eye on Cinq Mars, and seeing plainly the effect of Louis's speech, he hastened to wipe it away. "To calculate petty dangers in a great undertaking," said he, "were as weak as to think over all the falls one may meet with in the chase, before we get on horseback."

Both Cinq Mars and the king were passionately fond of the noble forest sport, so that the simile of Fontrailles went directly home, more especially to the king, who, following the idea thus called up, made a personal application of it to him who introduced it. " Jesu, that were folly indeed! " he exclaimed, in answer to the count's observation. " But you are not fond of the chase, either, Monsieur de Fontrailles, if I think right; I never saw you follow boar or stag, that I can call to mind."

" More my misfortune than my fault, sire," replied Fontrailles. " Had I ever been favored with an invitation to follow the royal hounds, your majesty would have found me as keen of the sport as even St. Hubert is said to have been of yore."

" Blessed be his memory! " cried the king. " But we will hunt to-day; we will see you ride, Monsieur de Fontrailles. What say you, Cinq Mars? The parties who went out to turn a stag last night presented this morning, that in the *bosquet* at the end of the forest, near Argenin, is quartered a fat stag of ten, and another by Boisjardin; but that by Argenin will be the best, for he has but one *refuite* by the long alley. Come, gentlemen, seek your boots, seek your boots; and as our *grand veneur* is not at Chantilly, you, Cinq Mars, shall superintend the chase. Order the *maître valet des chiens* to assemble the old pack and the *relais* at the *Carrefour d'Argenin,* and then we will quickly to horse." So saying, he turned away to prepare for his favorite sport, but scarcely had gone many paces ere he slackened his pace, and allowed the two gentlemen to rejoin him. " What think you, friend? " said he, addressing Cinq Mars; " they tell me the cardinal is sick. Have you heard of it? "

" I have heard a vague report of the kind," replied Cinq Mars, watching his master's countenance, " but as yet nothing certain. May I crave what information your majesty possesses? "

" Why, he is sick, very sick," replied Louis, " and perchance may die. May his soul find mercy! Perchance he may die, and then——" And the king fell into deep thought.

Fontrailles watched the alteration of the king's countenance, and, skilful at reading the mind's workings by the face, he added, as if finishing the sentence which Louis had left unconcluded, but taking care to blend what he said with an air of raillery towards the master of the horse, lest he should offend the irritable monarch—" and then," said he, " Cinq Mars shall be a duke. Is it not so, sire? "

Louis started. His thoughts had been engaged in far greater schemes; and yet rewarding his friends and favorites always formed a great part of the pleasure he anticipated in power, and he replied, without anger, " Most likely it will be so. Indeed," he added, " had my wishes, as a man, been followed,"—and he turned kindly towards the master of the horse,—" it should have been so long ago, Cinq Mars. But kings, you know, are obliged to yield their private inclinations to what the state requires."

Fontrailles glanced his eye towards the grand ecuyer, as if desiring him to remark the king's words. Cinq Mars bent his head in token that he comprehended, and replied to the king: " I understand your majesty; but, believe me, sire, no honor or distinction could more bind Cinq Mars to his king than duty, gratitude, and affection do at this moment."

" I believe thee, friend,—I believe thee, from my soul," said Louis. " God forgive us that we should desire the death of any man! And surely do not I that of the cardinal, for he is a good minister, and a man of powerful mind. But, withal, we may wish that he was more gentle and forgiving. Nevertheless, he is a great man. See how he thwarts and rules half the kings in Europe; see how he presses the emperor, and our good brother-in-law, Philip of Spain; while the great Gustavus, this northern hero, is little better than his general."

" He is assuredly a great man, sire," replied Cinq Mars. " But permit me to remark that a great bad man is worse than one of less talents, for he has the extended capability of doing harm; and perhaps, sire, if this minister contented himself with thwarting kings abroad, he would do better than by opposing the will of his own sovereign at home."

The time, however, was not yet come for Louis to make even an attempt toward liberating himself from the trammels to which he had been so long accustomed. Habit in this had far more power over his mind than even the vast and aspiring talents of Richelieu. No man in France, perhaps, more contemned or hated the cardinal than the royal slave whom he had so long subjugated to his burdensome sway. Yet Louis, amidst all his dreams for the future, looked with dread upon losing the support of a man whom he detested, but upon whose counsels and abilities he had been accustomed to rely with confidence and security.

Cinq Mars saw plainly the state of his master's mind: and as he entered the palace he again began to doubt whether he should at all lend himself to the bold and dangerous measure which Fontrailles had suggested. While the king's mind, as he returned to the Château de Chantilly, was agitated by vague hopes and fears; and while the thoughts of Cinq Mars ran over all the difficulties and dangers of the future prospect, reverted to the obligations Richelieu had once conferred upon him, or scanned the faults and crimes of the minister, till the struggle of patriotism and gratitude left nothing but doubt behind: the imagination of Fontrailles was very differently occupied. It was not that he pondered the means of engaging more firmly the wavering mind of

Cinq Mars. No, for he had marked him for his own:
and, from that morning's conversation, felt sure of his
companion. The occupation of his mind as they approached the castle was of a more personal nature. The
truth is, that so far from discomposing himself upon the
score of distant evils, the sole trouble of his thoughts was
the hunting-party into which he had entrapped himself.
Being by no means a good horseman, and caring not one
sous for a pastime which involved far too much trouble
and risk to accord in any degree with his idea of pleasure,
Fontrailles had professed himself fond of hunting merely
to please the king, without ever dreaming that he should
be called upon to give further proof of his veneration for
the royal sport.

He saw plainly, however, that his case admitted of
no remedy. Go he must; and, having enough philosophy
in his nature to meet inevitable evils with an unshrinking
mind, he prepared to encounter all the horrors of the
chase, as if they were his principal delight.

He accordingly got on his boots with as much alacrity
as their nature permitted, for, each weighing fully eight
pounds, they were somewhat ponderous and unmanage-
able. He then hastily loaded his pistols, stuck his *couteau de chasse* in his belt, and throwing the feather from
his hat, was the first ready to mount in the court-yard.

" Why, how is this, Monsieur de Fontrailles? " said the
king, who in a few minutes joined him in the area where
the horses were assembled. " The first at your post!
You are, indeed, keen for the sport. Some one see for
Cinq Mars. Oh! here he comes. Mount, gentlemen,
mount! Our ordinaries of the chase and lieutenants
await us at the *Carrefour d'Argenin.* Mount, gentlemen, mount! Ha! have you calculated your falls for
to-day, Monsieur de Fontrailles, as you spoke of this
morning? " And the king's eyes glistened with almost
childish eagerness for his favorite pastime.

In the meanwhile Cinq Mars had approached with a

slow step and a gloomy countenance, showing none of the alacrity of Fontrailles, nor the enthusiastic ardor of the king. ". There are other dangers than falls to be met with in chase, my liege," said the Master of the Horse, with a bitter expression of displeasure in his manner; "and that Claude de Blenau could inform your majesty."

"I know not what you mean, Cinq Mars," answered the king. "De Blenau is a gallant cavalier; as stanch to his game as a beagle of the best; and though he shows more service to our queen than to ourself, he is no less valued for that."

"He is one cavalier out of ten thousand," replied Cinq Mars, warmly: "my dearest companion and friend; and whilst Cinq Mars has a sword to wield, De Blenau shall never want one to second his quarrel."

"Why, what ails thee, Cinq Mars?" demanded the king with some surprise. "Thou art angry; what is it now?"

"It is, sire," replied the master of the horse, "that I have just had a courier from St. Germain, who bears me word that, three days since past, the count as your majesty and I have often done, was hunting in the neighborhood of Mantes, and was there most treacherously attacked by an armed band, in which adventure he suffered two wounds that nearly drained his good heart of blood. Shall this be tolerated, sire?"

"No, indeed! no, indeed!" replied the king with much warmth. "This shall be looked to. Our kingdom must not be overrun with robbers and brigands."

"Robbers!" exclaimed Cinq Mars, indignantly. "I know not—they may have been robbers; but my letters say that one of them wore colors of Isabel and silver."

"Those are the colors of Chavigni's livery," replied the king, who knew the most minute difference in the bearing of every family in the kingdom with wonderful precision. "This must be looked to, and it *shall*, or I am not deserving of my name. But now mount, gentlemen, mount! we are waited for at the rendezvous."

5

The *Carrefour d'Argenin,* at which the king and his attendants soon arrived, was a large open space in the forest, where four roads crossed. Louis had chosen this spot for the rendezvous perhaps as much on account of its picturesque beauty as for any other reason. Deprived as he was of courtly splendor and observance, his mind, unperverted by the giddy show and tinsel pomp that generally surround a royal station, regarded with a degree of enthusiasm the real loveliness of nature; and now it was some time before even the preparations for his favorite sport could call his attention from the picturesque beauty of the spot.

The policy of Richelieu, which had led him to deprive the king of many of the external marks of sovereignty, as well as of the real power, taught him also to encourage all those sports which might at once occupy Louis's mind, and place him at a distance from the scene of government. Thus, the hunting equipage of the king was maintained in almost more than regal luxury.

The first objects that presented themselves, in the *Carrefour d'Argenin,* were a multitude of dogs and horses, grouped together with the lieutenants of the forest, and the various officers of the hunt, under those trees which would best afford them shade as the sun got up. Various *piqueurs* and valets were seen about the ground, some holding the horses, some laying out the table for the royal *déjeûner,* and some busily engaged in cutting long straight wands from the more pliable sort of trees, and peeling off the bark for a certain distance, so as to leave a sort of handle or hilt still covered, while the rest of the stick, about three feet in length, remained bare. These, called " batons de chasse," were first presented to the king, who, having chosen one, directed the rest to be distributed among his friends and attendants, for the purpose of guarding their heads from the boughs, which in the rapidity of the chase, while it continued in the forest, often inflicted serious injuries.

The *maître valet des chiens*, and his ordinaries, each armed with a portentous-looking horn, through the circles of which were passed a variety of dog couples, were busily occupied in distributing the hounds into their different relays, and the grooms and other attendants were seen trying the girths of the heavy hunting saddles, loading the pistols, or placing them in the holsters, and endeavoring to distinguish themselves fully as much by their bustle as by their activity.

After examining the preparations with a critical eye, and inquiring into the height, age, size, and other distinctive signs of the stag which was to be hunted, Louis placed himself at the breakfast-table which had been prepared in the midst of the green, and motioning Cinq Mars and Fontrailles to be seated, entered into a lively discussion concerning the proper spots for placing the relays of horses and dogs. At length it was determined that six hounds and four hunters should be stationed at about two leagues and a half on the high-road; that twelve dogs and four *piqueurs*, with an ordinary of the chase, should take up a position upon the side of a hill under which the stag was likely to pass; and that another relay should remain at a spot called *Le Croix de Bois*, within sight of which the hunt would be obliged to come, if the animal, avoiding the open country, made for the other extremity of the forest.

It fell upon Cinq Mars to communicate these directions to the officers of the hunt, which he did in that sort of jargon, which the sports of the field had made common in those days, but which would now be hardly intelligible. He was engaged in giving general orders, that the horses should be kept in the shade and ready to be mounted at a moment's notice, in case the king, or any of his suite should require them, and that the ordinary should by no means let slip any of the dogs of the relay upon the stag, even if it passed his station, without especial orders from the *piqueurs* of the principal hunt—when suddenly he

stopped, and pointing with his hand, a man was discovered
standing in one of the avenues, apparently watching the
royal party.

The circumstance would have passed without notice,
had it not been for the extraordinary stature of the in-
truder, who appeared fully as tall as Cinq Mars himself.
Attention was further excited by his disappearing as soon
as he was observed; and some grooms were sent to bring
him before the king, but their search was in vain, and the
matter was soon forgotten.

The stag, poor silly beast, who had been dozing away
his time in a thicket, at about half a mile distance, was
soon roused by the very unwished-for appearance of the
huntsmen, and taking his path down the principal
avenue, bounded away towards the open country. The
horns sounded loud, the couples were unloosed, the
dogs slipped, and away went man and beast in the pursuit. For a moment or two the forest was filled with
clang, and cry, and tumult:—as the hunt swept away, it
grew fainter and fainter, till the sound, almost lost in indistinct distance, left the deep glades of the wood to re-
sume their original silence.

They did not, however, long appear solitary, for in a
few minutes after the hunt had quitted the forest, the
same tall figure, whose apparition had interrupted Cinq
Mars in his oratory concerning the relays, emerged from
one of the narrower paths, leading a strong black horse,
whose trappings were thickly covered with a variety of
different figures in brass, representing the signs of the
zodiac, together with sundry triangles, crescents, and
other shapes, such as formed part of the astrological
quackery of that day. The appearance of the master was
not less singular in point of dress than that of the horse.
He wore a long black robe, somewhat in the shape of that
borne by the order of Black Friars, but sprinkled with
silver signs. This, which made him look truly gigantic,
was bound round his waist by a broad girdle of white
leather, traced all over with strange characters, that might

have been called hieroglyphics, had they signified anything; but which were, probably, as unmeaning as tho
science they were intended to dignify.

To say the truth, the wearer did not seem particularly
at his ease in his habiliments; for when, after having
looked cautiously around, he attempted to mount his
horse, the long drapery of his gown got entangled round
his feet at every effort, and it was not till he had vented
several very ungodly execrations, and effected a long rent
in the back of his robe, that he accomplished the ascent
into the saddle. Once there, however, the dexterity of
his horsemanship, and his bearing altogether, made him
appear much more like the captain of a band of heavy
cavalry than an astrologer, notwithstanding the long
snowy beard which hung down to his girdle, and the
profusion of white locks that, escaping from his fur cap,
floated wildly over his face, and concealed the greater
part of its features.

The horseman paused for a moment, seemingly immersed in thought, while his horse, being a less considerate beast than himself, kept pawing the ground, eager
to set off. "Let me see," said the horseman; "the stag
will soon be turned on the high-road by the carriers for
Clermont, and must come round under the hill, and then
I would take the world to a *chapon de Maine*, that that
fool Andrieu lets slip his relay, and drives the beast to
water. If so, I have them at the *Croix de Bois*. At all
events one must try." And thus speaking, he struck his
horse hard with a thick kind of truncheon he held in his
hand, and was soon out of the forest.

In the meanwhile the king and his suite followed close
upon the hounds; the monarch and Cinq Mars animated
by the love of the chase, and Fontrailles risking to break
his neck rather than be behind. The road for some way
was perfectly unobstructed, and as long as it remained
so, the stag followed it without deviation; but at length a
train of carriers' wagons appeared, wending their way

towards Clermont.   The jingling of the bells on the yokes
of the oxen, and the flaunting of the red and white ribbons on their horns, instantly startled the stag, who, stopping short in his flight, stood at gaze for a moment, and
then darting across the country, entered a narrow track
of that unproductive sandy kind of soil, called in France
landes, which bordered the forest.   It so happened that a
large herd of his horned kindred were lying out in this
very track, enjoying the morning sunshine, and regaling
themselves upon the first fruits that fell from some chest-
nut-trees, which in that place skirted the forest.

Now the stag, remembering an old saying, which sig-
nalizes the solace of " company in distress" dashed
among his fellows, and away all went, flying in every
direction.

The hunters had as little cause to be pleased with this
manœuvre as the stags ; for the hounds being young, were
deceived by a strong family likeness between one of the
herd and the one they had so long followed, and all of the
dogs but four, yielding up the real object of pursuit, gave
chase to a strange stag, who, darting off to the left, took
his way towards the river.   Cinq Mars and most of the
piqueurs, misled by seeing the young hounds have so great
a majority, followed also.   It was in vain the king called
to him to come back that he was hunting the wrong
beast, and was as great a fool as a young hound ; he
neither heeded nor heard, and was soon out of sight.

" *Sacristi!* " cried Louis, " there they go, just like the
world, quitting the true pursuit to follow the first fool
that runs, and priding themselves on being in the right,
when they are most in error ; but come, Monsieur de Fontrailles, we will follow the true stag of the hunt."

But Fontrailles too was gone.   The separation of the
hounds had afforded an opportunity of quitting the sport
not to be neglected, and he had slunk away towards the
palace by the nearest road, which, leading through a narrow dell, skirted the side of the hill opposite to that over

"Que Diable!" cried the king viewing the strange figure of the astrologer. "What do you want? and who are you?" Page 71.

Richelieu.

which the king's stag had taken his course. However, he still heard from time to time the dogs give tongue, and the hunting cry of the king; who, without considering that no one followed, gave the exact number of *mots* on his horn, followed by the halloo, and the "*Il dit vrai! il dit vrai!*" which the *piqueurs* ordinarily give out, to announce that the dog who cried was upon the right scent. Still Fontrailles pursued his way, when suddenly he perceived the stag, who, having distanced the king, was brought to bay under the bank over which his road lay.

At that season of the year, the stag is peculiarly dangerous, but Fontrailles did not want personal courage, and, dismounting from his horse, he sprang to the bottom of the bank; where, drawing his *couteau de chasse*, he prepared to run in upon the beast; but remembering at the moment that the king could not be far distant, he paused, and waiting till Louis came up, held the stirrup and offered his weapon to the monarch, who instantly running in, presented the knife with all the dexterity of an experienced sportsman, and in a moment laid the stag dead at his feet.

It was now the task of Fontrailles to keep off the hounds, while the king, anxious to have all the honors of the day to himself, began what is called in France the "*section,*" and "*curée aux chiens,*" without waiting for *piqueurs* or ordinaries. Nevertheless, he had only time to make the longitudinal division of the skin, and one of the transverse sections from the breast to the knee, when the sound of a horse's feet made him raise his head from his somewhat unkingly occupation, thinking that some of the other hunters must be now come up.

"*Que Diable!*" cried the king, viewing the strange figure of the astrologer we have already noticed in this profound chapter. "*Je veux dire, Vive Dieu!* What do you want? and who are you?"

A friend to the son of Henri Quatre," replied the stranger, advancing his horse closer to the king, who stood gazing on him with no small degree of awe—for be it remembered, that the superstitious belief in all sorts of necromancy was at its height both in England and France.

"A friend to the son of Henri Quatre! and one who comes to warn him of near-approaching dangers."

"What are they, friend?" demanded the king, with a look of credulous surprise. "Let me know whence they arise and how they may be avoided, and your reward is sure."

"I seek no reward," replied the stranger, scornfully. "Can all the gold of France change the star of my destiny? No! Monarch, I come uncalled, and I will go unrewarded. The planets are still doubtful over your house, and therefore I forewarn you ere it be too late. A Spaniard is seeking your overthrow, and a woman is plotting your ruin—a prince is scheming your destruction, and a queen is betraying your trust."

"How!" exclaimed Louis. "Am I to believe—"

"Ask me no questions," cried the stranger, who heard the trampling of horses' feet approaching the scene of conference. "In this roll is written the word of fate. Read it, O king! and timely guard against the evil that menaces." So saying, he threw a scroll of parchment before the king, and spurred on his horse to depart; but at that moment the figure of Cinq Mars, who by this time had run down the stag he had followed, presented itself in his way. "What mumming is this?" cried the master of the horse, regarding the stranger.

"Stop him! Cinq Mars," cried Fontrailles, who foresaw that the stranger's predictions might derange all his schemes. "He is an impostor: do not let him pass!" And at the same time he laid his hand upon the astrologer's bridle. But in a moment, the stranger, spurring on his charger, overturned Fontrailles, shivered the hunting sword, which Cinq Mars had drawn against him, to atoms with one blow of his truncheon, and scattering the grooms and huntsmen like a flock of sheep, was soon out of reach of pursuit.

"What means all this?" exclaimed Cinq Mars; "explain, Fontrailles! Sire, shall we follow yon impostor?"

But Louis's eyes were fixed with a strained gaze upon the scroll, which he held in his hand, and which seemed to absorb every faculty of his soul. At length he raised them, mounted his horse in silence, and still holding the parchment tight in his hand, rode on, exclaiming, "To Chantilly."

CHAPTER VI.

Showing how the green-eyed monster got hold of a young lady's heart, and what he did with it.

THE fatigues of her journey had long worn off, and left Pauline de Beaumont all the glow of wild youthful beauty, which had adorned her in her native hills. But the cheerful gaiety which had distinguished her, the light buoyancy of spirit, that seemed destined to rise above all the sorrows of the world, had not come back with the rose of her cheek, or the lustre of her eye.

At first, Madame de Beaumont fancied that the melancholy of her daughter was caused by the sudden change from many loved scenes, endeared by all the remembrances of infancy, to others in which, as yet, she had acquired no interest. But as a second week followed the first, after their arrival at St. Germain, and the same depression of spirits still continued, the marchioness began to fear that Pauline had some more serious cause of sorrow; and her mind reverted to the suspicions of De Blenau's constancy, which she had been the first to excite in her daughter's bosom.

It was one of those still evenings, when the world, as if melancholy at the sun's decline, seems to watch in silence the departure of his latest beams, and Pauline felt a sensation of quiet, pensive melancholy steal over all her thoughts, harmonizing them with the calmness of the scene.

The window at which she sat looked towards St. Denis, where lay the bones of many a race of kings, who had, in turn, worn that often contested diadem, which to the winner had generally proved a crown of thorns. But her thoughts were not of them. The loss of early hopes, the blight of only love, was the theme on which her mind brooded, like a mother over the tomb of her child.

"Pauline!" said a voice close behind her. She started, turned towards the speaker, and with an impulse stronger than volition, held out her hand to Claude de Blenau. "Pauline," said he, printing a warm kiss on the soft white hand that he held in his, "dear, beautiful Pauline, we have met at last."

From the moment he had spoken, Pauline resolved to believe him true to her; but still she wanted him to tell her so. It was not coquetry! but she was afraid that after what she had seen, and what she had heard, she ought not to be satisfied. Common propriety, she thought, required that she should be jealous till such time as he proved to her that she had no right to be so. She turned pale, and red, and drew back her hand without reply.

De Blenau gazed on her for a moment in silence. "Do you not speak to me, Pauline?" said he at length. "Or is it that you do not know me? True, true! years work a great change at our time of life. But I had fancied— perhaps foolishly fancied—that Pauline de Beaumont would know Claude de Blenau wheresoever they met, as well as De Blenau would know her."

While he spoke, Pauline knew not well what to do with her eyes; so she turned them towards the terrace, and they fell upon Mademoiselle de Hauteford, who was walking slowly along before the palace.

Before Mademoiselle de Hauteford, with all the graceful dignity for which she was conspicuous, had taken three steps along the terrace, Pauline's doubts had become almost certainties; and turning round, with what she fancied to be great composure, she replied, "I have the pleasure of knowing you perfectly, Monsieur de Blenau; I hope you have recovered entirely from your late wounds."

"Monsieur de Blenau! The pleasure of knowing me!" exclaimed the count. "Good God, is this my re-

ception? Not three months have gone, since your letters
flattered me with the title of 'Dear Claude.' My
wounds are better, Mademoiselle de Beaumont, but you
seem inclined to inflict others of a more painful nature."

Pauline strove to be composed, and strove to reply, but
it was all in vain; nature would have way, and she burst
into tears and sobbed aloud. "Pauline, dearest Pauline!" cried De Blenau, catching her to his bosom unre-
pulsed: "this must be some mistake—calm yourself, dear
girl, and, in the name of Heaven, tell me, what means this
conduct to one who loves you as I do?"

"One who loves me, Claude?" replied Pauline, wiping
the tears from her eyes. "Oh no, no—But what right
had I to think that you would love me? None, none, I
will allow. Separated from each other so long, I had no
title to suppose that you would ever think of the child to
whom you were betrothed, but of whom you were afterwards commanded not to entertain a remembrance—
would think of her, after those engagements were broken
by a power you could not choose but obey. But still, De
Blenau, you should not have written those letters filled
with professions of regard, and vows to retain the engagements your father had formed for you, notwithstanding
the new obstacles which had arisen. You should not indeed, unless you had been very sure of your own heart;
for it was cruelly trifling with mine," and she gently disengaged herself from his arms. "I only blame you," she
added, "for ever trying to gain my affection, and not for
now being wanting in love to a person you have never
seen since she was a child."

"Never seen you!" replied De Blenau with a smile:
"Pauline, you are as mistaken in that as in any doubt
you have of me. A year has not passed since last we met.
Remember that summer sunset on the banks of the
Rhône: remember the masked cavalier who gave you the
ring now on your finger: remember the warm hills of
Languedoc, glowing with a blush only equalled by your

cheek, when he told you that that token was sent by one who loved you dearly, and would love you ever—that it came from Claude de Blenau, who had bid him place the ring on your finger, and a kiss on your hand, and renew the vow that he had long before pledged to you.—Pauline, Pauline, it was himself."

"But why, dear Claude," demanded Pauline eagerly, forgetting coldness, and pride, and suspicion, in the memory his words called up, "why did you not tell me? why did you not let me know that it was you?"

"Because if I had been discovered," answered the count, "it might have cost me my life, years of imprisonment in the Bastile, or worse—the destruction of her I loved! The slightest cry of surprise from you might have betrayed me.

"But how did you escape without your journey being known?" demanded Pauline; "they say in Languedoc that the cardinal has bribed the evil spirits of the air to be his spies on men's actions."

"It is difficult indeed to say how he acquires his information," replied De Blenau; "but, however, I passed undiscovered. It was thus it happened: I had gone as a volunteer to the siege of Perpignan, or rather, as one of the *arrière-ban* of Languedoc which was led by the young and gallant Duc d'Enghien, to whom, after a long resistance, that city delivered its keys. As soon as the place had surrendered I asked permission to absent myself for a few days. His Highness granted it immediately, and I set out—for what think you, Pauline? what, but to visit that spot round which all the hopes of my heart, all the dreams of my imagination, had hovered for many a year. Taking the two first stages of my journey towards Paris, I suddenly changed my course, and embarking on the Rhône, descended as far as the Château de Beaumont. You remember that my page, Henry La Mothe, is the son of your mother's *fermier*, old La Mothe, and doubtless know full well his house among the oaks on the borders of the great wood. It was here I took up my abode, and formed a thousand plans of seeing you undiscovered. At length fortune favored me. Oh! how my heart beat as, standing by one of the trees in the long avenue, Henry first pointed out to me two figures coming slowly down the path from the château—yourself and your mother—and as, approaching towards me, they gradually grew more and more distinct, my impatience almost overpowered me, and I believe I should have started forward to meet you, had not Henry reminded me of the danger. You passed close by—O Pauline! I had indulged many a waking dream. I had let fancy deck you in a thousand imaginary charms—but at that moment I found all I had imagined, or dreamed, a thousand times excelled. I found the beautiful girl that had been torn from me so many years before, grown into woman's most surpassing loveliness; and the charms which fancy and memory had scattered from their united stores faded away before the reality, like stars on the rising of the sun. But this was not enough. I watched my opportunity. I saw you as you walked alone on the terrace by the side of the glittering Rhône,—I spoke to you,—I heard the tones of a voice to be remembered for many an after hour, and placing the pledge of my affection on your hand, I tore myself away."

De Blenau paused. Insensibly, whilst he was speaking, Pauline had suffered his arm again to glide round her waist. Her hand somehow became clasped in his, and as he told the tale of his affection, the tears of many a mingled emotion rolled over the dark lashes of her eye, and chasing one another down her cheek, fell upon the lip of her lover, as he pressed a kiss upon the warm sunny spot which those drops bedewed.

De Blenau saw that those tears were not tears of sorrow, and had love been with him an art, he probably would have sought no farther; for in the whole economy of life, but more especially in that soft passion love, holds

good the homely maxim to let *well* alone. But De Blenau
was not satisfied, and, like a foolish youth, he teased
Pauline to know why she had at first received him coldly.
In good truth she had by this time forgotten all about it;
but as she was obliged to answer, she soon again conjured
up all her doubts and suspicions. She hesitated, drew
her hand from that of the count, blushed deeper and
deeper, and twice began to speak without ending her
sentence.

" I know not what to think," said she at .length, " De
Blenau: I would fain believe you to be all you seem,—I
would fain reject every doubt of what you say."

Her coldness, her hesitation, her embarrassment,
alarmed De Blenau's fears, and he, too, began to be suspicious.

" On what can you rest a doubt?" demanded he, with
a look of bitter mortification; and perceiving that she
still paused, he added sadly, but coldly, " Mademoiselle
de Beaumont, you are unkind. Can it be that you are
attached to another? Say, am I so unhappy?"

" No, De Blenau!" replied Pauline, struggling for
firmness; " but answer me one question, explain to me but
this one thing, and I am satisfied."

" Ask me any question, propose to me any doubts," answered the count, " and I will reply truly, upon my
honor."

" Then tell me," said Pauline,——But just as she was
about to proceed she felt some difficulty in proposing her
doubts. She had a thousand times before convinced herself they were very serious and well founded; but all
jealous suspicions look so very foolish in black and white,
or what is quite as good, in plain language, though they
may seem very respectable when seen through the twilight
of passion, that Pauline knew not very well how to give
utterance to hers. " Then tell me," said Pauline, with no
small hesitation—" then tell me what was the reason you
would suffer no one to open your hunting-coat, when you

were wounded in the forest—no, not even to stanch the bleeding of your side?"

"There was a reason, certainly," replied De Blenau, not very well perceiving the connection between his hunting-coat and Pauline's coldness; "there was a reason, certainly; but how in the name of heaven does that affect you, Pauline?"

"You shall see by my next question," answered she. "Have you or have you not received a letter, privately conveyed to you from a lady? and has not Mademoiselle de Hauteford visited you secretly during your illness?"

It was now De Blenau's turn to become embarrassed; he faltered and looked confused, and for a moment his cheek, which had hitherto been pale with the loss of blood, became of the deepest crimson, while he replied, "I did not know that I was so watched."

"It is enough, Monsieur de Blenau," said Pauline rising, her doubts almost aggravated to certainties. "To justify myself, sir, I will tell you that you have not been watched. Pauline de Beaumont would consider that man unworthy of her affection whose conduct would require watching. What I know has come to my ears by mere accident. In fact," and her voice trembled the more, perhaps, that she strove to preserve its steadiness—"in fact, I have become acquainted with a painful truth through my too great kindness for you, in sending my own servant to inquire after your health, and not to watch you, Monsieur de Blenau."

"Stop, stop, Pauline! in pity, stop," cried De Blenau, seeing her about to depart. "Your questions place me in the most embarrassing of situations. But, on my soul, I have never suffered a thought to stray from you, and you yourself will one day do me justice. But at present, on this point, I am bound by every principle of duty and honor not to attempt an exculpation."

"None is necessary, Monsieur de Blenau," replied Pauline. "It is much better to understand each other at

once. I have no right to any control over you. You
are, of course, free, and at liberty to follow the bent of
your own inclinations. Adieu! I shall always wish your
welfare." And she was quitting the apartment, but De
Blenau still detained her, though she gently strove to
withdraw her hand.

"Yet one moment, Pauline," said he. "You were once
kind, you were once generous, you have more than once
assured me of your affection. Now, tell me, did you bestow that affection on a man destitute of honor? on a man
who would sully his fame by pledging his faith to what
was false?" Pauline's hand remained in his without an
effort, and he went on. "I now pledge you my faith,
and give you my honor, however strange it may appear
that a lady should visit me in private, I have never loved
or sought any but yourself. Pauline, do you doubt me
now?"

Her eyes were fixed upon the ground, and she did not
reply, but there was a slight motion in the hand he held,
as if it would fain have returned his pressure had she
dared. "I could," he continued, "within an hour obtain
permission to explain it all. But oh, Pauline, how much
happier would it make me to find, that you trust alone to
my word, that you put full confidence in a heart that loves
you!"

"I do! I do!" exclaimed Pauline, with all her own
wild energy, at the same time placing her other hand also
on his, and raising her eyes to his face: "Say no more,
De Blenau. I believe I have been wrong; at all events,
I cannot, I will not doubt, what makes me so happy to
believe." And her eyes, which again filled with tears,
were hidden on his bosom.

De Blenau pressed her to his heart, and again and again
thanked the lips that had spoken such kind words, in the
way that such lips may best be thanked. "Dearest Pauline," said De Blenau, after enjoying a moment or two of
that peculiar happiness which shines but once or twice

6

even in the brightest existence, giving a momentary taste of heaven, and then losing itself, either in human cares, or less vivid joys.

"Dearest Pauline," said De Blenau, "I leave you for a time, that I may return and satisfy every doubt. Within one hour all shall be explained."

As he spoke the door of the apartment opened, and one of the servants of the Palace entered, with a face of some alarm. "Monsieur de Blenau," said he, "I beg a thousand pardons for intruding, but there have been, but now, at the Palace gate, two men of the cardinal's guard inquiring for you: so I told them that you were most likely at the other side of the park, for—for—" and after hesitating a moment, he added, "they are the same who arrested Monsieur de Vitry."

De Blenau started. "Fly, fly, Claude!" exclaimed Pauline, catching him eagerly by the arm—"Oh, fly, dear Claude, while there is yet time. I am sure they seek some evil towards you."

"You have done well," said De Blenau to the attendant. "I will speak to you as I come down.—Dearest Pauline," he continued when the man was gone—"I must see what these gentlemen want. Nay, do not look frightened; you are mistaken about their errand. I have nothing to fear, believe me. Some trifling business, no doubt. In the meantime, I shall not neglect my original object. In half an hour all your doubts shall be satisfied."

"I have none, Claude," replied Pauline; "indeed I have none, but about these men."

De Blenau endeavored to calm her, and assured her again and again that there was no danger. But Pauline was not easy, and the count himself had more suspicions concerning their object than he would suffer to appear.

CHAPTER VII.

Containing a great deal that would not have been said had it not been necessary.

In front of the Palace of St. Germain's, but concealed from the park and terrace by an angle of the building, stood the Count de Chavigni, apparently engaged in the very undignified occupation of making love to a pretty-looking soubrette, no other than Louise, the waiting-maid of Mademoiselle de Beaumont. But, notwithstanding the careless nonchalance with which he affected to address her, it was evident that he had some deeper object in view than the trifling of an idle hour.

" Well, *ma belle*," said he, after a few words of a more tender nature, " you are sure the surgeon said, though the wound is in his side, his heart is uninjured? "

" Yes, exactly," said Louise, " word for word ; and the queen answered, ' I understand you.' But I cannot think why you are so curious about it."

" Because I take an interest in the young count," replied Chavigni. " But his heart must be very hard if it can resist such eyes as yours."

" He never saw them," said Louise, " for I was not with my lady when they picked him up wounded in the forest."

" So much the better," replied Chavigni, " for that is he turning that angle of the palace : I must speak to him ; so farewell, *belle Louise*, and remember the signal. Go through that door, and he will not see you."

Speaking thus, Chavigni left her, and a few steps brought him up to De Blenau, who at that moment traversed the angle in which he had been standing with Louis, and was hurrying on with a rapid pace in search of the queen.

"Good morrow, Monsieur de Blenau," said Chavigni; "you seem in haste."

"And am so, sir," replied De Blenau proudly; and added, after a moment's pause, "Have you any commands for me?" for Chavigni stood directly in his way.

"None in particular," answered the other with perfect composure—"only if you are seeking the queen, I will go with you to her majesty; and as we go, I will tell you a piece of news you may perhaps like to hear."

"Sir Count de Chavigni, I beg you would mark me," replied De Blenau. "You are one of the king's council —a gentleman of good repute, and so forth; but there is not that love between us that we should be seen taking our evening's walk together, unless, indeed, it were for the purpose of using our weapons more than our tongues."

"Indeed, Monsieur de Blenau," rejoined Chavigni, his lip curling into a smile which partook more of good humor than scorn, though, perhaps, mingled somewhat of each—"indeed you do not do me justice; I love you better than you know, and may have an opportunity of doing you a good turn some day, whether you will or not. So with your leave I walk with you, for we both seek the queen."

De Blenau was provoked. "Must I tell you, sir," exclaimed he, "that your company is disagreeable to me? —that I do not like the society of men who herd with robbers and assassins?"

"Psha!" exclaimed Chavigni, somewhat peevishly. "Captious boy, you'll get yourself into the Bastile some day, where you would have been long ago, had it not been for me."

"When you tell me, sir, how such obligations have been incurred," answered the count, "I shall be happy to acknowledge them."

"Why, twenty times, Monsieur de Blenau, you have nearly been put there," replied Chavigni, with that air of

candor which it is very difficult to affect when it is not
genuine. " Your hot and boiling spirit, sir, is always
running you into danger. Notwithstanding all your late
wounds, a little bleeding, even now, would not do you any
harm. Here the first thing you do is to quarrel with a
man who has served you, is disposed to serve you, and of
whose service you may stand in need within five minutes.

" But to give you proof at once that what I advance is
more than a mere jest—do you think that your romantic
expedition to Languedoc escaped me? Monsieur de
Blenau, you start, as if you dreamed that in such a country as this, and under such an administration, anything
could take place without being known to some member of
the government. No, no, sir! there are many people in
France even now who think they are acting in perfect
security, because no notice is apparently taken of the plans
they are forming, or the intrigues they are carrying on;
while, in reality, the hundred eyes of Policy are upon
their every action, and the sword is only suspended over
their heads that it may eventually fall with more severity."

" You surprise me, I own," replied De Blenau, " by
showing me that you are acquainted with an adventure
which I thought buried in my own bosom, or only con-
fided to one equally faithful to me."

" You mean your page," said Chavigni, with the same
easy tone in which he had spoken all along. " You have
no cause to doubt him. He has never betrayed you (at
least to my knowledge). But these things come about
very simply, without treachery on any part. The stag
never flies so fast, nor the hare doubles so often, but
they leave a scent behind them for the dogs to follow,—
and so it is with the actions of man; conceal them as he
will, there is always some trace by which they may be
discovered; and it is no secret to any one now-a-days that
there are people in every situation of life, in every town
of France, paid to give information of all that happens;
so that the schemes must be well concealed indeed which

some circumstance does not discover. I see you shake your head, as if you disapproved of the principle.

"De Blenau, you and I are engaged in different parties. You act firmly convinced of the rectitude of your own cause—do me the justice to believe that I do the same. You hate the minister—I admire him, and feel fully certain that all he does is for the good of the State. On the other hand, I applaud your courage, your devotion to the cause you have espoused, and your proud unbending spirit—and I would bring you to the scaffold to-morrow if I thought it would really serve the party to which I am attached."

The interesting nature of his conversation, and the bold candor it displayed, had made De Blenau tolerate Chavigni's society longer than he had intended, and even his dislike to the statesman had in a degree worn away before the easy dignity and frankness of his manner. But still he did not like to be seen holding any kind of companionship with one of the queen's professed enemies; and taking advantage of the first pause, he replied—

"You are frank, Monsieur de Chavigni, but my head is well where it is. And now may I ask to what does all this tend?"

"You need not hurry the conversation to a conclusion," replied Chavigni. "You see that we are in direct progress towards that part of the park where her Majesty is most likely to be found." But seeing that De Blenau seemed impatient of such reply, he proceeded: "However, as you wish to know to what my conversation tends, I will tell you. If you please, it tends to your own good. The cardinal wishes to see you——"

He paused, and glanced his eye over the countenance of his companion, from which, however, he could gather no reply, a slight frown being all the emotion that was visible.

Chavigni then proceeded. "The cardinal wishes to see you. He entertains some suspicion of you. If you

will take my advice, you will set out for Paris immediately, wait upon his eminence, and be frank with him
—nay, do not start! I do not wish you to betray any
one's secrets, or violate your own honor. But be wise;
set out instantly."

"I suspected something of this," replied De Blenau,
"when I heard that there were strangers inquiring for
me. But whatever I do, I must first see the queen;" and
observing that Chavigni was about to offer some opposition, he added decidedly, "It is absolutely necessary—on
business of importance."

"May I ask," said Chavigni, "is it of importance to
her majesty or yourself?"

"I have no objection to answer that at once," replied
De Blenau; "it concerns myself alone."

"Stop a moment," cried Chavigni, laying his hand on
the count's arm, and pausing in the middle of the avenue,
at the farther extremity of which a group of three or four
persons was seen approaching. "No business can be of
more importance than that on which I advise you to go.
Monsieur de Blenau, I would save you pain. Let me once
more press you to set out without having any farther
conversation with her majesty than the mere *etiquette* of
taking leave for a day."

De Blenau well knew the danger which he incurred,
but still he could not resolve to go without clearing the
doubts of Pauline, which five minutes' conversation with
the queen would enable him to do. "It is impossible,"
replied he, thoughtfully; "besides. let the cardinal send
for me. I do not see why I should walk with my eyes
open into the den of a lion."

"Well, then, sir," answered Chavigni, with somewhat
more of coldness in his manner, "I must tell you his
eminence has sent for you, and that, perhaps, in a way
which may not suit the pride of your disposition. Do
you see those three men that are coming down the avenue? they are not here without an object. Come, once

more, what say you, Monsieur le Comte? Go with me to
take leave of the queen, for I must suffer no private conversation. Let us then mount our horses, and ride as
friends to Paris. There pay your respects to the cardinal,
and take Chavigni's word that, unless you suffer the heat
of your temper to betray you into anything unbecoming,
you shall return safe to St. Germain's before to-morrow
evening. If not, things must take their course."

" You offer me fair, sir," replied the count, " if I understand you rightly, that the cardinal has sent to arrest me;
and of course I cannot hesitate to accept your proposal.
I have no particular partiality for the Bastile, I can
assure you."

" Then you consent? " said Chavigni. De Blenau
bowed his head. " Well, then, I will speak to these gentlemen," he added, " and they will give us their room."

By this time the three persons, who had continued to
advance down the avenue, had approached within the
distance of a few paces of Chavigni and the count. Two
of them were dressed in the uniform of the cardinal's
guard; one as a simple trooper, the other being the lieutenant who bore the *lettre de cachet* for the arrest of De
Blenau. The third we have had some occasion to notice
in the wood of Mantes, being no other than the tall Norman, who on that occasion was found in a rusty buff
jerkin, consorting with the banditti. His appearance,
however, was now very much changed for the better.
The neat trimming of his beard and mustaches, the smart
turn of his broad beaver, the flush newness of his long-
waisted blue silk vest, and even the hanging of his sword,
which, instead of offering its hilt on the left hip, ever
ready for the hand, now swung far behind, with the tip
of the scabbard striking against the right calf,—all denoted a change of trade and circumstances, from the poor
bravo who won his daily meal at the sword's point, to
the well-paid bully who fattened at his lord's second table,
on the merit of services more real than apparent.

De Blenau's eye fixed full upon the Norman, certain that he had seen him somewhere before; but the change of dress and circumstances embarrassed his recollection.

"In the meanwhile, Chavigni advanced to the Cardinal's officer. "Monsieur Chauville," said he, "favor me by preceding me to his eminence of Richelieu. Offer him my salutation, and inform him, that Monsieur le Comte de Blenau and myself intend to wait upon him this afternoon."

Chauville bowed, and passed on, while the Norman, uncovering his head to Chavigni, instantly brought back to the mind of De Blenau the circumstances under which he had first seen him.

"You have returned, I see," said Chavigni. "Have you found an occasion of fulfilling my orders?"

"To your heart's content, Monseigneur," replied the Norman; "never was such an astrologer, since the days of Intrim of Blois."

"Hush!" said Chavigni, for the other spoke aloud. "If you have done it, that is enough. But for a time, keep yourself to Paris, and avoid the court, as some one may recognize you, even in these fine new feathers."

"Oh, I defy them," replied the Norman, in a lower tone than he had formerly spoken, but still so loud that De Blenau could not avoid hearing the greater part of what he said—"I defy them; for I was so wrapped up in my black robes and my white beard, that the Devil himself would not know me for the same mortal in the two costumes. But I hope, Monsieur le Comte, that my reward may be equal to the risk I have run, for they sought to stop me, and had I not been too good a necromancer for them, I suppose I should have been roasting at a stake by this time. But one wave of my magic wand sent the sword of Monsieur de Cinq Mars out of his hand, and opened me a passage to the wood; otherwise I should have fared but badly amongst them."

"You must not exact too much, Monsieur Marteville,"

replied Chavigni. "But we will speak of this to-night.
I shall be in Paris in a few hours; at present, you see, I
am occupied;" and leaving the Norman, he rejoined De
Blenau, and proceeded in search of the queen.

"If my memory serves me right," Monsieur de Chavigni," said De Blenau, in a tone of some bitterness, "I
have seen that gentleman before, and with his sword
shining at my breast."

"It is very possible," answered Chavigni, with the
most indifferent calmness. "I have seen him in the same
situation with respect to myself."

"Indeed!" rejoined De Blenau, with some surprise;
"but probably not with the same intention," he added.

"I do not know," replied the statesman, with a smile.
"His intentions in my favor were to run me through the
body."

"And is it possible, then," exclaimed De Blenau, "that
with such a knowledge of his character and habits, you
can employ and patronize him?"

"Certainly," answered Chavigni, "I wanted a bold
villain. Such men are very necessary in a State. Now, I
could not have better proof that this man had the qualities required, than his attempting to cut my throat. But
you do him some injustice; he is better than you suppose
—is not without feeling—and has his own ideas of
honor."

De Blenau checked the bitter reply which was rising to
his lips, and letting the conversation drop, they proceeded
in silence, in search of the queen. They had not gone
much farther, when they perceived her leaning familiarly
on the arm of Madame de Beaumont, and seemingly occupied in some conversation of deep interest. However,
her eye fell upon the count and Chavigni as they came up,
and, surprised to see them together, she abruptly paused
in what she was saying.

"Look there, De Beaumont," said she: " something is
not right. I have seen more than one of these creatures

of the cardinal hanging about the park to-day. I fear for poor De Blenau. He has been too faithful to his queen to escape long."

" I salute, your majesty," said Chavigni, as soon as they had come within a short distance of the queen, and not giving De Blenau the time to address her: " I have been the bearer of a message from his eminence of Richelieu to Monsieur de Blenau, your majesty's chamberlain, requesting the pleasure of entertaining him for a day in Paris. The count has kindly accepted the invitation; and I have promised that the cardinal shall not press his stay beyond to-morrow. We only now want your majesty's permission and good leave, which in his eminence's name I humbly crave for Monsieur de Blenau."

" His eminence is too condescending," replied the queen. " He knows that his will is law; and we, humble kings and queens, as in duty, do him reverence. I doubt not that his intentions towards our chamberlain are as mild and amiable as his general conduct towards ourself."

" The truth is, your majesty," said De Blenau, " the cardinal has sent for me, and (however Monsieur de Chavigni's politeness may color it) in a way that compels my attendance."

" I thought so," exclaimed the queen, dropping the tone of irony which she had assumed towards Chavigni, and looking with mingled grief and kindness upon the young cavalier, whose destruction she deemed inevitable from the moment that Richelieu had fixed the serpent eyes of his policy upon him—" I thought so. Alas, my poor De Blenau! all that attach themselves to me seem devoted to persecution."

" Not so, your majesty," said Chavigni, with some degree of feeling; " I can assure you, Monsieur de Blenau goes at perfect liberty. He is under no arrest; and, unless he stays by his own wish, will return to your majesty's court to-morrow night. The cardinal is far from wishing to give unnecessary pain."

"Talk not to me, Sir Counsellor," replied the queen, angrily. "Do I not know him? I, who of all the world have best cause to estimate his baseness? Have I not under his own hand, the proof of his criminal ambition? but no more of that——" And breaking off into Spanish, as was frequently her custom when angry, she continued, "No sè si es la misma vanidad, la sobervia, ó la arrogancia, Que todo esto, segun creo es el cardenal."

"It is useless, madam," said De Blenau, as soon as the queen paused in her angry vituperation of the minister, "to distress you further with this conversation. I know not what the cardinal wants, but he may rest assured that De Blenau's heart is firm, and that no human means shall induce him to swerve from his duty; and thus I humbly take my leave."

"Go then, De Blenau," said the queen: "go, and whether we ever meet again or not, your faithful services and zealous friendship shall ever have my warmest gratitude; and Anne of Austria has no other reward to bestow." Thus saying, she held out her hand to him. De Blenau in silence bent his head respectfully over it, and turned away. Chavigni bowed low, and followed the count, to whose hotel they proceeded, in order to prepare for their departure.

In the orders which De Blenau gave on their arrival, he merely commanded the attendance of his page.

"Pardon me, Monsieur de Blenau, if I observe upon your arrangements," said Chavigni, when he heard this order. "But let me remind you, once more, that you are not going to a prison, and that it might be better if your general train attended you, as a gentleman of high station about to visit the prime minister of his sovereign. They will find plenty of accommodation in the Hôtel de Bouthiliers."

"Be it so, then," replied De Blenau, scarcely able to assume even the appearance of civility towards his companion. "Henry de La Mothe," he proceeded, "order a dozen of my best men to attend me, bearing my full colors in their sword-knots and scarfs. Trick out my horses gaily, as if I were going to a wedding, for Claude de Blenau is about to visit the cardinal; and remember," he continued, his anger at the forced journey he was taking overcoming his prudence, " that there be saddled for my own use the good black barb that carried me so stoutly when I was attacked by assassins in the wood of Mantes;" and as he spoke, his eye glanced towards the statesman, who sitting in the window seat, had taken up the poems of Rotrou, and apparently inattentive to all that was passing, read on with as careless and easy an air, as if no more important interest occupied his thoughts, and no contending passions struggled in his breast. Though the attendants of the Count de Blenau did not expend much time in preparing to accompany their master, the evening was nevertheless too far spent, before they could proceed, to permit the hope of reaching Paris ere the night should have set in. It was still quite light enough, however, to show all the preparations for the count's departure to the boys of St. Germain, who had not beheld for many a good day such a gay cavalcade enliven the streets of that almost deserted town.

Chavigni and De Blenau mounted their horses together; and the four or five servants which the statesman had brought with him from Paris, mingling with those of De Blenau, followed the two gentlemen as they rode from the gate. Having the privilege of the park, Chavigni took his way immediately under the windows of the palace, thereby avoiding a considerable circuit, which would have occupied more time than they could well spare at that late hour of the evening.

The moment Pauline de Beaumont had seen her lover depart, the tears, which she had struggled to repress in his presence, flowed rapidly down her cheeks. She wept then—but her tears were from a very different cause to that which had occasioned them to flow before. However, her eyes were still full, when a servant entered to inform her that the queen desired her society with the other ladies of her scanty court. Pauline endeavored to efface the marks which her weeping had left, and slowly obeyed the summons, which being usual at that hour, she knew was on no business of import; but on entering the closet, she perceived that tears had also been in the bright eyes of Anne of Austria.

The circle, which consisted of Madame de Beaumont, Mademoiselle de Hauteford, and another lady of honor, had drawn round the window at which her majesty sat, and which, thrown fully open, admitted the breeze from the park.

"Come hither, Pauline," said the queen as she saw her enter, "what! have you been weeping too? Nay, do not blush, sweet girl; for surely a subject need not be ashamed of doing *once* what a queen is obliged to do every day. Why, it is the only resource that we women have. But come here: there seems a gay cavalcade entering the park gates. These are the toys with which we are taught to amuse ourselves. Who are they, I wonder? Come near, Pauline, and see if your young eyes can tell."

Pauline approached the window, and took her station by the side of the queen, who, rising from her seat, placed her arm kindly through that of Mademoiselle de Beaumont, and leaning gently upon her, prevented the possibility of her retiring from the spot where she stood.

In the meanwhile the cavalcade approached. The gay trappings of the horses, and the rich suits of their riders, with their silk scarfs and sword-knots of blue and gold, soon showed to the keen eyes of the queen's ladies that the young Count de Blenau was one of the party; while every now and then a horseman in Isabel and silver appearing amongst the rest, told them, to their no small surprise, that he was accompanied by the Count de Chavigni, the sworn friend of Richelieu, and one of the principal lead-

ers of the cardinal's party. The queen, however, evinced
no astonishment, and her attendants of course did not
attempt to express the wonder they felt at such a companionship.

The rapid pace at which the two gentlemen proceeded,
soon brought them near the palace; and Chavigni, from
whose observant eye nothing passed without notice, instantly perceived the queen and her party at the window,
and marked his salutation with a profound inclination,
low almost to servility, while De Blenau raised his high-
plumed hat and bowed, with the dignity of one conscious
that he had deserved well of all who saw him.

Chavigni led the way to Marly, and thence to Ruel,
where night began to come heavily upon the twilight; and
long before they entered Paris, all objects were lost in
darkness. "You must be my guest for to-night, Monsieur de Blenau," said Chavigni, as they rode on down
the Rue St. Honoré, "for it will be too late to visit the
cardinal this evening."

However, as they passed the Palais Royal (then called
the Palais Cardinal), the blaze of light, which proceeded
from every window of the edifice, told that on that night
the superb minister entertained the court;—a court, of
which he had deprived his king, and which he had appropriated to himself. De Blenau drew a deep sigh as he
gazed upon the magnificent edifice, and compared the
pomp and luxury which everything appertaining to it
displayed, with the silent, desolate melancholy which
reigned in the royal palaces of France.

Passing on down the Rue St. Honoré, and crossing the
Rue St. Martin, they soon reached the Place Royale, in
which Chavigni had fixed his residence. Two of De
Blenau's servants immediately placed themselves at the
head of his horse, and held the bridle short, while Henry
de La Mothe sprang to the stirrup. But at that moment
a gentleman who seemed to have been waiting the arrival
of the travellers, issued from the Hôtel de Bouthiliers,
and prevented them from dismounting.

"Do not alight, gentlemen," exclaimed he; "his eminence the Cardinal de Richelieu has sent me to request that Messieurs De Blenau and Chavigni will partake a small collation at the Palais Cardinal, without the ceremony of changing their dress."

De Blenau would fain have excused himself, alleging that the habit which he wore was but suited to the morning, and also was soiled with the dust of their long ride. But the cardinal's officer overbore all opposition, declaring that his eminence would regard it as a higher compliment, if the count would refrain from setting foot to the ground till he entered the gates of his palace.

"Then we must go back," said Chavigni. "We are honored by the cardinal's invitation. Monsieur de Blenau, pardon me for having brought you so far wrong. Go in, Chatenay," he added, turning to one of his own domestics, "and order flambeaux."

In a few moments all was ready; and preceded by half a dozen torch-bearers on foot, they once more turned towards the dwelling of the minister. As they did so, De Blenau's feelings were not of the most agreeable nature, but he acquiesced in silence, for to have refused his presence would have been worse than useless.

The Palais Royal, which, as we have said, was then called the Palais Cardinal, was a very different building when occupied by the haughty minister of Louis the Thirteenth, from that which we have seen it in our days. The unbounded resources within his power gave to Richelieu the means of lavishing on the mansion which he erected for himself, all that art could produce of elegant, and all that wealth could supply of magnificent.

On the evening in question almost every part of that immense building was thrown open to receive the multitude that interest and fear gathered round the powerful and vindictive minister. Almost all that was gay, almost all that was beautiful, had been assembled there. All to whom wealth gave something to secure—all to whom rank gave something to maintain— all whom wit rendered anxious for distinction—all whom talent prompted to ambition. Equally those that Richelieu feared or loved, hated or admired, were brought there by some means, and for some reason.

The scene which met the eyes of De Blenau and Chavigni, as they ascended the grand staircase and entered the saloon, can only be qualified by the word princely. The blaze of jewels, the glare of innumerable lights, the splendid dresses of the guests, and the magnificent decorations of the apartments themselves, all harmonized together, and formed a *coup-d'oeil* of surpassing brilliancy.

The rooms were full, but not crowded; for there were attendants stationed in various parts for the purpose of requesting the visitors to proceed, whenever they observed too many collected in one spot. Yet care was taken that those who were thus treated with scant ceremony should be of the inferior class admitted to the cardinal's fête. Each officer of the minister's household was well instructed to know the just value of every guest, and how far he was to be courted, either for his mind or influence.

To render to all the highest respect was the general order, but some were to be distinguished. Care was also taken that none should be neglected, and an infinite number of servants were seen gliding through the apartments, offering the most costly and delicate refreshments to every individual of the mixed assembly.

De Blenau followed Chavigni through the grand saloon, where many an eye was turned upon the elegant and manly figure of him, who on that night of splendor and finery, presumed to show himself in a suit, rich indeed and well-fashioned, but evidently intended more for the sports of the morning than for the gay evening circle in which he then stood. Yet it was remarked, that none of the ladies drew back as the cavalier passed them, notwithstanding his riding-dress and his dusty boots; and one

7

fair demoiselle, whose rank would have sanctioned it, had it been done on purpose, was unfortunate enough to entangle her train on his spurs. The Count de Coligni stepped forward to disengage it, but De Blenau himself had already bent one knee to the ground, and easily freeing the spur from the robe of Mademoiselle de Bourbon, he remained for a moment in the same attitude. "It is but just," said he, "that I should kneel, at once to repair my awkwardness, and sue for pardon."

"It was my sister's own fault, De Blenau," said the Duc d'Enghien, approaching them, and embracing the young count. "We have not met, dear friend, since the rendering of Perpignan. But what makes you here? Does your proud spirit bend at last to ask a grace of my Lord Uncle Cardinal?"

No, your highness," replied De Blenau; "no further grace have I to ask, than leave to return to St. Germain as soon as I may."

"What!" said the duke, in the abrupt heedless manner in which he always spoke, "does he threaten you too with that cursed bugbear of a Bastile? a bugbear, that makes one man fly his country, and another betray it; that makes one man run his sword into his heart, and another marry;" alluding without ceremony to his own compelled espousal of the cardinal's niece. "But there stands Chavigni," he continued, "waiting for you, I suppose. Go on, go on; there is no stopping when once you have got within the cardinal's magic circle—Go on, and God speed your suit: for the sooner you are out of that same circle the better."

Quitting the young hero, who had already, on more than one occasion, displayed that valor and conduct which in after-years procured for him the immortal name of the Great Condé, the Count de Blenau passed another group, consisting of the beautiful Madame de Montbazon and her avowed lover, the Duke of Longueville, who soon after, notwithstanding his unconcealed passion for an-

other, became the husband of Mademoiselle de Bourbon.
Here also was the Duke of Guise, who afterwards played
so conspicuous a part in the revolution of Naples, and by
his singular adventures, his gallantry and chivalrous
courage, acquired the name of *l'Hero de la Fable,* as
Condé had been called l'Hero de l'Histoire.   Still passing
on, De Blenau rejoined Chavigni, who waited for him
at the entrance of the next chamber.

It was the great hall of audience, and at the farther
extremity stood the Cardinal de Richelieu himself, leaning for support against a gilt railing, which defended
from any injurious touch the beautiful picture of Raphael,
so well known by the title of " La Belle Jardinière."   He
was dressed in the long purple robes of his order, and
wore the peculiar hat of a cardinal; the bright color of
which made the deadly hue of his complexion look still
more ghastly.   But the paleness of his countenance, and
a certain attenuation of feature, were all that could be
discerned of the illness from which he suffered.   The
powerful mind within seemed to conquer the feebleness
of the body.   His form was erect and dignified, his eye
beaming with that piercing sagacity and haughty confidence in his own powers, which so distinguished his
policy; and his voice clear, deep, and firm, but of that
peculiar quality of sound, that it seemed to spread all
round, and to come no one knew from whence, like the
wind echoing through an empty cavern.

It was long since De Blenau had seen the cardinal; and
on entering the audience-chamber, the sound of that voice
made him start.   Its clear hollow tone seemed close to
him, though Richelieu was conversing with some of his
immediate friends at the further end of the room.

As the two cavaliers advanced, De Blenau had an opportunity of observing the manner in which the minister
treated those around him: but far from telling aught of
dungeons and of death, his conversation seemed cheerful, and his demeanor mild and placid.   " And can this

be the man," thought the count, " the fabric of whose power is cemented by blood and torture?"

They had now approached within a few paces of the spot where the cardinal stood; and the figure of Chavigni catching his eye, he advanced a step, and received him with unaffected kindness. Towards De Blenau his manner was full of elegant politeness. He did not embrace him as he had done Chavigni; but he held him 'y the hand for a moment, gazing on him with a dignified approving smile. Those who did not well know the heart of the subtle minister would have called that smile benevolent, especially when it was accompanied by many kind inquiries respecting the young nobleman's views and pursuits. De Blenau had been taught to judge by actions, not professions; and the cardinal had taken care to imprint his deeds too deeply in the minds of men to be wiped out with soft words. To dissemble was not De Blenau's forte; and yet he knew that to show a deceiver he cannot deceive, is to make him an open enemy forever. He replied, therefore, calmly and politely; neither repulsed the cardinal's advances, nor courted his regard; and after a few more moments of desultory conversation, prepared to pursue his way through the various apartments.

" There are some men, Monsieur le Comte," said the cardinal, seeing him about to pass on, " whom I might have scrupled to invite to such a scene as this, in their riding-dress. But the Count de Blenau is not to be mistaken."

" I felt no scruple," answered De Blenau, " in presenting myself thus, when your eminence desired it; for the dress in which the Cardinal de Richelieu thought fit to receive me, could not be objected to by any of his circle." The cardinal bowed; and De Blenau, adding that he would not intrude further at that moment, took his way through the suite of apartments to Richelieu's left hand. Chavigni was about to follow, but a sign from the cardinal stopped him, and the young count passed on alone.

Each of the various rooms he entered was thronged with its own peculiar groups. In one was an assembly of famous artists and sculptors; in another, a close convocation of philosophers, discussing a thousand absurd theories of the day; and in the last he came to was a buzzing hive of poets and *beaux esprits*, each trying to distinguish himself, each jealous of the other, and all equally vain and full of themselves.

Passing on down a broad flight of steps, De Blenau found himself in the gardens of the palace. These, as well as the whole front of the building, were illuminated in every direction. Bands of musicians were dispersed in the different walks, and a multitude of servants were busily engaged in laying out tables for supper with all the choicest viands of the season, and in trimming the various lamps and tapers which hung from the branches of the trees, or were displayed on fanciful frames of wood, so placed as to give the fullest light to the banquets which were situated near them.

Scattered about in various parts of the garden, but more especially near the palace, were different groups of gentlemen, all speaking of plays, assemblies, or fêtes, and all taking care to make their conversation perfectly audible, lest the jealous suspicion ever attendant on usurped power should attribute to them schemes which, it is probable, fear alone prevented them from attempting.

Nevertheless, in the gardens, as we have said, containing several acres of ground, there were many parts comparatively deserted. It was towards these more secluded spots that De Blenau directed his steps, wishing himself many a league away from the Palais Cardinal and all its splendor. Just as he had reached a part where few persons were to be seen, some one struck him slightly on the arm, and turning round, he perceived a man who concealed the lower part of his face with his cloak, and tendered him what seemed to be a billet.

At the first glance De Blenau thought he recognized
the Count de Coligni, a reputed lover of Mademoiselle de
Bourbon, and imagined that the little piece of gallantry
he had shown that lady on his first entrance might have
called upon him the wrath of the jealous Coligni. But
no sooner had he taken the piece of paper than the other
darted away amongst the trees, giving him no time to
observe more, either of his person or his dress.

Approaching a spot where the number of lamps gave
him sufficient light to read, De Blenau opened the note,
which contained merely these words:—" Beware of
Chavigni;—they will seek to draw something from you
which may criminate you hereafter."

As he read, De Blenau heard a light step advancing,
and hastily concealing the note, turned to see who approached. The only person near was a lady, who had
thrown a thick veil over her head, which not only covered
her face, but the upper part of her figure. She passed
close by him, but without turning her head, or by any
other motion seeming to notice him; but as she did so,
De Blenau heard a low voice from under the veil, desiring him to follow. Gliding on, without pausing for a
moment, the lady led the way to the very extreme of the
garden. De Blenau followed quick upon her steps, and
as he did so, endeavored to call to mind where he had
seen that graceful and dignified figure before. At length
the lady stopped, looked round for a moment, and, raising
her veil, discovered the lovely countenance of Mademoiselle de Bourbon.

" Monsieur de Blenau," said the princess, " I have but
one moment to tell you that the cardinal and Chavigni are
plotting the ruin of the queen; and they wish to force or
persuade you to betray her. After you had left the cardinal, by chance I heard it proposed to arrest you even
to-night; but Chavigni said that he had given his word
that you should return to St. Germain to-morrow. Take
care, therefore, of your conduct while here, and if you

have any cause to fear, escape the moment you are at liberty. Fly to Flanders, and place yourself under the protection of Don Francisco de Mello."

"I have to return your highness a thousand thanks," replied De Blenau; "but as far as innocence can give security, I have no reason to fear."

"Innocence is nothing here," rejoined the lady. "But you are the best judge, Monsieur de Blenau. I sent Coligni to warn you, and taking an opportunity of escaping from the supper-table, came to request that you will offer my humble duty to the queen, and assure her that Marie de Bourbon is ever hers. But here is some one coming—Good God, it is Chavigni!"

As she spoke, Chavigni came rapidly upon them. Mademoiselle de Bourbon drew down her veil, and De Blenau placed himself between her and the statesman, who, affecting an excess of gaiety, totally foreign to his natural character, began to rally the count upon what he termed his gallantry. "So, Monsieur de Blenau," cried he, "already paying your devoirs to our Parisian dames. Nay, I must offer my compliments to your fair lady on her conquest;" and he endeavored to pass the count towards Mademoiselle de Bourbon.

De Blenau drew his sword. "Stand off, sir," exclaimed he, "or by Heaven you are a dead man!" And the point came flashing so near Chavigni's breast that he was fain to start back a step or two. The lady seized the opportunity to pass him, for the palisade of the garden had prevented her escaping the other way. Chavigni attempted to follow, but De Blenau caught his arm, and held him with a grasp of iron.

"Not one step, sir!" cried he. "Monsieur de Chavigni, you have strangely forgot yourself. How is it you presume, sir, to interrupt my conversation with any one? And let me ask, what affair it is of yours, if a lady chose to give me five minutes of her company even here? You have slackened your gallantry not a little."

" But was the cardinal's garden a place fitted for such love stories ? " demanded Chavigni.

It had been Chavigni's determination, on accompanying De Blenau to the Palais Cardinal, not to lose sight of his companion for a moment, in order that no communication might take place between him and any of the queen's party till such time as the cardinal had personally interrogated him concerning the correspondence which they supposed that Anne of Austria carried on with her brother, Philip of Spain. Chavigni, however, had been stopped, as we have seen, by the cardinal himself, and detained for some time in conversation, the principal object of which was the Count de Blenau himself, and the means of either persuading him by favor, or of driving him by fear, not only to abandon, but to betray the party he had espoused. The cardinal thought ambition would do all; Chavigni said that it would not move De Blenau; and thus the discussion was considerably prolonged.

As soon as Chavigni could liberate himself, he hastened after the count, and found him as we have described. To have ascertained who was his companion, Chavigni would have risked his life; but now that she had escaped him, the matter was past recall; and willing again to throw De Blenau off his guard, he made some excuses for his intrusion, saying he had thought that the lady was not unknown to him.

" Well, well, let it drop," replied De Blenau, fully more desirous of avoiding further inquiries than Chavigni was of relinquishing them. " But the next time you come across me on such an occasion, beware of your heart's blood, Monsieur de Chavigni." And thus saying, he thrust back his sword into the scabbard.

Chavigni, however, was resolved not to lose sight of him again, and passing his arm through that of the count, " You are still too hot, Monsieur de Blenau," said he; " but nevertheless let us be friends again."

" As far as we ever were friends, sir," replied De

Blenau. "The open difference of our principles in every respect, must always prevent our greatly assimilating."

Chavigni, however, kept to his purpose, and did not withdraw his arm from that of De Blenau, nor quit him again during the whole evening.

Whether the statesman suspected Mademoiselle de Bourbon or not, matters little; but on entering the banquet-room, where the principal guests were preparing to take their seats, they passed that lady with her brother and the Count de Coligni, and the eye of Chavigni glanced from the countenance of De Blenau to hers. But they were both upon their guard, and not a look betrayed that they had met since De Blenau's spur had been entangled in her train.

At that moment the master of the ceremonies exclaimed with a loud voice, " Place au Comte de Blenau," and was conducting him to a seat higher than his rank entitled him to take, when his eye fell upon the old Marquis de Brion; and with the deference due not only to his station but to his high military renown, De Blenau drew back to give him precedence.

" Go on, go on, *mon cher De Blenau*," said the old soldier; and lowering his voice to a whisper, he added, " Honest men like you and I are all out of place here; so go on, and never mind. If it were in the field, we would strive which should be first; but here there is no knowing which end of the table is most honorable."

" Wherever it were, I should always be happy to follow Monsieur de Brion," replied De Blenau; " but as you will have it, so let it be." And following the master of the ceremonies, he was soon placed amongst the most distinguished guests, and within four or five seats of the cardinal. Like the spot before a heathen altar, it was always the place either of honor or sacrifice; and De Blenau scarcely knew which was to be his fate. At all events, the distinction which he met with, was by no means pleasing to him, and he remained in silence during greater part of the banquet.

Everything in the vast hall where they sat was magnificent beyond description. It was like one of those scenes in fairy romance, where supernatural powers lend their aid to dignify some human festival. All the apartment was as fully illuminated as if the broad sun had shone into it in his fullest splendor; yet not a single light was to be seen. Soft sounds of music also occasionally floated through the air, but never so loud as to interrupt the conversation.

At the table all was glitter, and splendor, and luxury; and from the higher end at which De Blenau sat, the long perspective of the hall decked out with all a mighty kingdom's wealth and crowded with the gay, the bright, and the fair, offered an interminable view of beauty and magnificence.

The Cardinal de Richelieu, who held in his hand the fate of all who sat around him, yielded to his guests the most marked attention, treating them with the profound humility of great pride; trying to quell the fire of his eye, till it should become nothing but affability; and to soften the deep tones of his voice, from the accent of command to an expression of gentle courtesy; but notwithstanding all his efforts, a degree of that haughtiness with which the long habit of despotic rule had tinged his manners, would occasionally appear, and still show that it was the lord entertaining his vassals. His demeanor towards De Blenau, however, was all suavity and kindness. He addressed him several times in the most marked manner during the course of the banquet, and listened to his reply with one of those approving smiles, so sweet upon the lips of power.

De Blenau was not to be deceived, it is true. Yet though he knew that kindness to be assumed on purpose to betray, and the smile to be as false as hell, there was a fascination in the distinction shown him, against which he could not wholly guard his heart. His brow unbent of its frown, and he entered into the gay conversation which was going on around; but at that moment he observed the cardinal glance his eye towards Chavigni with a meaning smile.

De Blenau marked it. " So," thought he " my lord cardinal, you deem me your own."   And as the guests rose, De Blenau took his leave, and returned with Chavigni to the Place Royale.

CHAPTER VIII.

Containing a conference, which ends much as it began.

The music of the cardinal's fête rang in De Blenau's ears all night, and the lights danced in his eyes, and the various guests flitted before his imagination, like the figures in some great phantasmagoria. At length, however, towards the approach of morning, the uneasy visions died away, and left him in deep sleep, from which he rose refreshed, and prepared to encounter the events of a new day.

De Blenau prepared his mind, as a man arming for a battle; and sent to notify to Chavigni, that he was about to visit the cardinal. In a few minutes after, the statesman himself appeared, and courteously conducted the young count to his horse, but did not offer to accompany him to the minister. "Monsieur de Blenau," said he, "it is better you should go alone. After your audience, you will doubtless be in haste to return to St. Germain; but if you will remain to take your noon meal at my poor table, I shall esteem myself honored."

De Blenau thanked him for his courtesy, but declined, stating that he was anxious to return home before night, if he were permitted to do so at all. "My word is passed for your safety," replied Chavigni; "so have no doubt on that head. But take my counsel, Monsieur le Comte: moderate your proud bearing towards the cardinal. Those who play with a lion, must take good care not to irritate him."

On arriving at the Palais Cardinal, De Blenau left his attendants in the outer court, and following an officer of the household, proceeded through a long suite of apartments to a large saloon, where he found several others waiting the leisure of the minister, who was at that moment engaged in conference with the ambassador from Sweden.

De Blenau's own feelings were not of the most comfortable nature; but on looking round the room, he guessed, from the faces of all those with whom it was tenanted, that such sensations were but too common there.

There was nothing consolatory in their looks, and De Blenau turned to the portraits which covered the walls of the saloon. The first that his eye fell upon was that of the famous Montmorency. He was represented as armed in steel, with the head uncovered; and from his apparent age it seemed that the picture had not been painted long before the unfortunate conspiracy which, by its failure, brought him to the scaffold. There was also an expression of grave sadness in the countenance, as if he had presaged his approaching fate. De Blenau turned to another; but it so happened that each picture in the room represented some one of the many whom Richelieu's unsparing vengeance had overtaken. Whether they were placed in that waiting-room in order to overawe those whom the minister wished to intimidate; or whether it was that the famous gallery, which the cardinal had filled with portraits of all the principal historical characters of France, would contain no more, and that in consequence the pictures of the later date had been placed in this saloon, without any deeper intent, matters not; but at all events they offered no very pleasant subject of contemplation.

De Blenau, however, was not long kept in suspense; for, in a few minutes, the door on the other side of the room opened, and the Swedish ambassador passed out. The door shut behind him, but in a moment after an attendant entered, and although several others had been waiting before him, De Blenau was the first summoned to the presence of the cardinal.

He could not help feeling as if he wronged those he left still in doubt as to their fate: but following the officer through an ante-room, he entered the audience-closet, and immediately perceived Richelieu seated at a table, over which were strewed a multitude of papers of different dimensions, some of which he was busily engaged in examining: reading them he was not, for his eye glanced so rapidly over their contents that his knowledge of each could be but general. He paused for a moment as De Blenau entered, bowed his head, pointed to a seat, and resumed his employment. When he had done, he signed the papers and gave them to a dull-looking personage, in a black silk purpoint, who stood behind his chair.

"Take these three death-warrants," said he, "to Monsieur Lafemas, and then these others to Poterie at the Bastile. But no—stop," he continued after a moment's thought; "you had better go to the Bastile first, for Poterie can put Caply to the torture while you are gone to Lafemas; and you can bring me back his confession as you return."

De Blenau shuddered at the sang-froid with which the minister commanded those things that make one's blood curdle even to imagine. But the attendant was practised in such commissions; and taking the packets, as a mere matter of course, he bowed in silence, and disappearing by a door on the other side, left De Blenau alone with the cardinal.

"Well, Monsieur de Blenau," said Richelieu, looking up with a frank smile, "your pardon for having detained you. There are many things upon which I have long wished to speak to you, and this caused me to desire your company. But I have no doubt that we shall part perfectly satisfied with each other."

The cardinal paused, as if for a reply. "I hope so too, my lord," said De Blenau. "I can, of course, have no cause to be dissatisfied with your eminence; and for my own part, I feel my bosom to be clear."

"I doubt it not, Monsieur le Comte," replied the minister, with a gracious inclination of the head—"I doubt it not; I know your spirit to be too frank and noble to mingle in petty faction and treasonable cabal. No one more admires your brave and independent bearing than myself. You must remember that I have marked you from your youth. You have been educated, as it were, under my own eye; and were it now necessary to trust the welfare of the state to the honor of any one man, I would confide it to the honor of De Blenau."

"To what, in the name of heaven, can this lead?" thought De Blenau; but he bowed without reply, and the cardinal proceeded.

"I have for some time past," he continued, "been thinking of placing you in one of those high stations to which your rank and consideration entitle you to aspire. At present none are vacant; but as a forerunner to such advancement, I propose to call you to the council, and to give you the government of Poitou."

De Blenau was now, indeed, astonished. The cardinal was not a man to jest: and yet what he proposed, as a mere preliminary, was an offer that the first noble in France might have accepted with gladness. The count was about to speak; but Richelieu paused only for a moment to observe the effect of what he said upon his auditor; and perhaps over-rating the ambition of De Blenau, he proceeded more boldly.

"I do not pretend to say, notwithstanding my sense of your high merit, and my almost parental feelings towards you, that I am wholly moved to this by my individual regard; but the truth is, that the state requires at this moment the services of one who joins to high talents a thorough knowledge of the affairs of Spain."

"So!" thought De Blenau, "I have it now. The government of Poitou, and a seat at the council, provided I betray the queen and sell my own honor." Richelieu seemed to wait an answer, and De Blenau replied:

"If your eminence means to attribute such knowledge to me, some one must have greatly misled you. I possess no information on the affairs of Spain whatever, except from the common reports and journals of the time."

This reply did not seem to affect Richelieu's intentions. "Well, well, Monsieur de Blenau," said he, with a smile, "you will take your seat at the council, and will, of course, as a good subject and an honorable man, communicate to us whatever information you possess on those points which concern the good of the state. We do not expect all at once; and everything shall be done to smooth your way and facilitate your views. Then, perhaps, if Richelieu live to execute the plans he has formed, you, Monsieur de Blenau, following his path, and sharing his confidence, may be ready to take his place, when death shall at length call him from it."

The cardinal counted somewhat too much on De Blenau's ambition, and not sufficiently on his knowledge of the world; and imagining that he had, the evening before, discovered the weak point in the character of the young count, he thought to lead him to anything, by holding out to him extravagant prospects of future greatness. The dish, however, was somewhat too highly flavored; and De Blenau replied, with a smile.

"Your eminence is exceeding good to think at all of me in the vast and more important projects which occupy your mind. But, alas! my lord, De Blenau would prove but a poor successor to Richelieu. No, my lord cardinal," he continued, "I have no ambition; that is a passion which should be reserved for such great and comprehensive minds as yours. I am contented as I am. High stations are always stations of danger."

"I had heard that the Count de Blenau was no way fearful," said Richelieu, fixing on him a keen and almost scornful glance. "Was the report a mistake? or is it lately he has become afraid of danger?"

De Blenau was piqued, and lost temper. "Of personal danger, my lord, I am never afraid," replied he. "But when along with risk to myself is involved danger to my friends, danger to my country, danger to my honor, and danger to my soul," and he returned the cardinal's glance full as proudly as it had been given, "then, my lord cardinal, I would say it were no cowardice, but true courage to fly from such peril—unless," he added, remembering the folly of opposing the irritable and unscrupulous minister, and thinking that his words had, perhaps, been already too warm—"unless, indeed, one felt within one's breast the mind of a Richelieu."

While De Blenau spoke the cardinal's brow knitted into a frown. A flush, too, came over his cheek; and untying the ribbon which served as a fastening, he took off the velvet cap he generally wore, as if to give himself air. He heard him, however, to the end, and then answered dryly. "You speak well, Monsieur de Blenau, and, I doubt not, feel what you say. But am I to understand you that you refuse to aid us at the council with your information and advice?"

"So far your eminence is right," replied the count, who saw that the storm was now about to break upon his head; "I must, indeed, decline the honors which you offer with so bountiful a hand. But do not suppose that I do so from unwillingness to yield you any information; for, truly, I have none to give. I have never meddled with politics. I have never turned my attention to state affairs; and therefore still less could I yield you any advice. Your eminence would be wofully disappointed when you expected to find a man well acquainted with the arts of government, and deep read in the designs of foreign states, to meet with one whose best knowledge is to range a battalion, or to pierce a boar; a soldier, and not a diplomatist; a hunter, and not a statesman. And as to the government of Poitou, my lord, its only good would be the emolument, and already my revenues are far more than adequate to my wants."

"You refuse my kindness, sir," replied the cardinal, with an air of deep determined haughtiness, very different from the urbanity with which he had at first received De Blenau; " I must now speak to you in another tone. And let me warn you to beware of what you say; for be assured that I already possess sufficient information to confound you if you should prevaricate."

"My lord cardinal," replied De Blenau, somewhat hastily, " I am not accustomed to prevaricate. Ask any questions you please, and, so long as my honor and my duty go with them, I will answer you."

"Then there are questions," said the cardinal, " that you would think against your duty to answer?"

" I said not so, your eminence," replied De Blenau. " In the examination I find I am to undergo, give my words their full meaning, if you please, but no more than their meaning."

" Well, then, sir, answer me as a man of honor and a French noble," said the cardinal—" are you not aware of a correspondence that has been, and is now, carried on between Anne of Austria and Don Francisco de Mello, Governor of the Low Countries?"

" I know not whom you mean, sir, by Anne of Austria," replied De Blenau. " If it be her majesty, your queen and mine, that you so designate, I reply at once that I know of no such correspondence, nor do I believe that it exists."

" Do you mean to say, Monsieur de Blenau," demanded the cardinal, fixing his keen sunken eyes upon the young count with that basilisk glance for which he was famous—" do you mean to say that you yourself have not forwarded letters from the queen to Madame de Chevreuse, and Don Francisco de Mello, by a private channel? Pause, Monsieur de Blenau, before you answer, and be well assured that I am acquainted with every particular of your conduct."

" Your eminence is, no doubt, acquainted with much

more intricate subjects than any of my actions," replied the count. "With regard to Madame de Chevreuse, her majesty has no need to conceal a correspondence with her, which has been fully permitted and sanctioned both by your eminence and the still higher authority of the king; and I may add, that to my certain knowledge letters have gone to that lady by your own courier. On the other point I have answered already; and have only to say once more that I know of no such correspondence, nor would I, assuredly, lend myself to any such measures, which I should conceive to be treasonable."

"I have always hitherto supposed you to be a man of honor," said the cardinal, coolly; "but what must I conceive now, Monsieur le Comte, when I tell you that I have those very letters in my possession?"

"You may conceive what you please, sir," replied De Blenau, giving way to his indignation; "but I will dare any man to lay before me a letter from her majesty to the person you mention, which has passed through the hands of De Blenau."

The cardinal did not reply, but opening an ebony cabinet, which stood on his right hand, he took from one of the compartments a small bundle of papers, from which he selected one, and laid it on the table before the count, who had hitherto looked on with no small wonder and expectation. "Do you know that writing, sir?" demanded the cardinal, still keeping his hand upon the paper in such a manner as to allow only a word or two to be visible.

De Blenau examined the line which the cardinal suffered to appear, and replied—"From what little I can see, I should imagine it to be the handwriting of her majesty. But that does not show that I have anything to do with it."

"But there is that in it which does," answered Richelieu, folding down a line or two of the letter, and pointing out to the count a sentence which said, "This will be conveyed to you by the Count de Blenau, who you know never fails."

"Now, sir!" continued the cardinal, "once more let me advise you to give me all you possess upon this subject. From a feeling of personal regard, I have had too much patience with you already."

"All I can reply to your eminence," answered the count, not a little embarrassed, "is that no letter whatever has been conveyed by me, knowingly, to the governor of the Low Countries."

De Blenau's eyes naturally fixed on the paper, which still lay on the table, and from which the cardinal had by this time withdrawn his hand; and feeling that both life and honor depended upon that document, he resolved to ascertain its authenticity, of which he entertained some doubt.

"Stop," said he hastily, "let me look at the superscription," and before Richelieu could reply he had raised it from the table and turned to the address. One glance was enough to satisfy him, and he returned it to the cardinal with a cool and meaning smile, repeating the words—"To Madame de Chevreuse."

At first the cardinal had instinctively stretched out his hand to stop De Blenau in his purpose, but he instantly recovered himself, nor did his countenance betray the least change of feeling. "Well, sir," replied he, "you said that you would dare any one to lay before you a letter from the queen to the person I mentioned. Did I not mention Madame de Chevreuse, and is not there the letter?"

"Your eminence has mistaken me," replied De Blenau, bowing his head, and smiling at the minister's art: "I meant Don Francisco de Mello. I had answered what you said in regard to Madame de Chevreuse before."

"I did mistake you then, sir," said the cardinal; "but it was from the ambiguity of your own words. However passing over your boldness in raising that letter with-

out my permission, I will show you that I know more of
your proceedings than you suspect. I will tell you the
very terms of the message you sent to the queen, after you
were wounded in the wood of Mantes, conveying to her
that you had not lost the packet with which you were
charged. Did not Seguin tell her, on your part, that
though the wound was in your side, your heart was not
injured?"

"I dare say he did, my lord," replied DeBlenau,
coolly; "and the event has proved that he was quite
right, for your eminence must perceive that I am quite
recovered, which, of course, could not have been the
case had any vital part been hurt. But I hope, your
eminence, that there is no offence, in your eyes, either
in having sent the queen, my mistress, an account of my
health, or in having escaped the attack of assassins."

A slight flush passed over Richelieu's cheek. "You
may chance to fall into less scrupulous hands than even
theirs," replied he. "I am certainly informed, sir, that
you, on the part of the queen, have been carrying on a
treasonable intercourse with Spain—a country at war
with France, to whose crown you are a born subject and
vassal; and I have to tell you that the punishment of such
a crime is death. Yes, sir, you may knit your brow.
But no consideration shall stay me from visiting with the
full severity of the law such as do so offend; and though
the information I want be but small, depend upon it, I
shall not hesitate to employ the most powerful means to
wring it from you."

De Blenau had no difficulty in comprehending the
nature of those means to which the cardinal alluded; but
his mind was made up to suffer the worst. "My lord
cardinal," replied he, "what your intentions are I know
not; but be sure that to whatever extremes you may go,
you can wring nothing from me but what you have
already heard. I once more assure you that I know of
no treasonable correspondence whatsoever; and firm in

my own in..ocence, I equally despise all attempts to bribe
or to intimidate me."

"Sir, you are insolent!" replied the cardinal, rising.
"Use no such language to me! Are you not an insect
I can sweep from my path in an instant? Ho, a guard
there without! We shall soon see whether you know
aught of Philip of Spain."

Had the cardinal's glance been directed towards De
Blenau, he would have seen that at the name of Philip of
Spain a degree of paleness came over his cheek; but
another object had caught Richelieu's eye, and he did
not observe it. It was the entrance of the attendant
whom he had despatched with the death-warrants which
now drew his notice; and well pleased to show De Blenau
the dreadful means he so unscrupulously employed to
extort confession from those he suspected, he eagerly
demanded, "What news?"

"May it please your eminence," said the attendant,
"Caply died under the torture. In truth, it was soon
over with him, for he did not bear it above ten minutes."

"But the confession, the confession!" exclaimed
Richelieu. "Where is the procès verbal?"

"He made no confession, sir," replied the man. "He
protested to the last his innocence, and that he knew
nothing."

"Pshaw!" said Richelieu; "they let him die too soon;
they should have given him wine to keep him up. Foolish
idiot," he continued, as if meditating over the death of
his victim; "had he but told what he was commanded,
he would have saved himself from a death of horror.
Such is the meed of obstinacy."

"Such," thought De Blenau, "is, unhappily, often the
reward of firmness and integrity. But such a death is
honorable in itself."

No one could better read in the face what was passing
in the mind than Richelieu, and it is probable that he

easily saw in the countenance of De Blenau the feelings excited by what had just passed. He remembered also the promise given by Chavigni; and if, when he called the guard, he had ever seriously proposed to arrest De Blenau, he abandoned his intention for the moment. Not that the high tone of the young count's language was either unfelt or forgiven, for Richelieu never pardoned; but it was as easy to arrest De Blenau at St. Germain as in Paris; and the wily minister calculated that by giving him a little liberty, and throwing him off his guard, he might be tempted to do those things which would put him more completely in the power of the government, and give the means of punishing him for his pride and obstinacy, as it was internally termed by a man long un-accustomed to any opposition.

De Blenau was principally obnoxious to the cardinal as the confidant of the queen, and from being the chief of her adherents both by his rank, wealth, and reputation. Anne of Austria having now become the only apparent object which could cloud the sky of Richelieu's political power, he had resolved either to destroy her, by driving her to some criminal act, or so to entangle her in his snares, as to reduce her to become a mere instrument in his hands and for his purposes. To arrest De Blenau would put the queen upon her guard; and therefore the minister, without hesitation, resolved to dissemble his resentment, and allow the count to depart in peace; reserving for another time the vengeance he had deter-mined should overtake him at last. Nor was his dis-sembling of that weak nature which those employ who have all the will to deceive without the art of deceiving.

Richelieu walked rapidly up and down the closet for a moment, as if striving to repress some strong emotion, then stopped, and turning to De Blenau with some frank-ness of manner, " Monsieur le Comte," said he, " I will own that you have heated me,—perhaps I have given way to it too much. But you ought to be more careful of your words, sir; and remember that with men whose power you cannot resist, it is sometimes dangerous even to be in the right, much more to make them feel it rudely. However, it is all past, and I will detain you no longer; trusting to your word, that the information which I have received is without foundation. Let me only add that you might have raised yourself this day to a height which few men in France would not struggle to attain. But that is past also, and may, perhaps, never return."

"I am most grateful, believe me," replied De Blenau, "for all the favors your eminence intended me; and I have no doubt that you will soon find some other person on whom to bestow them, much more worthy of them than myself."

Richelieu bowed low, and fixed his eyes upon the count without reply—a signal that the audience was over, which was not lost upon De Blenau, who very gladly took his leave of the minister, hoping most devoutly never to see his face again. The ambiguity of his last sentence, however, had not escaped the cardinal.

"So, Monsieur de Blenau!" said he, as soon as the count had left him, "you can make speeches with a double meaning also! Can you so? You may rue it though, for I will find means to bend your proud spirit, or to break it; and that before three days be over. Is everything prepared for my passage to Chantilly?" he continued, turning to the attendant.

"All is prepared, please your eminence," replied the man; "and as I passed I saw Monsieur de Chavigni getting into his chaise to set out."

"We will let him be an hour or two in advance," said the cardinal. "Send in the Marquis de Goumont;" and he again applied himself to other affairs.

CHAPTER IX.

"An entire new comedy, with new scenery, dresses, and decorations."

THE little village of Mesnil St. Loup, all insignificant as it is, was at the time of my tale a place of even less consequence than it appears nowadays, when nine people out of ten have scarcely ever heard of its existence.

Mesnil St. Loup was little known to strangers, for its simplicity had no attractions for the many. Nevertheless, on one fine evening, somewhere about the beginning of September, the phenomenon of a new face showed itself at Mesnil St. Loup. The personage to whom it appertained was a horseman of small, mean appearance, who, having passed by the church, rode through the village to the auberge, and having raised his eyes to the garland over the door, he divined from it that he himself would find there good Champagne wine, and his horse would meet with entertainment equally adapted to his peculiar taste. Thereupon the stranger alighted and entered the place of public reception, without making any of that bustle about himself which the landlord seemed well inclined to do for him; but, on the contrary, sat himself down in the most shady corner, ordered his bottle of wine, and inquired what means the house afforded of satisfying his hunger, in a low, quiet tone of voice, which reached no farther than the person he addressed.

"As for wine," the host replied, " monsieur should have such wine that the first merchant of Epernay might prick his ears at it; and in regard to eatables, what could be better than stewed eels, out of the river hard by, and a civet de lievre? Monsieur need not be afraid," he added; " it was a real hare he had snared that morning himself in the forest under the hill. Some dishonorable inn-

keepers," he observed—"innkeepers unworthy of the
name, would dress up cats and rats, and such animals, in
the form of hares and rabbits; even as the devil had been
known to assume the appearance of an angel of light;
but he scorned such practices, and could not only show
his hare's skin, but his hare in the skin. Further, he
would give monsieur an ortolan in a vine leaf, and a dish
of stewed sorrel."

The stranger underwent the innkeeper's oration with
most exemplary patience, signified his approbation of the
proposed dinner, without attacking the hare's reputation;
and when at length it was placed before him, he ate his
meal and drank his wine in profound silence, without a
word of praise or blame to either one or the other. The
landlord, with all his sturdy loquacity, failed in more
than one attempt to draw him into conversation; and the
hostess, though none of the oldest or ugliest, could scarce
win a syllable from his lips, even by asking if he were
pleased with his fare. The taciturn stranger merely
bowed his head, and seemed little inclined to exert his
oratorical powers, more than by the simple demand of
what he wanted; so that both mine host and hostess gave
him up in despair—the one concluding that he was "an
odd one," and the other declaring that he was as stupid
as he was ugly.

This lasted some time, till one villager after another,
having exhausted every excuse for staying to hear
whether the stranger would open his lips, dropped away
in his turn, and left the apartment vacant. It was then,
and not till then, that mine host was somewhat surprised,
by hearing the silent traveller pronounce in a most audible
and imperative manner, "Gaultier, come here." The
first cause of astonishment was to hear him speak at all;
and the next to find his own proper name of Gaultier
so familiar to the stranger, forgetting that it had been
vociferated at least one hundred times that night in his
presence. However, Gaultier obeyed the summons with

all speed, and approaching the stranger with a low reverence, begged to know his good will and pleasure.

"Your wine is good, Gaultier," said the stranger, raising his clear gray eyes to the rosy round of Gaultier's physiognomy. Even an innkeeper is susceptible of flattery; and Gaultier bent his head down towards the ground.

"Gaultier, bring me another bottle," said the stranger.

The bottle of wine was not long in making its appearance; and as Gaultier set it on the table before the stranger, he asked if he could serve him further.

"Can you show me the way to the old Château of St. Loup?" demanded the stranger.

"Surely, I can, sir," replied the innkeeper; "that is to say, as far as knowing where it is. But I hope monsieur does not mean to-night."

"Indeed do I," answered the stranger; "and pray why not? The night is the same as the day to an honest man."

"No doubt, no doubt!" exclaimed Gaultier, with the greatest doubt in the world in his own mind. "No doubt! But, Holy Virgin! Jesu preserve us!"—and he signed the cross most devoutly—"we all know that there are spirits, and demons, and astrologers, and the devil, and all those sort of things; and I would not go through the Grove where old Père Le Rouge, the sorcerer, was burnt alive, not to be prime minister, or the Cardinal de Richelieu, or any other great man, that is to say, after nightfall. In the day I would go anywhere, or do anything. I am no coward, sir; I dare to anything. My father served in the blessed League against the cursed Huguenots. So I am no coward; but, bless you, sir, I will tell you how it happened, and then you will see——"

"I know all about it," replied the stranger, in a voice that made the innkeeper start, and look over his left shoulder; "I know all about it. But sit down and drink with me, to keep your spirits up, for you must show me the way this very night. Père Le Rouge was a dear friend of mine, and before he was burnt for a sorcerer, we had made a solemn compact to meet once every ten years. Now, if you remember aright, it is just ten years, this very day, since he was executed; and there is no bond in hell fast enough to hold him from meeting me to-night at the old château. So sit you down and drink!" And he poured out a full cup of wine for the innkeeper, who looked aghast at the portentous compact between the stranger and Père Le Rouge. However, whether it was that Gaultier was too much afraid to refuse, or had too much esprit de corps not to drink with any one who would drink with him, can hardly be determined now; but so it was, that sitting down, according to the stranger's desire, he poured the whole goblet of wine over his throat at one draught, and, as he afterwards averred, could not help thinking that the stranger must have enchanted the liquor, for no sooner had he swallowed it, than all his fears of Père Le Rouge began to die away, like morning dreams.

"Would you choose another bottle, sir?" demanded Gaultier; and as his companion nodded his head in token of assent, was about to proceed on this errand—with the laudable intention also of sharing all his newly arisen doubts and fears with his gentle helpmate, who, for her part, was busily engaged in the soft domestic duties of scolding the stable-boy and boxing the maid's ears. But the stranger stopped him, perhaps divining, and not very much approving, the aforesaid communication. He exclaimed, "La Bourgeoise!" in a tone of voice which overpowered all other noises: the abuse of the dame herself—the tears of the maid—the exculpation of the stable-boy—the cackle of the cocks and hens, which were on a visit in the parlor—and the barking of a prick-eared cur included. The fresh bottle soon stood upon the table; and while the hostess returned to her former tender avocations, the stranger, whose clear gray eye seemed reading deeply into Gaultier's heart, continued to drink from the scanty remains of his own bottle, leaving mine host to fill from that which was hitherto uncontaminated by any other touch than his own. This Gaultier did not fail to do, till such time as the last rays of the sun, which had continued to linger fondly amidst a flight of light feathery clouds overhead, had entirely left the sky, and all was gray.

At that moment the stranger drew forth his purse, let it fall upon the table with a heavy sort of clinking sound, showing that the louis-d'ors within had hardly room to jostle against each other. It was a sound of comfortable plenty, which had something in it irresistibly attractive to the ears of Gaultier; and as he stood watching while the stranger insinuated his finger and thumb into the little leathern bag, drawing forth first one broad piece and then another, so splendid did the stranger's traffic with the devil begin to appear in the eyes of the inn-keeper, that he almost began to wish that he had been brought up a sorcerer also.

The stranger quietly pushed the two pieces of gold across the table till they got within the innkeeper's sphere of attraction, when they became suddenly hurried towards him, with irresistible velocity, and were plunged into the abyss of a large pocket on his left side, close upon his heart.

The stranger looked on with philosophic composure, as if considering some natural phenomenon, till such time as the operation was complete. " Now, Gaultier," cried he, " put on your beaver, and lead to the beginning of the Grove. I will find my way through it alone. But hark ye, say no word to your wife."

Gualtier was all complaisance, and having placed his hat on his head, he opened the door of the auberge, and brought forth the stranger's horse, fancying that what with a bottle of wine, and two pieces of gold, he could meet Beelzebub himself, or any other of those gentlemen of the lower house, with whom the curé used to frighten the little boys and girls when they went to their first communion. However, the stranger had scarcely passed the horse's bridle over his arm, and led him a step or two on the way, when the cool air and reflection made the inn-keeper begin to think differently of the devil, and be more inclined to keep at a respectful distance from so grave and antique a gentleman. A few steps more made him as frightened as ever; and before they had got to the end of the village, Gaultier fell hard to work, crossing himself most laboriously, and trembling every time he remembered that he was conducting one sorcerer to meet another, long dead and delivered over in form, with fire and fagot, into the hands of Satan.

It is probable that he would have run, but the stranger was close behind, and cut off his retreat.

At about a mile and a half from the little village of Mesnil, stood the old Château of St. Loup, situated upon an abrupt eminence, commanding a view of almost all the country round. The valley at its foot, and the slope of the hill up to its very walls, were covered with thick wood, through which passed the narrow deserted road from Mesnil, winding in and out with a thousand turns and divarications, and twice completely encircling the hill itself, before it reached the castle gate, which once, in the hospitable pride of former days, had rested constantly open for the reception equally of the friend and the stranger, but which now only gave entrance to the winds and tempests—rude guests, that contributed, even more than Time himself, the great destroyer, to bring ruin and desolation on the deserted mansion.

But, beyond all these, and removed without the pre-cincts of consecrated ground, was a heap of shards and flints—the sorcerer's grave! Above it, some pious hand had raised the symbol of salvation—a deed of charity, truly, in those days, when eternal mercy was farmed by the Church, like a turnpike on the high-road, and none

could pass but such as paid toll. But, however, there it
rose,—a tall white cross, standing, as that symbol should
always stand, high above every surrounding object, and
full in view of all who sought it.

As the aubergiste and his companion climbed the hill,
which, leading from the village of Meslin, commanded
a full prospect of the rich woody valley below, and over-
hung that spot which, since the tragedy of poor Père Le
Rouge, had acquired the name of the Sorcerer's Grove,
it was this tall white cross that first caught their attention. It stood upon the opposite eminence, distinctly
marked on the background of the evening sky, catching
every ray of light that remained, while behind it, pile
upon pile, lay the thick clouds of a coming storm.

" There, monsieur," cried Gaultier, " there is the cross
upon the sorcerer's grave!" And the fear which agitated him while he spoke, made the stranger's lip curl
into a smile of bitter contempt. But as they turned the
side of the hill, which had hitherto concealed the castle
itself from their sight, the teeth of Gaultier actually chat-
tered in his head, when he beheld a bright light shining
from several windows of the deserted building.

" There!" exclaimed the stranger, " there, you see
how well Père Le Rouge keeps his appointment. I am
waited for, and want you no farther. I can now find my
way alone. I would not expose you, my friend, to the
dangers of that Grove."

The innkeeper's heart melted at the stranger's words,
and he was filled with compassionate zeal upon the occasion. " Pray don't go," cried Gaultier, almost blub-
bering betwixt fear and tender-heartedness; " pray don't
go! Have pity upon your precious soul! You'll go
to the devil, indeed you will!—or at least to purgatory
for a hundred thousand years, and be burnt up like an
overdone rabbit. You are committing murder, and conspiracy, and treason "—the stranger started, but Gaultier
went on—" and heresy, and pleurisy, and sorcery, and

you will go to the devil, indeed you will—and then you'll remember what I told you."

"What is fated, is fated!" replied the stranger, in a solemn voice, though Gaultier's speech had produced that sort of tremulous tone, excited by an inclination either to laugh or to cry. "I have promised, and I must go. But let me warn you," he continued, sternly, "never to mention one word of what has passed to-night, if you would live till I come again. For if you reveal one word, even to your wife, the ninth night after you have done so, Père Le Rouge will stand on one side of your bed, and I on the other, and Satan at your feet, and we will carry you away body and soul, so that you shall never be heard of again."

When he had concluded, the stranger waited for no reply, but sprang upon his horse, and galloped down into the wood.

In the meantime, the landlord climbed to a point of the hill, from whence he could see both his own village, and the ruins of the castle. There, the sight of the church steeple gave him courage, and he paused to examine the extraordinary light which proceeded from the ruin. In a few minutes, he saw several figures flit across the windows, and cast a momentary obscurity over the red glare which was streaming forth from them upon the darkness of the night. "There they are!" cried he, "Père Le Rouge, and his pot companion!—and surely the devil must be with them, for I see more than two, and one of them has certainly a tail—Lord have mercy upon us!"

As he spoke, a vivid flash of lightning burst from the clouds, followed instantly by a tremendous peal of thunder. The terrified innkeeper was startled at the sound, and more than ever convinced that man's enemy was on earth, took to his heels, nor ceased running till he reached his own door, and met his better angel of a wife, who boxed his ears for his absence, and vowed he had been gallanting.

CHAPTER X.

The motto of which should be, " Out of the frying-pan into the fire."

THE jingle of Claude de Blenau's spurs, as he descended with a quick step the staircase of the Palais Cardinal, told as plainly as a pair of French spurs could tell,
that his heart was lightened of a heavy load since he had
last tried their ascent; and the spring of his foot, as he
leaped upon his horse, spoke much of renewed hope and
banished apprehension.

De Blenau, striking his spurs into the sides of his
horse, cantered off towards St. Germain as gaily as if
all doubt and danger were over, and began to look upon
bastilles, tortures, and racks, with all the other et-cetera
of Richelieu's government, as little better than chimeras
of the imagination, with which he had nothing further
to do.

As De Blenau began to reflect, he unconsciously drew
in the bridle of his horse: and before he had proceeded
one league on the way to St. Germain, the marks of deep
thought were evident both in the pace of the courser and
the countenance of the rider; De Blenau knitting his
brow and biting his lip, as the various dangers that surrounded him crossed his mind; and the gentle barb, seemingly animated by the same spirit as his master, bending
his arched neck and throwing out his feet with as much
consideration as if the firm Chemin de St. Germain had
been no better than a quagmire.

De Blenau well knew that even in France a man might
smile, and smile, and be a villain; and that the fair words
of Richelieu too often preceded his most remorseless actions. He remembered also the warning of Mademoiselle de Bourbon, and felt so strongly how insecure a

9

warranty was conscious innocence for his safety; but
still he possessed that sort of chivalrous pride which
made him look upon flight as degrading under any circumstances, and more especially so when the danger was
most apparent.

As long as any hesitation had remained in the mind of
De Blenau, he had proceeded, as we have seen, with a
slow unequal pace; but the moment his determination
was fixed, his thoughts turned towards St. Germain, and
all his ideas concentrating into one of those day-dreams,
that every young heart is fond to indulge, he spurred on
his horse, eager to realize some at least of the bright
promises which hope so liberally held forth. It was late,
however, before he arrived at the end of his journey, and
internally cursing the etiquette which required him to
change his dress before he could present himself at the
palace, he sent forward his page to announce his return,
and beg an audience of the queen.

His toilet was not long, and without waiting for the
boy's return, he set out on foot, hoping to join the queen's
circle before it separated for the evening. In this he was
disappointed. Anne of Austria was alone; and though
her eyes sparkled with gladness for his unexpected return, and her reception was as kind as his good services
required, De Blenau would have been better pleased to
have been welcomed by other lips.

"I could scarce credit the news till I saw you, mon
chambellan," said the queen, extending her hand for him
to kiss; "nor can I truly believe it is you that I behold
even now. How have you escaped from that dreadful
man?"

"I will tell your majesty all that has happened." replied the count; "and as I have a boon to ask, I think
I must represent my sufferings in your majesty's cause
in the most tremendous colors. But without a jest, I
have had little to undergo beyond a forced attendance
at the cardinal's fête, where the only hard word I re-

ceived was from L'Angeli, the Duke of Enghien's fool,
who, seeing my riding-dress, asked if I were Puss in
Boots." De Blenau then shortly related all that had
occurred during his stay in Paris. "And thus, madam,"
he added, "you see that Chavigni has kept his word; for
had it not been for that promise, I doubt not I should
have been even now comfortably lodged in the Bastile,
with a table at his majesty's expense."

The queen mused for a moment without making any
reply; but from her countenance it seemed that she was
not a little troubled by what she had heard.

"De Blenau," said she at length, in a calm but melancholy voice, "there is something concealed here. The
cardinal has deeper plans in view. As Marie de Bourbon told you, they are plotting my ruin. When first I
entered France, that man of blood and treachery resolved
to make me his slave. He flattered my tastes, he prevented my wishes, like an insidious serpent he wound
himself into my confidence; and I was weak enough to
dream that my husband's minister was my best friend.
With as much vanity as insolence, he mistook condescension for love. He sought his opportunity, and dared to
insult my ears with his wishes. I need not tell you, De
Blenau, what was my reply; but it was such as stung him
to the soul. He rose from where he had been kneeling
at my feet, and threatened such vengeance, that, as he
said, my whole life should be one long succession of
miseries. Too truly has he kept his word."—The queen
paused, and as was often her custom when any circumstance called her memory back to the bitter events of her
past life, fell into a deep reverie, from which it was not
easy to rouse her.

"Too much of this," said she at length; "we must
look to the present, De Blenau. As the mother of two
princes, Richelieu both hates and fears me; and I see
that they are plotting my ruin. But yours shall not be
involved therein. De Blenau, you must fly till the storm
has passed by."

"Pardon me, madam," replied the count, "but in this I cannot yield your majesty that obedience I would willingly show under any other circumstances. I cannot, I must not fly. My own honor, madam, requires that I should stay; for if flight be not construed into an evidence of guilt, it may at least be supposed a sign of cowardice."

"Indeed, indeed! De Blenau," said the queen, earnestly, "you must do as I require; nay," she added, with a mixture of sweetness and dignity, "as I command. If they can prove against you that you have forwarded letters from me to my brother the King of Spain, they will bring you to the block, and will most likely ruin me."

"I trust to the promise your majesty gave me when first I undertook to have those letters conveyed to your royal brother King Philip," answered De Blenau: "you then pledged to me your word that they were alone of a domestic nature, and that they should always continue so, without ever touching upon one subject of external or internal policy, so that my allegiance to my king, and my duty to my country, should alike remain pure and inviolate. I doubt not that your majesty has pointedly kept this promise; and De Blenau will never fly, while he can lay his hand upon his heart and feel himself innocent."

"Yes, but remember, my good youth," replied the queen, "that this cardinal,—my husband's tyrant rather than his subject,—has commanded me, his queen, to forbear all correspondence with my brother, and has narrowly watched me to prevent that very communication between Philip and myself, which your kindness has found means to procure. Remember too his remorseless nature; and then judge whether he will spare the man who has rendered his precautions vain."

"Madam," replied De Blenau, "I do not fear; nothing shall make me fly. Though there be no bounds to what

the cardinal dare attempt, yet his power does not extend
to make me a coward!"

"But for my sake," still persevered Anne of Austria,
laboring to persuade him to a measure on which she too
well knew his safety depended. "Remember, that if
there be proved against me even so small a crime as
having sent those letters, my ruin is inevitable, and there
are modes of torture which will wrench a secret from
the most determined constancy."

"I fear me," replied De Blenau, "that some act of
mine must have much degraded me in your majesty's
opinion."

"No, no, my friend!" said the queen; "not so, indeed.
I do not doubt you in the least: but I would fain persuade
you, De Blenau, to that which I know is best and safest."

"Your majesty has now given me the strongest reasons for my stay," replied De Blenau, with a smile; "I
have now the means of proving my fidelity to you, and
nothing shall tempt me to leave you at this moment. But
in the meantime there is one favor—I have to request."

"Name it," replied the queen: "indeed, De Blenau,
you might command it."

"Your majesty is too good," said the count. "I will
make my story as brief as possible, but I must explain
to you that Mademoiselle de Beaumont and myself were
plighted to each other when very young."

"I know it, I know it all," interrupted the queen, "and
that you love each other still; and believe me, my dear De
Blenau, neither time nor disappointment has so frozen
my heart that I cannot enter warmly into all you feel.
Perhaps you never discovered that Anne of Austria was
an enthusiast. But tell me what difficulty has occurred
between you?"

"Why, in truth, madam," answered De Blenau, "the
difficulty arises with your majesty."

"With me!" cried the queen. "With me, De Blenau!
Impossible! Nothing could give me more pleasure than

to see your union. This Pauline of yours is one of the sweetest girls that ever I beheld; and with all her native unbought graces, she looks amongst the rest of the court like a wild rose in a flower garden: not so cultivated, in truth, but more simply elegant, and sweeter than them all."

De Blenau's heart beat, and his eye sparkled, and he paused a moment ere he could reply; nor indeed were his first sentences very distinct. He said a great deal about her majesty's goodness, and his own happiness, and Pauline's excellence, all in that simple sort of confused way which would make it appear simple nonsense were it written down; but which very clearly conveyed to the queen how much he loved Pauline, and how much obliged he was to her majesty for praising her.

After this he entered rather more regularly into a detail of those circumstances which had induced Mademoiselle de Beaumont to suspect him. "The point which seems to affect her most," continued De Blenau, " is the visit with which Mademoiselle de Hauteford honored me by your majesty's command, in order to receive from me the last letter from your majesty to the King of Spain, which I was unhappily prevented from forwarding by my late wounds. Now this, as affecting the character of the lady your majesty employed in the business, does certainly require some explanation. In regard to everything else, Pauline will, I feel sure, consider my word sufficient."

" Oh, leave it all to me, leave it all to me!" exclaimed the queen, laughing. " What! jealous already is she, fair maid? But fear not, De Blenau. Did she know you as well as I do, she would doubt herself sooner than De Blenau. However, I undertake to rob the rose of its thorn for you, and leave love without jealousy. A woman is very easily convinced where she loves, and it will be hard if I cannot show her that she has been in the wrong. But take no unworthy advantage of it, De

Blenau," she continued; " for a woman's heart will not
hesitate at trifles when she wishes to make reparation to
a man she loves."

" All the advantage I could ever wish to take, replied
the count, " would be to claim her hand without delay."

" Nay, nay, that is but a fair advantage," said the
queen. " Yet," continued she, after a moment's pause,
" it were not wise to draw the eyes of suspicion upon us
at this moment. But there are such things as private
marriages, De Blenau——"

There was no small spice of romance in the character
of Anne of Austria; and this, on more than one occasion,
led her into various circumstances of danger, affecting
both herself and the state. Of an easy and generous
spirit, she always became the partisan of the oppressed,
and anything that interested or excited her feelings was
certain to meet encouragement and support, however
chimerical or hazardous; while plans of more judgment
and propriety were either totally discountenanced or im-
properly pursued.

It was, perhaps, this spirit of romance more than any
political consideration which in the present instance made
her suggest to the Count de Blenau the idea of a private
marriage with Pauline de Beaumont; and he, as ardent
as herself, and probably as romantic, caught eagerly at
a proposal which seemed to promise a more speedy union
with the object of his love than was compatible with all
the tedious ceremonies and wearisome etiquette attendant
upon a court-marriage of that day.

" I shall not see your Pauline to-night," said the queen,
continuing the conversation which this proposal had induced. " She excused herself attending my evening circle on account of a slight indisposition; but to-morrow I
will explain everything on your part, and propose to her
myself what we have agreed upon."

" She is not ill, I trust?" said De Blenau.

" Oh no!" replied the queen, smiling at the anxiety of
his look, " not enough even to alarm a lover, I believe."

This answer, however, was not sufficient for De
Blenau, and taking leave of the queen, he sent for one of
Madame de Beaumont's servants, through whose inter-
vention he contrived to obtain an audience of no less a
person than Louise, Pauline's suivante. Now Louise was
really a pretty woman, and doubtless her face might have
claimed remembrance from many a man who had nothing
else to think of. De Blenau remembered it too, but without any reference to its beauty, which, indeed, he had
never stayed to inquire into.

It must be remembered that the morning previous to
his journey to Paris, the moment before he was joined
by Chavigni, his eye had been attracted by that nobleman engaged in earnest conversation with a girl habited
in the dress of dear Languedoc ; and he now found in the
soubrette of Mademoiselle de Beaumont the very individual he had seen in such circumstances. All this did not
very much enhance the regard of De Blenau towards
Louise, and he satisfied himself with a simple inquiry
concerning her mistress's health, adding a slight recom-
mendation to herself to take care whom she gossiped with
while she remained at St. Germain, conveyed in that
stately manner which made Louise resolve to hate him
most cordially for the rest of her life, and declare that he
was not half so nice a gentleman as Monsieur de Chavigni, who was a counsellor into the bargain.

After a variety of confused dreams concerning queens
and cardinals, Bastiles and private marriages, De Blenau
woke to enjoy one of those bright mornings which often
shine out in the first of autumn—memorials of summer,
when summer itself is gone. It was too early to present
himself at the palace ; but he had now a theme on which
his thoughts were not unwilling to dwell, and therefore
as soon as he was dressed he sauntered out, most lover-
like, into the park, occupied with the hope of future happiness, and scarcely sensible of any external thing, save
the soothing influence of the morning air, and the cheerful hum of awakening nature.

As time wore on, however—and probably it did so faster than he fancied—his attention was called towards the palace by an unusual degree of bustle and activity amongst the attendants, who were now seen passing to and fro along the terrace, with all the busy haste of a nest of emmets disturbed in their unceasing industry.

His curiosity being excited, he quitted the principal alley in which he had been walking, and ascending the flight of steps leading to the terrace, entered the palace by the small door of the left wing. As none of the servants immediately presented themselves, he proceeded by one of the side staircases to the principal saloon, where he expected to meet some of the valets de chambre, who generally at that hour awaited the rising of the queen.

On opening the door, however, he was surprised to find Anne of Austria already risen, together with the dauphin and the young Duke of Anjou, the principal ladies of the court, and several menial attendants, all habited in travelling costume; while various trunk-mails, saddle-bags, portmanteaus, etc., lay about the room, some already stuffed to the gorge with their appropriate contents, and others opening their wide jaws to receive whatever their owners chose to cram them withal.

As soon as De Blenau entered this scene of unprincely confusion, the quick eyes of Anne of Austria lighted upon him, and, advancing from the group of ladies to whom she had been speaking, she seemed surprised to see him in the simple morning costume of the court.

" Why, De Blenau! " exclaimed she, " we wait for you, and you have neither boots nor cloak. Have you not seen the page I sent to you? "

" No, indeed, madam," replied De Blenau; " but having loitered in the park some time, I have probably thus missed receiving your commands."

" Then you have not heard," said the queen; " we have been honored this morning by a summons to join the king at Chantilly."

"Indeed!" rejoined De Blenau, thoughtfully; "what should this mean, I wonder? It is strange! Richelieu was to be there last night: so I heard it rumored yesterday in Paris."

"I fear me," answered the queen in a low tone, "that the storm is about to burst upon our head. A servant informs me, that riding this morning, shortly after sunrise, near that small open space which separates this, the forest of Laye, from the great wood of Mantes, he saw a large party of the cardinal's guard winding along towards the wooden bridge at which we usually cross the river."

"Oh, I think nothing of that," replied the count. "Your majesty must remember that this cardinal has his men scattered all over the country; but, at all events, we can take the stone bridge farther down. At what time does your majesty depart? I will but pay my compliments to these ladies, and then go to command the attendance of my train, which will at all events afford some sort of escort."

During this dialogue the queen had looked from time to time towards the group of ladies who remained in conversation at the other end of the apartment; and with that unsteadiness of thought peculiar to her character, she soon forgot all her fears and anxieties as she saw the dark eye of Pauline de Beaumont wander every now and then with a furtive glance towards De Blenau, and then suddenly fall to the ground, or fix upon vacancy, as if afraid of being caught in such employment.

Easily reading every line expressive of a passion to which she had once been so susceptible, the queen turned with a playful smile to De Blenau. "Come," said she, "I will save you the trouble of paying your compliments to more than one of those ladies, and she shall stand your proxy to all the rest. Pauline—Mademoiselle de Beaumont," she continued, raising her voice, "come hither, Flower! I would speak a word with you."

Pauline came forward—not unhappy, in truth, but with the blood rushing up into her cheeks and forehead till timidity became actual pain, while the clear cold blue eye of Mademoiselle de Hauteford followed her across the room, as if she wondered at feelings she herself had apparently never experienced.

De Blenau advanced and held out his hand. Pauline instantly placed hers in it, and in the confusion of the moment laid the other upon it also.

"Well," said the queen, with a smile, "De Blenau, you must be satisfied now. Nay, be not ashamed, Pauline; it is all right, and pure, and natural."

"I am not ashamed, madam," replied Pauline, seeming to gain courage from the touch of her lover; "I have done De Blenau wrong in ever doubting one so good and so noble as he is: but he will forgive me now, I know, and I will never do him wrong again."

I need not proceed further with all this. De Blenau and Pauline enjoyed one or two moments of unmingled happiness, and then the queen reminded them that he had yet to dress for his journey, and to prepare his servants to accompany the carriages. This, however, was soon done, and in less than half an hour De Blenau rejoined the party in the saloon of the palace.

"Now, De Blenau," said the queen, as soon as she saw him, "you are prepared for travelling at all points. For once be ruled, and instead of accompanying me to Chantilly, make the best of your way to Franche Comté, or to Flanders, for I much fear that the cardinal has not yet done with you. I will take care of your interests while you are gone, even better than I would my own; and I promise you that as soon as you are in safety Madame de Beaumont and Pauline shall follow you, and you may be happy, surely, though abroad for a few short years, till Richelieu's power or his life be passed away."

De Blenau smiled. "Nay, nay," replied he, "that would not be like a gallant knight and true, either to de-

sert my queen or my lady love. Besides, I am inclined
to believe that this journey to Chantilly bodes us good
rather than harm.   For near three months past the king
has been there almost alone with Cinq Mars, who is as
noble a heart as e'er the world produced, and is well
affected towards your majesty. So I am looking forward to brighter days."

   " Well, we shall see," said the queen, with a doubtful
shake of the head.   " You are young, De Blenau, and
full of hopes—all that has passed away with me.   Now
let us go.   I have ordered the carriages to wait at the
end of the terrace, and we will walk thither:—perhaps it
may be the last time I shall ever see my favorite walk;
for who knows if any of us will ever return ? "

   With these melancholy anticipations, the queen took
the arm of Madame de Beaumont, and, followed by the
rest, led the way to the terrace, from which was to be
seen the vast and beautiful view extending from St. Germain over Paris to the country beyond, taking in all the
windings of the river Seine, with the rich woods through
which it flowed.

   It is ever a bright scene, that view from St. Germain,
and many have been the royal and the fair, and the noble,
whose feet have trod the terrace of Henry the Fourth;
but seldom, full seldom, has there been there a group of
greater loveliness or honor than that which then followed
Anne of Austria from the palace.   The melancholy which
hung over the whole party took from them any wish for
further conversation, than a casual comment upon the
beauties of the view; and thus they walked on nearly in
silence, till they had approached within a few hundred
yards of the extremity, where they were awaited by the
carriages prepared for the queen and her ladies, together
with the attendants of De Blenau.

   At that moment the quick clanging step of armed men
was heard following, and all with one impulse turned to
see who it was that thus seemed to pursue them.

The party which had excited their attention consisted of a soldier-like old man, who seemed to have ridden hard, and half-a-dozen chasseurs of the guard, who followed him at about ten or twelve paces' distance.

"It is the Count de Thiery," said De Blenau; "I know him well: as good an old soldier as ever lived."

Notwithstanding De Blenau's commendation, Anne of Austria appeared little satisfied with the count's approach, and continued walking on towards the carriages with a degree of anxiety in her eye, which speedily communicated feelings of the same kind to her attendants. Pauline, unacquainted with the intrigues and anxieties of the court, saw from the countenances of all around that something was to be apprehended; and magnifying the danger from uncertainty in regard to its nature, she instinctively crept close to De Blenau, as certain of finding protection there.

Judging at once the cause of De Thiery's coming, De Blenau drew the arm of Pauline through his, and lingered a step behind, while the rest of the party proceeded."

"Dear Pauline!" said he, in a low but firm tone of voice, "my own Pauline! prepare yourself for what is coming! I think you will find that this concerns me. If so, farewell! and remember, whatever be my fate, that De Blenau has loved you ever faithfully, and will love you till his last hour—beyond that—God only knows, but if ever human affection passed beyond the tomb, my love for you will endure in another state."

By this time they had reached the steps, at the bottom of which the carriages were in waiting, and at the same moment the long strides of the Count de Thiery had brought him to the same spot.

"Well, Monsieur de Thiery!" said Anne of Austria, turning sharp round, and speaking in that shrill tone which her voice assumed whenever she was agitated either by fear or anger; "your haste implies bad news. Does your business lie with me?"

" No, so please your majesty," replied the old soldier;
" no farther than to wish you a fair journey to Chantilly,
and to have the pleasure of seeing your majesty to your
carriage."

The queen paused, and regarded the old man for a
moment, with a steady eye, while he looked down upon
the ground and played with the point of his gray beard,
in no very graceful embarrassment.

" Very well! " replied she at length; " you, Monsieur
de Thiery, shall hand me to my carriage.   So, De Blenau,
I shall not need your attendance.   Mount your horse
and ride on."

" Pardon me, your majesty," said De Thiery, stepping
forward with an air of melancholy gravity, but from
which all embarrassment was now banished.   " Monsieur
de Blenau," he continued, " I have a most unpleasant task
to accomplish: I am sorry to say you must give me up
your sword; but be assured that you render it to a man
of honor, who will keep it as a precious and invaluable
charge, till he can give it back to that hand which he is
convinced will always use it nobly."

" I foresaw it plainly! " cried the queen, and turned
away her head.   Pauline clasped her hands and burst
into tears: but amongst the attendants of De Blenau, who
during this conversation had one by one mounted the
steps of the terrace, there was first a whisper, then a loud
murmur, then a shout of indignation, and in a moment
a dozen swords were gleaming in the sunshine.

Old De Thiery laid his hand upon his weapon, but De
Blenau stopped him in his purpose.

" Silence! " cried he, in a voice of thunder; " Traitors,
put up your swords!—My good friends," added he, in a
gentler tone, as he saw himself obeyed, " those swords
which have before so well defended their master, must
never be drawn in a cause that De Blenau could blush to
own.   Monsieur le Comte de Thiery, he continued, unbuckling his weapon, " I thank you for the handsome

manner in which you have performed a disagreeable duty. I do not ask to see the lettre de cachet, which, of course, you bear; for in giving you the sword of an honorable man, I know I could not place it in better hands; and now, having done so, allow me to lead her majesty to her carriage, and I will then follow you whithersoever you may have commands to bear me."

"Most certainly," replied De Thiery, receiving his sword; "I wait your own time, and will remain here till you are at leisure."

De Blenau led the queen to the carriage in silence, and having handed her in, he kissed the hand she extended to him, begging her to rely upon his honor and firmness. He next gave his hand to Pauline de Beaumont, down whose cheeks the tears were streaming unrestrained. "Farewell, dear Pauline! farewell!" he said. Her sobs prevented her answer, but her hands clasped upon his with a fond and lingering pressure, which spoke more to his heart than the most eloquent adieu.

Madame de Beaumont came next, and embraced him warmly. "God protect you, my son!" said she, "for your heart is a noble one."

Mademoiselle de Hauteford followed, greeting De Blenau with a calm cold smile and a graceful bow; and the rest of the royal suite having placed themselves in other carriages, the cavalcade moved on. De Blenau stood till they were gone. Raising his hat, he bowed with an air of unshaken dignity as the queen passed, and then turning to the terrace, he took the arm of the Count de Thiery, and returned a prisoner to the palace.

"Well, sir," said De Blenau, smiling with feelings mingled of melancholy resignation to his fate and proud disdain for his enemies, "imprisonment is too common a lot, nowadays, to be matter of surprise, even where it falls on the most innocent. Our poor country, France, seems to have become one great labyrinth, with the Bastile in the centre, and all the roads terminating there. I suppose that such is my destination."

" I am sorry to say it is," replied his companion. " My orders are to carry you thither direct; but I hope that your sojourn will not be long within its walls. Without doubt, you will soon be able to clear yourself."

" I must first know of what I am accused," replied the count. " If they cry in my case, as in that of poor Clement Marot, Prenez le, il a mangé le lard, I shall certainly plead guilty; but I know of no state crime which I have committed, except eating meat on a Friday. It is all well, perhaps, Monsieur de Thiery," continued he, falling into graver tone, " to take these things lightly. I cannot imagine that the cardinal means me harm; for he must well know that I have done nothing to deserve ill, either from my king or my country. Pray God his eminence's breast be as clear as mine!"

" Umph!" cried the old soldier, with a meaning shake of the head, " I should doubt that, De Blenau. You have neither had time nor occasion to get it so choked up as doubtless his must be. But these are bad subjects to talk upon: though I swear to Heaven, sir count, that when I was sent upon this errand, I would have given a thousand livres to have found that you had been wise enough to set out last night for some other place."

" Innocence makes one incautious," replied De Blenau; " but I will own, I was surprised to find that the business had been put upon you."

" So was I," rejoined the other. " I was astonished, indeed, when I received a lettre de cachet. But a soldier has nothing to do but to obey, Monsieur de Blenau. It is true, I one time thought to make an excuse; but, on reflection, I found that it would do you no good, and that some one might be sent to whom you would less willingly give your sword than to old De Thiery. But here we are at the palace, sir. There is a carriage in waiting; will you take any refreshment before you go?"

The prospect of imprisonment for an uncertain period, together with a few little evils, such as torture, and death, in the perspective, had not greatly increased De Blenau's appetite, and he declined accepting the Count de Thiery's offer, but requested that his page might be allowed to accompany him to Paris. The orders of Richelieu, however, were strict in this respect, and De Thiery was obliged to refuse. "But," added he, "if the boy has wit, he may smuggle himself into the Bastile afterwards. Let him wait for a day or two, and then crave of the jailer to see you. The prison is not kept so close as those on the outside of it imagine. I have been in more than once myself to see friends who have been confined there. There was poor La Forte, who was afterwards beheaded, and the Chevalier de Caply, who is in there still. I have seen them both in the Bastile."

"You will never see the Chevalier de Caply again," replied De Blenau, shuddering at the remembrance of his fate. "He died yesterday morning under the torture."

"Grand Dieu!" exclaimed De Thiery; "this cardinal prime minister stands on no ceremonies. Here are five of my friends he has made away within six months. There was La Forte, whom I mentioned just now, and Boissy, and De Reineville, and St. Cheron; and now, you tell me, Caply too; and if you should chance to be beheaded, or die under the torture, you will be the sixth."

"You are kind in your anticipations, sir," replied De Blenau, smiling at the old man's bluntness, yet not particularly enjoying the topic. "But having done nothing to merit such treatment, I hope I shall not be added to your list."

"I hope not, I hope not!" exclaimed De Thiery, "God forbid! I think, in all probability, you will escape with five or six weeks' imprisonment: and what is that?"

"Why, no great matter, if considered philosophically," answered De Blenau, thoughtfully. "And yet, Monsieur de Thiery, liberty is a great thing. The very freedom of walking amidst all the beauties of the vast creation, of wandering at our will from one perfection to an-

10

other, is not to be lost without a sigh. But it is not that alone—the sense, the feeling of liberty, is too innately dear to the soul of man to be parted with as a toy."

While De Blenau thus spoke, half reasoning with himself, half addressing his conversation to the old soldier by his side, who, by long service had been nearly drilled into a machine, and could not, consequently, enter fully into the feelings of his more youthful companion, the carriage which was to convey them to Paris was brought round to the gate of the palace at which they stood.

The preparations that had been made for De Blenau's journey to Chantilly, now served for this less agreeable expedition; and the various articles which he conceived would be necessary to his comfort, were accordingly disposed about the vehicle, whose roomy interior was not likely to suffer from repletion.

Had it been possible, De Blenau would fain have quitted St. Germain without encountering the fresh pain of taking leave of his attendants; but those who had seen his arrest, had by this time communicated the news to those who had remained in the town, and they now all pressed round to kiss his hand, and take a last look of their kind-hearted lord, before he was lost to them, as they feared, forever. There was something affecting in the scene, and a glistening moisture rose even in the eye of the old Count de Thiery, while De Blenau, with a kind word to say to each bade them farewell, one after another, and then sprang into the carriage that was to convey him to a prison.

The vehicle rolled on for some way in silence, but at length De Blenau said, " Monsieur de Thiery, you must excuse me if I am somewhat grave. Even conscious rectitude cannot make such a journey as this very palatable. And besides," he added, " I have to-day parted with some that are very dear to me."

" I saw that, I saw that," answered the old soldier. " It was bad enough parting with so many kind hearts as stood round you just now, but that was a worse fare-well at the end of the terrace. Now out upon the policy that can make such bright eyes shed such bitter tears. I can hardly get those eyes out of my head, old as it is. Oh, if I were but forty years younger! "

" What then? " demanded De Blenau, with a smile.

" Why, perhaps I might have ten times more pleasure in lodging you safe in the Bastile than I have now," answered De Thiery. " Oh, Monsieur de Blenau, take my word for it, age is the most terrible misfortune that can happen to any man; other evils will mend, but this is every day getting worse."

The conversation between De Blenau and his companion soon dropped, as all conversation must do, unless it be forced, where there exists a great dissimilarity of ideas and circumstances. It is true, from time to time, Monsieur de Thiery uttered an observation which called for a reply from De Blenau; but the thoughts which crowded upon the young count were too many, and too overpowering in their nature, to find relief in utterance. The full dangers of his situation, and all the vague and horrible probabilities which the future offered, presented themselves more forcibly to his mind, now that he had leisure to dwell upon them, than they had done at first, when all his energies had been called into action; and when, in order to conceal their effect from others, he had been obliged to fly from their consideration himself.

A thousand little accessory circumstances also kept continually renewing the recollection of his painful situation. When he dropped his hand, as was his custom, to rest it upon the hilt of his sword, his weapon was gone, and he had to remember that he had been disarmed; and if by chance he cast his eyes from the window of the carriage, the passing and repassing of the guards continually reminded him that he was a prisoner.

Thus passed the hours away as the carriage rolled on towards Paris. It may be well supposed that such a

vehicle did not move with any great celerity; but it so
happened that the machine itself was the personal property of Monsieur de Thiery, who always styled it une
belle voiture; and looking upon it as the most perfect
specimen of the coach-building art, he was mighty cautious concerning its progression. This the postilion was
well aware of, and therefore never ventured upon a
greater degree of speed than might carry them over the
space of two miles in the course of an hour; but notwithstanding such prudent moderation, the head of Monsieur
de Thiery would often be protruded from the window,
whenever an unfriendly rut gave the vehicle a jolt, exclaiming loudly, " Holla! Postillon! gardez vous de
casser ma belle voiture; " and sundry other adjurations,
which did not serve to increase the rapidity of their
progress.

Such tedious waste of time, together with the curious
gazing of the multitude at the State-prisoner, and uncertain calculations as to the future, created for De Blenau
a state of torment to which the Bastile at once would
have been relief; so that he soon began most devoutly to
wish his companion and the carriage and the postilion
all at the devil together for going so slowly. Night over-
took the travellers when they were about a league from
Paris, and the heaviest day De Blenau had ever yet
known found its end at last.

Avoiding the city as much as possible, the carriage
passed round and entered by the Porte St. Antoine; and
the first objects which presented themselves to the eyes
of De Blenau after passing the gates, were the large
gloomy towers of the Bastile, standing lone and naked
in the moonlight, which showed nothing but their dark
and irregular forms, strongly contrasted with the light
and rippling water that flowed like melted silver in the
fosse below.

One of the guards had ridden on, before they entered
the city, to announce their approach; and as soon as the

carriage came up, the outer drawbridge fell with a heavy clang, and the gates of the court opening, admitted them through the dark gloomy porch into that famous prison, so often the scene of horror and of crime. At the same time, two men advancing to the door, held each a lighted torch to the window of the carriage, which, flashing with a red gleam upon the rough stone walls, and gloomy archways on either side, showed plainly to De Blenau all the frowning features of the place, rendered doubly horrible by the knowledge of its purpose.

A moment afterwards, a fair, soft-looking man, dressed in a black velvet pourpoint (whom De Blenau discovered to be the governor), approached the carriage with an official paper in his hand, and lighted by one of the attendant's torches read as follows, with that sort of hurried drawl which showed it to be a matter of form:—

"Monsieur le Comte de Thiery," said he, "you are commanded by the king to deliver into my hands the body of Claude Count de Blenau, to hold and keep in strict imprisonment, until such time as his majesty's will be known in his regard, or till he be acquitted of the crimes with which he is charged, by a competent tribunal; and I now require you to do the same."

This being gone through, De Thiery descended from the carriage, followed by the Count de Blenau, whom the governor instantly addressed with a profound bow and servile smile.

"Monsieur de Blenau," said he, "you are welcome to the Bastile; and anything I can do for your accommodation, consistent with my duty, you shall command."

"I hope you will let it be so, sir governor," said old De Thiery; "for Monsieur de Blenau is my particular friend, and without doubt he will be liberated in a few days. Now, Monsieur de Blenau," continued he, "I must leave you for the present, but hope soon to see you in another place. You will, no doubt, find several of your friends here; for we all take it in turn: and indeed,

nowadays, it would be almost accounted a piece of ignorance not to have been in the Bastile once in one's life.
So, farewell!" And he embraced him warmly, whispering as he did so, "Make a friend of the governor—gold
will do it!"

De Blenau looked after the good old soldier with feelings of regret, as he drove through the archway. Immediately after, the drawbridge rose, and the gates closed
with a clang, sounding on De Blenau's ears as if they
shut out from him all that was friendly in the world;
and overpowered by a feeling of melancholy desolation,
he remained with his eyes fixed in the direction De Thiery
had taken, till he was roused by the governor laying his
hand upon his arm. "Monsieur de Blenau," said he,
"will you do me the favor of following me? and I will
have the honor of showing you your apartment."

De Blenau obeyed in silence, and the governor led the
way into the inner court, and thence up the chief staircase to the second story, where he stopped at a heavy
door plated with iron, and sunk deep in a stone wall, from
the appearance of which De Blenau did not argue very
favorably of the chambers within. His anticipations,
however, were agreeably disappointed, when one of the
attendants, who lighted them, pulled aside the bolts, and
throwing open the door, exposed to his view a large neat
room, fitted up with every attention to comfort, and even
some attempt at elegance. This, the governor informed
him, was destined for his use while he did the Bastile the
honor of making it his abode; and he then went on in the
same polite strain to apologize for the furniture being in
some disorder, as the servants had been very busy in the
château, and had not had time to arrange it since its last
occupant had left them, which was only the morning before. So far De Blenau might have imagined himself
in the house of a polite friend, had not the bolts and bars
obtruded themselves on his view wherever he turned,
speaking strongly of a prison.

The end of the governor's speech also was more in ac-
cordance with his office. " My orders, Monsieur de
Blenau," said he in continuation, " are, to pay every attention to your comfort and convenience, but at the same
time to have the strictest guard over you. I am therefore obliged to deny you the liberty of the court, which
some of the prisoners enjoy, and I must also place a sentinel at your door. I will now go and give orders for
the packages which were in the carriage to be brought
up here, and will then return immediately to advise with
you on what can be done to make your time pass more
pleasantly."

Thus saying, he quitted the apartment, and De Blenau
heard the heavy bolts of the door grate into their sockets
with a strange feeling of reluctance; for though he felt
too surely that liberty was gone, yet he would fain have
shrunk from those outward marks of captivity which
continually forced the recollection of it upon his mind.
The polite attentions of the governor, however, had not
escaped his notice, and his thoughts soon returned to that
officer's conduct.

" Can this man," thought he, " continually accustomed
to scenes of blood and horror, be really gentle in his nature, as he seems to show himself? or can it be that he
has especial orders to treat me with kindness? Yet here
I am a prisoner,—and for what purpose, unless they intend to employ the most fearful means to draw from me
those secrets which they have failed in obtaining otherwise?"

Such was the nature of his first thoughts for a moment
or two after the governor had left him; but rousing himself, after a little, from reveries which threw no light
upon his situation, he began to examine more closely the
apartment which bade fair to be his dwelling for some
time to come.

It was evidently one of the best in the prison, consisting of two spacious chambers, which occupied the

whole breadth of the square tower in the centre of the
Bastile. The first, which opened from the staircase and
communicated with the second by means of a small door,
was conveniently furnished in its way, containing, besides a very fair complement of chairs and tables of the
most solid manufacture, that happy invention of our an-
cestors, a corner cupboard, garnished with various articles of plate and porcelain, and a shelf of books, which
last De Blenau had no small pleasure in perceiving.

On one of the tables were various implements for writing, and on another the attendant who had lighted them
thither had placed two silver lamps, which, though of
an antique fashion, served very well to light the whole
extent of the room. Raising one of these, De Blenau
proceeded to the inner chamber, which was fitted up as
a bedroom, and contained various articles of furniture in
a more modern taste than that which decorated the other.
But the attention of the prisoner was particularly attracted by a heavy iron door near the head of the bed,
which, however, as he gladly perceived, possessed bolts
on the inside, so as to prevent the approach of any one
from without during the night.

So much of our happiness is dependent on the trifles
of personal comfort, that De Blenau, though little caring
in general for very delicate entertainment, nevertheless
felt himself more at ease when, on looking round his
apartment, he found that at all events it was no dungeon
to which he had been consigned ; and from this he drew a
favorable augury, flattering himself that no very severe
measures would ultimately be pursued towards him, when
such care was taken of his temporary accommodation.

De Blenau had just time to complete the survey of his
new abode, when the governor returned, followed by two
of the subordinate ministers of the prison, carrying the
various articles with which Henry de La Mothe had
loaded the coach of Monsieur de Thiery ; and as the faithful page had taken care to provide fully for his master's
comfort, the number of packages was not small.

As soon as these were properly disposed about the apartment, the governor commanded his satellites to withdraw, and remained alone with his prisoner, who, remembering the last words of the old Count de Thiery, resolved, as far as possible, to gain the good-will of one who had it in his power not only to soften or to aggravate the pains of his captivity, but even perhaps to serve him more essentially. De Thiery had recommended gold, all-powerful gold, as the means to be employed: but at first De Blenau felt some hesitation as to the propriety of offering sordid coin to a man holding so responsible a situation, and no small embarrassment as to the manner. These feelings kept him silent for a moment, during which time the governor remained silent also, regarding his prisoner with a polite and affable smile, as if he expected him to begin the conversation.

"I will try the experiment at all events," thought De Blenau. "I could almost persuade myself that the man expects it."

Luckily it so happened, that amongst the baggage which had been prepared for Chantilly, was comprised a considerable sum of money, besides that which he carried about him: and now drawing forth his purse, the contents of which might amount to about a thousand livres, he placed it in the hands of the governor.

"Let me beg you to accept of this, Monsieur le Gouverneur," said he, "not as any inducement to serve me contrary to your duty, but as a slight remuneration for the trouble which my being here must occasion."

The smooth-spoken governor neither testified any surprise at his proceeding, nor any sort of reluctance to accept what De Blenau proffered. The purse dropped unrejected into his open palm, and it was very evident that his future conduct would greatly depend upon the amount of its contents, according as it was above or below his expectation.

"Monseigneur," replied he, "you are very good, and

seem to understand the trouble which prisoners sometimes give, as well as if you had lived in the Bastile all
your life; and you may depend upon it, as I said before,
that everything shall be done for your accommodation—
always supposing it within my duty."

" I doubt you not, sir," answered De Blenau, who
from the moment the governor's fingers had closed upon
the purse, could hardly help regarding him as a menial
who had taken his wages: " I doubt you not; and at the
present moment I should be glad of supper, if such a
thing can be procured within your walls."

" Most assuredly it can be procured to-night, sir," replied the governor; " but I am sorry to say, that we have
two meagre days in the week, at which times neither
meat nor wine is allowed by government, even for my
own table; which is a very great and serious grievance,
considering the arduous duties I am often called upon
to perform."

" But of course such things can be procured from
without," said De Blenau, " and on the days you have
mentioned. I beg that you would not allow my table to
bear witness of any such regulations; and farther, as I
suppose that you, sir, have the command of all this, I
will thank you to order your purveyor to supply all that
is usual for a man of my quality and fortune, for which
he shall have immediate payment through your hands."

The tone in which De Blenau spoke was certainly
somewhat authoritative for a prisoner; and feeling, as
he proceeded, that he might give offence where it was
his best interest to conciliate regard, he added, though
not without pain,—

" When you will do me the honor to partake my fare,
I shall stand indebted for your society. Shall I say to-
morrow at dinner, that I shall have the pleasure of your
company ? "

The governor readily accepted the invitation, more
especially as the ensuing day chanced to be one of those

meagre days, which he held in most particular abhor-
rence. And now, having made some further arrangements with De Blenau, he left him, promising to send the
meal which he had demanded.

There is sometimes an art in allowing one's self to be
cheated, and De Blenau had at once perceived that the
best way to bind the governor to his interest, was, not
only to suffer patiently, but even to promote everything
which could gratify the cupidity of his jailer or his un-
derlings; and thus he had laid much stress upon the pro-
vision of his table, about which he was really indifferent.

Well contented with the liberality of his new prisoner,
and praying God most devoutly that the cardinal would
spare his life to grace the annals of the Bastile for many
years, the governor took care to send De Blenau immediately the supper which had been prepared for himself,
an act of generosity, of which few jailers, high or low,
would have been guilty.

It matters little how De Blenau relished his meal; suffice it, that the civility and attention he experienced,
greatly removed his apprehensions for the future, and
made him imagine that no serious proceedings were intended against him. In this frame of mind, as soon as
the governor's servants had taken away the remains of
his supper, and the bolts were drawn upon him for the
night, he took a book from the shelf, thinking that his
mind was sufficiently composed to permit of his thus occupying it with some more pleasing employment than the
useless contemplation of his own fate. But he was mistaken. He had scarcely read a sentence, before his
thoughts, flying from the lettered page before his eyes,
had again sought out all the strange uncertain points of
his situation, and regarding them under every light,
strove to draw from the present some presage for the
future. Thus finding the attempt in vain, he threw the
book hastily from him, in order to give himself calmly
up to the impulse he could not resist. But as the volume

fell from his hand upon the table, a small piece of written paper flew out from between the leaves, and after having made a circle or two in the air, fell lightly to the ground.

De Blenau carelessly took it up, supposing it some casual annotation; but the first few words that caught his eye riveted his attention. It began:

"To the next wretched tenant of these apartments I bequeath a secret, which, though useless to me, may be of service to him. To-day I am condemned, and to-morrow I shall be led to the torture or to death. I am innocent: but knowing that innocence is not safety, I have endeavored to make my escape, and have by long labor filed through the lock of the iron door near the bed, which was the sole fastening by which it was secured from without. Unfortunately, this door only leads to a small turret staircase communicating with the inner court; but should my successor in this abode of misery be, like me, debarred from exercise, and also from all converse with his fellow-prisoners, this information may be useful to him. The file with which I accomplished my endeavor is behind the shelf which contains these books. Adieu, whoever thou art! Pray for the soul of the unhappy Caply!"

As he read, the hopes which De Blenau had conceived from the comforts that were allowed him fled in air. There also, in the same apartment, and doubtless attended with the same care, had the wretched Caply lingered away the last hours of an existence about to be terminated by a dreadful and agonizing death. "And such may be my fate," thought De Blenau with an involuntary shudder, springing from that antipathy which all things living bear to death. But the moment after, the blood rushed to his cheek, reproaching him for yielding to such a feeling though no one was present to witness its effects. "What!" thought he, "I who have confronted death a thousand times, to tremble at it now! However, let me see the truth of what this paper tells;"

and entering the bedroom, he approached the iron door, of which he easily drew back the bolts, Caply having taken care to grease them with oil from the lamp, so that they moved without creating the smallest noise.

The moment that these were drawn, the slightest push opened the door, and De Blenau beheld before him a little winding stone staircase, filling the whole of one of the small towers; which containing no chambers and only serving as a back access to the apartments in the square tower, had been suffered in some degree to go to decay. The walls were pierced with loopholes, which being enlarged by some of the stones having fallen away, afforded sufficient aperture for the moonlight to visit the interior with quite enough power to permit of De Blenau's descending without other light. Leaving the lamp, therefore, in the bedroom, he proceeded down the steps till they at once opened from the turret into the inner court, where all was moonlight and silence, it being judged unnecessary, after the prisoners were locked in for the night, to station even a single sentry in a place which was otherwise so well secured.

Without venturing out of the shadow of the tower, De Blenau returned to his apartment, feeling a degree of satisfaction in the idea that he should not now be cut off from all communication with those below in case he should desire it. He no longer felt so absolutely lonely as before, when his situation had appeared almost as much insulated as many of those that the lower dungeons of that very building contained, who were condemned to drag out the rest of their years in nearly unbroken solitude.

Having replaced the paper in the book, for the benefit of any one who might be confined there in future, De Blenau fastened the iron door on the inside, and addressing his prayers to Heaven, he laid himself down to rest. For some time his thoughts resumed their former train, and continued to wander over his situation and its prob-

able termination, but at length his ideas became confused, memory and perception gradually lost their activity, while fatigue and the remaining weakness from his
late wounds overcame him, and he slept.

CHAPTER XI.

Which shows a new use for an old Castle; and gives a good receipt for leading a man by the nose.

It was in the old chateau of St. Loup, near the village of Mesnil, on a sultry evening about the beginning of September, that a party was assembled, who in point of rank and greatness of design, had seldom been equalled within those walls, even when they were the habitation of the great and beautiful of other days.

The chamber that had been chosen for a place of meeting on the present occasion was one which, more than any other, had escaped the hand of desolation. The casements, it is true, had long ceased to boast of glass, and part of the wall itself had given way, encumbering with its broken fragments the farther end of the great saloon, as it had once been called. The rest, however, of the chamber was in very tolerable repair, and contained also several pieces of furniture, consisting of more than one rude seat, and a large uncouth table, which evidently had never belonged to the castle in its days of splendor.

At the head of this table sat Gaston Duke of Orleans, the younger brother of the king, leaning his head upon his hand in an attitude of listless indifference, and amusing himself by brushing the dust which had gathered on the board before him, into a thousand fanciful shapes with the feather of a pen—now forming fortifications with lines and parallels, and half moons and curtains—and then sweeping them all heedlessly away—offering no bad image of the many vast and intricate plans he had engaged in, all of which he had overthrown alike by his caprice and indecision.

Near him sat his two great favorites and advisers,

Montressor and St. Ibal; the first of whom was really the inconsiderate fool he seemed; the second, though not without his share of folly, concealed deeper plans under his assumed carelessness. These two men, whose pride was in daring everything, affected to consider nothing in the world worth trouble or attention, professing at the same time perfect indifference to danger and uncomfort, and contending that vice and virtue were merely names, which signified anything according to their application. Such was the creed of their would-be philosophy; and Montressor lost no opportunity of evincing that heedlessness of everything serious which formed the principal point of his doctrine. In the present instance he had produced a couple of dice from his pocket, and was busily engaged in throwing with St. Ibal for some pieces of gold which lay between them.

Two more completed the party assembled in the old chateau of St. Loup. The first of these was Cinq Mars: his quick and ardent spirit did not suffer him to join in the frivolous pastimes of the others, but on the contrary, he kept walking up and down the apartment, as if impatient for the arrival of some one expected by all; and every now and then, as he turned at the extremity of the chamber, he cast a glance upon the weak duke and his vicious companions, almost amounting to scorn.

Beside the master of the horse, and keeping an equal pace, was the celebrated president, De Thou, famed for unswerving integrity and the mild dignity of virtuous courage. His personal appearance, however, corresponded ill with the excellence of his mind; and his plain features, ill-formed figure, and inelegant movements, contrasted strongly with the handsome countenance and princely gait of Cinq Mars, as well as the calm pensive expression of his downcast eye, with the wild and rapid glance of his companion's.

As the time wore away, the impatience of Cinq Mars visibly increased; and every two or three minutes he would stop, and look out from one of the open casements, and then approaching the table would take one of the torches, of which there were several lighted in the room, and strike it against the wall to increase the flame. "It is very extraordinary," cried he at length, "that Fontrailles has not yet arrived."

"Oh! no, Cinq Mars," replied De Thou, "we are a full hour before the time. You were so impatient, my good friend, that you made us all set off long before it was necessary."

"Why, it is quite dark," said the master of the horse, "and Fontrailles promised to be here at nine.—It is surely nine, is it not, Montressor?"

"Seize ace," said the gambler, "quatre à quatre, St. Ibal. I shall win yet!"

"Pshaw!" cried Cinq Mars—"who will tell me the time? I wish we could have clocks made small enough to put in our pockets."

"I will show you what will tell us the hour as well as if we had," answered De Thou. "Look out there in the west! Do you see what a red light the sun still casts upon those heavy masses of cloud that are coming up? Now the sun goes down at seven! so you may judge it can scarce be eight yet."

"Cinq quatre!" cried Montressor, throwing. "I have lost, after all—Monsieur de Thou, will you bet me a thousand crowns that it is not past eight by the village clock of Mesnil St. Loup?"

"No, indeed!" replied the president; "I neither wish to win your money, Monsieur Montressor, nor to lose my own. Nor do I see how such a bet could be determined."

"Oh! if you do not take the bet, there is no use of inquiring how it might be determined," rejoined Montressor. "Monseigneur," he continued, turning to the Duke of Orleans, who had just swept away his last fortification, and was laying out a flower-garden in its place; "can you tell how in the name of fortune these chairs

11

and this table came here, when all the rest of the place is
as empty as your highness's purse?"

"Or as your head, Montressor," answered the duke.
"But the truth is, they were the property of poor old
Père Le Rouge, who lived for many years in these ruins,
half-knave, half-madman,—till they tried and burnt him
for a sorcerer down in the wood there at the foot of the
hill. Since then it has been called the Sorcerer's Grove,
and the country people are not fond of passing through
it, which has doubtless saved the old conjurer's furniture
from being burnt for firewood; for none of the old
women in the neighborhood dare come to fetch it, or infallibly it would undergo the same fate as its master."

"So, that wood is called the Sorcerer's Grove," said
St. Ibal, laughing: "that is the reason your highness
brought us round the other way, is it not?"

Gaston of Orleans colored a good deal at a jest which
touched too near one of his prevailing weaknesses; for
no one was more tinctured with the superstition of the
day than himself, yet no one was more ashamed of such
credulity. "No, no!" answered he; "I put no faith in
Père Le Rouge and his prophecies. He made too great
a mistake in my own case to show himself to me since
his predictions have proved false, I will answer for
him."

"Why, what did he predict about you, monseigneur?"
asked De Thou, who knew the faith which the duke still
placed in astrology.

"A great deal of nonsense," answered the duke, affecting a tone very foreign to his real feelings. "He pre-
dicted that I should marry the queen, after the death of
Louis. Now, you see, I have married some one else, and
therefore his prophecy was false. But, however, as I
said, these chairs belonged to him: where he got them I
know not—perhaps from the devil; but at all events, I
wish he were here to fill one now; he would be a good
companion in our adventures." As he spoke, a bright

flash of lightning blazed through the apartment, followed by a loud and rolling peal of thunder, which made the duke start, exclaiming, " Jesu! what a flash! "

" Your highness thought it was Père Le Rouge," said St. Ibal; " but he would most likely come in at the door, if he did come; not through the window."

Gaston of Orleans heard the jests of his two companions without anger; and a moment or two after, Cinq Mars, who stood near one of the dilapidated casements, turned round exclaiming, " Hark! I hear the sound of horse's feet: it is Fontrailles at last. Give me a torch; I will show him where we are."

" If it should be the devil now——" said Montressor, as Cinq Mars left the room.

" Or Père Le Rouge," added St. Ibal.

" Or both," said the Duke of Orleans.

" Why for cunning and mischief they would scarcely supply the place of one Fontrailles," rejoined St. Ibal. " But here comes one or the other,—I suppose it is the same to your royal highness which."

" Oh, yes! " answered the duke, " they shall all be welcome. Nothing like keeping good company, St. Ibal."

As he spoke, Cinq Mars returned, accompanied by Fontrailles, both laughing with no small glee. " What makes you so merry, my lords? " exclaimed Montressor; " a laugh is too good a thing to be lost. Has Monsieur de Fontrailles encountered his old friend Sathanus by the road-side, or what? "

" Not so," answered Cinq Mars, " he has only bamboozled an innkeeper. But come, Fontrailles, let us not lose time: will you read over the articles of alliance to which we are to put our names; and let us determine upon them to-night, for, if we meet frequently in this way, we shall become suspected ere our design be ripe."

" Willingly for my part," replied Fontrailles, approaching the table, and speaking with some degree of emphasis, but without immediately deviating into declamation.

"There certainly never was a case when speedy decision was more requisite than the present. Every man in this kingdom, from the king to the peasant, has felt, and does now feel, the evils which we are met to remedy. It is no longer zeal, but necessity, which urges us to oppose the tyranny of this daring minister. It is no longer patriotism, but self-defence. In such a case, all means are justifiable; for when a man (as Richelieu has done) breaks through every law, human and divine, to serve the ungenerous purpose of his own aggrandizement; when he sports with the lives of his fellow-creatures with less charity than a wild beast; are we not bound to consider him as such, and to hunt him to the death for the general safety?"

De Thou shook his head, as if there was something in the proposition to which he could not subscribe; but Cinq Mars at once gave his unqualified assent, and all being seated round the table, Fontrailles drew forth some papers, and proceeded.

"This, then, is our first grand object," said he: "to deprive this tyrant, whose abuse of power not only extends to oppress the subject, but who even dares, with most monstrous presumption, to curb and overrule the royal authority, making the monarch a mere slave to his will, and the monarch's name but a shield behind which to shelter his own crimes and iniquities—I say, to deprive this usurping favorite of the means of draining the treasures, sacrificing the honor, and spilling the blood of France; thereby to free our king from bondage, to restore peace and tranquillity to our country, and to bring back to our homes long-banished confidence, security, and ease—to this you all agree?"

A general assent followed, and Fontrailles went on.

"Safely to effect our purpose, it is not only necessary to use every energy of our minds, but to exert all the local power we possess. Every member, therefore, of our association will use all his influence with those who are attached to him by favor or connection, and prepare all his vassals, troops, and retainers to act in whatsoever manner shall hereafter be determined, and will also amass whatever sums he can procure for the general object. It will also be necessary to concentrate certain bodies of men on particular points, for the purpose of seizing on some strong fortified places. And further, it will be advisable narrowly to watch the movements of the cardinal, in order to make ourselves masters of his person."

"But whose authority shall we have for this?" demanded De Thou; "for while he continues prime minister by the king's consent, we are committing high treason to restrain his person."

"We must not be so scrupulous, De Thou," rejoined Cinq Mars; "we must free his majesty from those magic chains in which Richelieu has so long held his mind, before we can expect him to do anything openly: but I will take it upon me to procure his private assent. I have sounded his inclinations already, and am sure of my ground. But proceed, Fontrailles, let us hear what arrangements you have made respecting troops, for we must have some power to back us, or we shall fail."

"Well, then," said Fontrailles, "I bring with me the most generous offers from the noble Duke of Bouillon. They are addressed to you, Cinq Mars, but were sent open to me. I may as well, therefore, give their contents at once, and you can afterwards peruse them at your leisure. The duke here offers to place his town and principality of Sedan in our hands, as a depot for arms and munition, and also as a place of retreat and safety, and a rendezvous for the assembling of forces. He further promises, on the very first call, to march his victorious troops from Italy, when, as he says, every soldier will exult in the effort to liberate his country."

"Generously promised of the duke," exclaimed Montressor, slapping the table with mock enthusiasm. "My head to a bunch of Macon grapes, he expects to be prime minister in Richelieu's place."

" The Duke of Bouillon, Monsieur de Montressor," replied Cinq Mars, somewhat warmly, " has the good of his country at heart; and is too much a man of honor to harbor the ungenerous thought you would attribute to him."

" My dear Cinq Mars, do not be angry," said Montressor. " Don't you see how much the odds were in my favor? Why, I betted my head to a bunch of grapes, and who do you think would be fool enough to hazard a full bunch of grapes against an empty head? But go on, Fontrailles; where are the next troops to come from? "

" From Spain! " answered Fontrailles, calmly; while at the name of that country, at open war with France, and for years considered as its most dangerous enemy, each countenance round the table assumed a look of astonishment and disapprobation, which would probably have daunted any other than the bold conspirator who named it.

" No, no! " exclaimed Gaston of Orleans, as soon as he had recovered breath. " None of the Spanish Catholicon for me; " alluding to the name which had been used to stigmatize the assistance that the league had received from Spain during the civil wars occasioned by the accession of Henry IV. to the throne. " No, no! Monsieur de Fontrailles, this is high treason at once."

St. Ibal was generally supposed, and with much appearance of truth, to have some secret connection with the Spanish court; and having now recovered from the first surprise into which he had been thrown by the bold mention of an alliance with that obnoxious country, he jested at the fears of the timid and unsteady duke, well knowing that by such means he was easily governed. " Death to my soul! " exclaimed he. " Your highness calls out against high treason, when it is what you have lived upon all your life! Why, it is meat, drink, and clothing to you. A little treason is as necessary to your comfort as a dice-box is to Montressor, a Barbary horse to Cinq Mars, or a bird-net and hawking-glove to the king. But to speak seriously, monseigneur," he continued, "is it not necessary that we should have some farther support than that which Monsieur de Bouillon promises? His enthusiasm may have deceived him;— his troops may not be half so well inclined to our cause as he is himself;—he might be taken ill;—he might either be arrested by the gout, to which he is subject; or by the cardinal, to whom we all wish he was not subject. A thousand causes might prevent his giving us the assistance he intends, and then what a useful auxiliary would Spain prove. Besides, we do not call in Spain to fight against France, but for France. Spain is not an enemy of the country, but only of the cardinal; and the moment that man is removed, who for his sole interest, and to render himself necessary, has carried on a war which has nearly depopulated the kingdom, a lasting and glorious peace will be established between the two countries; and thus we shall confer another great benefit on the nation."

"Why, in that point of view, I have no objection, replied the Duke of Orleans. "But do you not think that Louis will disapprove of it?"

"We must not let him know it," said Montressor, "till Richelieu is removed, and then he will be as glad of it as any one."

"But still," rejoined the duke with more pertinacity than he generally displayed, "I am not fond of bringing Spanish troops into France. Who can vouch that we shall ever get rid of them?"

"That will I," answered St. Ibal. "Has your highness forgot what good faith and courtesy the Spanish government has shown you in your exile; as also the assistance it yielded to your late royal mother? Besides, we need not call in a large body of troops. What number do you propose, Fontrailles?"

"The offer of Spain is five thousand," replied Fontrailles; "with the promise of ten thousand more, should

we require it. Nothing can be more open and noble than
the whole proceeding of King Philip. He leaves it entirely to ourselves what guarantee we will place in his
hands for the safety of his troops."

"Well, well," said the Duke of Orleans, getting tired
of the subject, "I have no doubt of their good faith. I
am satisfied, St. Ibal; and whatever you think right, I
will agree to. I leave it all to you and Montressor."

"Well then," said Fontrailles hastily, "that being settled, we will proceed——"

"Your pardon, gentlemen," interposed De Thou, "I
must be heard now—your schemes extend much farther
than I had any idea of—Cinq Mars, I was not informed
of all this—had I been so, I would never have come here.
To serve my country, to rid her of a minister who, as I
conceive, has nearly destroyed her, who has trampled
France under his feet, and enthralled her in a blood-
stained chain, I would to-morrow lay my head upon the
block. Frown not, Monsieur de Fontailles—Cinq Mars,
my noble friend, do not look offended—but I cannot, I
will not be a party to the crime into which mistaken zeal
is hurrying you. Are we not subjects of France? and is
not France at war with Spain? and though we may all
wish and pray God that this war may cease, yet to treat
or conspire with that hostile kingdom is an act which
makes us traitors to our country and rebels to our King.
Old De Thou has but two things to lose—his life and his
honor. His life is valueless. He would sacrifice it at
once for the least benefit to his country. He would sacrifice it, Cinq Mars, for his friendship for you. But his
honor must not be sullied: and as through life he has kept
it unstained, so shall it go with him unstained to his last
hour. Were it merely personal danger you called upon
me to undergo, I would not bestow a thought upon the
risk: but my fame, my allegiance, my very salvation are
concerned, and I will never give my sanction to a plan
which begins by the treasonable proposal of bringing
foreign enemies into the heart of the land."

"As to your salvation, Monsieur le President," said Montressor, "I'll undertake to buy that for you for a hundred crowns. You shall have an indulgence to commit sins ad libitum, in which high treason shall be specified by name. Now, though these red-hot heretics of Germany, who seem inclined to bring that fiery place upon earth, which his holiness threatens them with in another world, and who are assisted by our Catholic cardinal with money, troops, ammunition, and all the hell-invented implements of war,—though these Protestants, I say, put no trust in the indulgences which their apostasy has rendered cheap in the market, yet I am sure you are by far too stanch a stickler for all antique abuses to doubt their efficacy. I suppose, therefore, when salvation can be had for a hundred crowns, good Monsieur de Thou, you can have no scruple on that score—unless indeed you are as stingy as the dog in the fable."

"Jests are no arguments, Monsieur de Montressor," replied De Thou, with stern gravity; "you have a bad habit, young sir, of scoffing at what wiser men revere. Had you any religion yourself of any kind, or any reason for having none, we might pardon your error, because it was founded on principle. As for myself, sir, what I believe, I believe from conviction, and what I do, I do with the firm persuasion that it is right; without endeavoring to cloak a bad cause with a show of spirit, or to hide my incapacity to defend it with stale jokes and profane raillery. Gentlemen, you act as you please; for my part I enter into no plan by which Spain is to be employed or treated with."

"I think it dangerous too," said the unsteady Duke of Orleans.

"Ten times more dangerous to attempt anything without it," exclaimed Fontrailles. "Should we not be fools to engage in such an enterprise without some foreign power to support us? We might as well go to the Palais Cardinal, and offer our throats to Richelieu at once."

Montressor and St. Ibal both applied themselves to
quiet the fears of the duke, and soon succeeded in removing from his mind any apprehensions on the score of
Spain: but he continued from time to time to look sus-
piciously at De Thou, who had risen from the table, and
was again walking up and down the apartment. At
length Gaston beckoned to Cinq Mars, and whispered
something in his ear.

"You do him wrong, my lord," exclaimed Cinq Mars
indignantly, "I will answer for his faith. De Thou," he
continued, "the duke asks your promise not to reveal
what you have heard this night; and though I think my
friend ought not to be suspected, I will be obliged by
your giving it."

"Most assuredly," replied De Thou; "his highness
need be under no alarm. On my honor, in life or in
death, I will never betray what I have heard here. But
that I may hear as little as possible, I will take one of
these torches, and wait for you in the lower apartments."

"Take care that you do not meet with Père le Rouge,
Monsieur de Thou," exclaimed St. Ibal as De Thou left
them.

"Cease your jesting, gentlemen," said Cinq Mars; "we
have had too much of it already. A man with the good
conscience of my friend, De Thou, need not mind whom
he meets. For my own part, I am resolved to go on with
the business I have undertaken; I believe I am in the
right; and if not, God forgive me, for my intentions are
good."

The rest of the plan was soon settled after the president
had left the room; and the treaty which it was proposed
to enter into with Spain was read through and approved.
The last question which occurred, was the means of conveying a copy of this treaty to the court of King Philip
without taking the circuitous route by the Low Countries.
Numerous difficulties presented themselves to every plan
that was suggested, till Fontrailles, with an affectation

of great modesty, proposed to be the bearer himself, if, as he said, they considered his abilities equal to the task.

The offer was of course gladly accepted, as he well knew it would be: and now being to the extent of his wish furnished with unlimited powers, and possessed of a document which put the lives of all his associates in his power, Fontrailles brought the conference to an end: it being agreed that the parties should not meet again till after his return from Spain.

A few minutes more were spent in seeking cloaks and hats, and extinguishing the torches; and then descending to the court-yard, they mounted their horses, which had found shelter in the ruined stable of the old castle, and set out on their various roads. By this time the storm had cleared away, leaving the air but the purer and the more serene; and the bright moon shining near her meridian, served to light Cinq Mars and De Thou on the way towards Paris, while the Duke of Orleans and his party bent their steps towards Bourbon, and Fontrailles set off for Troyes to prepare for his journey to Spain.

CHAPTER XII.

Intended to prove that keen-sighted politicians are but buzzards after all, and show how Philip the woodman took a ride earlier than usual.

It was a common custom with Louis the Thirteenth to spend a part of the morning in that large circular piece of ground at Chantilly, called then, as now, the Manège; while his various hunters, in which he took great delight, were exercised before him. Here, while the few gentlemen that generally accompanied him, stood a step behind, he would lean against one of the pillars that surrounded the place, and remark, with the most minute exactitude, every horse as it passed him, expressing his approbation to the grooms when anything gave him satisfaction. But on the same morning which had witnessed at St. Germain the arrest of De Blenau, something had gone wrong with the king at Chantilly. He was impatient, cross, and implacable: and Lord Montague, an English nobleman, who was at that time much about him, remarked in a low voice to one of the gentlemen in waiting, "His majesty is as peevish as a crossed child, when Cinq Mars is absent."

The name of his grand ecuyer, though spoken very low, caught the king's ear.

"Do any of you know when Cinq Mars returns?" demanded he. "We never proceed well when he is not here. Look at that man now, how he rides," continued Louis, pointing to one of the grooms; "would not any one take him for a monkey on horseback? Do you know where Cinq Mars is gone, milor?"

"I hear, sire," replied Lord Montague, "that he is gone with Monsieur de Thou to Troyes, where he has an estate, about which there is some dispute, which Monsieur de Thou, who is learned in such matters, is to determine."

"To Troyes!" exclaimed the king, "that is a journey of three days. Did not some of you tell me, that Chavigni arrived last night, while I was hunting?"

"I did so, please your majesty," replied one of the gentlemen; "and I hear, moreover, that the cardinal himself slept at Luzarches last night, with the purpose of being here early this morning."

"The cardinal at Luzarches!" said the king, a cloud coming over his brow. "It is strange I had not notice. We shall scarce have room for them all—I expect the queen to-night—and the cardinal and her majesty are as fond of each other as a hawk and a heron poulet."

Louis was evidently puzzled. After thinking for a moment about the queen and cardinal, and their mutual hatred, and their being pent up together in the small space of Chantilly, and seeing no end to it whatever, he suddenly burst forth—

"Come, messieurs, I'll go hunt. Quick! saddle the horses!" and casting kingly care from his mind, he began humming the old air, Que ne suis-je un Berger! while he walked across the manège towards the stables. But just at that moment Chavigni presented himself, doffing his hat with all respect to the king, who could not avoid seeing him.

Louis was brought to bay, but still he stood his ground. "Ah! good day, Monsieur de Chavigni," exclaimed he, moving on towards the stables. "Come in good time to hunt with us. We know you are free of the forest."

"I humbly thank your majesty," replied the statesman: "but I am attending the cardinal."

"And why not attend the king, sir? ha!" exclaimed Louis, his brow gathering into a heavy frown. "It is our will that you attend us, sir."

Chavigni did not often commit such blunders, but it was not very easy to remember at all times to pay those external marks of respect which generally attend real power, to a person who had weakly resigned his authority into the hands of another: and as the cardinal not only possessed kingly sway, but maintained kingly state, it sometimes happened that the king himself was treated with scanty ceremony.

This, however, always irritated Louis not a little. He cared not for the splendor of a throne, he cared not even for the luxuries of royalty; but of the personal reverence due to his station, he would not bate an iota, and clung to the shadow when he had let the substance pass away. The statesman now hastened to repair his error, and bowing profoundly, he replied, " Had I not thought that in serving the cardinal I best served your majesty, I should not have ventured on so bold an answer; but as your majesty is good enough to consider my pleasure in the chase, and the still greater pleasure of accompanying you, your invitation will be more than an excuse for breaking my appointment with the cardinal."

To bear the burthen of forcing one of the council to break his engagement with the prime minister, and all for so trifling a cause as an accidental hunting-party, was not in the least what the king wished or intended, and he would now very willingly have excused Chavigni's attendance; but Chavigni would not be excused.

The wily statesman well knew, that Richelieu had that day a point to carry with the king of the deepest importance as to the stability of his power. The queen, whom the cardinal had long kept in complete depression, being now the mother of two princes, her influence was increasing in the country to a degree that alarmed the minister for his own sway. It was a principle with Richelieu always to meet an evil in its birth; and seeing plainly that as the king's health declined—and it was then failing fast—the party of Anne of Austria would increase if he did not take strong measures to annihilate it —he resolved at once to ruin her with her husband, to deprive her of her children, and, if possible, even to send her back to Spain. "And then," thought he, "after the king's death I shall be regent.—Regent? King! ay, and one more despotic than ever sat upon the throne of France. For twenty years this young dauphin must be under my guidance; and it will be strange indeed if I cannot keep him there till my sand be run." And the proud man, who reasoned thus, knew not that even then he trembled on the verge of the grave.

However, the object of his present visit to Chantilly was to complete the ruin of the queen; and Chavigni, who suffered his eyes to be blinded to simple right and wrong by the maxims of state policy, lent himself entirely to the cardinal's measures, little imagining that personal hatred had any share in the motives of the great minister whose steps he followed.

A moment's reflection convinced Chavigni that he might greatly promote the object in view by accompanying the king in the present instance. He knew that in difficult enterprises the most trifling circumstances may be turned to advantage; and he considered it a great thing gained at that moment, to lay Louis under the necessity of offering some amends, even for the apparent trifle of making him break his appointment with Richelieu. In riding with the king, he would have an opportunity of noting the monarch's state of mind, which he perceived was unusually irritated, and also of preparing the way for those impressions which Richelieu intended to give: and accordingly he avoided with consummate art any subject which might open the way for Louis to withdraw his previous order to accompany him.

Having already followed one royal hunt somewhat too minutely, we will not attempt to trace the present; only observing that during the course of the day, Chavigni had many opportunities of conversing with the king, and took care to inform him that the campaign in the Netherlands was showing itself much against the arms of

France; that no plan was formed by the Government, which did not by some means reach the ears of the Spanish generals, and consequently that all the manœuvres of the French troops were unavailing; and from this, as a natural deduction, he inferred, that some one at the court of France must convey information to the enemy; mingling these pleasant matters of discourse, with sundry sage observations respecting the iniquity and baseness of thus betraying France to her enemies.

Louis was exactly in the humor that the statesman could have wished. Peevish from the absence of Cinque Mars, and annoyed by the unexpected coming of Richelieu, he listened with indignation to all that Chavigni told him, of any one in France conveying intelligence to a country which he hated with the blindest antipathy.

The predominant passion in the king's mind had long been his dislike to Spain, but more especially to Philip, whom he regarded as a personal enemy: and Chavigni easily discerned, by the way in which the news he conveyed was received, that if they could cast any probable suspicion on the queen (and Chavigni really believed her guilty), Louis would set no bounds to his anger. But just at the moment he was congratulating himself upon the probable success of their schemes, a part of the storm he had been so busily raising fell unexpectedly upon himself.

" Well, Monsieur de Chavigni," said the king, after the chase was over, and the royal party were riding back slowly to Chantilly, " this hunting is a right noble sport: think you not so, sir? "

" In truth I do, sire," replied Chavigni; " and even your majesty can scarce love it better than myself."

" I am glad to hear it, sir," rejoined the king, knitting his brows; " 'tis a good sign. But one thing I must tell you, which is, that I do not choose my royal forests to be made the haunt of worse beasts than stags and boars.— No wolves and tigers.—Do you take me, sir? "

"No, indeed, sire," replied Chavigni, who really did not comprehend the king's meaning, and was almost tempted to believe that he had suddenly gone mad. "Allow me to remind your majesty that wolves are almost extinct in this part of France, and that tigers are altogether beasts of another country."

"There are beasts of prey in every part of the world," answered the king. "What I mean, sir, is, that robbers and assassins are beginning to frequent our woods; especially, sir, the wood of Mantes. Was it that, or was it the forest of Laye in which the young Count de Blenau was attacked the other day?"

It was not easy on ordinary occasions to take Chavigni by surprise, and he was always prepared to repel open attack, or to parry indirect questions, with that unhesitating boldness, or skilful evasion, the proper application of which is but one of the lesser arts of diplomacy; but on the present occasion the king's question was not only so unexpected as nearly to overcome his habitual command of countenance, but was also uttered in such a tone as to leave him in doubt whether Louis's suspicions were directed personally towards himself. He replied, however, without hesitation: "I believe it was the wood of Mantes, sire; but I am not perfectly sure."

"You, of all men, ought to be well informed on that point, Monsieur de Chavigni," rejoined the king," since you took care to send a servant to see it rightly done."

The matter was now beyond a doubt, and Chavigni replied boldly: "Your majesty is pleased to speak in riddles, which I am really at a loss to comprehend."

"Well, well, sir," said Louis, hastily, "it shall be inquired into, and made plain both to you and me. Anything that is done legally must not be too strictly noticed; but I will not see the laws broken, and murder attempted, even to serve state purposes."

Thus speaking, the king put his horse into a quicker pace, and Chavigni followed with his mind not a little

12

discomposed, though his countenance offered not the slightest trace of embarrassment. How he was to act now became the question; and running over in his own mind all the circumstances connected with the attack upon the Count de Blenau, he could see no other means by which Louis could have become acquainted with his participation therein, than by the loquacity of Philip, the woodman of Mantes; and as he came to this conclusion, Chavigni internally cursed that confident security which had made him reject the advice of Lafemas when the sharp-witted judge had counselled him to arrest Philip on first discovering that he had remarked the livery of Isabel and silver amongst the robbers.

In the present instance, the irritable and unusually decided humor of the king made him fear that inquiries might be instituted immediately, which would not only be dangerous to himself personally, but might probably overthrow all those plans which he had been laboring, in conjunction with the cardinal, to bring to perfection. Calculating rapidly, therefore, all the consequences which might ensue, Chavigni resolved at once to have the woodman placed in such a situation as to prevent him from giving any further evidence of what he had seen. But far from showing any untimely haste, though he was the first to dismount in the courtyard in order to offer the king his aid in alighting, yet that ceremony performed, he loitered, patting his horse's neck, and giving trifling directions to his groom, till such time as Louis had entered the palace, and his figure had been seen passing the window at the top of the grand staircase. That moment, however, Chavigni darted into the chateau, and seeking his own apartments, he wrote an order for the arrest of Philip the woodman, which with the same despatch he placed in the hands of two of his most devoted creatures, adding a billet to the governor of the Bastile, in which he begged him to treat the prisoner with all kindness, and allow him all sort of liberty within the prison, but on no account to let him escape till he received notice from him.

We have already had occasion to see that Chavigni was a man who considered state-policy paramount to every other principle; and naturally not of an ungentle disposition or ignoble spirit, he had unfortunately been educated in a belief that nothing which was expedient for the statesman could be discreditable to the man. However, the original bent of his mind generally showed itself in some degree, even in his most unjustifiable actions, as the ground-work of a picture will still shine through, and give a color to whatever is painted above it. In the present instance, as his only object was to keep the woodman out of the way till such time as the king's unwonted mood had passed by, he gave the strictest commands to those who bore the order for Philip's arrest, to use him with all possible gentleness, and to assure his wife and family that no harm was intended to him. He also sent him a purse, to provide for his comfort in the prison, which he well knew could not be procured without the potent aid of gold.

The two attendants, accustomed to execute commands which required despatch, set out instantly on their journey, proceeding with all speed to Beaumont, and thence to Pontoise, where, crossing the river Oise, they soon after arrived at Meulan: and here a dispute arose concerning the necessity of calling upon two exempts of that city to assist in arresting Philip the woodman, the one servant arguing that they had no such orders from their lord, and the other replying that the said Philip might have twenty companions for aught they knew, who might resist their authority, they not being legally entitled to arrest his majesty's lieges. This argument was too conclusive to be refuted; and they therefore waited at Meulan till the two exempts were ready to accompany them. It being night when they arrived at Meulan, and the two exempts being engaged in " potations deep and strong,"

drinking long life to the Cardinal de Richelieu, and success to the royal prisons of France, some time was of
course spent before the party could proceed. However,
after the lapse of about an hour, discussed no matter
how, they all contrived to get into their saddles, and passing the bridge over the Seine, soon reached the first little village, whose white houses, conspicuous in the moonlight, seemed, on the dark background of the forest, as
if they had crept for protection into the very bosom of
the wood; while it, sweeping round them on every side,
appeared in its turn to afford them the friendly shelter
that they sought.

All was silence as they passed through the village, announcing plainly that its sober inhabitants were comfortably dozing away the darkness. This precluded them
from asking their way to Philip's dwelling; but Chavigni
had been so precise in his direction, that notwithstanding
the wine-pots of Meulan, the two servants, in about half
an hour after having entered the wood, recognized the
abreuvoir and cottage, with the long-felled oak and piece
of broken ground, and all the other et-cetera which entered into the description they had received.

Having discovered the cottage, they held a profound
council before the door, disputing vehemently as to the
mode of proceeding until one of the exempts, not bearing clearly in mind the subject of discussion, knocked
violently at the door, declaring it was tiresome to stand
disputing on their feet, and that they could settle how
they should gain admission after they had got it and sat
down.

The moment after the woodman appeared at the window, and seeing some travellers, as he imagined, he bade
them wait till he had lighted a lamp, and he would come
to them. Accordingly, in a moment or two Philip opened
the door, purposing either to give them shelter, or to
direct them on their way, as they might require; but
when the light gleamed upon the black dresses of the ex-

empts, and then upon the well-known colors of Isabel and silver, the woodman's heart sank, and his cheek turned pale, and he had scarcely power to demand their errand.

"I will tell you all that presently," replied the principal servant of the two, who, like many another small man in many another place, thought to become great by much speaking. " First let us come in and rest ourselves; for, as you may judge by our dusty doublets, we have ridden far and hard: and after that I will expound to you, good friend, the cause of our coming, with sundry other curious particulars, which may both entertain and affect you."

Philip suffered them to enter the house, one after another, and setting down the lamp, he gazed upon them in silence, his horror at gentlemen in black coats and long straight swords, as well as those dressed in Isabel and silver, being quite unspeakable.

" Well, Monsieur Philip le Bucheron," said the spokesman, throwing himself into the oaken settle with that sort of percussion of breath denoting fatigue; " you seem frightened, Monsieur Philip; but, good Monsieur Philip, you have no cause for fear. We are all your friends, Monsieur Philip."

" I am glad to hear it, sir," replied the woodcutter; "but may I know what you want with me?"

" Why, this is the truth, Monsieur Philip," replied the servant, " it seems that his majesty the king, whom we have just left at Chantilly, is very angry about something, —Lord knows what! and our noble employer, not to say master, the Count de Chavigni, having once upon a time received some courtesy at your hands, is concerned for your safety, and has therefore deemed it necessary that you should be kept out of the way for a time."

" Oh, if that be the case," cried Philip, rubbing his hands with gladness, " though I know not why the king's anger should fall on me, I will take myself out of the way directly."

" No, no, Monsieur Philip, that won't do exactly," answered the servant. " You do not know how fond my master is of you; and so concerned is he for your safety, that he must be always sure of it, and therefore has given us command to let you stay in the Bastile for a few days."

At that one word Bastile, Philip's imagination set to work plunging him into greatest distress of mind. However, the purse which Chavigni's attendants gave him in behalf of their master, for they dared not withhold his bounty, however much they might be inclined, greatly allayed the fears of the woodman.

There is something wonderfully consolatory in the chink of gold at all times; but in the present instance Philip drew from it the comfortable conclusion that they could not mean him any great harm, when they sent him money.

" I know not what to think," cried he.

" Why, think it is exactly as I tell you," replied the servant, " and that the count means you well. But after you have thought as much as you like, get ready to come with us, for we have no time to spare."

Of course, on all such occasions there must follow a very tender scene between husband and wife, and such there was in the present instance; only Joan, availing herself of one especial privilege of the fair sex, did not fail, between her bursts of tears and sobs, to rail loudly at the cardinal, the king, and all belonging to them, talking - more high treason in five minutes, than would have cost any man an hour to compose; nor did she spare even the exempts, or the two gentlemen in Isabel and silver, but poured forth her indignation upon all alike.

However, as all things must come to an end, so did this; and Philip was carried away amidst the vain entreaties his wife at length condescended to use.

The only difficulty which remained was, how to mount their prisoner, having all forgot to bring a horse from

Meulan for that purpose; and Philip not choosing to
facilitate his own removal by telling them that he had a
mule in the stable.

However it was at length agreed, that one of the exempts should walk to the next town, and that Philip
should mount his horse till another could be obtained.
As the party turned away from the hut, the chief servant,
somewhat moved by the unceasing tears of Joan, took
upon him to say that he was sure that Charles the woodman's son, who stood with his mother at the door, would
be permitted to see his father in the Bastile, if they would
all agree to say, that they did not know what was become
of him, in case of any impertinent person inquiring for
him during his absence.

This they all consented to, their grief being somewhat
moderated by the prospect of communicating with each
other, although separated; and Philip once more having
bid his wife and children adieu, was carried on to a little
village, where a horse being procured for him, the whole
party took the road to Marley, and thence proceeded to
Paris with all possible diligence.

Day had long dawned before they reached the Bastile,
and Philip, who was now excessively tired, never having
ridden half the way in his life, was actually glad to arrive
at the prison, which he had previously contemplated with
so much horror.

Here he was delivered, with the lettre de cachet, and
Chavigni's note, to the governor; and the servant again,
in his own hearing, recommended that he should be
treated with all imaginable kindness, and allowed every
liberty consistent with his safe custody.

All this convinced the woodcutter, as well as the conversation he had heard on the road, that Chavigni really
meant well by him: and without any of those more refined feelings, which, however they may sometimes open
the gates of the heart to the purest joys, but too often

betray the fortress of the breast to the direst pains, he now felt comparatively secure, and gazed up at the massy walls and towers of the Bastile with awe indeed, but awe not unmingled with admiration.

CHAPTER XIII.

Which show that diadems are not without their thorns.

DURING the absence of the king and Chavigni in the chase, two arrivals had taken place at Chantilly very nearly at the same moment. Luckily, however, the queen had just time to alight from her carriage, and seek her apartments, before the Cardinal de Richelieu entered the court-yard, thus avoiding an interview with her deadly enemy on the very threshold,—an interview, from which she might well have drawn an inauspicious augury, without even the charge of superstition.

As soon as Chavigni had (as far as possible) provided for his own safety by despatching the order for Philip's arrest, he proceeded to the apartments of Richelieu, and there he gave that minister an exact account of all he had heard, observed, and done; commenting particularly upon the violent and irascible mood of the king, and the advantages which might be thence derived, if they could turn his anger in the direction that they wished.

In the meanwhile Louis proceeded to the apartments of the queen, not indeed hurried on by any great affection for his wife, but desirous of seeing his children, whom he sincerely loved, notwithstanding the unaccountable manner in which he so frequently absented himself from them.

Never very attentive to dress, Louis the Thirteenth, when anything disturbed or irritated him, neglected entirely the ordinary care of his person. In the present instance he made no change in his apparel, although the sports in which he had been engaged had not left it in a very fit state to grace a drawing-room. Thus, in a pair of immense jack-boots, his hat pressed down upon his brows, and his whole dress soiled, deranged, and covered with dust, he presented himself in the saloon where Anne of Austria sat surrounded by the young princes and the ladies who had accompanied her to Chantilly.

The queen immediately arose to receive her husband, and advanced towards him with an air of gentle kindness, mixed however with some degree of apprehension; for to her eyes, long accustomed to remark the various changes of his temper, the disarray of his apparel plainly indicated the irritation of his mind.

Louis saluted her but coldly, and without taking off his hat. "I am glad to see you well, madam," said he, and passed on to the nurse who held in her arms the young dauphin.

The child had not seen its father for some weeks, and now perceiving a rude-looking ill-dressed man, approaching hastily towards it, became frightened, hid its face on the nurse's shoulder, and burst into tears.

The rage of the king now broke the bounds of common decency.

"Ha!" exclaimed he, stamping on the ground with his heavy boot, till the whole apartment rang: "is it so, madam? Do you teach my children, also, to dislike their father?"

"No, my lord, no, indeed!" replied Anne of Austria, in a tone of deep distress, seeing this unfortunate contretemps so strangely misconstrued to her disadvantage. "I neither teach the child to dislike you, nor does he dislike you; but you approached Louis hastily, and with your hat flapped over your eyes, so that he does not know you. Come hither, Louis," she continued, taking the dauphin out of the nurse's arms. "It is your father; do not you know him? Have I not always told you to love him?"

The dauphin looked at his mother, and then at the king, and perfectly old enough to comprehend what she said, ne began to recognize his father, and held out his little arms towards him. But Louis turned angrily away.

"A fine lesson of dissimulation!" he exclaimed; and advanced towards his second son, who then bore the title of Duke of Anjou. "Ah, my little Philip," he continued, as the infant received him with a placid smile,—"you are not old enough to have learned any of these arts. You can love your father without being told to show it, like an ape at a puppet-show."

At this new attack, the queen burst into tears.

"Indeed, indeed, my lord," she said, "you wrong me. Oh, Louis! how you might have made me love you once!" and her tears redoubled at the thought of the past. "But I am a weak fool," she continued, wiping the drops from her eyes, "to feel so sensibly what I do not deserve —At present your majesty does me deep injustice. I have always taught both my children to love and respect their father. That name is the first word that they learn to pronounce; and from me they learn to pronounce it with affection. But oh, my liege! what will these dear children think in after years, when they see their father behave to their mother, as your majesty does towards me?"

"Pshaw!" exclaimed the king, "let us have no more of all this. I hate these scenes of altercation. Fear not, madam; the time will come, when these children will learn to appreciate us both thoroughly."

"I hope not, my lord,"—replied the queen fervently— "I hope not. From me, at least, they shall never learn all I have to complain of in their father."

Had Anne of Austria reflected, she would have been silent; but it is sometimes difficult to refrain when urged by taunts and unmerited reproach. In the present case the king's pale countenance flushed with anger. "Beware, madam, beware!" exclaimed he. "You have already been treated with too much lenity—Remember the affair of Chalais!"

"Well, sir!" replied the queen, raising her head with an air of dignity; "your majesty knows, and feels, and has said, that I am perfectly guiltless of that miserable plot. My lord, my lord! if *you* can lay your head upon your pillow conscious of innocence like mine, you will sleep well; *my* bosom at least is clear."

"See that it be, madam," replied Louis, darting upon her one of those fiery and terrible glances in which the whole vindictive soul of his Italian mother blazed forth in his eyes with the glare of a basilisk. "See that it be, madam; for there may come worse charges than that against you. I have learned from a sure source that a Spaniard is seeking my overthrow, and a woman is plotting my ruin," he continued, repeating the words of the astrologer: "that a prince is scheming my destruction, and a queen is betraying my trust—so, see that your bosom be clear, madam." And passing quickly by her, he left the apartment, exclaming loud enough for all within it to hear, "Where is his eminence of Richelieu? Some one, give him notice that the king desires his presence when he has leisure."

Anne of Austria clasped her hands in silence, and looking up to heaven seemed for a moment to petition for support under the new afflictions she saw ready to fall upon her; and then without a comment on the painful scene that had just passed, returned to her ordinary employments.

CHAPTER XIV.

Containing a great many things not more curious and interesting than
true.

In the old Chateau of Chantilly was a long gallery,
which went by the name of the Cours aux cerfs, from
the number of stags' heads which appeared curiously
sculptured upon the frieze, with their long branching
horns projecting from the wall, and so far extended on
both sides as to cross each other and form an extraordinary sort of trellis-work architrave, before they
reached the ceiling.

The windows of this gallery were far apart, and narrow, admitting but little light into the interior, which,
being of a dingy stone color, could hardly have been
rendered cheerful even by the brightest sunshine; but
which, both from the smallness of the windows and the
projection of a high tower on the other side of the court,
was kept in continual shadow, except when in the long-
est days of summer the sun just passed the angle of the
opposite building and threw a parting gleam through the
last window, withdrawn as quickly as bestowed.

But at the time I speak of, namely, two days after the
queen's arrival at Chantilly, no such cheering ray found
entrance. It seemed, indeed, a fit place for melancholy
imaginings; and to such sad purpose had Anne of Austria
applied it. For some time she had been standing at
one of the windows, leaning on the arm of Madame de
Beaumont, and silently gazing with abstracted thoughts
upon the open casements of the corridor on the other
side, when the figures of Richelieu and Chavigni, passing
by one of them, in their full robes, caught her eye; and
withdrawing from the conspicuous situation in which she

was placed, she remarked to the marchioness what she had seen, and observed that they must be going to the council-chamber.

Thus began a conversation which soon turned to the king, and to his strange conduct, which ever since their arrival had continued in an increasing strain of petulance and ill-temper.

"Indeed, madam," said the Marchioness de Beaumont, "you majesty's gentleness is misapplied. Far be it from me to urge aught against my king; but there be some dispositions to have their vehemence checked and repelled; and it is well also for themselves, when they meet with one who will oppose them firmly and boldly."

"Perhaps, De Beaumont," replied the queen, "if I had taken that course many years ago, it might have produced a happy effect; but now, alas! it would be in vain; and God knows whether it would have succeeded even then!"

As she spoke, the door of the gallery opened, and an officer of the council appeared, notifying to the queen that his majesty the king demanded her presence in the council-chamber.

Anne of Austria turned to Madame de Beaumont with a look of melancholy foreboding. "More, more, more still to endure," she said; and then added, addressing the officer, "His majesty's commands shall be instantly obeyed; so inform him, sir. De Beaumont, tell Mademoiselle de Hauteford that I shall be glad of her assistance too. You will go with me, of course."

Mademoiselle de Hauteford instantly came at the queen's command, and approaching her with a sweet and placid smile, said a few words of comfort to her royal mistress in so kind and gentle a manner, that the tears rose in the eyes of Anne of Austria.

"De Hauteford!" said she, "I feel a presentiment that we shall soon part, and therefore I speak to you now of what I never spoke before. I know how much I have to thank you for—I know how much you have rejected

for my sake—The love of a king would have found few
to refuse it. You have done so for my sake, and you will
have your reward."

The eloquent blood spread suddenly over the beautiful
countenance of the lady of honor. "Spare me, spare me,
your majesty," cried she, kissing the hand the queen held
out to her. "I thought that secret had been hidden in
my bosom alone. But, oh, let me hope that, even had it
not been for my love for your majesty, I could still have
resisted. Yes! yes!" continued she, clasping her hands,
and murmuring to herself the name of a higher and holier
king, "yes! yes! I could have resisted!"

The unusual energy with which the beautiful girl
spoke, on all ordinary occasions so calm and imperturba-
ble, showed the queen how deeply her heart had taken
part in that to which she alluded; and perhaps female
curiosity might have led her to prolong the theme, though
a painful one to both parties, had not the summons of
the king required her immediate attention.

As they approached the council-chamber, Madame de
Beaumont observed that the queen's steps wavered.

"Take courage, madam," said she. "For Heaven's
sake, call up spirit to carry you through, whatever may
occur."

"Fear not, De Beaumont," replied the queen, though
her tone betrayed the apprehension she felt. "They
shall see that they cannot frighten me."

At that moment the huissier threw open the door of the
council-chamber, and the queen with her ladies entered,
and found themselves in the presence of the king and all
his principal ministers. In the centre of the room,
strewed with various papers and materials for writing,
stood a long table, at the top of which, in a seat slightly
raised above the rest, sat Louis himself, dressed, as was
usual with him, in a suit of black silk, without any ornament whatever, except three rows of sugar-loaf buttons
of polished jet,—if these could be considered as orna-

mental. His hat, indeed, which he continued to wear, was looped up with a small string of jewels; and the feather, which fell much on one side, was buttoned with a diamond of some value; but these were the only indications by which his apparel could have been distinguished from that of some poor avoué, or greffier de la cour.

On the right hand of the king was placed the Cardinal de Richelieu, in his robes; and on the left was the Chancellor Seguier. Bouthilliers, Chavigni, Mazarin, and other members of the council, filled the rest of the seats round the table; but at the farther end was a vacant space, in front of which the queen now presented herself, facing the chair of the king.

There was an angry spot on Louis's brow, and as Anne of Austria entered, he continued playing with the hilt of his sword, without once raising his eyes towards her. The queen's heart sank, but still she bore an undismayed countenance, while the cardinal fixed upon her the full glance of his dark commanding eyes, and rising from his seat, slightly inclined his head at her approach.

The rest of the council rose, and Chavigni turned away his eyes, with an ill-defined sensation of pain and regret; but the more subtle Mazarin, ever watchful to court good opinion, whether for present, or for future purposes, glided quietly round, and placed a chair for her at the table. It was an action not forgotten in after days.

A moment's pause ensued. As soon as the queen was seated, Richelieu glanced his eye towards the countenance of the king, as if to instigate him to open the business of the day: but Louis's attention was deeply engaged in his sword-knot, or at least seemed to be so, and the cardinal was at length forced to proceed himself.

" Your majesty's presence has been desired by the king, who is like a God in justice and in equity," said Richelieu, proceeding in that bold and figurative style, in which all

his public addresses were conceived, " in order to enable
you to cast off, like a raiment that has been soiled by a
foul touch, the accusations which have been secretly
made against you, and to explain some part of your conduct, which, as clouds between the earth and sun, have
come between your royal self and your royal husband,
intercepting the beams of his princely approbation. All
this your majesty can doubtless do, and the king has
permitted the council to hear your exculpation from
your own lips, that we may trample under our feet the
foul suspicions that appear against you."

" Lord cardinal," replied the queen, calmly, but firmly,
" I wonder at the boldness of your language. Remember,
sir, whom it is that you thus presume to address—The
wife of your sovereign, sir, who sits there, bound to protect her from insult and from injury."

" Cease, cease, madam! " cried Louis, breaking silence.
" First prove yourself innocent, and then use the high
tone of innocence, if you will."

" To you, my lord," replied the queen, " I am ready to
answer everything, truly and faithfully, as a good wife,
and a good subject; but not to that audacious vassal, who,
in oppressing and insulting me, but degrades your authority and weakens your power."

" Spare your invectives, madam," said the cardinal
calmly, " for, if I be not much mistaken, before you leave
this chamber you will be obliged to acknowledge all that
is contained in the paper before me; in which case, the
bad opinion of your majesty would be as the roar of idle
wind, that hurteth not the mariner on shore."

" My lord and sovereign," said the queen, addressing
Louis, without deigning to notice the cardinal, " it seems
that some evil is laid to my charge; will you condescend
to inform me of what crime I am accused, that now calls
your majesty's anger upon me?—If loving you too well,
—if lamenting your frequent absence from me,—if giving
my whole time and care to your children, be no crimes,
tell me, my lord, tell me, what I have done."

13

"What you have done, madam, is easily told," exclaimed Louis, his eyes flashing fire. "Give me that paper, lord cardinal;" and passing hastily from article to article of its contents, he continued: "Have you not contrary to my express command, and the command of the council, corresponded with Philip of Spain? Have you not played the spy upon the plans of my government and caused the defeat of my armies in Flanders, the losses of the Protestants in Germany, the failure of all our schemes in Italy, by the information you have conveyed? Have you not written to Don Francisco de Mello, and your cousin the archduke? Have you not——"

"Never, never!" exclaimed the queen, clasping her hands, "never, so help me Heaven!"

"What!" cried Louis, dashing the paper angrily upon the table. "Darest thou deny what is as evident as the sun in the noonday sky? Remember, madam, that your minion, de Blenau, is in the Bastile, and will soon forfeit his life upon the scaffold, if his obstinacy does not make him die under the question."

"For poor De Blenau's sake, my lord," replied the queen,—" for the sake of as noble, and as innocent a man as ever was the victim of tyranny, I will tell you at once, that I have written to Philip of Spain—my own dear brother. And who can blame me, my lord, for loving one who has always loved me? But I knew my duty better than ever once to mention even the little that I knew of the public affairs of this kingdom: and far less, your majesty, did I pry into secret plans of state policy for the purpose of divulging them. My letters, my lord, were wholly domestic. I spoke of myself, of my husband. of my children; I spoke as a woman, a wife, and a mother; but never my lord, as a queen; and never, never as a spy.

"As to De Blenau, my lord, let me assure you, that before he undertook to forward those letters, he exacted from me a promise, that they should never contain anything which could impeach his honor, or his loyalty. This, my lord, is all my crime, and this is the extent of his."

There was a degree of simplicity and truth in the manner of the queen, which operated strongly on the mind of Louis. "But who," said he, "will vouch that those letters contained nothing treasonable? We have but your word, madam; and you well know that we are at war with Spain, and cannot procure a sight of the originals."

"Luckily," replied Anne of Austria, her countenance brightening with a ray of hope, "they have all been read by one whom your majesty yourself recommended to my friendship. Clara de Hauteford, you have seen them all. Speak! Tell the king the nature of their contents without fear and without favor."

Mademoiselle de Hauteford advanced from behind the queen's chair; and the king, who, it was generally believed, had once passionately loved her, but had met with no return, now fixed his eyes intently upon the pale, beautiful creature, that, scarcely like a being of the earth, glided silently forward and placed herself directly opposite to him. Clara de Hauteford was devotedly attached to the queen. Whether it sprang from that sense of duty which in general governed all her actions, or whether it was personal attachment, matters little, as the effect was the same, and she would, at no time, have considered her life too great a sacrifice to the interest of her mistress.

She advanced then before the council, knowing that the happiness, if not the life of Anne of Austria, might depend upon her answer; and clasping her snowy hands together, she raised her eyes towards heaven, "So help me God at my utmost need!" she said, with a clear, slow, energetic utterance, "no line that I have ever seen of her majesty's writing—and I believe I have seen almost all she has written within the last five years—no line that I have seen, ever spoke anything but the warmest attachment to my lord the king; nor did any ever contain the slightest allusion to the politics of this kingdom, but were confined entirely to the subject of her domestic life;— nor even then," she continued, dropping her full blue eyes to the countenance of the king, and fixing them there, with a calm serious determined gaze, which overpowered the glance of the monarch, and made his eyelid fall—"nor even then did they ever touch upon her domestic sorrows."

Richelieu saw that the king was moved; he knew also the influence of Mademoiselle de Hauteford, and he instantly resolved upon crushing her by one of those bold acts of power which he had so often attempted with impunity. Nor had he much hesitation in the present instance, knowing that Louis's superstitious belief in the predictions of the astrologer had placed the monarch's mind completely under his dominion. "Mademoiselle de Hauteford," said he in a stern voice, "answer me. Have you seen all the letters that the queen has written to her brother, Philip, King of Spain, positively knowing them to be such?"

"So please your eminence I have," replied Mademoiselle de Hauteford.

"Well then," said Richelieu, rising haughtily from his chair while he spoke, "in so doing you have committed misprision of treason, and are therefore banished from this court and kingdom forever; and if within sixteen days from this present, you have not removed yourself from the precincts of the realm, you shall be considered guilty of high treason, and arraigned as such, inasmuch as, according to your own confession, you have knowingly and wilfully, after a decree in council against it, concealed and abetted a correspondence between persons within the kingdom of France, and a power declaredly its enemy."

As the cardinal uttered his sentence in a firm, deep, commanding voice, the king, who had at first listened to him with a look of surprise, and perhaps of anger, soon began to feel the habitual superiority of Richelieu, and shrunk back into himself, depressed and overawed; the queen pressed her hand before her eyes; and Chavigni half raised himself, as if to speak, but instantly resumed his seat as his eye met that of the cardinal.

It was Mademoiselle de Hauteford alone that heard her condemnation without apparent emotion. She merely bowed her head with a look of the most perfect resignation. "Your eminence's will shall be obeyed," she replied, "and may a gracious God protect my innocent mistress!" Thus saying, she again took her place behind the queen's chair, with hardly a change of countenance—always pale, perhaps her face was a little paler, but it was scarcely perceptible.

"And now," continued Richelieu in the same proud manner, assuming at once that power which he in reality possessed,—"and now let us proceed to the original matter, from which we have been diverted to sweep away a butterfly. Your majesty confesses yourself guilty of treason, in corresponding with the enemies of the kingdom. I hold in my hand a paper to that effect, or something very similar, all drawn from irrefragable evidence upon the subject. This you may as well sign, and on that condition no further notice shall be taken of the affair; but the matter shall be forgotten as an error in judgment."

"I have not confessed myself guilty of treason, arrogant prelate," replied the queen, "and I have not corresponded with Philip of Spain as an enemy of France, but as my own brother. Nor will I, while I have life, sign a paper so filled with falsehoods as any one must be that comes from your hand."

"You majesty sees," said Richelieu, turning to the king, from whom the faint sparks of energy he had lately shown were now entirely gone. "Is there any medium to be kept with a person so convicted of error, and so obstinate in the wrong? And is such a person fit to educate the children of France? Your majesty has promised that the Dauphin and the Duke of Anjou shall be given into my charge."

" I have," said the weak monarch, " and I will keep my promise."

" Never! never! " cried the queen vehemently, " never while Anne of Austria lives! Oh! my lord! " she exclaimed, advancing, and casting herself at the feet of the king with all the overpowering energy of maternal love, " consider that I am their mother!—Rob me not of my only hope,—rob me not of those dear children who have smiled and cheered me through all my sorrows. Oh, Louis! if you have the feelings of a father, if you have the feelings of a man, spare me this! "

The king turned away his head, and Richelieu, gliding behind the throne, placed himself at the queen's side. " Sign the paper," said he, in a low deep tone, " sign the paper, and they shall not be taken from you."

" Anything! anything! but leave me my children! " exclaimed the queen, taking the pen he offered her. " Have I your promise? "

" You have," replied he decidedly. " They shall not be taken from you."

" Well, then," said Anne of Austria, receiving the paper, " I will sign it; but I call heaven to witness that I am innocent; and you, gentlemen of the council, to see that I sign a paper the contents of which I know not, and part of which is certainly false." Thus saying, with a rapid hand she wrote her name at the bottom of the page, threw down the pen, and quitted the apartment.

The queen walked slowly, and in silence, to the apartments allotted to her use, without giving way to the various painful feelings that struggled in her bosom; but once arrived within the shelter of her own saloon, she sank into a chair and burst into a flood of tears. Mademoiselle de Hauteford, who stood beside her, endeavored in vain for some time to calm her agitation, but at length succeeding in a degree.

"Oh, Clara!" said the queen, "you have ruined yourself for my sake."

"I hope, madam," replied the young lady, "that I have
done my duty, which were enough in itself to reconcile
me to my fate; but if I could suppose that I have served
your majesty, I should be more than rewarded for anything I may undergo."

"You have served me most deeply on this and every
occasion," answered the queen; "and the time may come
when the affection of Anne of Austria will not be what
it is now—the destruction of all that possess it. But why
comes Mademoiselle de Beaumont in such haste?" she
continued, as Pauline, who had been absent in the gardens
of the palace, and unconscious of all that had lately
passed, entered the saloon with hurry and anxiety in her
countenance.

"Please, your majesty," said Pauline, and then suddenly stopped, seeing that the queen had been weeping.

"Proceed, proceed! wild rose," said Anne of Austria;
"they are but tears—drops that signify nothing."

"As I was walking in the gardens but now," continued
Pauline, "a little peasant boy came up to me, and asked
if I could bring him to speech of your majesty. I was
surprised at his request, and asked him what was his
business; when he told me that he brought you a letter
from the Bastile. This seemed so important that I made
bold to take him into the palace by the private gate, and
concealed him in my apartments till I had informed you
of it all."

"You did right, Pauline, you did right," replied the
queen. "It must surely be news from De Blenau. Bring
the boy hither directly—not by the ante-room, but by the
inner apartments. You, Clara, station Laporte at the top
of the staircase, to see that no one approaches."

Pauline flew to execute the queen's commands, and in a
few minutes a clatter was heard in the inner chamber,
not at all unlike the noise produced by that most unfortu-

nate animal a cat, when some mischievous boys adorn her
feet with walnut-shells.

The moment after the door opened, and Pauline appeared leading in a fine curly-headed boy of about ten
years old. He was dressed in hodden grey, with a broad
leathern belt round his waist, in which appeared a small
axe and a knife, while his feet, displaying no stockings,
but with the skin tanned to the color of Russia leather,
were thrust into a pair of unwieldy sabots, or wooden
shoes, which had caused the clatter aforesaid.

"Take off his sabots, take off his sabots," cried the
queen, putting her hands to her ears. "They will alarm
the whole house."

"Dame oui!" cried the boy, slapping his feet out of
their encumbrances. "J'avons oublié, et vous aussi,
mademoiselle," turning to Pauline, who, anxious to hear
of De Blenau, would have let him come in if he had been
shod like a horse.

The little messenger now paused for a moment, then
having glanced his eye over the ladies at the other end
of the room, as if to ascertain to which he was to deliver
his credentials, advanced straight to the queen, and falling down upon both his knees, tendered her a sealed
packet.

"Well, my boy," said Anne of Austria, taking the
letter, "whom does this come from?"

"My father, the woodman of Mantes," replied the boy,
"told me to give it into the queen's own hand; and when
I had done so to return straight to him, and not to wait,
for fear of being discovered."

"And how do you know that I am the queen?" asked
Anne of Austria, who too often suffered her mind to be
distracted from matters of grave importance by trifling
objects of amusement. "That lady is the queen," she
continued, pointing to Madame de Beaumont, and playing upon the boy's simplicity.

"No, no," said Charles, the woodman's son, "she

stands and you sit; and besides, you told them to take off my sabots, as if you were used to order all about you."

"Well," rejoined the queen, "you are right, my boy; go back to your father, and as a token that you have given the letter to the queen, carry him back that ring," and she took a jewel from her finger and put it into the boy's hand. "Mademoiselle de Beaumont," she continued, "will you give this boy into the charge of Laporte, bidding him take him from the palace by the most private way, and not to leave him till he is safe out of Chantilly."

According to Anne of Austria's command, Pauline conducted Charles to the head of the staircase, at which had been stationed Laporte, the confidential servant of the queen, keeping watch to give notice of any one's approach. To him she delivered her charge with the proper directions, and then returned to the saloon, not a little anxious to learn the contents of De Blenau's letter.

"Come hither, my wild rose," said the queen, as she saw her enter. "Here is a letter from De Blenau, full of sad news indeed. His situation is perilous in the extreme; and though I am the cause of all, I do not know how to aid him."

Pauline turned pale, but cast down her eyes, and remained without speaking.

"Surely, Pauline," said the queen, misinterpreting her silence, "after the explanations I gave you some days ago, you can have no further doubt of De Blenau's conduct?"

"Oh no, indeed! madam," replied Pauline, vehemently, "and now that I feel and know how very wrong those suspicions were, I would fain do something to atone for having formed them."

"Thou canst do nothing, my poor flower," said the queen, with a melancholy smile. "However, read that letter, and thou wilt see that something must soon be done to save him, or his fate is sealed. De Blenau must be informed that I have acknowledged writing to my brother, and all the particulars connected therewith; for well I know that Richelieu will not be contented with my confession, but will attempt to wring something more from him, even by the peine forte et dure."

Pauline read and re-read the letter, and each time she did so the color came and went in her cheek, and at every sentence she raised her large dark eyes to the queen, as if inquiring what could be done for him. Each of the queen's ladies was silent for a time, and then each proposed some plan which was quickly discussed and rejected, as either too dangerous, or totally impracticable. One proposed to bribe the governor of the Bastile to convey a letter to De Blenau, but that was soon rejected: another proposed to send Laporte, the queen's valet de chambre, to try and gain admittance; but Laporte had once been confined there himself, and was well known to all the officers of the prison: and another mentioned Seguin, Anne of Austria's surgeon; but he also was not only too well known, but it appeared, from what De Blenau had informed the queen of his conference with Richelieu, that the very words of the message which had been sent by him on the night of the young count's rencontre with the robbers, had been communicated to the cardinal; and the whole party forgot that Louise, the soubrette, had been present when it was delivered.

In the meanwhile, Pauline remained profoundly silent, occupied by many a bitter reflection, while a thousand confused schemes flitted across her mind like bubbles floating on a stream, and breaking as soon as they were looked upon. At length, however, she started, as if some more feasible plan presented itself to her thoughts——" I will go!" exclaimed she—"Please your majesty, I will go."

"You, Pauline!" said the queen, "you, my poor girl! You know not the difficulties of such an undertaking. What say you, Madame de Beaumont?"

"That I am pleased, madam, to see my child show forth the spirit of her race," replied the marchioness. "Nor do I doubt of her success; for sure I am Pauline would not propose a project which had no good foundation."

"Then say how you intend to manage it," said the queen, with little faith in the practicability of Pauline's proposal. "I doubt me much, my sweet girl, they will never let you into the Bastile. Their hearts are as hard as the stones of the prison that they keep, and they will give you no ingress for love of your bright eyes."

"I do not intend to make that a plea," replied Pauline, smiling in youthful confidence; "but I will borrow one of my maid's dresses, and doubtless shall look as like a soubrette as any one. Claude directs us, here, to ask at the gate for Philip the woodman of Mantes. Now he will most likely be able to procure me admission; and if not, I can but give the message to him and be sent away again."

"Oh, no, no!" cried the queen, "give no messages but in the last extremity. How do we know that this woodman might not betray us, and raise Richelieu's suspicions still more? If you can see De Blenau, well—I will give you a letter for him; but if not, only tell the woodman to inform him, that I have confessed all. If that reach the tyrant's ears, it can do no harm. Your undertaking is bold, Pauline: think you your courage will hold out?"

The boundaries between emulation and jealousy are very frail, and Madame de Beaumont, who regarded the services which Mademoiselle de Hauteford had rendered the queen with some degree of envy, now answered for her daughter's courage with more confidence than perhaps she felt. But Pauline's plan yet required great arrangement, even to give it the probability of success. With a thousand eyes continually upon their actions, it was no very easy matter even to quit Chantilly without calling down that observation and inquiry which would have been fatal to their project.

To obviate this difficulty, however, it was agreed that Pauline should accompany Mademoiselle de Hauteford, whose sentence of banishment required her immediate presence in Paris, for the arrangement of her affairs. On their arrival in that city, the two ladies were to take up their abode with the old Marchioness de Senecy, one of the queen's most devoted adherents, and to determine their future proceedings by the information they received upon the spot.

The greatest rapidity, however, was necessary to any hope of success, and neither Pauline nor Mademoiselle de Hauteford lost any time in their preparations. The queen's letter to De Blenau was soon written. Pauline borrowed from her maid Louise, the full dress of a Languedoc peasant, provided herself with a considerable sum of money, that no means might be left untried, and having taken leave of her mother, whose bold counsels tended to raise her spirits and uphold her resolution, she placed herself in the carriage beside Mademoiselle de Hauteford, buoyed up with youthful confidence and enthusiasm.

It was rather an anxious moment, however, as they passed the gates of the palace, which by some accident were shut. This caused a momentary delay, and several of the cardinal's guard (for Richelieu assumed that of a bodyguard amongst other marks of royalty) gathered round the vehicle with the idle curiosity of an unemployed soldiery. Pauline's heart beat fast, but the moment after she was relieved by the appearance of the old concierge, or porter, who threw open the gates, and the carriage rolled out without any question being asked. Her mind, however, was not wholly relieved till they were completely free of the town of Chantilly, and till the carriage, slowly mounting the first little hill, took a slight turn to avoid a steeper ascent, showing them the towers of the château and the course of the road they had already passed, without any human form that could afford subject for alarm.

Pauline, seeing that they were not followed, gave herself up to meditations of the future, firmly believing that their departure had entirely escaped the observation of the cardinal. This, however, was not the case. He had been early informed that one of the queen's carriages was in preparation to carry some of the ladies of honor to Paris; but concluding that it was nothing more than the effect of that sentence of banishment which he had himself pronounced against Mademoiselle de Hauteford, he suffered Pauline and her companion to depart without inquiry or obstruction; although some of the many tools of his power had shut the palace gates, as if by accident, till his decision was known.

As the carriage rolled on, and Pauline reflected in silence upon the task she had undertaken, the bright coloring of the moment's enthusiasm faded away; the mists in which hope had concealed the rocks and precipices around her path, no longer intercepted her view, and the whole difficulties and dangers to which she exposed herself, presented themselves one after another to her sight. But the original motives still remained in full force. Her deep romantic attachment to De Blenau, her sense of duty to the queen, and that generosity of purpose which would have led her at any time to risk her life to save the innocent—much more the innocent and loved—of these, nothing could deprive her; and these kept up her resolution, although the very interest which her heart took in the success of her endeavor, made her magnify the dangers, and tremble at the thought of failure.

CHAPTER XV.

Which shows what they did with De Blenau in the Bastile, and what he himself did to get out of it.

THE sleep of the Count de Blenau was fully as sound within the Bastile as ever it had been in his own hotel at St. Germain: nor was it till the day was risen high that he awoke, on the first morning after his imprisonment.

It was some minutes before he could remember his precise situation, so profound had been his sleep. But the unpleasant parts of our fate soon recall themselves to our senses, though we may forget them for a time; and the narrow windows, the iron door, and the untapestried walls, speedily brought back to De .Blenau's recollection many a painful particular, to which sleep had given a temporary oblivion.

On rising, he missed in some degree the attendance to which he was accustomed; but nevertheless he contrived to get through the business of the toilet, without much difficulty; although no page was ready at his call, no groom prepared to adjust every part of his apparel. He then proceeded into the outer chamber, which he mentally termed his saloon, and would willingly have ordered his breakfast, but his apartments afforded no means of communicating with those below, except by the iron door already mentioned, the secret of which was of too great importance to be lost upon so trifling an occasion.

No remedy presented itself but patience, and proceeding to the window, which opened at will to admit the air, but which was strongly secured on the outside with massy iron bars, he endeavored to amuse the time by looking into the court below, in which he could occasionally

catch a glimpse of some of his fellow-prisoners, appearing and disappearing, as they sometimes emerged into
the open space within his sight, and sometimes retired
into the part, which the thickness of the walls in which
the window was placed, hid from his view.

They were now apparently taking their morning's
walk, and enjoying the privilege of conversing with each
other—a privilege which De Blenau began to value more
highly than ever he had done. Amongst those that he
beheld were many whom he recognized, as having either
known them personally, or having seen them at the court,
or with the army; and the strange assemblage of all different parties which met his eye in the court-yard of the
Bastile, fully convinced him, that under the administration of a man who lived in constant fear that his ill-
gotten power would be snatched from him, safety was to
be found in no tenets and in no station.

Here he beheld some that had been of the party of
Mary de Medicis, and some who had been the avowed
followers of Richelieu himself; some that the minister
suspected of being too much favored by the king, and
some, as in his own case, who had been attached to the
queen. One he saw who was supposed to have favored
the Huguenots in France, and one that had assisted the
Catholic party in Germany.

" Well," thought De Blenau," I am but one out of the
many, and whatever plan I had pursued, most probably I
should have found my way here somehow. Wealth and
influence, in despotic governments, are generally like
the plumes of the ostrich, which often cause her to be
hunted down, but will not help her to fly."

Whilst engaged in such reflections, De Blenau heard
the bolts of the door undrawn, and the governor of the
prison entered, followed by his servant loaded with the
various requisites for so substantial a meal as a breakfast
of that period. De Blenau and the governor saluted each
other with every outward form of civility; and the count,

perceiving that his custodier still lingered after the servant had disposed the various articles upon the table and
had taken his departure, luckily remembered that this
was one of the jours maigres of which he had heard, and
invited his companion to partake of his morning meal.
The governor agreed to the proposal sans cérémonie, and
having done ample justice to the dish of stewed part-
ridges, which formed the principal ornament of the table,
he himself finished a bottle of the celebrated wine of
Suresnes, which is one of the things now lost to the bons
vivants of Paris.

De Blenau was not so much importuned by hunger as
to envy the governor the very large share he appropriated
of the viands before him; and he had plenty of leisure to
remark, that his companion performed his feats of masti-
cation with a wonderful degree of velocity. But the
governor had a reason for thus wishing to hurry, what
was to him a very agreeable occupation, to its conclusion;
for he had scarcely poured out the last goblet of his wine,
and was still wiping and folding up his case-knife (which,
by-the-way, was the constant companion of high and low
in those days, and the only implement they had for cutting their food), when the door opened, and a servant
appeared, giving the governor a significant nod, which
was answered by a sign of the same kind.

Upon this the man retired, and the door being closed,
the well-filled official turned to De Blenau,—" I did not
tell you before, Monsieur le Comte," said he, " for fear of
taking away your appetite; but we have had a message
this morning from Monsieur Lafemas,—you have heard
of Monsieur Lafemas, doubtless?—importing that he
would soon be here to put some questions to you. Now,
Monsieur de Blenau, you are a gentleman for whom
I have a great regard, and I will give you a hint
which may be of service to you. If in the examination which you are about to undergo, there be any questions to which you do not find it convenient to reply, do

not refuse to answer them, but speak always in such a manner as to bear two interpretations, by which means I have known many a prisoner avoid the torture, and sometimes go on from examination to examination, till they gave him his liberty from pure weariness."

De Blenau bowed, already determined as to the course he should pursue. "When do you expect this worthy judge?" he demanded. "I am perfectly unconcerned as to his coming, let me assure you, though I feel obliged by your consideration for my appetite."

"He is here now, sir," replied the governor; "we had better, if you please, join him in the audience-hall. That servant came to announce his arrival."

"I will follow you instantly," replied the count; upon which the governor rose and opened the door.

The moment De Blenau had passed out, the guard, who had been stationed at the head of the stairs, followed at the distance of a couple of paces, while the governor led the way. In this order they proceeded to the inner court, which they had to pass before they could reach the audience-chamber. This open space was still filled by the prisoners, who, glad of the little liberty allowed them, seldom retired to their cells, except when obliged by the regulations of the prison. The moment De Blenau appeared in the court, there was a slight stir amongst its tenants, and the question of, "Who is he? who is he?" circulated rapidly among them.

"It is the Count de Blenau, by St. Louis?" exclaimed a deep voice, which De Blenau remembered to have heard somewhere before; but, though on looking round he saw several persons that he knew, he could not fix upon any one in particular as the one who had spoken.

He had not time, however, for more than a momentary glance, and was obliged to pass on to the door of the audience-hall, which opened into a little narrow passage leading from the court. Here De Blenau paused for an instant to collect his thoughts, and then followed the governor, who had already entered.

14

The audience-hall of the Bastile was a large oblong chamber, dimly lighted by two high Gothic windows, which looked into the outer court. The scanty gleam of daylight which would have thus entered, had the space been open, was impeded by the dust and dirt of many a century, and by the thick crossing of the leaden framework, while its progress into the hall itself was also farther obstructed by several heavy columns which supported the high pointed arches of the roof.

The pavement of this melancholy hall was damp and decayed, many of the stones having strayed from their bed of mortar, and become vagrant about the apartment; and the furniture, if it might be so called, far from filling it, served only to show its size and emptiness. At the farther extremity was a long table, at the end of which, in a chair somewhat elevated, sat the Judge Lafemas, with a clerk at a desk below him; and two or three exempts standing round about.

Near the end next De Blenau was another chair, which he conceived to be placed for his use; while between two of the pillars, sitting on a curious machine, the use of which De Blenau at once suspected, appeared an ill-favored muscular old man, whose lowering brow and doggedness of aspect seemed to speak of many a ruthless deed.

As the count entered the door closed after him with a loud clang; and advancing to the table, he took his seat in the vacant chair, while the governor placed himself at a little distance between him and the judge.

"Well, Monsieur de Blenau," said Lafemas, in that sweet mild tone which he always assumed when not irritated by the taunts of Chavigni. "This is the last place where I could have wished to meet a nobleman whose general character has always engaged my most affectionate esteem."

De Blenau knew Lafemas to be one of the meanest and most viperous of the cardinal's tools, and not feeling much moved to exchange courtesies with him, he merely acknowledged the judge's salutation by a silent bow, while the other proceeded: "I have requested the pleasure of your society for a space, in order to ask you a few questions; your reply to which will, doubtless, soon procure your liberation from this unpleasant place."

"I trust so, sir," replied the count, "as the detention of an innocent person must occasion fully as much discredit to his majesty's government, as it does inconvenience to the person himself."

"You are quite right, you are quite right," rejoined the sweet-tongued judge. "Indeed, my very object in coming is to obtain such answers from you as will convince the Cardinal de Richelieu, who, though a profound minister, is somewhat suspicious withal,—to convince him, I say, that you are innocent; of which, on my conscience, and as I believe in the Saviour, I have no doubt myself. —In the first place, then," he continued, "tell me as a friend, have you any acquaintance in Brussels?"

"I have!" replied De Blenau, decidedly.

"That is honorable,—that is candid," said the judge. "I told you, Monsieur le Gouverneur, that we should have no difficulty, and that Monsieur de Blenau would enable me easily to establish his innocence.—Pray do you correspond with these friends," he continued, "and by what means?"

"I do correspond with them; but seldom: and then by any means that occur."

"Monsieur de Blenau," exclaimed Lafemas, "I am enchanted with this frankness; but be a little more specific about the means. If you have no particular objection to confide in me, mention any channel that you call to mind, by which you have sent letters to the Low Countries."

De Blenau felt somewhat disgusted with the sweet and friendly manner of a man whose deeds spoke him as cruel and as bloody-minded as a famished tiger; and unwilling to be longer mocked with soft words, he replied, " Sometimes by the king's courier, sir; sometimes by the cardinal's; and once I remember having sent one by your cousin De Merceau, but I believe that letter never reached its destination; for you must recollect that De Merceau was hanged by Don Francisco de Mello, for ripping open the bag, and purloining the despatches."

"We have nothing to do with that, my dear count," said Lafemas, struggling to maintain his placidity of demeanor. "The next thing I have to inquire is,"—and he looked at a paper he held in his hand: "Have you ever conveyed any letters to the Low Countries for any one else?"

De Blenau answered in the affirmative; and the judge proceeded with a series of questions, very similar to those which had been asked by Richelieu himself, artfully striving to entangle the prisoner by means of his own admissions, so as to force him into farther confessions by the impossibility of receding. But beyond a certain point De Blenau would not proceed.

"Monsieur Lafemas," said he in a calm firm tone, "I perceive that you are going into questions which have already been asked me by his eminence the cardinal prime minister. The object in doing so is evidently to extort from me some contradiction which may criminate myself; and therefore henceforward I will reply to no such questions whatsoever. The cardinal is in possession of my answers; and if you want them, you must apply to him."

"You mistake entirely, my dear count," said Lafemas; "on my salvation, my only object is to serve you. You have already acknowledged that you have forwarded letters from the queen,—why not now inform me to whom those letters were addressed? If those letters were not of a treasonable nature, why did she not send them by one of her own servants?"

"When a queen of France is not allowed the common attendants which a simple gentlewoman can command, she may often be glad to use the servants and services of her friends. My own retinue, sir, trebles that which the queen has ever possessed at St. Germain. But, without going into these particulars, your question is at once replied to by reminding you, that I am her majesty's chamberlain, and therefore her servant."

"Without there were something wrong, Monsieur de Blenau," said Lafemas, "you could have no objection to state whether you have or have not conveyed some letters from her majesty to Don John of Austria, Don Francisco de Mello, or King Philip of Spain. It is very natural for a queen to write to her near relations, surely!"

"I have already said," replied De Blenau, "that I shall reply to no such questions, the object of which is alone to entangle me."

"You know not what you are exposing yourself to," rejoined the judge; "there are means within this prison which would easily compel an answer."

"None," replied De Blenau, firmly. "My resolution is taken, and no power on earth can shake it."

"Really, Monsieur de Blenau, it would hurt me to the heart to leave you to the dreadful fate which your mistaken determination is likely to call upon you. I could weep, truly I could weep, to think of what you are calling upon your own head;" and the judge glanced his eye towards the machine, which we have already noticed, and from which the old man rose up, as if preparing for his task.

"You mean the torture?" said De Blenau, looking at it without a change of countenance. "But let me tell you, Monsieur Lafemas, that you dare not order it to a man of my rank, without an express warrant for the purpose; and, even if you had such authority, not all the torture in the world would wring one word from me. Ask that instrument of tyranny, sir," and he pointed to the executioner,—"ask him how the noble Caply died; and so would De Blenau also."

Lafemas looked at the governor, and the governor at the executioner, and so round. One of the dreadful secrets of the Bastile had evidently escaped beyond those precincts to which they were fearfully confined; no one could divine how this had occurred, and each suspected the other. A temporary silence ensued, and then Lafemas proceeded:

"The torture! no, Monsieur de Blenau: God forbid that I should think of ordering such a thing! But let me advise you to answer; for I must, of course, report your refusal to the cardinal prime minister, and you know that he is not likely to consider either your rank or your fortune, but will, in all probability, order you the question ordinary and extraordinary instantly."

"The guilt be his then!" said De Blenau. "I have already told you my resolution, sir; act upon it as you think fit."

Lafemas seemed at a loss, and a whispering consultation took place between him and the secretary, who seemed to urge more vigorous measures than the judge himself thought proper to pursue; for their conference was terminated by Lafemas exclaiming in a tone not sufficiently low to escape De Blenau's ear, "I dare not, I tell you—I dare not—I have no orders. Monsieur de Blenau," he continued aloud, "you may now retire, and I must report your answers to the cardinal. But let me advise you, as a sincere friend, to be prepared with a reply to the questions you have now refused to answer, before we next meet; for by that time I shall have received his eminence's commands, which, I fear, will be more severe than my heart could wish."

De Blenau made no reply, but withdrew, escorted as before; and it were needless to deny, that, notwithstanding the coolness with which he had borne his examination, and the fortitude with which he was prepared to repel the worst that could be inflicted, his heart beat high as the door of the audience-hall closed behind him, and he looked forward to returning to his apartments with more pleasure than a captive usually regards the place of his confinement.

The many agitating circumstances which had passed since, had completely banished from his thoughts the voice which he had heard pronounce his name, on the first time of his crossing the court; but as he returned, his eye fell upon the form of a tall, strong man, standing under the archway; and he instantly recognized the woodman of the forest of Mantes.

De Blenau had spoken to him a thousand times in his various hunting-excursions, and he could not help being astonished to meet him in such a place, little dreaming that he himself was the cause. " What, in the name of heaven!" thought he, " can that man have done to merit confinement here? Surely, Richelieu, who affects to be an eagle of the highest flight, might stoop on nobler prey than that."

As these thoughts crossed his mind, he passed by the foot of the little tower, containing the staircase which communicated with his apartments by the iron door in the inner chamber. This had evidently been long disused: and on remembering the position of the two chambers which he occupied, he conceived that they must have been at one time quite distinct, with a separate entrance to each, the one being arrived at by the turret, and the other by the chief staircase. He had, however, only time to take a casual glance, and wisely refrained from making that very apparent; for the governor who walked beside him, kept his eyes almost constantly fixed upon him, as if to prevent any communication even by a sign with the other prisoners.

On arriving at his chamber, the governor allowed him to pass in alone, and having fastened the door, returned to Lafemas, leaving De Blenau to meditate over his situation in solitude. The first pleasure of having escaped from immediate danger having subsided, there was nothing very cheering to contemplate in his position. His fate, though postponed, seemed inevitable. Richelieu, he knew, was no way scrupulous; and the only thing which honor could permit him to do, was to defend the queen's secret with his life.

The queen herself indeed might relieve him from his difficulty, if he could find any way of communicating with her. But in looking round for the means, absolute impossibility seemed to present itself on all sides. In vain he sought for expedients; his mind suggested none that a second thought confirmed. He once contemplated inducing the governor to forward a letter by the temptation of a large bribe; but a moment's reflection showed him that it was a thousand to one that the smooth-spoken officer both accepted his bribe and betrayed his trust.

Many other plans were rejected in a like manner, from a conviction of their impracticability, till at length a vague thought of gaining an interview with the woodman of Mantes, and, if possible, engaging him to bribe some of the inferior officers of the prison, crossed De Blenau's mind; and he was still endeavoring to regulate his ideas on the subject, when the bolts were once more withdrawn, and the governor again entered the apartment.

"Let me congratulate you, Monsieur de Blenau," said he, with a look of sincere pleasure, which probably sprang more from the prospect of continued gain to himself than any abstract gratification in De Blenau's safety. "Monsieur Lafemas is gone, and as the cardinal is at Chantilly, you will be safe for three or four days at least, as nothing can be decided till his eminence returns."

De Blenau well knew how to estimate the kindness of his friend the governor; but though he put its proper value upon it, and no more, he felt the necessity of striving to make his interested meanness act the part of real friendship.

"Well, Monsieur le Gouverneur," said he, assuming a cheerful air, "I suppose, then, that I shall remain with you a day or two longer nor should I, indeed, care so much for the confinement, where I am so well treated, if I had some one to wait upon me as I have been accustomed to."

" I do not know how that could be arranged," replied the governor, thoughtfully; " I would do anything to serve you, Monsieur de Blenau, consistent with my duty, but this is quite contrary to my orders; and if I were to allow you one of my own servants, it would put me completely in his power."

" Oh, that would not do at all," said De Blenau; " but are there not some of the inferior prisoners—" The governor's brow darkened. " Of course," continued the count, " you would have to pay them for their trouble— and I, of course, would reimburse you. If you think that three hundred crowns would induce one of them to wait on me for the time I am here, I would willingly pay the money into your hands, and you could make all the necessary arrangements for the purpose."

The countenance of the governor gradually cleared up as De Blenau spoke, like a sheltered lake that, after having been agitated for a moment by some unwonted breeze, soon relapses into its calm tranquillity, when that which disturbed it has passed away. The idea of appropriating, with such unquestioned facility, the greater part of three hundred crowns was the sun which thus speedily dispersed the clouds upon his brow; and he mused for a moment, calculating shrewdly the means of attaining his object.

" The worst of it is," said he at length, " that we have no inferior prisoners. They are all prisoners of state in the Bastile—— But stay," he added, a felicitous idea crossing his mind, " I remember there was a man brought here this morning by Chavigni's people, and they told me to give him all possible liberty, and employ him in the prison if I could."

" That will just do, then," said De Blenau, inwardly

praying that it might be the honest woodman of Mantes. " He can visit me here occasionally during the day, to see if I have need of him, and the guard at the door can take good care that I do not follow him out, which is all that your duty demands."

" Of course, of course," replied the governor; " it is your safe custody alone which I have to look to: and further, I am ordered to give you every convenience and attention, which warrants me in allowing you an attendant at least. But here comes your dinner, sir."

" Dinner! " exclaimed De Blenau; " it surely is not yet noon." But so it proved: the time had passed more quickly than he thought; nor indeed had he any reason to regret the appearance of dinner, for the substantial and luxurious meal which was served up at his expense on that jour maigre did not prove any bad auxiliary in overcoming whatever scruple yet lingered about the mind of Monsieur le Gouverneur. At every mouthful of becasse, his countenance became more placable and complacent, and while he was busily occupied in sopping the last morsels of his dorade in the sauce au cornichons, and conveying them to the capacious aperture which stood open to receive them, our prisoner obtained his full consent that the person he had mentioned should have egress and regress of the apartment; for which liberty, however, De Blenau was obliged to pay down the sum of three hundred crowns under the specious name of wages to the attendant.

This arrangement, and the dinner, came to a conclusion much about the same time; and the governor, who had probably been engaged with De Blenau's good cheer much longer than was quite consistent with his other duties, rose and retired, to seek the inferior prisoner whose name he could not remember, but whom he piously resolved to reward with a crown per diem, thinking that such unparalleled liberality ought to be recorded in letters of gold.

In regard to De Blenau, the governor looked upon him as the goose with the golden eggs; but more prudent than the boy in the fable, he resolved to prolong his life to the utmost of his power, so long, at least, as he continued to produce that glittering ore which possessed such wonderful attraction in his eyes. De Blenau, however, was not the goose he thought him; and though he waited with some impatience to see if the person on whom so much might depend were or were not his honest friend the woodman, yet his thoughts were deeply engaged in revolving every means by which the cupidity of the governor might be turned to his own advantage.

At length the bolts were undrawn, and the prisoner, fixing his eyes upon the door, beheld a little old man enter, with withered cheeks and sunken eyes; a greasy night-cap on his head, and a large knife suspended by the side of a long thin sword, which sometimes trailed upon the ground, and sometimes with reiterated blows upon the tendons of his meagre shanks, seemed to reproach them for the bent and cringing posture in which they carried the woodcock-like body that surmounted them.

"Well, sir," said De Blenau, not a little disappointed with this apparition; "are you the person whom the governor has appointed to wait upon me?"

"Oui, monsieur," said the little man, laying his hand upon his heart, with a profound inclination of his head, in which he contrived to get that organ completely out of sight, and, like a tortoise, to have nothing but his back visible. "Oui, monsieur; I am cuisinier vivandier, that is to say, formerly vivandier; at present, cuisinier aubergiste ici à la porte de la Bastile, tout près. I have the honor to furnish the dinner for monseigneur, and I have come for the plates."

"Oh, is that all!" cried De Blenau; "take them, take them, my good friend, and begone."

The little man vowed that monsieur did him too much honor, and gathering up his dishes with admirable dexterity, he held the heap with his left arm, reserving his right to lay upon his heart, in which position he addressed another profound bow to De Blenau, and left the apartment. The prisoner now waited some time, getting more and more impatient as the day wore on. At length, however, the door once more opened, and Philip the woodman himself appeared.

Between Philip and the young count there was of course much to be explained, which, requiring no explanation to the reader, shall not be here recapitulated. Every circumstance, however, that Philip told, whether of his writing the letter to inform him of the plots of Chavigni and Lafemas, or of the manner and apparent reason of his being dragged from his cottage to the Bastile, concurred to give De Blenau greater confidence in his new ally; and perhaps Philip himself, from having suffered a good deal on De Blenau's account, felt but the greater inclination to hazard still more. Between two persons so inclined preliminaries are soon adjusted: nor had De Blenau time to proceed with diplomatic caution, even had he had reason to suspect the sincerity of the woodman. The dangers of his situation admitted no finesse; and, overleaping all ceremonies, he at once demanded if Philip would and could convey a letter from him to the queen.

Of his willingness, the woodman said, there was no doubt; and after a moment's thought he added, that he had reason to hope that opportunity also would be afforded him. "It will be dangerous," said he, "but I think I can do it."

"Tell me how, good friend," demanded De Blenau, "and depend upon it, whatever risks you run on my account, whether I live or die, you will be rewarded."

"I want no reward, sir," answered Philip, "but a good cause and a good conscience; and I am sure, if I serve you, I am as well engaged as if I were cutting all the fagots in Mantes. But my plan is this: They tell me that my children shall always be allowed to see me. Now I know my boy Charles, who is as active as a picvert, will not be long before he follows me. He will be here before nightfall, I am sure, and he shall take your letter to the queen."

De Blenau remained silent for a moment. "Was it your son who brought your letter to me?" demanded .he. The woodman assented; and the count continued: "He was a shrewd boy, then. At all events, it must be risked. "Wait, I will write, and depend upon you."

The woodman, however, urged that if he stayed so long suspicion might be excited; and De Blenau suffered him to depart, desiring him to return in an hour, when the letter would be ready. During his absence the prisoner wrote that epistle which we have already seen delivered. In it he told his situation, and the nature of the questions which had been asked him by Lafemas. He hinted also that his fate was soon likely to be decided; and desired that any communication which it might be necessary to make to him might be conveyed through the woodman of Mantes.

More than one hour elapsed after this letter was written before Philip again appeared. When he did so, however, he seemed in some haste. "Monsieur le Comte," said he, "my son is here. They have let me take him into my cell to rest, but I dare not be absent more than a moment, for fear they suspect something. Is the letter ready?"

De Blenau placed it in his hand, and would fain have added some gold. "The queen is at Chantilly," said he, "and your son will want money for his journey."

"No, no, sir," replied Philip, "that is no stuff for a child. Let him have a broad-piece, if you like, to help him on, but no more."

"Well, then," said the count, "accept the rest for your services. I have more in that valise."

"Not so, either, monseigneur," answered the woodman. "Pay for what is done when it is done;" and
taking the letter and one gold piece, he left the apartment.

CHAPTER XVI.

Which shows that Accident holds Wisdom by the leg, and like a pig-driver with a pig, often makes her go forward by pulling her back.

THE heavy carriage which conveyed Pauline de Beaumont towards Paris rolled on with no great rapidity, and the time, to her anxious mind, seemed lengthened to an inconceivable degree. Towards night, every little town they entered she conceived to be the capital, and was not undeceived till Mademoiselle de Hauteford observed, that they had set out so late she was afraid they would be obliged to pass the night at Ecouen.

In her companion Pauline found but little to console or soothe her under the anxiety and fear which the dangerous enterprise she had undertaken naturally produced. Mademoiselle de Hauteford had little either of warmth of heart or gentleness of disposition; and such were the only qualities which could have assimilated with Pauline's feelings at that time.

In combating the passionate love with which the king had regarded her, Mademoiselle de Hauteford had entirely triumphed over her own heart, and having crushed every human sensation that it contained, she substituted a rigid principle of duty, which like the mainspring of a piece of clock-work, originated all her actions, making them regular without energy and correct without feeling.

In the present instance, she seemed to look upon the task which Pauline had undertaken as a thing which ought to be done, and therefore that no doubt or hesitation of any kind could remain upon her mind. She talked calmly of all the difficulties and dangers which presented themselves, and of the best means of obviating them; but did not offer the least consolation to the fears of a young and inexperienced girl, who had taken upon

herself a bold and perilous enterprise, in which her own
happiness was at stake, as well as the lives and fortunes
of others. The indifferent coolness with which she spoke
of risks and obstacles was far from reassuring Pauline,
who soon dropped the conversation, and sinking into herself, revolved all the circumstances in her mind; her
heart sometimes beating high with hope, sometimes sick-
ening at the thought of failure.

Thus in silence the travellers proceeded to Ecouen,
where, from the lateness of the hour, they were obliged
to pass the night; but leaving it early the next morning,
they reached Paris, in a short time, and alighted at the
hotel of the Marchioness de Senecy. That lady, it appeared, was absent, having left Paris some time before
for a distant part of the country; but this was no disadvantage, as Mademoiselle de Hauteford was well known
to the servants that remained in the house, and she did not
in the least hesitate to take up her abode there on the
service of the queen, though the mistress of the mansion
herself was absent.

At Ecouen, Pauline had dressed herself in the clothes
of her maid Louise, and on alighting at the Hôtel de
Senecy, was taken by the servants for the soubrette of
Mademoiselle de Hauteford. All this was to her wish;
and not a little delighted with the first success of her disguise, she affected the ton paysan, and treated the domestics with the same familiarity which they showed
towards her.

An old and confidential servant of the queen was the
only male attendant who accompanied them to Paris,
and he took especial care not to undeceive the others in
regard to Mademoiselle de Beaumont's rank, though he
had more than once nearly betrayed the secret by smiling
at the lady's maid airs which Pauline contrived to assume.
This task, however, was not of long duration; for Pauline's anxiety would not suffer her to remain inactive, and
she accordingly pressed her companion to set out speedily

for the Bastile, afraid that under any long delay her courage, which she felt to be failing every moment, might give way entirely, and that she might at length prove unequal to accomplish her undertaking.

Mademoiselle de Hauteford, whose acquaintance with the city qualified her to act as guide, readily agreed to proceed immediately on their expedition; and Pauline's disguise as soubrette not permitting her to make use of a mask like her companion, she covered her head as far as she could with a large capuchin of brown tafetas, which, however, was all-insufficient to conceal her face. This being done, she followed the lady of honor into the street, and in a moment found herself immersed in all the bustle and confusion of the capital.

Poor Pauline's senses were almost bewildered by the crowd; but Mademoiselle de Hauteford, leaning on her arm, hurried her on as far as the Rue St. Antoine, where she stopped opposite to the church of St. Gervais, or rather the narrow dirty street which leads towards it.

Here she directed Pauline straight on to the Bastile, and pointing out the church, told her that she would wait there for her return, offering up prayers for the success of her enterprise.

Totally ignorant of Paris and all that it contained; young, beautiful and timid; engaged in an undertaking full of danger and difficulty, and dressed in a manner to which she was unaccustomed; Pauline de Beaumont shrank from the glance of the numerous passengers that thronged the Rue St. Antoine; and every eye which, attracted by her loveliness, or by the frightened haste with which she proceeded, gazed on her with more than common attention, she fancied could see into her bosom, and read the secret she was so anxious to conceal.

At length, however, her eye rested on a group of heavy towers, presenting nothing but massy stone walls, pierced with loop-holes, and surmounted at various distances with embrasures, through the aperture of which the threat-

15

ening mouths of some large cannon were occasionally visible. Sweeping round this gloomy building was a broad fosse filled with water, which prevented all approach but at one particular point, where a drawbridge, suspended by two immense chains, gave access to the outer court. But even here no small precaution was taken to guard against any who came in other than friendly guise; for the gate which terminated the bridge on the inner side, besides the security afforded by its ponderous doors and barricadoes, possessed two flanking-towers, the artillery of which commanded the whole course of the approach.

Pauline had often heard the Bastile described, and its horrors detailed, by the guests who occasionally visited her mother's château in Languedoc; but, whatever idea she had formed of it, the frowning strength and gloomy horrors which the original presented, far outbid the picture her imagination had drawn; and so strong was the sensation of fear which it produced upon her mind, that she had nearly turned back and run away the moment she beheld it. An instant's reflection, however, reawakened her courage.

"Claude de Blenau," she thought, "immured within those walls! and do I hesitate when his life, perhaps, depends upon my exertion?" That thought was enough to recall all her resolution; and rapidly crossing the drawbridge, she passed what is called the grille. But here her farther progress was stayed by a massy door covered with plates and studs of iron, which offered none of those happy contrivances either of modern or ancient days, by which people within are called upon to communicate with people without. With shaking knees and trembling hands Pauline tried for some moments to gain admission, but in vain. The gate resisted all her weak efforts, her voice was scarcely audible, and vexed, wearied, and terrified, and not knowing what to do, she burst into a flood of tears,

At about a hundred yards on the other side of the fosse, forming one corner of the Rue St. Antoïne, on the face of which it seemed a wart, or imposthume, stood a little narrow house of two stories high, the front of which displayed an immense board covered with a curious and remarkable device. This represented no other than the form of an immense wild boar, with a napkin tucked under his chin, seated at a table, on which smoked various savory dishes, of which the above ferocious gentleman appeared to be partaking with a very wild-boarish appetite. Underneath all was written, in characters of such a size that those who ran might read, Au Sanglier Gourmand, and then followed a farther inscription, which went to state that Jacques Chatpilleur, autrefois Vivandier de l'Armée de Perpignan, à present Aubergiste Traiteur, fed the hungry, and gave drink to those that thirsted, at all hours of the day and night.

Every one will allow that this man must have been blessed with a charitable disposition; and it so happened that, standing at his own door, with his heart opened by the benign influence of having cooked a dinner for the Count de Blenau, he beheld the ineffectual efforts of Pauline de Beaumont to gain admission into the Bastile.

The poor little man's heart was really moved; and skipping across the drawbridge, he was at her side in a moment. "What seek you, charmante demoiselle?" demanded the aubergiste, making her a low bow; and then observing her tears, he added, "Ma pauvre fille, do not weep. Do you wish to get in here?"

"Yes, indeed," replied Pauline; "but I cannot make them hear."

"There are many who want to get out, who cannot make them hear either," said the aubergiste: "but they shall hear me, at all events." So saying he drew forth his knife, with a flourish which made Pauline start back, and applied the handle with such a force to the gate of the prison, that the whole place echoed with the blows.

Immediately a little wicket was opened, and the head of a surly-looking porter presenter itself at the aperture.

"Philip the woodman! Philip the woodman!" said he, as soon as he heard Pauline's inquiries. "Who is he, I wonder? We have nothing to do with woodmen here. Oh, I remember the man. And we are to break through all rules and regulations for him, I suppose? But I can tell Monsieur Chavigni, or whoever gave the order, that I shall not turn the key for any one except at proper hours; so you cannot see him now, young woman—you cannot see him now."

"And is not this a proper hour?" asked Pauline. "I thought mid-day was the best time I could come."

"No!" answered the porter, "I tell you no, my pretty demoiselle; this is the dinner-hour, so you must come again."

"When can I come then, sir?" demanded Pauline, "for I have journeyed a long way to see him."

"Why, then you are in need of rest," replied the other, "so you will be all the better for waiting till evening. Come about seven o'clock and you shall see him."

"Cannot I see him before that?" asked the young lady, terrified at the delay.

"No! no! no!" roared the porter, and turned to shut the wicket; but bethinking him for a moment, he called after Mademoiselle de Beaumont—"Who shall I tell him wants him, when I see him?"

Pauline was unprepared with an answer, but the necessity of the moment made her reply, "His daughter!" trusting that, as there must be some understanding between him and De Blenau, the woodman would conceive her errand, and not betray any surprise, whether he had a daughter or not.

During this conversation, the aubergiste had remained hard by, really compassionating Pauline's disappointment.

"Ma pauvre fille," said he, as the wicket closed, "I am very sorry that they treat you so; but they are great brutes in these prisons. Bon Dieu! you look very pale. Come in with me here to my little place, and take some soup, and rest yourself till the time comes round."

Pauline thanked him for his offer, but declined it, of course; telling him, that she was going to the house of a friend who waited for her; and then taking leave of the good aubergiste, she left him interested in her sorrow, and enchanted by her sweet manner.

In the meanwhile, Pauline returned to the church of St. Gervais, where she found Mademoiselle de Hauteford still on her knees in the chapel of St. Denis.

Pauline's recital of what had happened, called forth but few remarks from her companion, who only observed that seven would be an unpleasant hour, for by that time night began to fall. To Mademoiselle de Beaumont, however, night seemed more favorable to her enterprise than day, when the trepidation which she felt was visible to every passing eye; and she congratulated herself on the prospect of the darkness covering the agitation which might lead to suspicion if observed.

I shall not follow the two ladies through the remaining part of the day. Suffice it, that Mademoiselle de Hauteford employed herself in preparations for the long journey which the cardinal's sentence of banishment required her to take, and that Pauline's time passed in anxiety and apprehension, till the hour came for her once more to visit the Bastile.

As soon as the long hand upon the dial pointed towards the Roman capitals IX. and the shorter one to VII. the two ladies set out in the same guise, and on the same route as in the morning, with only this difference in their proceedings, that the old domestic of the queen, who had accompanied them to Paris, received orders to follow at a few paces distance, well armed with sword and pistol.

It was now quite dark, and the streets not being so crowded as when she before passed through them, Pauline proceeded more calmly except when the torch-bearers of some of the gay world of Paris flashed their flambeaux in her eyes as they lighted their lords along to party or spectacle. At the church of St. Gervais she again left Mademoiselle de Hauteford with the servant; and now, well acquainted with the way, ran lightly along till she arrived at the Bastile, where, not giving her resolution time to fail, she passed the drawbridge, and entered the outer gate, which was at that moment open. Before her stood the figure of the porter, enjoying the cool evening air that blew through the open gate into the court. His hand rested upon the edge of the door, and the moment Pauline entered, he pushed it to with a clang that made her heart sink.

"Whom have we here," said he, "that comes in so boldly? Oh, so! is it you, ma belle demoiselle?" he continued as the light of the lanterns which hung under the arch fell upon her countenance:—"well, you shall see your father now. But first, I think, you had better go and speak to the governor; he is a man of taste, and would like such a pretty prisoner, no doubt; perhaps he might find a warrant for your detention."

Pauline's heart sank at the idea of being carried before the governor, well knowing how little competent she was to answer any inquiries concerning her errand; but the excess of fear will often give courage, and the most timid animals turn and resist when pressed to extremity. Thus Pauline summoned up all her resolution, and remembering the allusion which the porter had made to Chavigni's orders in favor of the woodman, she replied boldly: "This is no time for jesting, sir! and as to detaining me, it would be as much as the governor's post is worth, if it came to Monsieur de Chavigni's ears that he ever thought of such a thing."

"So, so!" cried the porter with a grin, "you are a friend of Monsieur de Chavigni's. So—I thought there was something made him so careful of yon sour old woodman. These great statesmen must have their little relaxations. So that is it, mademoiselle? He takes especial care of the father for the daughter's sake."

There was a drop or two of the warm blood of Languedoc flowing in Pauline's veins with all her gentleness, and her patience now became completely exhausted. "Well, sir!" she answered, "all I have to say to you is, that if I meet with any insolence, it may cost you dear. So bring me to see my father, or refuse me at once."

"I am not going to refuse you, my pretty demoiselle," replied the porter; "though, truly, you speak more like a lady of quality than a woodman's daughter. Now I'll swear you are Madame la Comtesse's suivante. Nay, do not toss your head so impatiently; your father will be here in a minute; he knows of your having called at the wicket this morning, and is to come here to see you at seven—but here is the governor, as I live—going to take a twilight walk, I suppose."

As he spoke, the governor approached: "Whom have you got here, porter?" he asked, while he eyed Pauline with one of those cool luxurious glances that made her shrink.

"This is the woodman's daughter, sir," replied the man, "who wishes to speak with her father."

"By the keys of St. Peter! which are something in my own way," exclaimed the governor, "thou art a beautiful daughter for a woodman. Art thou sure thy mother did not help thee to a better parentage? What is thy father's name?"

Terrified, confused, and ignorant of the woodman's name, Pauline faltered forth, unconscious of what she said, "I do not know."

"Ha! ha! ha! thou sayest well, my pretty damsel," cried the governor, laughing, and thinking that she answered his jest in kind. "It is a wise father that knows his own child; and why not a wise child that knows his own father? But without a joke, what is your supposed father's name?"

"My supposed father!" repeated Pauline, in the same state of perturbation; "oh, Philip the woodman."

"Nay, nay," replied the governor, "that does not answer my meaning either. What is the surname of this Philip the woodman?"

The impossibility of answering overpowered her. Pauline had not the most remote idea of Philip's name, and another instant would indubitably have betrayed all; but at the moment the governor asked his question, Philip had entered the court. He had heard the last sentence, saw Pauline's embarrassment, and divining its cause, with quick presence of mind caught her in his arms, and kissed her on both cheeks, with that sort of fatherly affection which would have deceived the governor's eyes by day, much less by the fainter light of the lanterns in the archway.

"My dear child!" cried he, "how art thou? and how is thy mother?" And then turning to the governor, without giving her time to reply, he went on, "My name, sir, which you were asking but now, is Philip Grissolles, but I am better known by the name of Philip the woodman, and some folks add the name of the wood, and call me Philip the woodman of Mantes."

"Philip Grissolles!" said the governor; "very well, that will do. It was your surname that I wished to know, for it is not put down in the order for your detention, and it must be inserted in the books. And now Monsieur Philip Grissolles, you may take your daughter to your cell; but remember that you have to wait upon the Count de Blenau in half an hour, by which time I shall have returned. You can leave your daughter in your cell till you have done attending the count, if you like."

He then proceeded to the gate, and beckoning to the porter, he whispered to him, "Do not let her go out till I come back. It is seldom that we have anything like that in the Bastile! Doubtless, that woodman would be glad to have her with him; if so, we will find her a cell."

Philip turned his ear to catch what the governor was saying, but not being able to hear it distinctly, he addressed himself to Pauline loud enough to reach every one round. " Come," said he, " ma fille, you are frightened at all these towers and walls and places; but it is not so unpleasant after one is in it either. Take my arm, and I'll show you the way."

Pauline was glad to accept of his offer, for her steps faltered so much that she could hardly have proceeded without assistance; and thus, leaning on the woodman, she was slowly conducted through a great many narrow passages, to the small vaulted chamber in which he was lodged.

As soon as they had entered, the woodman shut the door, and placing for Pauline's use the only chair that the room contained, he began to pour forth a thousand excuses for the liberty he had taken with her cheek. " I hope you will consider, mademoiselle, that there was no other way for me to act, in order to bring us out of the bad job we had fallen into. The porter of the prison told me this morning that my daughter was coming to see me, and knowing very well I had no daughter, I guessed that it was some one on the Count de Blenau's account; but little did I think that it was you, mademoiselle—you that I saw in the wood of Mantes on the day he was wounded."

Pauline was still too much agitated with all that had passed to make any reply, and sitting with her hands pressed over her eyes, her thoughts were all confusion, though one terrible remembrance still predominated, that she was there—in the very heart of the Bastile—far from all those on whom she was accustomed to rely— habited in a disguise foreign to her rank—acting an assumed character, and engaged in an enterprise of life and death.

All this was present to her, not so much as a thought, but as a feeling; and for a moment or two it deprived her, not only of utterance, but of reflection. As her mind grew more calm, however, the great object for which she came began again to recover the ascendancy; and she gradually regained sufficient command over her ideas to comprehend the nature of the excuses which Philip was still offering for his presumption, as he termed it.

"You did perfectly right," replied Pauline; "and, having extricated us from a dangerous predicament, merit my sincere thanks. But now," she continued, "without loss of time I must see the Count de Blenau."

"See the Count de Blenau!" exclaimed Philip in astonishment. "Impossible, mademoiselle! utterly impossible! I can deliver a letter or a message; but that is all I can do."

"Why not?" demanded Pauline. "For pity's sake, do not trifle with me. If you have free admission to his prison, why cannot you open the way to me?"

"Because, mademoiselle, there is a sentinel at his door who would not allow you to pass," replied Philip. "I have no wish to trifle with you, indeed; but what you ask is merely impossible."

Pauline thought for a moment. "Cannot we bribe the sentinel?" she demanded. "Here is gold."

"That is not to be done either," answered Philip. "He is not allowed to speak to any one, or any one to speak to him. The first word, his fusil would be at my breast; and the second, he would fire: such are his orders, mademoiselle, and be sure he would obey them."

"Well, then," cried Pauline, "fly to the Count de Blenau, tell him that there is a lady here from the queen, with a letter which she must not trust to any one else, and ask him what is to be done—but do not stay long, for I am afraid of remaining here by myself."

The woodman promised not to be a moment, and hastened to the Count de Blenau's apartment, where the wary sentinel, as usual, examined him well to ascertain his identity before he gave him admission. He then entered and communicated as rapidly as possible to De Blenau the message he had received.

"It is Mademoiselle de Hauteford, without doubt," said De Blenau, thoughfully; "I must see her by all means."

"See her, sir!" exclaimed Philip. "The guard will never let her pass. It is quite impossible."

"Not so impossible as you think. The gates of the inner court do not shut, I think, till nearly nine. Is there any one in the court?"

"No one, sir," answered the woodman; "all the state prisoners were locked up at six."

"Well, then, Philip," proceeded De Blenau, "do you know a small tower in the court, where you just see through the archway part of an old flight of steps?"

"Oh, yes, I know it well," replied Philip. "The tower is never used now, they tell me. There is a heap of rubbish in the doorway."

"Exactly," said the count. "Now, my good Philip, bring the lady with all speed to that tower, and up the old flight of steps till you come to a small iron door: push that with your hand, and you will find that it brings you into the inner room, where I will wait for you."

Philip's joy and astonishment found vent in three bon Dieu's! and three est-il possible's! and rushing away without more loss of time, he flew to Pauline, whose stay in his cell had been undisturbed by anything but her own anxious fears. These, however, magnified every sound into the approach of some one to be dreaded. Even the footstep of the woodman made her heart beat with alarm; but the news he brought far more than compensated for it, and, inspired with new hope, she followed him gladly through the gloomy passages which led to the inner court.

The darkness which pervaded the unlighted avenues of the Bastile was so great, that Pauline was obliged to follow close upon Philip's footsteps for fear of losing her way. The woodman, however, was a little in advance, when a faint light showed that they were approaching the open air, and Pauline began to catch an indistinct glimpse of the dark towers that surrounded the inner court. But at that moment Philip drew back:—" There is some one in the court," he whispered. " Hark ! "—and listening, she clearly heard the sound of measured steps crossing the open space before her.

" It is the guard," said the woodman, in the same low voice; " they are going to relieve the sentinel at the count's door." He now waited till they were heard ascending the stairs, and then, " Quick, follow me across the court, mademoiselle," he said; " for they go through this passage on their return."

Pauline was about to follow him as he desired, but her dress caught upon one of the staples of the doorway. Philip attempted to disentangle it for her, but in vain: his efforts only fixed it the more. Pauline herself tried to tear it away, but the soubrette's stout serge-dress would not tear. In the meantime they heard the " Qui vive ? " of the sentinel, the countersign returned, the relief of the guard; and by the time that Philip had by main strength torn away the dress from the staple that had caught it, the steps of the soldiers were again heard descending the staircase from the prison of De Blenau.

" For God's sake, mademoiselle," whispered the woodman, run back as quickly as you can to my cell, for we cannot pass without their seeing us. I will wait here, for they would hear my heavy feet in the passage, and follow us both; but if I can stop them a while, I will, to give you time."

Pauline doubted not that she could remember the turnings, and, gliding along as fast as possible, she endeavored to find her way back. As she went she heard some words pass between Philip and the guard, and immediately after she distinguished that they had entered the passage, for the echoing tramp of their feet, reverberated by the low arches, seemed following close upon

her. Terrified and agitated, she flew on with the speed
of lightning. But we all know how difficult it is to retrace
any course we have pursued in the dark; and in her haste
and confusion Pauline lost the turning she ought to have
taken, and, afraid of going back, even after she discovered her mistake, she paused for a moment in a state
of alarm and suspense little short of agony.

She could now distinctly hear the guard approaching,
and not knowing where the passage might terminate, or
what might obstruct the path, she felt her way with her
hand along the wall, till at length she discovered a small
recess, apparently one of those archways which gave
entrance to the various cells, for beneath her fingers she
felt the massy bolts and fastenings which secured it from
without. She had scarce a moment to think, but, placing
herself under the arch, she drew back as far as possible,
in the hope that, sheltered by the recess, and concealed by
the darkness, the guard would pass her by unnoticed.

It was a dreadful moment for poor Pauline. The soldiers were not so near as the echoes of the place had led
her to imagine; and she had several minutes to wait,
holding her breath, and drawing herself in, as if to nothing, while the tramp of the armed feet came nearer and
nearer, till at length she felt, or fancied that she felt, their
clothes brush against her as they passed; and then heard
their steps becoming fainter and more faint as they proceeded to some other part of the building.

It was not till all was again silent that Pauline ventured,
still trembling with the danger she had just escaped, to
seek once more the path she had lost in her terror. But
her search was now in vain; she had entirely forgot the
turnings that she had taken in her flight, and in the darkness only went wandering on from one passage to another, starting at every sound, and always convinced that
she was mistaken, but not knowing in what direction to
seek the right.

At length, however, she found herself at a gateway

which led into what seemed an open court, and imagining
from the towers she saw round about, that she had arrived
once more at the spot from which she had been frightened
by the approach of the guards, she resolved again to seek
more cautiously the cell of the woodman, to which, of
course, he would return in search of her. But as she
turned to put this resolve in execution, she perceived a
light coming down the passage towards her; and without
giving herself a moment to reflect that it might possibly
be the woodman himself, fear seized her again, and darting across the court, she looked round for some place of
concealment.

Exactly opposite, she perceived another archway similar to the one she had left, and concealing herself within
it, she paused to see who it was that followed, it just
occurring to her mind at that instant, that perhaps she
was in full career away from the very person she wished
to find. But, the moment after, the light appeared in the
archway, and glancing on the face of the man who
carried it, discovered to her the features of the governor.

This sight was not calculated to allay her fears; but her
alarm was infinitely increased when she perceived that he
began crossing the court towards the spot where she
stood. Flight again became her resource, and, turning to
escape through the passages to which she supposed that
archway led, as well as the others, she struck her foot
against some steps and had nearly fallen. Recovering
herself, however, without loss of time she began ascending the steps that lay before her, nor stopped, till reaching a small landing-place, she loked through one of the
loopholes in the wall, and beheld the governor directing
his course to another part of the building.

Satisfied that he did not follow her, but faint and out
of breath with the speed she had employed in her flight,
Pauline paused for a moment's repose; and stretching out
her hand, she leaned against a door which stood at the
top of the staircase; however, it afforded her no support,

for the moment she touched it, it gave way under her hand, and flying open, discovered to her a well-lighted apartment. New terror seized upon Pauline; her eyes were dazzled by the sudden glare, and drawing back she would have fallen headlong down the stairs, but at that instant she was caught in the arms of De Blenau.

The tumult of joy and surprise—the mutual explanations—the delight of De Blenau—the relief to Pauline—with the thousand little et ceteras of such a meeting, I must leave to the reader's imagination. Neither shall I dilate upon the surprise of Philip the woodman, when, on coming to inform De Blenau that he had lost the lady in the windings of the Bastile, he discovered that she had found her way to the object of her search without his sage guidance. One piece of information, however, he conveyed, which hurried their conference towards a conclusion. The governor, he said, who had been absent, had returned, and was then engaged in visiting the western wards; and therefore he might be shortly expected in that part of the prison.

This unpalatable news reminded Pauline to deliver the letter from the queen, which in the joy and agitation of their first meeting she had neglected to do. De Blenau looked it over with a hurried glance. " She commands me," said he, " to confess all exactly as it occurred; but on one or two points I have already refused to answer, and if I do so now without producing the queen's warrant for my conduct, I shall be held a base coward, who betrays his trust for fear of the torture."

" And do you hesitate, Claude? " demanded Pauline rather reproachfully—" do you hesitate to take the only means which can save you? Do you think nothing of what I feel? You, Claude, may be proof against corporeal torture; but I cannot endure much longer the mental agony I have suffered since you have been confined here, especially when I reflected that even while you were acting most nobly, I was suspecting you ungenerously. If you love me as you profess, dear Claude, you will take the means that the queen directs to ensure your safety."

"Well, dearest Pauline," replied De Blenau, yielding to the all-persuasive eloquence of woman's lips, "I will do as you wish, and endeavor to pursue such measures as will be both safe and honorable. But now conclude what you were telling me, of having lost yourself in the prison, and how you found your way hither."

It may be necessary to explain, that while this conversation had taken place between De Blenau and Pauline in the inner apartment, Philip the woodman had remained in the outer chamber, keeping watch with his ear to the door which communicated with the staircase, in order to apprise them in time of the governor's approach. Pauline now had not time to conclude her little history of perilous escapes and dangers ere Philip entering from the outer chamber interrupted her: "Fly down the stairs, mademoiselle," cried he, "and wait at the bottom till I join you. The governor is coming, for I hear other steps on the stairs as well as those of the sentinel at the top."

Prisons are not places for great ceremonies, nor for all the mighty delicacies of general society; so Pauline suffered De Blenau to press his lips upon hers unreproved, and then fled down the back staircase with the speed of light; after which the count shut and bolted the iron door, and passed into the outer chamber, while the woodman bustled about in the inner one, arranging the count's apparel for the night, and appearing much more busy than he really was.

Thus everything was as it should be when the governor entered; but still there was an angry spot upon his brow, and with but a slight inclination to De Blenau, he looked through the door between the two chambers, saying, "Well, Mr. Woodman of Mantes, where is your daughter? She is not in your cell."

"You have made sure of that in person, I suppose," replied Philip, in his usual surly manner.

"Whether I have or not," answered the governor, "does but little signify. I ask where is your daughter? We must have no strangers wandering about the Bastile."

"I know my child's beauty as well as you do, monsieur," replied Philip, "and was too wise to leave her in my cell, where every one that chose would have liberty and time to affront her, while I was attending upon Monsieur le Comte here: so I made her come with me, and set her under the archway of the old tower to wait till I was done. Now, if monsieur has done with me, I will go and conduct her to the outer gate, and never with my will shall she set her foot within these walls again."

"I have no farther need of you to-night Philip," said De Blenau, as the woodman stood at the door ready to depart; and then seeing that the governor turned to follow him out, he added, "Monsieur le Governeur, will you sup with me this evening?"

Philip quitted the room, but the governor was obliged to stay to reply. "With pleasure, sir, with pleasure," said he. "I will be back with you immediately, before my servant brings the plates; but I must first take the liberty of seeing this demoiselle out of the prison gates." He then left De Blenau, and having bolted the door, followed the woodman quickly down the steps. Philip, however, had gained so much upon him, that he had time to whisper to Pauline, whom he found waiting in the archway: "The governor is coming, but do not be alarmed. Let him think that I bade you wait for me here till I had attended the çount."

Pauline, however, could not help being alarmed. While the excitement of her enterprise had continued, it afforded a false sort of courage, which carried her through; but now that her object was gained, all her native timidity returned, and she thought of encountering the governor again with fear and trembling. Nor had she much time to recall her spirits before he himself joined them.

"Well, my fair demoiselle," he cried, "I think if I
16

had known that you were waiting here all alone in the dark, I should have paid you a visit; and he raised the lamp close to Pauline's face, which was as pale as death. "Why, you look as terrified," proceeded the governor, "as if you had been committing murder. Well, I will light you out, and when you come to-morrow, you will not be so frightened. At what hour do you come, eh?"

"I desire that you would not come at all," said Philip aloud, as he followed the governor, who was escorting Pauline along with an air of gallantry and badinage which did not at all set off his thin demure features to advantage, especially in the unbecoming light of the lamp that flickered upon them but at intervals, tipping all the acute angles of his countenance with not the most agreeable hue. "I desire that you would not come at all: you have been here once too often already. Let your brother Charles come the next time."

The governor darted a glance at Philip, which certainly evinced that his face could take on, when it liked, an expression of hatred, malice, and all uncharitableness; and in a minute or two after, by some means, the lamp went out in his hands. "Here, Philip," cried he, "take the lamp, and get a light."

"Your pardon, sir," answered the sturdy woodman: "not till I have seen my daughter beyond the gates."

"Philip Grissolles, or Philip the Woodman, or whatever you call yourself," cried the governor, "are you mad? Do you know what you are about? Go and fetch me a light instantly, or refuse me at your peril."

"I do refuse then," replied the woodman, who had learned by conversation with the porter and turnkeys, how much power the governor had placed in his hands by permitting him to attend upon the Count de Blenau; "I am your prisoner, sir," he continued, "but not your servant."

"I have allowed you to act as such in the prison," said the governor, "and there are no servants here but mine."

" In suffering me to attend upon the Count de Blenau,"
rejoined Philip boldly, " you have outstepped your duty,
and broken the express order of the cardinal. So much
have I learned since I came here—therefore allow my
daughter to depart quietly, sir. We shall find a. light in
the porter's room."

" By heavens! I have a mind to detain the girl all
night, for your insolence," cried the governor, stamping
with rage.

" Oh, for God's sake do not ! " exclaimed Pauline, clasping her hands; but Philip came close up to him,—" You
dare not," said he, in a low voice; " for your head, you
dare not." And then added aloud to Pauline, " Come
along, my child; Monsieur le Gouverneur will let you out."

During this altercation they had continued to proceed;
and the governor, knowing that his violation of the
cardinal's commands with regard to the strict confinement of De Blenau, might bring his head to the block if
sifted thoroughly, thought it best to abstain from irri-
tating a person who not only possessed, but knew that he
possessed, so much power. Not that he would not willingly have silenced the woodman by some of those infal-
lible means which were much resorted to in that day;
but that he knew Chavigni was not easily satisfied on
such points; and thus being in a situation which is
popularly expressed by " the horns of a dilemma," like
a good Christian as he was, he chose rather to risk discovery than commit a murder which would undoubtedly
be found out. Under these circumstances, he permitted
Philip and Pauline to proceed to the gates, and ordered
the porter to give the young lady egress, taking care,
however, to follow them all the way till they arrived at
the last gate opening upon the drawbridge, which at the
time they arrived, had not been yet raised for the evening.

Pauline's heart beat with glad impatience as the janitor
put his key into the lock, whose bolt grating harshly, as it
was withdrawn, produced to her ears most excellent
music.

It so unfortunately happened, however, that at the moment the gate swung heavily back upon its hinges, Charles, the woodman's son, presented himself for admission; and having before had free access to his father, was proceeding calmly through the open door, without taking any notice of Mademoiselle de Beaumont, whom he did not recognize in her disguise.

"What!" exclaimed the governor, whose Bastile habits rendered him quick to the slightest suspicion, " do you not speak to your sister?"

"Sister!" said the boy, confounded; "I have no sister!"

Pauline saw that in another moment all would be lost; and darting past the governor, she was through the gate, and over the draw-bridge in a moment.

"Nom de Dieu!" cried the governor: "follow her, Letrames!—quick, quick!"

The turnkey was on Pauline's footsteps in a minute; but she had gained so much in the first instance, that she would certainly have escaped with ease, if an envious stone had not obstructed her path at the bottom of the glacis, and striking her foot, occasioned her to fall. Pauline uttered a scream of both pain and fear; and two steps would have brought the turnkey to the spot where she lay, when suddenly a small strange-shaped figure in white skipped over her prostrate form, and interposed between her and her pursuer.

"Ventre Saint Gris!" cried the redoubtable Jacques Chatpilleur, cuisinier aubergiste, who thus came to her assistance. " You shall not touch her!" and drawing the long rapier that hung beside his carving-knife, he made a pass so near the breast of the turnkey, that the official started back full ten paces, not knowing in the dim light of the hour, what hobgoblin shape thus crossed his purpose. "Maraud!" continued the aubergiste, "who are you that dare to injure this demoiselle? under the very walls of the Bastile, too, contrary to the peace and quiet of his majesty's true subjects! Get thee gone! or I will spit thee like a chapon de maine, or rather skewer thee like an ortolan under the wings."

This professional allusion, together with a moment's reflection, enabled Letrames, the turnkey, to call to mind the ancient vivandier; and showering upon him a thousand harsh epithets for his interference, he called upon him to stand aside, and let him secure his prisoner; still, however, standing aloof from the point of the weapon,—for Jacques Chatpilleur, while vivandier to the army, had shown that he could gather laurels with his sword, as well as with his knife.

In the present instance, he either did not, or would not, know the turnkey; and continued vociferating to him to hold off, and tell who he was, with such reiteration, that for some time the other had no opportunity of replying. At length, however, he roared, rather than said, " Jacques Diable! you know me well enough; I am Letrames, géolier au château."

The aubergiste looked over his shoulder, and seeing that Pauline was no longer visible, he very quietly put up his rapier, saying, " Mais mon Dieu! mon ami, why did you not tell me that before? Je vous en demande mille pardons; " and seizing the turnkey in his arms, he embraced him, making a thousand excuses for having mistaken him, and hugging him with a sort of malicious affection, which quite put a stop to his pursuit of Pauline.

The only benediction that the jailer thought proper to bestow on the little aubergiste was a thousand curses, struggling all the time to free himself from the serpent folds of Chatpilleur's embrace. But it was not till the aubergiste had completely satisfied himself, that he suffered Letrames to escape, and then very composedly offered to assist him in the pursuit, which he well knew would now be ineffectual.

The darkness of the night had prevented this scene from being visible from the gates of the Bastile, and

Letrames, on his return to the prison was too wise to complain of the conduct of our friend Chatpilleur; a vivandier at the gates of the Bastile being much too convenient an acquaintance to be quarrelled with upon trifles.

During his absence the wrath of the governor turned upon Philip the woodman. "What is the meaning of this? Villain!" exclaimed he, "this is none of your daughter! Fouchard! La Heuterie!" he called aloud to some of his satellites—"quick! bring me a set of irons! we shall soon hear who this is, Monsieur Philip Grissolles!"

"You will never hear anything from me more than you know already, replied Philip; "so put what irons on me you like. But you had better beware, Sir Governor; those that meddle with pitch will stick their fingers. You do not know what you may bring upon your head."

"Silence, fool!" cried the governor, in a voice that made the archway ring; "you know not what you have brought upon your own head.—Fouchard! La Heuterie! I say, why are you so long? Oh, here you come at last. Now secure that fellow, and down with him to one of the black dungeons!—Porter, turn that young viper out," he continued, pointing to Charles, who stood trembling and weeping by his father's side; "turn him out, I say!—we will have no more of these traitors than we have occasion for."

At the word the "dark dungeon," Philip's courage had almost failed him, and it was not without an effort that he kept his sturdy limbs from betraying his emotion, while the jailers began to place the irons on his wrists and ankles: but when he heard the order to drive forth his son, he made a strong effort and caught the boy in his arms: "God bless you, Charles! God bless you, my boy! and fear not for me," he exclaimed, "while there is a power above."

It was a momentary solace to embrace his child, but the porter soon tore the boy from his arms, and pushing

him through the gate closed it after him, rejoicing that
he should no more have to turn the key for any of the
woodman's family. "Now," said he, "now we shall
have no more trouble; I hate to see all our good old rules
and regulations broken through. I dare say if his eminence the cardinal—God protect him!—were to follow
this Monsieur Chavigni's advice, we should have everything out of order; and all the good store of chains and
irons here in the lodge would get rusty for want of use."

"Peace, peace!" cried the governor: "La Heuterie,
take that fellow down as I told you. He shall have the
question to-morrow, and we shall see if he finds that so
easy to bear. Away with him, quick!—A fool I was to
be so deceived!—I suspected something when she stam-
mered so about her father's name." So saying, he turned
to hear the report of Letrames, who at that moment returned from his unsuccessful pursuit of Pauline.

In the meanwhile the jailers led Philip, who moved
with difficulty in his heavy irons, across the first and
second court, and opening a low door in the western
tower displayed to his sight a flight of steps leading down
to the lower dungeons. At this spot La Heuterie, who
seemed superior in rank to his fellow-turnkey, lighted
a torch that he had brought with him at his companion's
lantern, and descending to the bottom of the steps, held
it up on high to let Philip see his way down. The woodman shuddered as he gazed at the deep gloomy chasm
which presented itself but half seen by the glare of the
torch, the light of which glancing upon the wall in different places, showed its green damp and ropy slime,
without offering any definite limit to the dark and fearful vacuity. But he had no time to make any particular
remark, for the second jailer, who stood at his side,
rudely forced him on; and descending the slippery stone
steps, he found himself in a large long vault, paved with
round stones, and filled with heavy subterranean air,
which at first made the torch burn dim, and took away the

woodman's breath. As the light, however, spread slowly through the thick darkness, he could perceive three doors on either hand, which he conceived to give entrance to some of those under-ground dungeons, whose intrinsic horror, as well as the fearful uses to which they were often applied, had given a terrific fame to the name of the Bastile, and rendered it more dreaded than any other prison in France.

During this time they had paused a moment, moving the torch slowly about, as if afraid that it would be extinguished by the damp, but when the flame began to rise again, La Heuterie desired his companion to bring the prisoner to number six, and proceeding to the extremity of the vault, they opened the farthest door on the left, which led into a low damp cell, cold, narrow, and unfurnished, the very abode of horror and despair. Into this they pushed the unfortunate woodman, following themselves, to see, as they said, if there was any straw.

"Have you brought some oil with you?" demanded La Heuterie, examining a rusty iron lamp that hung against the wall. "This is quite out."

"No, indeed," replied Fouchard, "and we cannot get any to-night; but he does not want it till day. It is time for him to go to sleep."

"No, no," rejoined the other, who seemed at least to have some human feeling; "do not leave the poor devil without light. Give him your lantern, man; you can fetch it to-morrow, when you come round to trim the lamps."

The man grumbled, but did as La Heuterie bade him; and having fastened the lantern on the hook where the lamp hung, they went away, leaving Philip to meditate over his fate in solitude.

"I have brought it on myself at last," thought the woodman, as looking round him he found all the horrors he had dreamed of the Bastile more than realized; and his spirit sank within him. Cut off from all communi-

cation with any human being, he had now no means of
making his situation known; and the horrible idea of the
torture shook all his resolution and unmanned his heart.

Sleep, however, was out of the question; and he sat
mournfully on the straw that had been placed for his bed,
watching the light in the lantern, as inch by inch it burned
away, till at last it gleamed for a moment in the socket—
sank—rose again with a bright flash, and then became
totally extinguished. He now remained in utter darkness,
and a thousand vague and horrible fancies crowded upon
his imagination while he sat there, calculating how near
it was to day, when he fancied that even the momentary
presence of the jailer would prove some relief to the
blank solitude of his situation. Hour after hour, however, passed away, and no glimpse of light told him it
was morning. At length the door opened and the jailer
appeared, bringing with him a fresh lighted lamp, thus
offering a frightful confirmation of Philip's fears that
the beams of day never penetrated to the place of his
confinement.

The jailer took down the lantern, and having fastened
the lamp in its place, gave to the unfortunate woodman
a loaf of bread and a pitcher of water. "Come!" exclaimed Fouchard, in a tone which spoke no great pleasure in the task; "get up; I am to take off your irons for
you: and truly, there is no great use of them, for if you
were the devil himself, you could not get out here."

"I suppose so," answered Philip. "But I trust that it
will not be long before I am released altogether."

"Why, I should guess that it would not," answered the
jailer, in somewhat of a sarcastic tone, still continuing to
unlock the irons; "people do not in general stay here very
long."

"How so?" demanded Philip, anxiously, misdoubting
the tone in which the other spoke.

"Why," replied he, "you must know there are three
ways, by one of which prisoners are generally released,

as you say, altogether; and one way is as common as another, so far as my experience goes. Sometimes they die under the torture; at other times they are turned out to have their head struck off; or else they die of the damp: which last we call being homesick." And with this very consolatory speech he bundled up the irons under his arm, and quitted the cell, taking care to fasten the door behind him.

CHAPTER XVII.

Showing what it is to be a day after the fair; with sundry other matters,
which the reader cannot fully comprehend without reading them.

Having now left the woodman as unhappy as we could
wish, and De Blenau very little better off than he was
before, we must proceed with Pauline, and see what we
can do for her in the same way.

It has been already said that, in the hurry of her flight,
she struck her foot against a stone and fell. This is an
unpleasant accident at all times, and more especially when
one is running away; but Pauline suffered it not to interrupt her flight one moment longer than necessary. Finding that some unexpected obstacle had delayed her pursuer as well as herself, she was upon her feet in a
moment; and leaving him to arrange his difference with
Monsieur Chatpilleur in the best way he could, she flew
on towards the Rue Saint Antoine, without stopping to
thank her deliverer; and, indeed, without knowing that
the good aubergiste, taking a sincere interest in her fate,
had, at the hour appointed, waited at the door of his
auberge till he saw her enter the Bastile, and then, from
some undefined feeling that all would not go right, had
watched anxiously to see her safe out again.

The interest not being reciprocal, Pauline had forgot
all about the aubergiste; and only seeing that some one
obstructed her pursuer, she fled, as I have said before,
to the Rue Saint Antoine. She passed Jacques Chatpilleur's little auberge and darted by the boutique of a
passementier with the same celerity. The next shop
was a marchand de broderie et de dentelle, with a little
passage, or cul de sac, between it and the following house,

which was occupied by a brocanteur, both which trades
requiring daylight in aid of their operations, were at that
hour firmly closed with bolt and bar, nor shed one solitary ray to light the passenger along the streets.

Just as she had come opposite to the first of these, Pauline found some one seize her robe behind, and the next
minute a large Spanish cloak was thrown over her head,
while a gigantic pair of arms embracing her waist, raised
her from the ground and bore her along the street. Naturally conceiving that she was in the power of some of
her pursuers from the Bastile, Pauline did not perceive,
in the dreadful agitation of the moment, that she was carried in a different direction; and, giving herself up for
lost, she yielded to her fate without scream or cry. Whoever it was that held her carried her like a feather; but
after striding along through several turnings, he paused,
placed her on the ground, and still holding the cloak over
her head with one hand, seemed to open a door with the
other. The next moment he raised her again, though in
a different position, and carried her up what was evidently
a small winding staircase, at the top of which he again
opened a door, where, even through the cloak, Pauline
could perceive that they had entered some place which
contained a powerful light. The moment the door was
open some one exclaimed, " It is her! Oh, Jesu! yes, it
is her!" in a voice which sounded so like that of her maid
Louise, that Pauline was more than ever bewildered.
The person who had carried her now placed her in a
chair, and taking the additional security of tying the
cloak over her head, communicated for a few minutes
with the other person in whispers; after which Pauline
fancied that some one quitted the room. The covering
was then removed from her eyes, and she found herself
in a small, meanly-furnished apartment, whose only occupant, besides herself, was a handsome man, of very
gigantic proportions, and of that sort of daring aspect
which smacked a little of the bravo. He was well dressed

in a pourpoint of green lustring, braided with gold lace, slightly tarnished; the haut-de-chausses was of the same, tied down the side with red ribbons; and the cloak which he removed from Pauline's head seemed to form a part of the dress, though he had deprived himself of it for the moment, to answer the purpose in which we have seen it employed. On the whole, he was a good-looking cavalier, though there was a certain air of lawlessness in his countenance and mien which made Pauline shrink.

"Nay, do not be afraid, mademoiselle," said he, with a strong Norman accent. "Point de danger, point de danger;" and he strove to reassure her to the best of his power. He possessed no great eloquence, however, at least of the kind calculated to calm a lady's fears; and the only thing which tended to give Pauline any relief was the manifest respect with which he addressed her, standing cap in hand, and reiterating that no harm was intended or could happen to her.

She listened without attending, too much frightened to believe his words to their full extent, and striving to gain from the objects round about some more precise, knowledge of her situation. She was evidently not in the Bastile, for the door of the room, instead of offering to her view bolts and bars, of such complicated forms that, like the mousetrap, they would have puzzled the man that made them, was only fastened by a single wooden lock, the key of which, like a dog's tongue in a hot day, kept lolling out with a negligent inclination towards the ground, very much at ease in its keyhole. The more Pauline gazed around her, the more she was bewildered; and after resolving twenty times to speak to the Norman, and as often failing in courage, she at last produced an articulate sound, which went to inquire where she was. The Norman, who had been walking up and down the room, as if waiting the arrival of some one, stopped in the midst, and making a low inclination, begged to assure mademoiselle that she was in a place of safety.

The ice being broken, Pauline demanded, " Did not I hear the voice of my maid Louise? "

" No; it was my wife, mademoiselle," replied her companion dryly; and recommencing his perambulations, the young lady sank back into herself. At length a tap was heard at the door, and the Norman starting forward went on the outside, closing it after him, though not completely; and of the conversation which ensued between him and some other man, Pauline could catch detached sentences, which, though they served but little to elucidate her position to herself, may be of service to the reader.

At first all was conducted in a whisper, but the Norman soon broke forth, " Sachristie! I tell you she got in. I did not catch her till she was coming out."

" Monseigneur will be precious angry with us both," answered the other. " How I missed you, I cannot imagine; I only went to call upon la petite Jeanette, and did not stay five minutes."

" And I just stepped into the Sanglier Gourmand," rejoined our Norman, " which is opposite, you know. There I thought I could see all that went on. But that maraud, Jacques Chatpilleur, was always at his door about something; so finding that I could not get my second bottle of wine, I went down to the cave for it myself; and she must have passed while I was below."

" How did you find out, then, that she had got into the Bastile? " demanded the other.

The Norman's reply was delivered in so low a tone that Pauline could only distinguish the words—" Heard a scream—saw her running past like mad—threw the cloak over her, and brought her here."

" Perhaps she was not in, after all," rejoined the other; " but at all events, we must tell monseigneur so. You swear you caught her just as she was going in, and I'll vow that I was there and saw you."

A new consultation seemed to take place; but the speakers proceeded so rapidly, that Pauline could not comprehend upon what it turned exactly, although she was herself evidently the subject of discussion. " Oh, she will not tell, for her own sake," said one of the voices. " She would be banished, to a certainty, if it was known that she got in; and as to the folks at the Bastile, be sure that they will hold their tongues."

Something was now said about a letter, and the voice of the Norman replied, " Monseigneur does not suppose that she had a letter. Oh, no! trust me, she had none. It was word of mouth work, be you sure. They were too cunning to send a letter which might be stopped upon her. No, no, they know something more than that."

" Well, then, the sooner we take her there, the better," rejoined the other; " the carriage is below, but you must blind her eyes, for she may know the liveries."

" Ah! your cursed livery betrayed us once before," answered the Norman. " Holla! la haut! mon Ange, give me a kerchief; I will tie her eyes with that, for the cloak almost smothers her, poor little soul! "

A light step was now heard coming down-stairs, and a third person was added to the party without. What they said Pauline could not make out; but though speaking in a whisper, she was still confident that she distinguished the voice of her maid Louise. " Harm! " said the Norman, after a moment, " we are going to do her no harm, chère amie! She will be down there in Maine, with the countess, and as happy as a princess. Give this gentleman the trunk-mail, and get yourself ready against I come back; for we have our journey to take too, you know, ma petite femme."

The Norman now laid his hand upon the lock; there was a momentary bustle as of the party separating; and then entering the room, he informed Pauline that she must allow him to blindfold her eyes. Knowing that resistance was in vain, Pauline submitted with a good grace; and, her fears considerably allayed by the conversation she had overheard, attempted to draw from the Nor-

man some further information. But here he was in-
flexible; and having tied the handkerchief over her eyes,
so as completely to prevent her seeing, he conducted
her gently down the stairs, taking care to keep her from
falling; and having arrived in the open air, lifted her
lightly into a carriage, placed himself by her side, and
gave orders to drive on.

The vehicle had not proceeded many minutes, when it
again stopped; and Pauline was lifted out, conducted
up a flight of stone steps, and then led into an apartment,
where she was placed in a fauteuil, the luxurious softness
of which bespoke a very different sort of furniture from
that of the chamber which she had just left. There was
now a little bustle, and a good deal of whispering, and
then every one seemed to leave the room. Fancying
herself alone, Pauline raised her hand, in order to remove the handkerchief from her eyes, at least for a
moment; but a loud " Prenez garde! " from the Norman,
stopped her in her purpose, and the next instant a door
opened, and she heard steps approaching.

" Shut the door," said a voice she had never heard before. " Marteville, you have done well. Are you sure
that she had no conversation with any one in the prison? "

" I will swear to it! " answered the Norman, with the
stout asseveration of a determined liar. " Ask your man
Chauvelin, monseigneur; he was by, and saw me catch
hold of her before she was at the gate."

" So he says," rejoined the other; " but now leave the
room. I must have some conversation with this demoiselle myself. Wait for me without."

" Pardie! " muttered the Norman, as he withdrew;
" he'll find it out now, and then I'm ruined."

" Mademoiselle de Beaumont," said the person that remained, " you have been engaged in a rash and dangerous
enterprise—had you succeeded in it, the Bastile must
have been your doom, and severe judgment according to
the law. By timely information on the subject, I have

been enabled to save you from such a fate; but I am sorry to say that, for the safety of all parties, you must endure an absence from your friends for some time."

He paused, as if expecting a reply; and Pauline, after a moment's consideration, determined to answer, in order to draw from him, if possible, some further information concerning the manner in which he had become acquainted with her movements, and also in regard to her future destination. "I perceive, sir," said she, "from your conversation, that you belong to the same rank of society as myself; but I am at a loss to imagine how any gentleman presumes to attribute dangerous enterprises, and actions deserving imprisonment, to a lady, of whom he neither does, nor can know anything."

"My dear young lady," replied her companion, "you make me smile. I did not think that I should have to put forth my diplomatic powers against so fair and so youthful an opponent. But allow me to remind you that, when young ladies of the highest rank are found masquerading in the streets at night, dressed in their servants' garments, they subject their conduct, perhaps, to worse misconstructions than that which I have put upon yours. But, Mademoiselle de Beaumont, I know you, and I know the spirit of your family too well to suppose that anything but some great and powerful motive could induce you to appear as you do now. Withdraw that bandage from your eyes (I have no fear of encountering them), and look if that be a dress in which Mademoiselle de Beaumont should be seen."

Pauline's quick fingers instantly removed the handkerchief, and raising her eyes, she found that she was placed exactly before a tall Venetian mirror, which offered her a complete portrait of herself, sitting in an immense armchair of green velvet, and disguised in the costume of a Languedoc paysanne. The large capote, or hood, which she had worn, had been thrust back by the Norman, in order to blindfold her eyes, and her dark hair, all dis-

17

hevelled, was hanging about her face in glossy confusion. The red serge jupe of Louise had acquired in the passages of the Bastile no inconsiderable portion of dust; and near the knee on which she had fallen at the foot of the glacis, it was stained with mire, as well as slightly torn. In addition to all this, appeared a large rent at the side, occasioned by the efforts of Philip the woodman to disengage it from the staple on which it had caught; and the black bodice had been broadly marked with green mold, in pressing against the wall while the guards passed so near to her.

Her face also was deathly pale, with all the alarm, agitation, and fatigue she had undergone; so that no person could be more different from the elegant and blooming Pauline de Beaumont than the figure which that mirror reflected. Pauline almost started when she beheld herself; but quickly recovering from her surprise, she cast her eyes round the room, which was furnished in the most splendid and costly manner, and filled with a thousand objects of curiosity or luxury, procured from all the quarters of the globe.

Her attention, however, rested not upon any of these. Within a few paces of the chair in which she sat, stood a tall elegant man, near that period of life called the middle age, but certainly rather below than above the point to which the term is generally applied. He was splendidly dressed, according to the custom of the day, and the neat trimming of his beard and moustaches, the regular arrangement of his dark flowing hair, and the scrupulous harmony and symmetry of every part of his apparel, contradicted the thoughtful, dignified expression of his eyes, which seemed occupied with much higher thoughts.

He paused for a moment, giving her time to make what examination she liked of everything in the apartment; and as her eye glanced to himself, demanded with a smile, " Well, Mademoiselle de Beaumont, do you recollect me ? "

" Not in the least," replied Pauline; " I think, sir, that
we can never have seen each other before."

" Yes, we have," answered her companion; " but it
was at a distance. However, now look in that glass, and
tell me—do you recollect yourself? "

" Hardly ! " replied Pauline, with a blush " hardly, indeed ! "

" Well, then, fair lady, I think that you will no longer
demand my reasons for attributing to you dangerous enterprises and actions, as you say, deserving imprisonment;
but to put an end to your doubts at once, look at that
order, where, I think, you will find yourself somewhat
accurately described." And he handed to Pauline a small
piece of parchment, beginning with the words of serious
import, " De par le roy," and going on to order the arrest
of the Demoiselle Pauline, daughter of the late Marquis
de Beaumont, and of the Dame Anne de la Hautière;
with all those good set terms and particulars, which left
no room for mistake or quibble, even if it had been examined by the eyes of the sharpest lawyer of the Cour des
Aides.

" What say you now, Mademoiselle de Beaumont? "
demanded her companion, seeing her plunged in embarrassment and surprise.

" I have nothing to say, sir," replied Pauline, " but
that I must submit. However, I trust that, in common
humanity, I shall be allowed to see my mother, either
when I am in prison, or before I am conveyed thither."

" You mistake me," said the other; " you are not
going to a prison. I only intend that you should take a
little journey into the country; during the course of
which all attention shall be paid to your comfort and convenience. Of course, young lady, when you undertook
the difficult task of conveying a message from the queen
to a prisoner in the Bastile, you were prepared to risk
the consequences. As you have not succeeded, no great
punishment will fall upon you; but as it is absolutely

necessary to the government to prevent all communication between suspected parties, you must bear a temporary
absence from the court, till such time as this whole business be terminated; for neither the queen, nor any one
else, must know how far you have succeeded or failed."

Pauline pleaded hard to be allowed to see her mother,
but in vain. The stranger was obdurate, and would
listen to neither entreaties, promises, nor remonstrances.
All she could obtain was, the assurance that Madame de
Beaumont should be informed of her safety, and that,
perhaps, after a time she might be permitted to write
to her. " Listen to me," said the stranger, cutting short
the prayers by which she was attempting to influence
him. " I expect the king and court from Chantilly within
an hour; and before that time you must be out of Paris.
For your convenience, a female servant shall attend you,
and you will meet with all the respect due to your rank;
but for your own sake, ask no questions, for I never
permit my domestics to canvass my affairs with any one—
nay, they are forbidden ever to mention my name, except
for some express and permitted purpose. I will now
leave you, and send Mathurine to your assistance, who
will help you to change your dress from that coffre. You
will then take some refreshment, and set out as speedily
as possible. At the end of your journey you will meet
with one to whose care I have recommended you, and you
will then learn in whose hands you are placed. At present, I have the honor of bidding you farewell! "

The uncertainty of her fate, the separation from her
mother, the vague uneasy fear attendant upon want of all
knowledge of whither she was going, and the impossibility of communicating with her friends under any event,
raised up images far more terrifying and horrible to the
mind of Pauline, than almost any specific danger could
have done; and, as her companion turned away, she hid
her face in her hands and wept.

Hearing her sob, and perhaps attributing her tears to

other motives, he returned for a moment, and said in a
low voice: "Do not weep, my dear child! I give you my
honor, that you will be well and kindly treated. But one
thing I forgot to mention. I know that your object was
to visit the Count de Blenau; and I know, also, that a
personal interest had something to do in the matter.
Now, Mademoiselle de Beaumont, I can feel for you;
and it may be some comfort to know, that M. de Blenau
has, at least, one person in the council, who will strive
to give to the proceedings against him as much leniency
as circumstances will admit."

This said, he quitted the apartment, and in a moment
after Pauline was joined by the female servant of whom
he had spoken. She was a staid, reputable-looking woman, of about fifty, with a little of the primness of ancient
maiden-hood, but none of its acerbity. And, aware of
Pauline's rank, she assisted her to disentangle herself
from her uncomfortable disguise with silent respect,
though she could not help murmuring to herself. "Mon
Dieu! Une demoiselle mise comme ça." She then called
the young lady's attention to the contents of the coffre,
asking which dress she would choose to wear; when, to
her surprise, Pauline found that it contained a considerable part of her own wardrobe. Forgetting the prohibition to ask questions, she could not help demanding
of Mathurine how her clothes could come there; but the
servant was either ignorant, or pretended to be so, and
Pauline could obtain no information. As soon as she
was dressed, some refreshments were placed on the table
by Mathurine, who received them from a servant at one
of the doors, which she immediately closed again, and
pressed Pauline to eat. Pauline at first refused; but at
length, to satisfy her companion, who continued to insist
upon it with a degree of quiet, persevering civility, that
would take no refusal, she took some of the coffee, which
was at that time served up as a rarity. As soon as ever
the domestic perceived that no entreaty would induce

her to taste anything else, she called in a servant to carry the coffre to the carriage, and then notified to Pauline that it was time for them to depart.

Pauline felt that all resistance or delay would be vain; and she accordingly followed Mathurine down a magnificent staircase into a courtyard, where stood a carriage, the door of which was held open by the Norman we have already mentioned, while two men-servants appeared ready mounted to follow the vehicle, as soon as it set out. Mathurine placed herself by Pauline's side when she had entered; and the Norman, having closed the door, opened the porte-cochère of the court, and the carriage drove out into the street.

We will not take the trouble of following Mademoiselle de Beaumont on her journey, which occupied that night and the two following days:—suffice it to say, that on the evening of the second day they arrived in the beautiful neighborhood of Château du Loir, and after putting her head more than once from the window, Mathurine, with a smile of pleasure, pointed forward exclaiming, " Voilà le château."

Pauline's eyes followed to the point where the other's hand directed them; and upon a high ground, rising gently above the trees which crowned a little projecting turn of the river, she beheld a group of towers and pinnacles, with the conical-slated roofs, multifarious weathercocks, long narrow windows, one turret upon the back of another, and all the other distinctive marks of an old French château. I can easily imagine myself, and I dare say the reader will not find much difficulty in fancying, that the Count de Blenau suffered not a little inquietude while he remained in uncertainty respecting Pauline's free exit from the Bastille.

Take and draw him, as Sterne did his captive. See him walking up and down the chamber with the anxiety of doubt upon his brow and in his heart, listening for every sound in the courtyard, catching the footstep of the

sentinel at his door, and fancying it the return of the
governor,—hope struggling against fear, and fear remaining victor,—conjuring up a thousand wild, improbable events, and missing the true one, and, in short,
making his bosom a hell wherein to torment his own
heart.

Thus did Claude de Blenau, during that lapse of time
which the governor might reasonably be supposed to be
occupied in the duties of his office. But when a longer
time passed, and still no news arrived of Pauline's escape,
the uncertainty became too great for mortal endurance;
and he was about to risk all, by descending into the court
through the turret, when the challenge of the sentinel
announced the approach of some one, and in the next
moment the governor entered the room, his pale features
flushed with anger, and his lip quivering with ill-subdued
rage.

"Monsieur de Blenau!" said he, in a tone that he had
never before presumed to use towards his wealthy prisoner, there is something wrong. There has been a
woman in the prison to-night, passing for that rascal
woodman's daughter: and I am given to understand, that
she has brought either letter or message to you. But I
will ascertain the truth—by heaven! I will ascertain the
truth!"

"Have you detained her, then?" exclaimed De Blenau,
losing all caution in his fears for Pauline.

"Oh, ho! Monsieur le Comte," said the governor,
fixing on him his keen and angry eye; "then you do
know that she has been here? But do you know, sir, that
it may cost me my head?"

"Very possibly, if you tell anybody," replied De Blenau;
who by this time had recovered his self-possession,
and had, upon reconsideration, drawn from the governor's speech a different conclusion from that which he
had formed at first; feeling sure, that if Pauline had not
escaped, his anger would have taken a calmer form.

"Listen to me, Sir Governor," continued he firmly, after having determined in his own mind the line of conduct which he ought to pursue: "let us deal straightforwardly towards each other, and like friends as we have hitherto done. We are both in some degree in each other's power. On your part, do not attempt to entrap me into any acknowledgment, and I will show you that I will not make use of any advantage you may have given me——"

"I do not understand your meaning, sir," cried the governor, still angrily: "I have given you no advantage. By heaven! I will have the apartment searched;—ay, sir, and your person too."

"Will you so?" replied De Blenau, coolly drawing from his bosom the queen's billet, and approaching the edge to the lamp so that it caught fire. The governor started forward to seize it; but the strong arm of the count held him at a distance, till the few lines the queen had written were irretrievably destroyed; and then freeing him from his grasp, he pointed to a chair, saying, "Now, Monsieur le Gouverneur, sit down and listen to a few words of common sense." The governor placed himself in the chair with a look of bitter malignity; but this softened down gradually into an expression of thoughtful cunning, as De Blenau proceeded—"Thus stands the case," said the count; "I was committed to your charge, I think, with positive orders not to allow me communication with any person whatsoever—was it not so?" The governor assented. "It so happened, however," continued the count with a smile, "that at our very first interview, you conceived a friendship for me of the most liberal and disinterested nature" (the governor bit his lip), "a sort of love at first sight; and, for the sake of my accommodation, you not only broke through the positive commands of the cardinal prime minister, in suffering me once to have communication with another person, but allowed such to take place at all times, according to my pleasure; and also took especial pains to procure the attendance of the person I wished, paying him with my money, for which, and other excellent purposes, you have, within the space of six days, received from me upwards of one thousand crowns."

The governor winced most desperately; and fully convinced that a tale so told would readily convey his head under the axe of the executioner, if it reached the ears of Richelieu, he cursed himself for a fool, De Blenau for a knave, and Philip the woodman for something between the two; most devoutly wishing both the others at the devil, so he could slip his own neck out of the halter.

De Blenau, without much skill in reading the mind's construction by the face, easily divined what was passing in his companion's bosom; and perceiving him to be much in the situation of a lame dog, he resolved still to apply the lash a little before he helped him over the stile. " Well, Sir Governor," continued he : " now we will suppose, as a mere hypothesis to reason upon, that, through this very liberty which your disinterested kindness has allowed me, I have received those communications from without which it was the cardinal's great object to prevent. How ought you to act under such circumstances ? Ought you to go to the stern, unrelenting Richelieu, and say to him—" May it please your eminence, I have intentionally and wilfully broken through every order you gave me—I have taken the utmost pains that they should not be observed; and I have so far succeeded in thwarting your designs, that Monsieur de Blenau, from whom I have received one thousand crowns, and from whom I expect a thousand more the moment he is liberated—I say, that this good friend of mine, and your enemy, has gained all the information which you wished to prevent." This would be a pretty confession of faith ! "

De Blenau paused, and the governor bit his lip; but after a moment he looked the count full in the face, and replied, " Perhaps it might be the best way."

De Blenau, however, was not to be deceived; he saw

terror in the deadly hue of the governor's pale cheek, and
the anxious rolling of his sunken eye, and he went on—
"Perhaps it might be the best way—to have your head
struck off without delay; for what would your confession
avail the cardinal now, after the mischief is done?
Would it not be better to say to yourself—"Here is a
young nobleman, whom I believe to be innocent—for
whom I have a regard—whom I have served already,
and who is both willing and able to reward any one who
does serve him; and who, lastly, will never betray me, let
happen what will. Under these circumstances, should
I not be a fool of the first water, to inquire into a matter
the truth of which I am very unlikely to discover, and
which, if I do, it will be my duty to disclose: whereas,
standing as the affair does now, without my knowledge
in the least, my ignorance makes my innocence and I betray no one. Even supposing that the whole be found
out, I am no worse than I was before, for the story can
but be told at last; while, if the count be liberated, which
most likely he will, instead of losing my office, or my
head, I shall gain a thousand crowns to indemnify me
for all the trouble I have had, and shall ensure his
friendship for life." Now, Monsieur le Gouverneur, this
is what you ought to say to yourself. In my opinion, the
strength of argument is all on one side. Even if there
were anything to know, you would be a fool to investigate
it, where you must of necessity be your own accuser;
where all is to be lost, and nothing can be gained."

"You argue well, Monsieur de Blenau," answered the
governor, thoughtfully; "and your reasoning would be
convincing if it extended to all the circumstances of the
case. But you do not know one half;—you do not know
that Chavigni, from whose eyes nothing seems hidden,
knew of this girl's coming, and sent me an order to detain her, which that sottish fool the porter never gave me
till she had escaped. How am I to get over that, pray?"

"Then, positively, she has escaped?" demanded De Blenau.

"Yes, yes, she has escaped!" replied the governor, pettishly: "you seem to consider nothing but her; but, let me tell you, Monsieur de Blenau, that you are fully as much concerned as I am, for if they discover that she has got in, you will have a touch of the peine forte et dure, to make you confess who she is, and what she came for."

"Truly, I know not what can be done," answered the count. "Chavigni seems to know all about it."

"No, no! he does not know all," replied the governor; "for he says here, in his note, that if a young lady dressed in a jupe of red serge, with a black bodice, comes to the gate of the prison, asking anything concerning the Count de Blenau, we are to detain her: now she never mentioned your name, and, God knows, I heeded not what she was dressed in."

"Then the matter is very simple," replied the count: "no such person as he bade you detain has been here. This is no matter of honor between man and man, where you are bound to speak your suspicions as well as your knowledge. No person has come to the gate of the prison asking anything concerning me; and so answer Chavigni."

"But the porter, Monsieur de Blenau," said the officer, anxiously,—"he may peach. All the other dependants on the prison are my own, placed by me, and would turn out were I to lose my office; but this porter was named by the cardinal himself. What is to be done with him?"

"Oh! fear not him," answered De Blenau; "as his negligence was the cause of your not receiving the order in time to render it effectual, your silence will be a favor to him."

"True! true!" cried the governor, rubbing his hands with all the rapture of a man suddenly relieved from a mortal embarrassment: "True! true! I'll go and bully

him directly—I'll threaten to inform the cardinal, and
Chavigni, and the whole council; and then—when he
begins to fancy that he feels the very rope round his
neck—I'll relent, and be charitable, and agree to conceal
his mistake, and to swear that the lady never came.—How
will Chavigni know? She will never confess it herself,
and at that hour it was too dark for any one to watch her
up to the gates.—Morbleu! that will do precisely."

"I see little or no danger attending upon it," said the
prisoner; "and, at all events, it is a great deal better
than conveying your neck into the noose, which you would
certainly do by confessing to Richelieu the circumstances
as they have occured."

"Well, well, we will risk it, at all events," replied the
governor, who, though not quite free from apprehension
respecting the result, had now regained his usual sweet
complacency of manner. "But one thing, Monsieur de
Blenau, I am sure you will promise me; namely, that
this attempt shall never be repeated, even if occasion
should occur; and for the rest—with regard to your
never betraying me, and other promises which your
words imply, I will trust to your honor."

De Blenau readily agreed to what the governor required, and repeated his promises never to disclose anything that had occurred, and to reward his assistance
with a thousand crowns, upon being liberated. Mindful
of all who served him, he did not forget Philip the woodman; and deeply thankful for the escape of Pauline, was
the more anxious to ascertain the fate of one who had
so greatly contributed to the success of her enterprise.

"Speak not of him!" speak not of him!" exclaimed
the governor, breaking forth into passion at De Blenau's
inquiries. "This same skilful plotter attends upon you
no longer. You will suffer some inconvenience for your
scheme; but it is your fault, not mine, and you must put
up with it as best you may."

"That I care not about," replied De Blenau. "But I

insist upon it that he be treated with no severity. Mark me, Monsieur le Gouverneur: if I find that he is ill used, Chavigni shall hear of the whole business. I will risk anything sooner than see a man suffer from his kindness for me."

"You paid him well, of course," said the governor, drawing up his lip, "and he must take his chance. However, do not alarm yourself for him: he shall be taken care of—only, with your good leave, Seigneur Comte, you and he do not meet again within the walls of the Bastile.—But in the name of Heaven! what clatter is this at the door?" he exclaimed, starting from his chair, at a most unusual noise which proceeded from the staircase.

The governor, indeed, had good reason to be astonished; for never was there a more strange and inconsistent sound heard within the walls of a prison than that which saluted their ears. First came the "Qui vive?" of the sentinel; to which a voice cried out, "Le diable!" "Qui vive?" cried the sentinel again in a still sharper key. The answer to this was nothing but a clatter, as the governor had expressed it, such as we might suppose produced by the blowing up of a steam-kitchen: then followed the discharge of the sentinel's firelock; and then sundry blows given and received upon some hard and sonorous substance, mingled with various oaths, execrations, and expletives then in use amongst the lower classes of his Christian majesty's lieges, making altogether a most deafening din.

At this sound the governor, as little able to conceive whence it originated as De Blenau himself, drew his sword, and throwing open the door, discovered the redoubtable Jacques Chatpilleur, cuisinier aubergiste, striding in triumph over the prostrate body of the sentinel, and waving over his head an immense stew-pan, being the weapon with which he had achieved the victory, and through which appeared a small round hole, caused by the ball of the soldier's firelock. In the meanwhile was to be seen the sentinel on the ground, his iron morion actually dented by the blows of his adversary, and his face and garments bedabbled, not with blood, indeed, but with the poulet en blanquette and its white sauce, which had erst been tenant of the stew-pan.

"Victoria! Victoria! Victoria!" shouted the aubergiste, waving his stew-pan. "Twice have I conquered in one night! Can Mielleraye or Bouillon say that? Victoria! Victoria!" But here his triumph received a check; for looking into the unhappy utensil, he suddenly perceived the loss of its contents, which had flown all over the place, the treacherous lid having detached itself during his conflict with the sentinel, and sought safety in flight down the stairs. "Mon poulet! mon poulet!" exclaimed he, in a tone of bitter despair, the nest is there, but the bird is flown. Hélas, mon poulet! mon pauvre poulet!" and quitting the body of his prostrate foe, he advanced into the apartment with that sort of zigzag motion which showed that the thin sinewy shanks which supported his woodcock-shaped upper man, were somewhat affected by a more than usual quantity of the generous grape.

The whole scene was so inexpressibly ludicrous, that De Blenau burst into an immoderate fit of laughter, in which the governor could not help joining, notwithstanding his indignation at the treatment the sentinel had experienced. Recovering himself, however, he poured forth his wrath upon the aubergiste in no measured terms, demanding how he dared to conduct himself so in the Royal Château of the Bastile, and what had become of the Count de Blenau's supper, adding a few qualificatory epithets, which may as well be omitted.

"Eh bien, monsieur! Eh bien!" cried the aubergiste, with very little respect for the governor: "as for the gentleman there, lying on his belly, he ought to have let me in, and not fired his piece at me. He knew me well enough. He might have cried qui vive? once,—that was well, as it is the etiquette."

"But why did you not answer him, sacré maraud?" cried the governor.

"I did answer him," replied the other, stoutly. "He cried, Qui vive? and I answered, Le diable, car le diable vive toujours. And as for the supper, I have lost it all. Je l'ai perdu entre deux matins. The first was a greedy Norman vagabond, who feeds at my auberge; and while I was out for a minute, he whips me up my matelot d'anguille from out of the casserole, and my dinde piquée from the spit, and when I came back five minutes after, there was nothing left but bare bones and empty bottles. Pardie! And now I have bestowed on the head of that varlet a poulet en blanquette that might have comforted the stomach of a king. Oh Dieu! Dieu! mes malheurs ne finiront jamais. Oh; but I forgot," he continued, "there is still a fricandeau à l'oseille with a cold paté, that will do for want of a better.—Monseigneur, votre serviteur," and he bowed five or six times to De Blenau; "Monsieur le Gouverneur, votre très humble," and bowing round and round to every one, even to the sentinel, who by this time was beginning to recover his feet, the tipsy aubergiste staggered off, escaping the wrath of the governor by the promise of the fricandeau, but not, however, without being threatened with punishment on the morrow.

CHAPTER XVIII.

The bureau of a councilor of state, or how things were managed in 1642.

"MARTEVILLE, you have served me essentially," said
the Count de Chavigni as soon as he had left Pauline in
what was called the ladies' hall of the Hôtel de Bouthilliers, addressing the tall Norman, whom the reader has
already recognized beyond a doubt. "You know I
never suffer any good service to go without its reward;
therefore I will now pay you yours, more especially as I
have fresh demands to make upon your zeal. Let us
see how our accounts stand;" and approaching a small
table, which served both for the purposes of a writing-
desk and also to support a strong ebony cabinet clasped
with silver, he drew forth a bunch of keys and opened a
drawer plated with iron, which contained a quantity of
gold and silver coin. Chavigni then seated himself at the
table, and the Norman standing on his right hand, they
began regularly to balance accounts, the items of the
Norman's charge being various services of rather a curious nature.

"For stopping the archduke's courier," said Chavigni,
"and taking from him his despatches—fifty crowns is
enough for that."

"I demand no more," said Marteville; "any common
thief could have done it."

"But, by-the-way, I hope you did not hurt him, for he
came with a safe conduct."

"Hurt him! no," replied the Norman; "we are the
best friends in the world. When I met him on the road,
I told him civilly that I must have his despatches; and that
I would either cut his throat or drink a bottle with him,

whichever he liked: so he chose the latter, and when we parted, he promised to give me notice the next time he came on the same errand."

"The rascal!" said Chavigni, "that is the way we are served. But now we come to this business of the Count de Blenau—what do you expect for the whole concern?"

"Nay but, monseigneur, you forget," exclaimed the other; "there is one little item before that. Put down, —for being an astrologer."

"Why, I have given you fifty crowns on that account already," rejoined the statesman; "you are exorbitant, Seigneur Marteville."

"That fifty crowns went for my expenses—all of it," replied the other. "There was my long black robe all covered with gimcracks; there was my leathern belt, painted with all the signs under heaven; there was my white beard, and wig, which cost me ten good crowns at the shop of Jansen the peruquier: besides the harness of my horse, which was made to suit, and my astrologer's bonnet, which kept all fast upon my head. Now, monseigneur, you cannot give me less than fifty crowns, for being out two nights, and running the risk of being burnt alive."

"I think not," said Chavigni, "so let that pass. But to come to the other business."

"Why, first and foremost," replied the Norman, marking each article as he named it, by laying the index of his right hand upon one of the immense fingers of his left,—"For making love to mademoiselle's maid."

"Nay, nay, nay!" cried Chavigni, "this is too much. That must be part of the dower I have promised with her, of which we will talk presently. But have you married her?"

"No," answered the Norman, "not yet. We will see about that hereafter."

Chavigni's cheek reddened, and his brow knit into a heavy frown. "No evasions, sir. I commanded you,

18

when you took her away last night from Chantilly, to
marry her directly, and you agreed to do so. Why is it
not done?"

"Well, well, monseigneur," replied the other, seeing
the fire that flashed in his lord's eye, "I will marry her:
foy de Normand! Don't be angry; I will marry her."

"Foy de Normand; will not do," said Chavigni. "It
must be this very night."

"Eh bien! Eh bien! Soit," cried the Norman, and then
muttered to himself with a grin, "I've four wives now
living; a fifth won't make much difference."

"What murmur you, sir?" demanded the statesman.
"Mark me! in one hour from hence you will find a priest
and two witnesses in the cardinal's chapel! When you
are married the priest will give you a certificate of the
ceremony, carry it to my intendant, and upon the sight
of it he will pay you the sum we agree upon. Now,
proceed with your demands."

"Well, then, monseigneur," continued Marteville,
"what is the information concerning mademoiselle's
coming to Paris worth?"

"It is worth a good deal," replied Chavigni, "and I
will always pay more for knowledge of that kind than
any acts of brute force. Set that down for a hundred
crowns, and fifty more for catching the young lady, and
bringing her here; making altogether two hundred and
fifty."

"Yes, sir, yes; but the dot—the dowry you mentioned,"
cried the Norman. "You have forgot that."

"No, I have not," replied Chavigni. "In favor of
Louise I will make the sum up one thousand crowns,
which you will receive the moment you have married
her."

"Oh! I'll marry her directly, if that be the case," cried
the Norman. "Morbleu! that makes all the difference."

"But treat her kindly," said Chavigni. "With the
stipend of a thousand crowns, which I allow you yearly,

and what you can gain by particular services, you may live very well; and perhaps I may add some little gratification, if you please me in your conduct towards your wife."

" Oh! I'll be the tenderest husband living," cried the Norman, " since my gratification depends upon hers. But I'll run and fetch her to be married directly, if you will send the priest, monseigneur."

" Nay, stop a moment," said the statesman. " You forget that I told you I had other journeys for you to take, and other services for you to perform."

" No, sir," answered the Norman, " all is prepared to set out this very night, if you will tell me my errand."

Chavigni paused for a moment, and remained in deep thought, gnawing his lip as if embarrassed by doubts as to the best manner of proceeding. " Mark me, Marteville," said he at length : " there are two or three sorts of scoundrels in the world, amongst whom I do not look upon you as the least." The Norman bowed with the utmost composure, very well aware of the place he held in Chavigni's opinion. " There are, however, some good points about you," continued the statesman; at which Marteville bowed again. " You would rob, kill, and plunder, I believe, without remorse, any one you hated or did not care about; but I do not think you would forget a kindness or betray a trust."

" Never! " said the Norman: " red hot pincers will not tear from me what is entrusted to my honor."

" So be it, then, in the present instance," said Chavigni; " for I am obliged to give you the knowledge of some things, and to enter into explanations with you which I do not often do with any one. You must know, then, I have information that on the same day that Monsieur de Cinq Mars set out from Chantilly with Monsieur de Thou, the Duke of Orleans, with Montressor and St. Ibal, took their departure from Moulins, and the Count de Fontrailles from Paris. They all journeyed towards the same point in Champagne. I can trace Fontrailles to Troyes, the duke and his companion to Villeneuve, and Cinq Mars and De Thou to Nogent, but no further. All this might be accidental, but there are circumstances that create suspicion in my mind. Cinq Mars, when he set forth, gave out that he went to his estate near Troyes, in which I find he never set his foot; and when he returned his conference with Louis was somewhat long. It might have been of hawks and hounds, it is true; but after it the king's manner both to the cardinal and myself was cold and haughty, and he suddenly took this resolution of coming to Paris himself to examine into the case of the young Count de Blenau:—in short, I suspect that some plot is on foot. What I require of you then is, to hasten down to Champagne; try to trace each of these persons, and discover if they had a conference, and where; find out the business that brought each of them so far, examine their track as you would the slot of a deer, and give me whatever information you collect; employ every means to gain a thorough knowledge of all their proceedings—force, should it be required—but let that be the last thing used. Here is this signet, upon the sight of which all the agents of government in the different towns and villages will communicate with you." And he drew from his finger a small seal ring, which the Norman consigned to his pocket, his hands being somewhat too large to admit of his wearing it in the usual manner.

"The Duke of Orleans and his pack I know well," answered Marteville, "and also Cinq Mars and De Thou; but this Count de Fontrailles—what like is he, monseigneur?"

"He is a little ugly mean-looking man," replied Chavigni; "he frequently dresses himself in gray, and looks like a sorcerer. Make him your first object; for if ever there was a devil of cunning upon earth, it is Fontrailles, and he is at the bottom of the plot if there be one."

"You traced him to Troyes, you say, monseigneur? Had he any pretence of business there?"

"None," answered Chavigni; "my account says that he had no attendants with him, lodged at the Auberge du Grand Soleil, and was poorly dressed."

"I will trace him if he were the devil himself," said the Norman; "and before I see you again monseigneur, I shall be able to account for each of these gentry."

"If you do," said Chavigni, "a thousand crowns is your reward; and if you discover any plot or treasonable enterprise, so that by your means they may be foiled and brought to justice the thousand shall grow into ten thousand, and you shall have a place that will give you a life of luxury."

The Norman's eyes sparkled at the anticipation, and his imagination portrayed himself and his five wives living together in celestial harmony, drinking the best vintages of Burgundy and Epernay, eating of the fat of the land, and singing like mad. These blissful ideas were first interrupted by the sound of horses' feet in the court. "Hark!" cried Chavigni, "they are putting the horses to the carriage; go down, and see that all be prepared for the young lady's journey."

"Instantly," answered the Norman, "and after that I will carry Louise to the priest, finger your lordship's cash, and we will set off for Troyes."

"Do you intend to take her with you?" demanded Chavigni, in some surprise.

"Nay, my lord, you would not wish me to leave my bride on our wedding night, surely," replied the Norman, in a mock sentimental tone. "But the truth is, I think she may be useful. Woman's wit will often find a way where man's wisdom looks in vain; and as I have now, thanks to your bounty, two good horses, I shall e'en set Louise upon one of them, and with the bridle rein over my arm lead her to Brie, where, with your good leave, we will sleep, and thence on upon our journey. Travelling with a woman, no one will suspect my real object, and I shall come sooner at my purpose."

"Well, so be it then," answered the statesman. "You are now, as you wished to be, intrusted with an affair of more importance than stopping a courier, or carrying off a weak girl; and as the reward is greater, so would be the punishment in case you were to betray your trust. I rely on your honor; but let me hint at the same time, that there is such a thing as the rack, which has more than once been applied to persons who reveal state secrets. Keep good account of your expenses, and such as are truly incurred for the government, the government will pay."

Thus ended the conference between Chavigni and the Norman, neither of whom we shall follow much farther at present. Of Chavigni it is only necessary to say, that immediately after the departure of Pauline he proceeded to the Louvre to wait the arrival of Louis the Thirteenth, who soon after entered Paris accompanied by the queen, Cinq Mars, and all the usual attendants of the court, and followed by the cardinal and those members of the council who had not previously arrived along with Chavigni.

In regard to the Norman, inspired by the agreeable prospect of a thousand crowns, he was not long in visiting the chapel of the Palais Cardinal, where the priest speedily united him to a black-eyed damsel that he brought in his hand.

XIX.

Showing how a great minister made a great mistake.

THE more the Count de Blenau reflected upon his situation, the more he was puzzled in regard to his future conduct. A fresh examination, either by Lafemas or some member of the council, was to be expected speedily, under which he must either still refuse to answer, which would infallibly be followed by the peine forte et dure; or he must acknowledge that the queen had privily conveyed him an order to confess all, which would involve his royal mistress and himself and Pauline in dangers, the extent of which he hardly knew; or he must reply to the questions he had before refused to answer, and disclose what had been intrusted to his honor, without showing that he was authorized to do so; in which case, the reproach of treachery and cowardice must inevitably fall upon his name. De Blenau was sadly chewing the cud of these bitter doubts, when he heard some one enter the outer chamber; and the moment after, the very privacy of his bedroom was invaded by the governor, who entered with a countenance pale and agitated; and who, like all people who have something horrible to communicate, begged him not to be alarmed, in a tone that was enough to frighten him out of his wits.

" Alarmed at what? " demanded the count, summoning courage to encounter the danger, whatever it might be.

" Why, Monsieur de Blenau," answered the governor, " you must prepare yourself to meet the cardinal himself; a messenger has just come to say that he will be here in person without loss of time. He arrived last night at the Palais Cardinal, and brought the king to Paris with him."

"You seem to hold this cardinal in some fear," said
De Blenau, almost smiling amidst his own embarrass‧
ment, at the evident terror of the governor. "I could
have wished that he had given me a little more time for
consideration; but I am not so frightened at him as you
seem to be, who have nothing to do with it."

"But pray remember, mon cher comte," cried the
governor, "that you promised not to betray me to the
cardinal in any case.

De Blenau's lip curled with contempt. "I think you
ought to know before this time, answered he, "that I am
not likely to betray any one.—But there seems a noise
and bustle in the court, in all probability caused by the
arrival of the cardinal. Go and receive him, and depend
upon me."—Of all misfortunes on the earth, thought De
Blenau, the curse of cowardice is the most dreadful.

In a few minutes his supposition respecting the arrival
of the cardinal was confirmed by a summons to appear
before the council in the hall of audience; and with his
mind still undecided, he followed the officer across the
court to the scene of his former examination. A differ‧,
ence, however, struck him in the present arrangements of
the prison, from those which he had before remarked.

The court, instead of being crowded by those prisoners
who had the liberty of walking in it, was now entirely
void; and, fixed like marble on each side of the door
opening into the audience-hall, was a soldier of the cardinal's guard, between whom stood a clerk, or greffier,
of the council-chamber, seemingly waiting for the approach of the prisoner. As soon as De Blenau was
within hearing, the doors were thrown open, and the
clerk pronounced, "Claude, Count de Blenau appear before the king in council."

"The king!" thought De Blenau; "this cardinal, not
content with taking the king's guards, must take his title
also:—but passing on through the open doors he entered
the hall, where a very different scene presented itself

from that which had before met his eyes in the same place.

The whole farther part of the chamber was filled with the officers and attendants of Richelieu: each side, as well as the interstices between the massy pillars that supported the roof, was occupied by a body of the cardinal's guard: in the chair at the head of the table sat the king himself with the prime minister on his right hand: Chavigni, Bouthilliers, Mazarin, and others occupied seats on either side; and to complete the array appeared several clerks, together with the officers of the prison, leaving, only the space of about three feet at the bottom of the table, which remained clear for the prisoner to present himself opposite the throne.

Extraordinary as it was for the king himself to sit upon the examination of a state prisoner, the whole demeanor and conduct of the monarch had undergone a change since the return of Cinq Mars, which astonished those about him more than even his resolution to be present at the council held that morning in the Bastile. Even those who were most accustomed to watch the changes of the king's variable disposition, would hardly have recollected in the sovereign, who, with the easy dignity and self-possession of a clear and intelligent mind, presided at the head of the council-table, the same man who in general yielded his very thoughts to the governance of Richelieu, and abandoned all his kingly duties to one whom he appeared both to dislike and dread. But so it was, that, stimulated by some unseen means, Louis seemed at once to have resumed the king; and as soon as De Blenau entered the audience-hall, he at once opened the business of the day himself with all those powers which his mind really possessed when called into activity.

"Monsieur de Blenau," said the king, "we are glad to see you. We have heard much of you, and that always a good report, from those that we love, and therefore our confidence in your honor and integrity is great. There

will be various questions asked of you to-day by the
members of the council present, which much affect the
welfare of the kingdom, and our own personal happiness;
and to these questions we command you, as a good subject and an honest man, to answer truly, and according
to your conscience, without any reservation whatsoever."

Before entering the audience-hall, De Blenau, well
knowing that every careless word might be subject to
misconstruction, had determined to speak as little as possible; and therefore merely answering the king's speech
by a profound inclination of the head, he waited in silence
for the questions to which he had alluded.

Richelieu, the keen searching glance of whose eyes
had been fixed upon him during the whole time, paused
for a moment in expectation of a reply; but seeing that
he said nothing, the minister proceeded himself. " I
have heard with astonishment, Monsieur de Blenau,"
said he, " that you have lately refused to answer questions, to which you had before replied in conversation
with me; and I can conceive no reason, sir, why you
should object to give satisfaction on these points one day
as much as another."

" Nor can I conceive," replied De Blenau, " any reason
why your eminence should cause questions to be put to
me again which I had before answered; and that reiteration even while the replies were yet new in your mind."

" My memory might want refreshing," answered the
cardinal; " and you must also remember that the circumstances were very different at the two periods in
which those questions were addressed to you. In the
first place, you spoke merely in conversation; in the
second case, you were a prisoner, and it was therefore
necessary that your deposition should be taken from your
own mouth.—But all this is irrelevant. The council is
not inclined to take notice of your former contumacy,
provided you now reply to what shall be asked you."

De Blenau was again silent, merely bowing to signify
that he comprehended, without pledging himself either
to answer or not; and Richelieu proceeded with his questions, placing his hand as he did so, upon a large packet
of open letters which lay on the table before him.

"You have already informed me, Monsieur de Blenau,
if I remember rightly," said the minister, "that you have
at various times forwarded letters for the queen, both by
the usual public conveyances and otherwise."

The king fixed his eyes intently upon the count, while
he replied at once, "I have done so!"

"Can you remember," continued the cardinal, "during
what period you have been accustomed to send these
letters for the queen? I mean, of what date was the
first?"

"I cannot precisely at this moment call to mind," answered De Blenau, "but it was shortly after your eminence appointed me, or rather recommended me to the
office of chamberlain to her majesty."

"You see, sire," said Richelieu, turning to the king
with a menacing glance, "just before the taking of Arras
by the Imperialists——"

"Exactly so, your eminence; I remember it by a circumstance that occurred at the time," interposed De
Blenau, misdoubting the effect of the cardinal's com-
ments.

Richelieu gave him a gracious smile for this confirmation of his remark. "Pray, what circumstance was that,
Monsieur de Blenau?" demanded he; but his smile was
soon clouded by the count's reply.

"It was that the lace lappets, in order to procure which
her majesty wrote that letter to Brussels, were seized at
Arras, that city having fallen into the enemy's hands.
The queen was much grieved thereat. You know, monseigneur, ladies set great store by their apparel."

Chavigni smiled, but Richelieu's brow gathered into a
heavy frown, and his reply was in that deep hollow tone

of voice, by which alone one could distinguish when he was affected by any powerful feeling. His brow at all times remained calm, except when he sought to awe or intimidate; his eye, too, was under command, scanning the passions of others, and expressing none of his own, but those which he himself wished to appear; but his voice betrayed him, and when internally agitated it would sink to so low and cavernous a sound that it seemed as if the dead were speaking. It was in this tone that he answered De Blenau.

"The contents of that letter, sir, are but too well known by their effects. But I am to conclude from your observation, that you are as well aware of what the queen's letters have contained, as the persons to whom they were addressed."

"Not so, your eminence," replied De Blenau. "The import of that letter I happened to be acquainted with by accident, but I pretend to no farther knowledge."

"Yes, yes, sir," said Richelieu, "it is very evident that you know well to be informed or not on any subject, as it suits your purpose."

"Nay, Monsieur le Cardinal," interposed the king, "I think the young gentleman answers with all candor and discretion. We do not seek to perplex him, but to hear the truth; and I am sure that he will not discredit his birth or honor by prevarication."

"Your majesty's own honorable mind does justice to mine," replied the count; "I will own that I am guarded in my speech; for surrounded by those who seek to draw matter from my mouth, on which to found some accusation against me, I were a fool to speak freely. Nevertheless, I will answer truly to whatsoever I do answer; and if there should come a question to which I cannot reply without betraying my duty, I will tell no falsehood, but, as I have done before, refuse to answer, and the consequences of my honesty be upon my own head."

"Well, sir," said the cardinal, "if you have done the

harangue with which you are edifying the council, I will
proceed with my questions; but first let me tell you that I
am not disposed to be dared with impunity. I think you
denied to me that you had ever forwarded any letters
to Don Francisco de Mello, Leopold Archduke of Austria,
or Philip King of Spain.—Beware what you say Claude
Count de Blenau!"

"If I understand your eminence rightly," said the
prisoner, "you do not ask me whether I ever did forward such letters, but whether I ever denied to you that
I did forward them; in which case, I must reply, that I did
deny having expedited any letter to Don Francisco de
Mello, but the two other names I never touched upon."

"Then you acknowledge that you have conveyed letters
from the queen to the archduke and King of Spain?"
demanded Richelieu.

"I have made no such acknowledgment," answered
De Blenau; "your eminence puts a forced construction on
my words."

"In vain you turn, sir, like a rebellious serpent that
strives in its windings to escape the hand that grasps it.
At once I ask you, have you or have you not ever, by
any means, expedited any letter from the queen, or other
person, to either the Archduke of Austria, or the King of
Spain? This, sir, is a question that you cannot get over!"

The eyes of the whole council fixed upon the count as
the cardinal spoke. De Blenau paused for a moment to
recollect himself, and then addressed himself directly to
the king. "As a good and faithful subject," he said,
"there is a great duty which I owe your majesty, and I
believe I have always performed it as I ought; but as a
servant of your royal consort the queen, I have other
duties, distinct, though I hope in no degree opposed to
those which bind me to my king. As a man of honor,
also, and a gentleman, I am bound to betray no trust reposed in me, whether that trust seem to me material or
not; and though I feel sure that I might at once answer

the questions proposed to me by his eminence of Richelieu
without any detriment or discredit to her majesty, yet so
sacred do I hold the confidence of another, that I must
decline to reply, whatever be the consequence. However, let me assure you, sire, that no word or deed of her
majesty the queen, which has ever come to my ears, has
been derogatory to your majesty's dignity, or contrary to
your interest."

"Then I am to conclude that you refuse to answer?"
said Richelieu, sternly; "think, Monsieur de Blenau,
before you carry your obstinacy too far."

"My conduct does not arise in obstinacy," replied De
Blenau, "but from a sense of what is due to my own
honor; and unless it can be shown me that it is her
majesty's desire I should inform your eminence of all I
know respecting her affairs, from henceforth I hold my
tongue, and answer no further questions whatever."

"Be the consequence on your own head then, young
man," exclaimed the cardinal. "We will now break up the
council. Monsieur de Blenau, take leave of the sun, for
you never see another morrow!"

De Blenau's courage was unshaken, but yet a cold
chilly feeling gathered round his heart as Richelieu bade
him take leave of the sun, and rose to break up the council. But still the king kept his seat, and Chavigni, hastily
writing a few words on a scrap of paper, handed it to
the cardinal, who, after reading it, appeared to think
for a moment, and then again addressed De Blenau.
"There is one hope still left for you, sir: did Monsieur
de Chavigni understand you rightly, that if you had the
queen's command to confess what you know of her affairs, you would answer the questions we put to you?"

De Blenau breathed freely. "Undoubtedly!" replied
he; "my honor will then be satisfied, and there will be
no subject on which I shall have a reserve."

"What will you consider a sufficient expression of her
majesty's commands to that effect?" asked Chavigni:

"I know that his eminence wishes to treat you with all possible lenity, although the mere command of the king in council ought to be sufficient warrant for you to yield any information that may be required."

"We think differently on many points, Monsieur de Chavigni," answered De Blenau; "but if you can show me her handwriting to any order, or if one of the officers of her household will bear me a message from her majesty to deliver what little I know of her affairs, I will do so without further hesitation."

There was now a momentary consultation carried on in a low voice amongst the various members of the council, apparently concerning which of the queen's attendants should be sent for; but at length Chavigni whispered to the cardinal, "Send for La Rivière; he is a friend of Lafemas, and will do anything he is bid."

"If Monsieur de La Rivière bear you the queen's commands, will you be satisfied, Sir Count?" demanded Richelieu.

"The queen's gentleman-usher," said De Blenau; "most assuredly; that will be sufficient."

"Go yourself, Chavigni," whispered Richelieu; "and as you come, tell him what to say. We will wait his arrival," he proceeded aloud; "but see, Monsieur de Chavigni, that he communicates with the queen, and be fully informed of her wishes."

De Blenau smiled, convinced from his late information through Pauline that the queen was still at Chantilly, and therefore that though La Rivière might be himself in Paris, and ready to swear anything that the cardinal dictated, he could have no communication with Anne of Austria, unless, what seemed improbable, she had returned to the capital with the king.

As soon as De Chavigni had retired for the purpose of seeking La Rivière, Richelieu ran his eye over some memoranda, as if about to put further questions to De Blenau; but the king, not noticing these indications of

his purpose, addressed the prisoner himself. " Well,
Monsieur le Comte," said he, " while Chavigni is gone,
there are two or three points on which I shall be glad to
speak with you.

Richelieu was surprised, and not particularly delighted,
thinking that the king was about to continue the examination himself, which might not be conducted precisely in
such a manner as to produce the effect he wished; but,
in the independent mood with which Louis was affected,
he dared not, with all his daring, attempt to interrupt the
course of his sovereign's proceedings, and therefore remained silent, watching the opportunity of interposing,
to give what turn he best could to the interrogatory that
appeared about to commence. In the meanwhile De
Blenau bowed his head, calmly prepared to bear the mental torture of a long cross-examination, where every word
might be subject to dangerous misconstruction.

" I understand, Monsieur de Blenau," continued the
king, while the whole council listened with attentive expectation—" I understand that you have the best breed of
boar-dogs in France. Pray are they of the Pomeranian
or the Exul race?—and how can they be procured? "

Richelieu bit his lip; but to De Blenau the king's question was like the clearing away of a threatened storm;
and habitually attached to the chase, as well as deeply
learned in all its mysteries, he was delighted to find that
Louis turned the conversation to a subject equally familiar
to both.

" Mine are the true Pomeranian breed, sire," he replied; " flewed an inch deep, with eyes like Sandarak—
would light your majesty home at night, if by chance you
lost your way. In truth, they are only fit for a monarch;
and Cinq Mars has now four couple of the best in education for your majesty, which, when well trained, and recovered from their wildness, he will present to your
majesty in my name; and I humbly hope that you will
accept them in aid of your royal sport."

"We shall, we shall; and thank you well, Sir Count,"
replied the king, smiling most graciously at the prospect
of possessing a breed which he had been long seeking for
in vain. "Monsieur le Cardinal, do you hear that? We
will hunt with them some day. You used to hunt in
your day too; have you quite given it over?"

"I have been too much busied, sire," answered Richelieu gravely, "in hunting from your majesty's dominions
Huguenot wolves and Spanish foxes, to pursue other
game."

Louis turned from him with an uneasy shrug, expressive of fully as much distaste for Richelieu's employments
as the statesman experienced for his; and once more addressing De Blenau, he plunged deep into the science of
hunting, hawking, and fowling; giving the young count
a thousand receipts, instructions, and anecdotes, which
he listened to with the most reverential deference, not
only inasmuch as they proceeded from his sovereign, but
also as coming from the most experienced sportsman of
the age.

In the meanwhile, Richelieu was fain to employ himself in writing notes and memoranda, to allay the spleen
and irritation that he felt at what he internally termed the
king's weak trifling; till at length he was relieved by the
return of Chavigni, bringing with him the queen's usher,
La Rivière.

De Blenau well knew that this person, who was by
birth just within the rank of a gentleman (which word
was then in France one of great significance), had been
placed in the service of Anne of Austria for the purpose
of acting as a spy upon her, from Richelieu's fear of her
correspondence with Spain; but informed, as the count
now was, of the queen's wishes, it was perfectly indifferent to him who appeared on her behalf; his only object
being, that his mistress's commands, publicly expressed,
should, in the minds of all, free him from the imputation
of having betrayed her.

19

La Rivière looked round him, as he entered, with a
glance not altogether free from apprehension; for though
Chavigni had given him full instructions and information
concerning the services he was sent for to perform, yet
there was something so terrible in the idea of the Bastile,
that he could hardly keep his limbs from trembling as he
passed the gates of the prison.

"Come hither, Monsieur de La Rivière," exclaimed the
cardinal, as soon as he appeared: "We are wasting too
much time here." La Rivière approached, and placed
himself in the spot to which Richelieu pointed, almost
exactly opposite to De Blenau.

The Cardinal then proceeded. "Have you seen her
majesty the queen since Monsieur de Chavigni informed
you of the wishes of the council?"

"I have, may it please your eminence," replied La
Rivière, in a tremulous voice.

"And what was her majesty's reply to our request?"
asked Richelieu. "Speak boldly!" he added, in a tone
only calculated to reach the ear of the usher, who stood
close beside him, and showed plainly, by his hesitating
manner, that he was under the influence of alarm. The
cardinal, however, attributed this to a wrong cause, thinking that La Rivière had not really seen the queen, and
was about to play his part, as prompted by Chavigni, but
that in all probability he would spoil it by his hesitation.

Just as La Rivière was proceeding to answer, however,
Chavigni, who had taken his place at the council-table the
moment he entered, and had been writing rapidly since,
conveyed a slip of paper across to the cardinal, who
raised his hand for the usher to be silent while he read.
The words which his friend had written greatly discomposed the minister's plans. They were, "I am afraid
it will not succeed: I have seen the queen, when she not
only told La Rivière, at once, to command the count, in
her name, to answer every question that related to her,

but has given him a letter under her own hand to that effect. She is either innocent, or relies devotedly on De Blenau; whichever is the case, her open conduct will clear her in the mind of the king. Act as you like."

"What is the matter, monsieur le cardinal?" demanded Louis, somewhat impatiently. "Why do we not proceed?"

"Because," answered Richelieu, "what Monsieur de Chavigni says is right, sire, though, I confess, it did not strike me before. Shall we not become contemptible in the eyes of the world by submitting to be dictated to by Monsieur de Blenau? And is it not a gross insult to your majesty's power, to obey the commands of the queen, when he has refused to obey your own? I am sorry that this did not appear to me earlier: but the objection now seems to me so forcible, that I can proceed no further in this course."

Louis paused. He was as jealous of the queen possessing any authority as Richelieu could wish; but in the present instance he was urged, by different motives, in an opposite direction. Some sparks of affection had revived in his bosom towards Anne of Austria, and he wished much to satisfy himself regarding the suspicions which had been urged against her. De Blenau was the dear friend of his favourite Cinq Mars; and his mind also had begun to yield to the arguments of those who sought the destruction of the minister. But, on the other hand, the habit of being ruled by Richelieu, and the specious arguments he produced, made Louis hesitate:— "what, then, do you intend to do?" demanded he, addressing the cardinal.

"In the first place, sire," replied Richelieu, sternly, "I propose to interrogate the prisoner once more, and if his contumacy still continues, let the question be his doom."

The king's naturally good feelings and love of justice here at once overcame all doubt. "No, God forbid!"

cried he, rousing himself to energy. "What, are we
Christians, Monsieur le Cardinal, and shall we put a
fellow-creature to the torture, when there is a straightforward way to gain the information that we want? Fie
upon it! No!"

Richelieu's ashy cheek grew still a shade paler. It
was the first time for many a year he had undergone rebuke. He felt that the trammels with which he had so
long held the king enthralled were but as green withes
twined round the limbs of a giant. He saw that the vast
fabric of his power was raised upon a foundation of
unsteady sand, and that even then it trembled to its very
base.

"Monsieur la Rivière, answer the king!" continued
Louis, in a dignified tone. "What says the queen to the
request of our council, that she would command her
chamberlain to answer those questions in regard to which
he has a scruple on her account?"

"Her majesty says, sire," answered La Rivière, "that
she is most willing to do anything that will please your
majesty; and she has not only ordered me to command,
in her name, Monsieur de Blenau to inform the council
of everything he knows concerning her conduct, but has
also written this letter, with her own hand, to the same
effect." And advancing to the table, he bent his knee
before the king, and presented the document of which
he was the bearer.

Louis took the letter, and read it through. "This
looks not like a guilty conscience," said he, frowning upon
Richelieu. "Give that to Monsieur de Blenau," he continued to one of the officers. "There, Sir Count, is your
warrant to speak freely; and though we think you carry
your sense of honor too far, so as to make it dangerous
to yourself, and almost rebellious towards us, we cannot
help respecting the principle, even though it be in excess."

"May I always have such a judge as your majesty!"
replied De Blenau. "Most humbly do I crave your royal

pardon, if I have been at all wanting in duty towards you. Believe me, sire, it has proceeded not from any fault of inclination, but from an error in judgment. I have now no further hesitation, all my duties being reconciled; and, I believe, the best way fully to reply to the questions which have been asked me, will be by telling your majesty that I have on several occasions forwarded letters from the queen, by private couriers of my own, or by any other conveyance that offered. None of these letters have been either to the archduke, to Don Francisco de Mello, or any other person whatever connected with the Spanish government, except her majesty's brother, Philip, King of Spain, to whom I have assuredly sent several; but before I even undertook to do so her majesty condescended to give me her most positive promise, and to pledge her royal word, that the tidings she gave her brother should on all occasions be confined to her domestic affairs, nor ever touch upon the external or internal policy of the government, so that my honor and allegiance should be equally unsullied. These letters have sometimes remained upon my person for weeks, waiting for the fit opportunity to send them; which circumstance having by some means been discovered, has caused me no small inconvenience at times. Further, I have nothing to tell your majesty, but that I have ever heard the queen express the greatest affection for your royal person, and the warmest wishes for your public and private welfare; and, on my honor, I have never observed her do, by word or action, anything which could be construed into a breach of the duty she owes your majesty, either as her sovereign or her husband."

"You see!" exclaimed the king, turning to Richelieu, as De Blenau concluded; "you see—exactly what she confessed herself—not one tittle of difference."

The anger of the cardinal at finding himself foiled swept away his political prudence. Irritated and weakened by a wearying disease, he was in no frame of mind to

see calmly a scheme he had formed with infinite care so
completely overthrown; and forgetting that the king's
energies were now aroused to oppose him, he resolved to
let his vengeance fall on the head of De Blenau as the
means of his disappointment. His brow darkened, and
his eye flashed, and he replied in that stern and haughty
manner which had so often carried command along with
it.

"If your majesty be satisfied, of course so am I, whose
sole wish was to purge the lily crown from the profaning
touch of strangers. But as for Monsieur de Blenau, he
has confessed himself guilty of a crime little short of
high treason, in forwarding those letters to a foreign
enemy. We have already condemned a woman to exile
for a less offence; and therefore the mildest sentence
that the council can pronounce, and which by my voice
it does pronounce, is, that Claude Count de Blenau be
banished forever from these realms; and that, if after
the space of sixteen days he be found within their precincts, he shall be considered as without the pale of law,
and his blood be required at the hand of no man that sheds
it!"

There was an indignant spot glowing in the king's
face while Richelieu spoke thus, that Chavigni marked
with pain; for he saw that the precipitant haste of the
minister was hurrying his power to its fall.

"Too much of this!" cried Louis angrily. "Lord
cardinal, you forget the presence of the king. Monsieur
de Blenau—We, by our royal prerogative, do annul and
make void the sentence you have just heard, merely commanding you to retire from this château of the Bastile,
without holding communication with any persons attached
to the court, and to render yourself within the limits of
our province of Bourbon, and there to wait our farther
pleasure. The council is over," he continued, rising.
Monsieur le Cardinal de Richelieu, by sending the war-

rant for the count's release some time in the day to our
governor of the Bastile, you will merit our thanks."

The officers cleared the way for the king—the huissiers
of the chamber threw wide the doors— and Louis, with
a firm and dignified step, proceeded slowly out of the hall,
followed by Richelieu, who, thunderstruck and confounded, kept his eyes bent upon the ground, in the silence
of deep astonishment. The rest of the council, equally
mute and surprised, accompanied the cardinal with
anxiety in every eye: while the officers of the Bastile and
the Count de Blenau remained the sole occupants of the
hall of audience. The silence that reigned in the audience-hall of the Bastile after the scene we have described,
endured several minutes, during which each person who
remained within its walls, commented mutely on the extraordinary events he had just witnessed. De Blenau's
feelings were of course mingled, of surprise at the king's
unusual conduct, and gratification at his own deliverance.
The governor's thoughts were differently employed, looking forward to the fall of Richelieu, speculating in regard to his successor, and trying to determine who would
be the best person to court in the changes that were likely
to ensue. "Like master, like man," says the adage; and
the inferior officers of the prison, in compliance therewith,
calculated upon the removal of the governor as a consequence of the ruin of the minister who had placed him
there, and laid their own minor plans for securing their
places.

De Blenau was the first to break silence. "Well, my
friend," said he, addressing the governor, "I am to be
your guest no longer, it seems; but be assured that I
shall not forget my promises."

"You are infinitely good, monseigneur," answered the
other, bowing almost to the ground. "I hope you will
believe that I have gone to the very extreme of what
my duty permitted, to afford you all convenience."

"I have no doubt of it," replied the count; "but let

me ask what has become of my good friend, Philip the
woodman? He must not be forgotten."

The knowledge of the severity he had exercised towards poor Philip, in the first heat of his anger, now
called up a quick flush in the pale cheek of the governor;
and he determined to shelter himself from the resentment of his late prisoner, by telling him that the woodman
had been liberated.

In those dangerous times, the acuteness of every one
was sharpened by continual exercise; and De Blenau's
eye fixing on the varying countenance of his companion,
soon detected that there was something amiss, by the
alteration which his question produced. "Monsieur le
Gouverneur," said he, "give me the truth. I promise
you that everything shall be forgotten, provided you have
not seriously injured him; but I must know that the man
is safe who has served me so faithfully."

"The fact then is this, monseigneur," replied the
governor; "thinking it best for all parties, I ordered this
Monsieur Philip Grissolles to be confined till after your
examination to-day, lest anything might transpire that
could injure you or me."

"You thought of yourself alone, sir," answered De
Blenau somewhat bitterly; "but see that he be restored
to that degree of liberty which you were ordered at first
to permit, or you will hear more of me—"

As he spoke, the door of the audience-hall communicating with the outer court, was thrown open so suddenly
as to make the governor start a pace back, and Chavigni
entered the room with a countenance, from which all his
efforts could not banish the anxiety of his mind.

On entering, he pointed with his hand towards the door
for the governor to leave them; and seeing that he did
not immediately obey, he exclaimed in no very placable
voice, "Begone! I wish Monsieur de Blenau's company
alone. What do you wait for? Oh, there is the order for
his liberation—There, take your pack with you." And he

pointed to the lower officers of the prison, who thus dismissed, quickly followed the governor as he shrunk away from the statesman's hasty and irritable glance.

"Monsieur de Blenau," said Chavigni, as soon as the door was closed, "it was not worth while to detain you here for an hour or two, till such time as the order could be sent for your emancipation; I therefore drew it out in the lodge. But you owe me nothing for that; he continued, seeing that De Blenau was about to thank him for the supposed service. "I made it an excuse to stay behind, in order to seek an answer to a question or two. Now, I make no pretence of asking you these questions as a friend, for I know that you consider me not as such; but I do it merely on my own account, wishing for information on some points regarding which you alone can satisfy me. It is your business, therefore, to consider before you answer, whether so to do be for your interest or not. The only thing I will promise, which I do honestly, is, not to let your replies go beyond my own breast."

"The method of your address is certainly extraordinary, Monsieur de Chavigni," replied De Blenau: "but however we may differ on many points, I give you credit for so much frankness, that I believe you would not betray even your enemy if he relied on you; neither do I know, or rather recollect, at this moment, any question I should hesitate to answer. Therefore propose what you think fit, and I will satisfy you, or not, as suits my convenience."

"Between you and me, Monsieur de Blenau, there is no need of fine words. I have always found you strictly honorable, and therefore I rely on what you tell me, as if it were within the scope of my own knowledge. In the first place, then, you have been witness to an extraordinary scene to-day. Are you at all aware from what cause the king has acted as he has done, so at variance with his conduct for fifteen years?"

" Particularly, I am aware of no cause, and can only
conjecture that his majesty is tired of being dictated to
by his servant? "

" Umph ! " said Chavigni, in a tone of dissatisfaction;
" there is no need to triumph, Monsieur de Blenau. Am
I to believe that you know of no one who has instigated
the king to take such singular steps in your favor? "

" Of none whatever ! " answered the count; " unless
it were her majesty the queen,—the effect of any application from whom, would be quite different, I should conceive."

" No, no, no ! " said Chavigni. " It was not on her
that my suspicions rested. I must have been mistaken.
One word more.—Have you had any late communication
with Monsieur de Cinq Mars? "

" About three weeks ago I wrote to him from St.
Germain, sending some young hounds for the king's
service: but that was long before I dreamed of finding
my way hither."

" I must have been mistaken," repeated Chavigni. " I
thank you, Monsieur de Blenau. This must be a whim of
the king's own—God grant it ! for then the humor will
soon pass.

" And now, sir," said De Blenau, " that I have answered
your questions, there are one or two subjects on which
you might give me satisfaction. Are you inclined to do
so? "

" If I can, without injuring myself or others, or disclosing any plan that I am desirous to conceal," replied
the statesman.

" My questions shall regard the past, and not the
future," said De Blenau; " and are intended merely to
gratify my own curiosity. In the first place then, I
once saw you at St. Germain, in conversation with a
demoiselle attached to Mademoiselle de Beaumont—to
what did your business with her refer? "

" I did not think you had seen us," replied Chavigni.

" I might answer that I was making love, and probably you thought so as well as she did herself; but my conversation referred to you. I found that she had been present when Seguin, the surgeon, brought the news of your having been wounded to the queen: and from her also I learned the words he made use of to let her know that you had not lost the packet which you had upon you in the wood of Mantes."

" Monsieur de Chavigni," said De Blenau, with more cordiality in his manner than he usually evinced towards the statesman; " the world is too well aware of your domestic happiness for any one to suspect you of degrading yourself to a soubrette; I thank you for your candor. Now tell me, is a poor man, called Philip the woodman, detained here on my account? and why is he so?"

" He is," replied Chavigni " and the reason is this:—he happened to recognize amongst those who attacked you a servant of mine, and was fool enough to tell it abroad, so that it reached the king's ears. Now, though everything is justifiable in the service of the state, I did not particularly wish that business investigated, and I therefore put Monsieur Philip in here to keep him out of the way for a time. You are now of course aware why you were attacked. It was to secure the papers on your person, which papers we supposed were part of a treasonable correspondence between the queen and the Spanish government. All that is now over; and therefore, if you will promise me not to stir the business of that affray in any way—which indeed would do you no good—this meddling woodman shall have his liberty."

" I never had the slightest intention of stirring it," replied De Blenau; " and therefore rest satisfied on that score. But at the same time I must tell you that the whole affair came to the king's ears through me, and not through the woodman, I believe. I observed your servant, as well as he did, and did not fail to write of it to several of my friends, as well as speak of it openly on

more than one occasion; and this, depend upon it, has
been the means by which it reached the ears of the king,
and not by poor Philip."

"Then I have done him wrong," said Chavigni, "and
must make him some amends.—Let me see.—Oh, he
shall be sub-lieutenant of the forest; it will just suit him.
And now, Monsieur de Blenau, as a friend, let me give
you one piece of advice. This country is in a troubled
and uncertain state, and there will be doubtless, many
plots and cabals going on. Retire, as you are commanded,
into Bourbon; and if any one attempt to lead you into any
conspiracy, so far from acceding, do not even listen to
them; for the cardinal owes you something for what has
happened to-day, and he is not one to forget such debts.
The eye of an angry man is upon you!—so be as guarded
as if you trod amongst vipers. The time will come
when you will say that Chavigni has advised you well."

"And it is certainly advice which I shall follow, both
from reason and inclination. But let me ask—am I to
consider the king's prohibition strict in regard to communicating with any one at the court?"

Chavigni thought for a moment, and De Blenau
imagined that he was considering the circumstances
under which Louis's command had been given; but it
was not so. The mind of the statesman rapidly reverted
to Pauline de Beaumont, all his precautions with regard
to whom turned out to be nugatory; and he now calculated the consequences which were likely to ensue
under the present state of affairs. He had no fear, indeed,
in regard to the responsibility he had taken upon himself;
for it would be easy to prove, in case of investigation,
that Pauline had attempted in disguise to communicate
privately with a state prisoner in the Bastile, which
would completely justify the measures he had pursued;
but he wished on all accounts to let a matter drop and be
forgotten which had already produced such disagreeable
events, and he therefore determined boldly to inform

Madame de Beaumont of what had been done, and the motives for doing it; and then—certain that for her own sake she would keep silence on the subject—to restore her daughter with all speed.

Though the thoughts of Chavigni were very rapid in combination, yet all these considerations occupied him so long, that De Blenau, perceiving his companion plunged into so profound a reverie, took the liberty of pulling him out by the ear, repeating his former question, whether he was to consider the king's prohibition in regard to communicating with the court as strictly to be observed.

"Undoubtedly!" replied Chavigni: "beyond all question! You do not want to get into the Bastile again, do you? Oh! I perceive it is Mademoiselle de Beaumont you are thinking of. But you cannot see her. She is neither in Paris, nor at St. Germain; but I will take care that when she joins her mother in Paris, she shall be informed of your safety; and you can write yourself when you get into the Bourbonnois."

The reader, who is behind the scenes, may probably take the trouble of pitying De Blenau for the anxiety he would suffer on hearing that Pauline was neither at St. Germain nor in Paris; but there is no occasion to distress himself. De Blenau knowing that Pauline had absented herself from the court for the purpose of conveying to him the epistle of the queen, naturally concluded that Chavigni had been deceived in regard to her absence, and that she was at all events in safety wherever she was.

In the meantime Chavigni proceeded. "You must of course go to St. Germain, to prepare for your journey; but stay even there as few hours as you well may. Remember, I have told you, the eye of an angry man is upon you! To-day is yours—to-morrow may be his—take care that by the least imprudence you do not turn your sunshine into storm. That you may make all speed, I will lend you a horse; for I own I take some interest in your fate—I know not why. It shall be at the gates in an hour, together with an order for the woodman's liberation: so now, farewell. I have wasted too much time on you already."

With this speech, half kind, half rude, Chavigni left De Blenau. Whether the statesman's motives were wholly friendly, or whether they might not be partly interested, proceeding from a nice calculation of the precarious state both of the cardinal's health and of his power, weighed with the authority the queen might gain from the failure of either, the count did not stay to investigate, although a suspicion of the latter kind flashed across his mind. In this, however, he did Chavigni injustice. In natural character he was not unlike De Blenau himself, frank, honorable, and generous; but education is stronger than nature; and education had made them different beings.

On the departure of the statesman the count returned once more to the apartment he had occupied while a prisoner, with no small self-gratulation on the change in his situation. Here he busied himself in preparations for his departure, and took pains to ascertain that the paper written by the unhappy Caply still remained in the book, as well as that the file was yet in the position which it described. Having finished this examination, which he looked upon as a duty to the next person destined to inhabit that abode, he waited impatiently till the hour should be passed which Chavigni had named as the time likely to elapse before the horse he promised would be prepared.

Ere it had flown much more than half, however, the governor entered the chamber, and with many profound bows and civil speeches, informed him that Monsieur de Chavigni had sent a horse for his use, and an order for the immediate release of Philip, the woodman. De Blenau was gratified by Chavigni's prompt fulfilment of his word in this last respect; and remembering the thousand crowns which he had promised the governor on his liberation, he placed them in his hand, which brought him very near to the end of the large sum of gold that his valise contained.

Now De Blenau was perfectly well convinced that the governor was as great a rogue as need be; but there is something so expansive in the idea of being liberated from prison, that he could not bear the thought of keeping his louis shut up in a bag any longer, and he poured them forth into the governor's palm with as much satisfaction as if he was emancipating so many prisoners himself.

The governor, even when he had safely clutched the promised fee, looked very wistfully at a little green silk bag, which De Blenau reserved in his left hand, and which he calculated must contain about the same sum, or more.

The count, however, held it firm; and having given directions to whom, and when, his baggage was to be delivered, he descended into the inner court, and cast his eyes round in search of his faithful friend Philip. But the woodman had received at once his emancipation from the dungeon where we last left him, and the news that De Blenau was free; and though he lingered in the court to see the young count depart, with something both of joy and pride in his feelings, yet there was a sort of timid delicacy in the peasant's mind which made him draw back from observation, amidst the crowd of prisoners that the court now contained, the moment that he perceived the governor, with many a servile cringe, marshalling the late prisoner towards the gate of the Bastile, while those less fortunate persons, still destined to linger out their time within its walls, stood off with curious envying looks, to allow a passage for him now freed from their sad fellowship. De Blenau, however, was by no means forgetful of the woodman, and not perceiving him amongst the rest, he inquired where he was of the obsequious governor, who instantly vociferated his name till the old arches echoed with the sound. "Philip! Philip the Woodman! Philip Grissolles!" cried the governor.

"Does he know that he is free altogether to return home?" demanded De Blenau, seeing him approach.

"No, I believe not," replied the governor. "I had the honor of waiting first upon your lordship."

Philip now came near, and De Blenau had the gratification of announcing to him, unforestalled, that the storm had blown over, and that he might now return to his cottage in peace. He also told him of the appointment with which Chavigni proposed to compensate his imprisonment—an office so elevated that the gayest daydreams of Philip's ambition had never soared to half its height. But the joy of returning to the bosom of his family, to the calm shelter of his native forest, and the even tenor of his daily toil, swallowed up all his feelings. A throne would not have made him happier; and the tears of delight streaming down his rough cheek, brought a glistening drop too into De Blenau's eye. Noble and aristocratic as he was, De Blenau felt that there was an aristocracy above all—the nobility of virtue; and he did not disdain to grasp the broad hand of the honest woodman. "Fare you well, Philip," he said. "Fare you well, till we meet again. I shall not easily forget you."

The woodman felt something more weighty in his palm than the hand of De Blenau, and looked at the heavy green purse which remained in it with a hesitating glance. But the count raised his finger to his lip with a smile. "Not a word," said he, "not a word, as you value my friendship." And turning round, he followed the governor through the various passages to the outer court, where stood Chavigni's horse caparisoned for his journey. De Blenau sprang into the saddle with the lightness of recovered freedom. The heavy gate was thrown open, the drawbridge fell, and, striking the sides of his

horse with his armed heel, the newly emancipated prisoner
bounded over the clattering boards of the pontlevé, and
with a lightened heart took the road to St. Germain.

His journey was soon made, and, as he approached
the place of his destination, all the well-known objects
round about seemed as if there shone upon them now a
brighter and more beautifying sun than when he last
beheld them. At his hotel all was gladness and delight,
and crowding round their loved lord, with smiles of welcome, his attendants could scarcely be made to comprehend that he was again about to quit St. Germain. De
Blenau's commands, however, immediately to prepare
for a long journey, recalled them to their duty: and eager
to accompany him wherever he went, their arrangements
were soon completed, and the majordomo announced that
all were ready.

Not so the count himself, who, notwithstanding the
king's command, could not resolve to quit St. Germain
without visiting the palace. Sending forward, therefore,
his train to the entrance of the forest, he proceeded on
foot to the gate of the park, and crossing the terrace, entered the chateau by the small door in the western quad-
rangle.

Perhaps De Blenau was not without a hope that
Pauline might have returned thither from Paris; and at
first, meeting none of the royal servants, he walked from
empty chamber to chamber, with a degree of undefined
expectation that in each he should find the object of
his wishes; but of course his search was in vain, and
descending to the lower part of the building, he proceeded
to the porter's chamber, who, having received no news to
the contrary, informed him that the whole court were
still at Chantilly.

Fancy presented to his mind a thousand forebodings
of evil, as with many a lingering look he turned again
and again towards the palace; and even when at length
he was joined by his train, who waited at the entrance of

20

the forest, he was still absorbed in gloomy meditations. However, he felt it was in vain, and springing on his horse, he turned his face resolutely on his onward way.

Skirting along the wood, he soon reached Versailles, and thence proceeding with little intermission, he arrived in time to pass the night at Etampes, from which place he set out early the next morning for Orleans. Continuing to trace along the course of the Loire with quick stages, he soon arrived at Nevers, where he crossed the river, and shortly after entered the Bourbonnois.

CHAPTER XX.

Which shows the truth of the French adage, " L'habit ne fait pas le moine."

At Troyes, the Norman's perquisitions were very successful. No Bow Street officer could have detected all
the proceedings of Fontrailles with more acuteness.
Step by step he traced him, from his first arrival at
Troyes, till the day he set out for Mesnil St. Loup; and
learning the road he had taken, he determined upon following the same track, for l.e shrewdly concluded, that
whatever business of import the conspirator had been
engaged in, had been transacted in the two days and one
night, which, according to the story of the garçon
d'auberge at the Hôtel du Grand Soleil, he had been
absent from the good city of Troyes.

Now, our friend Monsieur Marteville had learned
another piece of news, which made him the more willing
to bend his steps in the direction pointed out as that which
Fontrailles had taken. This was no other than that a
considerable band of robbers had lately come down into
that part of the country to collect their rents; and that
their principal haunt was supposed to be the thick woods
which lay on the borders of the high road to Troyes, in
the neighborhood of Mesnil.

True it is, the Norman had abandoned his free companions of the forest, and received the wages of Monsieur
de Chavigni; but still he kept up a kind of desultory correspondence with his former associates, and had not
lost sight of them till certain reports got about, that the
lieutenant criminel was going to visit the forest of Laye,

which induced them to leave the vicinity of St. Germain, for fear that there should not be room enough in the forest for them and the lieutenant too. The Norman had a strange hankering after his good old trade, and was very well inclined to pass a day or two in the free forest, and do Chavigni's work into the bargain. There was a little embarras indeed in the case, respecting Louise, for whom, in these first days of possession, he did feel a certain degree of attachment; and did not choose to leave her behind, though he did not like to take her with him, considering the society he was going to meet. " Pshaw ! " said he at length, speaking to himself, " I'll leave her at Mesnil."

This resolution he began to put in execution, by placing Louise upon one horse, and himself upon the other, together with their several valises; and thus, in the same state and order in which they had arrived at Troyes, so they quitted it for Mesnil St. Loup. All the information that Marteville possessed to guide him in his farther inquiries, amounted to no more than this (which he learned from the aforesaid garçon d'auberge), namely, that the little gentleman in gray had taken the road apparently to Mesnil; that he had been absent, as before said, two days and one night; and that his horse, when it came home, appeared to have been furnished with a new shoe en route. This, however, was quite sufficient as a clue, and the Norman did not fail to turn it to its full account.

Passing through the little villages of Mehun and Langly, the Norman eyed every blacksmith's forge as he went; but the one was next to the post-house, and the other was opposite the inn; and the Norman went on, saying within himself—" A man who was seeking concealment, would rather proceed with his beast unshod than stop there." So, resuming his conversation with Louise, they jogged on, babbling, not of green fields, but of love and war; both of which subjects were much within the knowledge of the Sieur Marteville, his battles being somewhat more numerous than his wives, and having had plenty of both in his day.

At all events, Louise was very well satisfied with the husband that Heaven had sent her, and looked upon him as a very fine gentleman, and a great warrior; and though, now and then, she would play the coquette a little, and put forth all the little minauderie which a Languedoc soubrette could assume, in order to prevent the Norman from having too great a superiority, yet Monsieur Marteville was better satisfied with her than any of his former wives; and as she rode beside him, he admired her horsemanship, and looked at her from top to toe in much the same manner that he would have examined the points of a fine Norman charger.

While they were thus shortening the road with sweet discourse, at the door of a little hovel by the side of the highway, half hidden from sight by a clumsy mud wall against which he leaned, half exposed by the lolloping position he assumed, appeared the large, dirty, unmeaning face and begrimed person of a Champenois blacksmith, with one hand grubbing amongst the roots of his grizzled hair, and the other hanging listlessly by his side, loaded with the ponderous hammer appropriated to his trade. " C'est ici," thought the Norman; " Quatre vingt dix neuf moutons et un Champenois font cent—ninety-nine sheep and a Champenois make a hundred; so we'll see what my fool will tell me.—Holloa! monsieur!"

" Plait-il?" cried the Champenois, advancing from his hut.

" Pray has Monsieur Pont Orson passed here to-day?" demanded the Norman.

" Monsieur Pont Orson! Monsieur Pont Orson!" cried the Champenois, trying to assume an air of thought, and rummaging in his empty head for a name that never was in it: " Pardie, I do not know."

" I mean," said the Norman, " the same little gentleman in gray, who stopped here ten days agone, to have a bay horse shod, as he was coming back from—what's the name of the place?"

"No!" cried the Champenois; "he was going, he was not coming, when he had his horse shod."

"But I say he was coming," replied the Norman. "How the devil do you know he was going?"

"Mais dame;" exclaimed the other; "How do I know he was going? Why, did not he ask me how far it was to Mesnil? and if he had not been going, why should he wish to know?"

"It was not he, then," said the Norman.

"Mais dame! oui!" cried the Champenois. "He was dressed all in gray, and had a bay horse, on whose hoof I put as nice a piece of iron as ever came off an anvil; and he asked me how far it was to Mesnil, and whereabouts was the old castle of St. Loup. Monsieur Pont Orson! Monsieur Pont Orson? Dieu! qui aurait déviné que c'etait Monsieur Pont Orson?"

"Mais je vous dis que ce n'était pas lui," cried the Norman, putting spurs to his horse. "Allons, chèrie. Adieu, Monsieur Champenois, adieu!"—Ha! ha! ha!" cried he, when at a little distance. "Ganache! he has told me all that I wanted to know. Then he did go to Mesnil—the old château of St. Loup! What could he want there? I've heard of this old château."

"But who is Monsieur Pont Orson?" demanded Louise, interrupting the broken cogitations of her husband.

"Nay, I know not, ma chère," replied her husband. "The man in the moon, with a corkscrew to tap yon fool's brains, and draw out all I wanted to know about the person whom I told you I was seeking for Monsieur de Chavigni.—It was a mere name. But there, I see a steeple on yon hill in the wood. Courage! we shall soon reach it. It is not above a league.—That must be Mesnil."

The Norman's league, however, proved at least two, and Louise, though a good horsewoman, was complaining most bitterly of fatigue, when they arrived in the little street of Mesnil St. Loup, and, riding up to the dwelling of our old friend Gaultier the innkeeper, alighted under the withered garland that hung over the door.

"Holla! Aubergiste! Garçon!" cried the Norman. "Holla!"

But no one came; and on repeating the summons, the sweet voice of the dame of the house was all that could be heard, screaming forth a variety of tender epithets, applicable to the garçon d'écurie, and intended to stimulate him to come forth and take charge of the strangers' horses. "Don't you know, lambin," cried she, "that that hog your master is lying upstairs dying for no one knows what? And I am to go out, maraud, and take people's horses with my hands all over grease, while you stand there? Cochon! if you do not go, I'll throw this pot-lid at you." And immediately a tremendous rattle on the boards at the further side of the stable announced that she had been as good as her word.

This seemed the only effectual method of arousing the occult sensibilities of the garçon d'écurie, who listened unconcerned to her gentler solicitations, but, yielding to the more potent application of the pot-lid, came forth and took the bridle of the horses, while our Norman lifted his lady to the ground.

The sight of such goodly limbs as those possessed by Monsieur Marteville, but more especially the blue velvet pourpoint to which we have formely alluded, and which he wore on the present occasion, did not fail to produce the most favorable impression on the mind of the landlady; and, bustling about with the activity of a grasshopper, she prepared to serve the athletic cavalier and his pretty lady to the best cheer of the auberge.

"Would madame choose some stewed escargots pour se restaurer? Would monsieur take un coup de vin before dinner to wash the dust out of his mouth? Would madame step upstairs to repose herself? Would monsieur

take a gouter?" These and a thousand other civil prof-
fers the hostess showered upon the Norman and Louise,
some of which were accepted, some declined; but the
principal thing on which the Norman seemed to set his
heart was the speedy preparation of dinner, which he
ordered with the true galloping profusion of a beggar on
horseback, demanding the best of everything. While this
was in progress, he forgot not the principal object of his
journey, but began with some circumlocution to draw
the hostess towards the subject of Fontrailles' visit to
Mesnil.

At the very mention, however, of a little man in gray,
the good landlady burst forth in such a torrent of in-
vective that she went well-nigh to exhaust her copious
vocabulary of epithets and expletives; while the Norman,
taken by surprise, stood gazing and shrugging his
shoulders, wondering at her facility of utterance. The
little man in gray, who had been there precisely ten days
before, was, according to her opinion, a liar, and a rogue,
and a cheat; a conjuror, a Huguenot, and a vagabond;
a man without honor, principle, or faith; a maraud, a
matin, a misérable; together with a great many other
titles the enumeration of which she summed up with " et
s'il n'est pas le diable, le diable l'emporte!"

" C'est vrai," cried the Norman every time she paused
to take breath; " c'est vrai. But how came you to find
out he was so wicked? "

The lady's reply was not of the most direct kind; but
from it the Norman gathered, with his usual acuteness,
that after our friend Gaultier had pointed out to Fontrailles the road to the old castle of St. Loup, he returned
home, his mind oppressed with the consciousness of
being the confidant of a sorcerer. He labored under the
load of this terrific secret for some days; and then, his
constitution not being able to support his mental struggles, he sickened and took to his bed, where he still lay in
a deplorable state, talking in his sleep of the conjuror in

gray, and of Père Le Rouge, and the devil himself, and
sundry other respectable people of the same class. But
when awake, it must be remarked, the aubergiste never
opened his lips upon the subject, notwithstanding all
the solicitations which his better half, being tempted by
the curiosity of her sex, did not fail to make. From all
this the good dame concluded that the little man in gray
had bewitched her husband and driven him mad, causing
him to lie up there upon his bed, neglecting his business,
and leaving her worse than a widow.

All this was corn, wine, and oil to the mind of the Norman, who, wisely reserving his opinion on the subject,
retired to consult with Louise, having a great esteem for
woman's wit in such cases. After some discussion, a
plan was manufactured between them, which, though
somewhat bold in conception, was happily brought to
issue in the following manner.

During the dinner, at which the bourgeoise waited
herself, she was not a little surprised to hear Louise more
than once call Marteville by the reverend appellation of
mon père; and if this astonished, how much was her
wonder increased when afterwards, during a concerted
absence of the Norman, the fair lady informed her, under
a promise of profound secrecy, that the goodly cavalier,
whose blue velvet doublet she had so much admired, was
neither more nor less than the celebrated Père Alexis,
directeur of the Jesuits of Alençon who was travelling in
disguise in order to place her (one of his penitents) in a
monastery at Rome.

True, Louise either forgot or did not know that they
were not precisely in the most direct road to Rome, but
she was very safe in the person she spoke to, who had
even less knowledge of where Rome stood than herself.
Be that as it may, the simple bourgeoise never doubted it
for a moment, and casting herself at the feet of Louise,
she entreated her, with tears in her eyes, to intercede with

the reverend directeur to confess and absolve her sinful
husband, who lay upstairs doing nothing.

Just at this moment the Norman re-entered the room;
and though his precise object in the little drama they
had got up, was neither more nor less than to confess
the unhappy aubergiste, yet, as a matter of form, he made
some difficulty to meddling with the penitent of another;
but after faintly advising that the curé of the village
should be sent for, he agreed, as the case was urgent, to
undertake the office of confessor himself, though he
mildly reproached Louise, in presence of the hostess, for
having betrayed his real character, and bade her be more
careful in future.

As soon as he had signified his consent, the bourgeoise
ran to tell her husband that the very reverend Père
Alexis, directeur of the Jesuits of Alençon, had kindly
consented to hear his confession and absolve him of his
sins; and in the meanwhile the Norman gave directions
to Louise, whose adroitness had often served him in
discovering the secrets of the palace, while she had
remained with Madame de Beaumont, to gain, in the
present instance, all the information she could from the
wife, while he went to interrogate the husband.

This being settled, as a blue velvet pourpoint was not
exactly the garb to play a confessor in, Louise ran in all
haste to strip the astrologer's robe we have already
mentioned of all its profane symbols, and the Norman,
casting its shadowy folds over his lusty limbs, and drawing the hood over his head, appeared to the eye as goodly
a friar as ever cracked a bottle. No great regard to
costume was necessary, for the landlady took it all for
granted; and when she beheld the Norman issue forth
from the room in which the valise had been placed,
clothed in his long dark robes, she cast herself at his
feet in a transport of reverence and piety.

Monsieur Marteville, otherwise the Père Alexis, did
not fail to give her his blessing with great gravity, and

with a solemn demeanor and slow step followed to the chamber of the sick man.

Poor Gaultier was no longer the gay rosy-cheeked inn-keeper which he had appeared to Fontrailles, but, stretched upon his bed, he lay pale and wan, muttering over to himself shreds and tatters of prayers, and thinking of the little man in gray, Père Le Rouge, and the devil. As soon as he beheld the pretended Père Alexis enter his chamber, he essayed to rise in his bed; but the Norman motioned him to be still, and sitting down by him, exhorted him to make a full confession of his sins, and then, to give greater authenticity to his character, he knelt down and composed an extempore prayer, in a language equally of his own manufacture, but which the poor aubergiste believed devoutly to be Latin, hearing every now and then the words sanctissimus, in secula seculorum, and benedictus, with which the Norman did not fail to season it richly, being the only stray Latin he was possessed of.

The Norman now proceeded to business, and putting down his ear to a level with the lips of Gaultier, he once more desired him to make a clear breast.

"Oh, mon père," cried Gaultier, "je suis un pauvre pécheur, un misérable!"

The good father exhorted him to take courage, and to come to a detail of his crimes.

"Oh, mon père," cried he, "I have sold cats for rabbits, and more especially for hares. I have moistened an old hareskin with warm water and bloodied it with chicken's blood, to make my cats and my badgers and my weasels pass for what they really were not. I have cooked up snakes for eels, and dressed vipers en matelot. I have sold bad wine of Boismarly for good wine of Epernay: and, oh, mon père, je suis un pauvre pécheur."

"Well, well, get on," cried the Norman, somewhat impatiently, "I'll give you absolution for all that. All innkeepers do the same. But what more have you done?"

"Oh, mon père, je suis un pauvre pécheur," proceeded Gaultier in a low voice; "I have charged my customers twice as much as I ought to charge. I have vowed that fish was dear when it was cheap; and I have——"

"Nom de Dieu!" cried the Norman, getting out of temper with the recapitulation of Gaultier's peccadilloes. "Nom de Dieu! that is to say, in the name of God, I absolve you from all such sins as are common to inn-keepers, masters of taverns, cooks, aubergistes and the like—sins of profession as they may be called—only appointing you to kneel before the altar of your parish church for two complete hours, repeating the Pater and the Ave during the whole time, by way of penance;" thought he, for making me hear all this nonsense. "But come," he continued, "bring up the heavy artillery—that is, let me hear your more uncommon sins. You have some worse things upon your conscience than any you have told, or I am mistaken."

"Oh, mon père! oh, mon bon père!" groaned Gaultier, "je suis un pauvre pécheur, un misérable."

"Now it comes," thought the Norman; "allons, allons, mon fils, ayez courage! l'eglise est pleine de miséricorde."

"There was an old owl in the barn," said Gaultier, "and woodcocks being scarce——"

"Ventre Saint Gris!" thought Marteville to himself, "this will never come to an end; Mais mon fils," he said aloud, "I have told you all that is pardoned. Speak, can you charge yourself with murder, treason, conspiracy, sorcery," — Gaultier groaned — "astrology" — Gaultier groaned still more deeply—"or of having concealed any such crimes when committed by others?" Gaultier groaned a third time. The Norman had now brought him to the point; and after much moaning, hesitation, and agony of mind, he acknowledged that he had been privy to a meeting of sorcerers; nay, that he had even conducted a notorious astrologer, a little man in gray, on the road to meet the defunct Père Le Rouge and his

companion the devil, at the old château of St. Loup; and
that it was his remorse of conscience for this crime, together with his terror at revealing it, after the menaces
of the sorcerer, that had thrown him into the lamentable
state in which he then lay.

By degrees the Norman drew from him every particular, and treasuring them up in his memory, he hastened
to give the suffering innkeeper absolution; which, though
not performed in the most orthodox manner, quite satisfied Gaultier; who concluded that any little difference of
form from that to which he had been used, proceeded
from the Norman being a Jesuit and a directeur; and
he afterwards was heard to declare that the Père Alexis
was the most pious and saintly of men, and that one
absolution from him was worth a hundred from any one
else; although the curé of the village, when he heard
how it had been administered, pronounced it to be
heterodox and heretical, and in short a damnable error.

As soon as he had concluded all the ceremonies he
thought right to perform, for the farther consolation of
Gaultier, he said to him—"Fear not, my son, the menaces
of the sorcerer; for I forbid all evil beings, even were
it the devil himself, to lay so much as the tip of a finger
upon you; and moreover, I will go this very night to the
old château of St. Loup, and will exercise Père Le Rouge
and drive his spirit forth from the place, and, morbleu! if
he dare appear to me I will take him by the beard, and
lead him into the middle of the village, and all the little
children shall drum him out of the regiment—I mean out
of the town."

With this bold resolution, Monsieur Marteville descended to the ground floor, and communicated his design
to Louise and the bourgeoise, who were sitting with
their noses together over a flagon of vin chaud. "Donnez
moi un coup de vin," said he, " et j'irai."

But Louise, who did not choose to trust her new
husband out of her sight, having discovered by a kind of

instinct, that in his case "absence was worse than death," declared she would go with him, and see him take Père Le Rouge by the beard. The Norman remonstrated, but Louise persisted with a sort of sweet pertinacity which was quite irresistible, and, though somewhat out of humor with her obstinacy, he was obliged to consent.

However, he growled audibly while she assisted to disembarrass him of his long black robe; and probably, had it not been for his assumed character, would have accompanied his opposition with more than one of those elegant expletives with which he was wont to season his discourse. Louise, notwithstanding all this, still maintained her point, and the horses being brought forth, the bags were placed on their backs, and the Norman and his spouse set forth for the old château of St. Loup, taking care to repeat their injunction to the landlady not to discover their real characters to any one, as the business of the père directeur required the utmost secrecy.

The landlady promised devoutly to comply, and having seen her guests depart, entered the public room, where several of the peasantry had by this time assembled, and told every one in a whisper that the tall gentleman they had seen get on horseback was the Père Alexis, directeur of the Jesuits of Alençon, and that the lady was Mademoiselle Louise de Crackmagnole, sa penitente. Immediately, they all ran in different directions, some to the door, some to the window, to see so wonderful a pair as the Père Alexis and his penitente. The bustle, rushing, and chattering which succeeded, and which the landlady could no way abate, called the attention of the Sieur Marteville, who, not particularly in a good humor at being contradicted by Louise, was so much excited into anger by the gaping of the multitude, that he had wellnigh drawn the portentous Toledo which hung by his side, and returned to satisfy their curiosity by presenting his person rather nearer than they might have deemed agreeable. He bridled in his wrath, however, or rather, to change the figure, kept it in store for some future occasion; and consoling himself with a few internal curses, in which Louise had her share, he rode on, and soon arrived at that part of the wood which we have already said was named the Sorcerer's Grove.

CHAPTER XXI.

Being a chapter of explanations, which the reader has no occasion to
peruse if he understands the story without it.

"GREAT news! Cinq Mars!" exclaimed Fontrailles.
"Great news! the cardinal is sick to the death, and goes
without loss of time to Tarascon; he trembles upon the
brink of the grave."

Cinq Mars was stretched upon three chairs, the farthest
of which he kept balanced on its edge by the weight of
his feet, idly rocking it backwards and forwards, while
his mind was deeply buried in one of the weak romances
of the day, the reading which was a favorite amusement
with the master of the horse, at those periods when the
energies of his mind seemed to sleep. "Too good news
to be true, Fontrailles, he replied, hardly looking up;
"take my word for it, the devil never dies."

"That may be," answered Fontrailles, "but nevertheless the cardinal, as I said, is dying, and goes instantly
to Tarascon to try another climate."

"Why, where hast thou heard all this? and when
didst thou come from Spain?" demanded Cinq Mars,
rousing himself. "Thou hast made good speed."

"Had I not good reason?" asked the other. "But
they tell me that I must question you for news; for that
it is something in regard to your friend, the young Count
de Blenau, which has so deeply struck the cardinal."

"Well then, I will give the story, in true heroic style,"
answered Cinq Mars, tossing the book from him.
"Thou dost remember, O my friend!" he continued,
imitating the language of the romance he had just been
reading, how stormy was the night, when last I parted

from thee, at the old château of Mesnil St. Loup; and
if the thunder-clouds passed away, and left the sky clear
and moonlighted, it was but to be succeeded by a still
more violent tempest. For, long after thou wert snugly
housed at Troyes, De Thou and myself were galloping on
through the storm of night. The rain fell, the lightning
glanced, the thunder rolled overhead, and the way seemed
doubly long, and the forest doubly dreary, when by a
sudden blaze of the red fire of heaven, I described some
one, mounted on a white horse, come rapidly towards us."

"Come, come, Cinq Mars!" exclaimed Fontrailles,
"for grace, leave the land of romance—remember I have
a long story to tell, and not much time to tell it in.
Truce with imagination, therefore, for we have more
serious work before us."

"It's truth—it's truth, thou unbelieving Jew," cried
Cinq Mars. "No romance, I can assure you. Well, soon
as this white horseman saw two others wending their
way towards him, he suddenly reined in his beast, and
turning round, galloped off as hard as he could go. Now,
if curiosity be a failing, it is one I possess in an eminent
degree; so, clapping spurs to my horse, after him I went,
full faster than he ran away. As for De Thou, he calls
out after me, loud enough to drown the thunder, crying,
"Cinq Mars, where are you going? In God's name,
stop—we know the place is full of banditti—if these are
robbers, they may murder you,"—and so on; but finding
that I did not much heed, he also was smitten with a
galloping fit, and so we followed each other, like a procession, though with no procession pace; the white horseman first—I next—and De Thou last—with about a hundred yards between each of us—going all at full speed,
to the great peril of our necks, and no small danger of
our heads from the boughs. I was best mounted, however, on my stout black horse Sloeberry—you know Sloeberry—and so distancing De Thou all to nothing, I began
to come closer to my white horseman, who, finding that

21

he could not get off, gradually pulled in, and let me come up with him. "Well, sir," said he directly, with all possible coolness, "you have ridden hard to-night."— "In truth, I have, my man," answered I, "and so have you, and I should much like to know why you did so."— "For the same reason that you did, I suppose," replied the boy, for such it was who spoke.—"And what reason is that?'" I asked.—"Because we both liked it, I suppose," replied he.—"That may be," answered I; "but we have all a reason for our likings."—"True, sir," said the boy, "and I dare say yours was a good one; pray, believe that mine was so also."—All the time he spoke, he kept looking round at me, till at last he got a good sight of my face. "Are not you Monsieur de Cinq Mars?" cried he at length.—"And if I am, what follows then?"—"Why, it follows that you are the person I want?" said the boy.—"And what want you with me?" —"Who is that?" demanded he, pointing to De Thou, who now came up. I soon satisfied him on that score, and he went on. "My name is Henry de La Mothe, and I am page to your good friend, the Count de Blenau, whom I have seen arrested and carried to the Bastile."

"Now, you know, Fontrailles, how dear I hold De Blenau; so you may guess how pleasantly this rang upon my ear. My first question to the page was, whether my friend had sent him to me. "No, no, seigneur," answered the boy; "but as I knew you loved my master, and the king loved you, I thought it best to let you know, in case you might wish to serve him. He was taken as he was about to go with the queen to Chantilly, and they would not let me or any other go with him, to serve him in prison. So I cast about in my mind, how I could serve him out of it, and consequently came off to seek you."— "But how did you know where to find me?" demanded I, not a little fearing that our movements were watched; but the boy relieved me from that by answering, "Why, sir, there was a messenger came from Chantilly to desire the queen's presence; and amongst all the questions I asked him, there was one which made him tell me that you had gone to Troyes upon some business of inheritance, and as I heard that the path through this wood would save me a league, I took it, hoping to reach the town to-night."

"Well, all the page's news vexed me not a little, and I thought of a thousand things to relieve De Blenau ere I could fix on any. But it happened, as it often does in this world, that chance directed me when reasoning failed. Having made the best of my way, I arrived with De Thou and the boy at Chantilly, at the hour of nine the next night, and passing towards my own apartments in the palace, I saw the king's cabinet open, and on inquiry, found that he had not yet retired to rest. My resolution was instantly taken; and without waiting even to dust my boots, I went just as I was, to pay my duty to his majesty. My short absence had done me no harm with Louis, who received me with more grace than ever; so while the newness was on, I dashed at the subject next my heart at once. Like a well-bred falcon, I soared my full pitch, hovered an instant in my pride of place, and then stooped at once with irresistible force. In short, Fontrailles, for the first time I believe in my life, I boasted. I told Louis how I loved him; I counted over the services I had done him. His noble heart—you may smile, sir, but he has a noble heart—was touched; I saw it, and gave him a moment to think over all old passages of affection between us, and to combine them with the feelings of the moment, and then I told him that my friend—my bosom friend—was suffering from the tyranny of the cardinal, and demanded his favor for De Blenau. "What can I do, Cinq Mars?" demanded he; "you know I must follow the advice of my ministers and councillors."

"It was an opportunity not to be lost," exclaimed Fontrailles, eagerly; "I hope you seized it."

"I did," replied Cinq Mars. "I plied him hard on every point that could shake the influence of Richelieu. I showed him the shameful bondage he suffered. I told him, that if he allowed the sovereign power, placed by God in his hands, to be abused by another, he was as guilty as if he misused it himself; and then I said, "I plead alone for the innocent, sire. Hear De Blenau yourself, and if you find him guilty, bring him to the block at once. But if he have done nothing worthy of death, I will trust that your majesty's justice will instantly set him free." Well, the king not only promised that he would go to Paris and examine De Blenau himself, but he added— "And I will be firm, Cinq Mars; I know the power is in my own hands, and I will exert it to save your friend, if he be not criminal."

"This was all fair, Fontrailles; I could desire no more; but Louis even outdid my expectation. Something had already irritated him against the cardinal—I think it was the banishment of Clara de Hauteford. However, he went to the Bastile with Richelieu, Chavigni, and others of the council. Of course I was not admitted; but I heard all that passed from one who was present. De Blenau bore him nobly and bravely, and downright refused to answer any questions about the queen, without her majesty's own commands. Well, Richelieu, according to custom, was for giving him the torture instantly. But the king had many good reasons for not suffering that to be done. Besides wishing to pleasure me, and being naturally averse to cruelty, he had a lingering inclination to cross Richelieu, and De Blenau's firmness set him a good example; so the cardinal was overruled; and the queen's commands to De Blenau to confess all being easily procured, he owned that he had forwarded letters from her majesty to her brother the King of Spain. Now, you see, Richelieu was angry, and irritated at being thwarted; and he did the most foolish thing that ever man did; for though he saw that Louis was roused, and just in the humor to cross him, he got up, and not considering the king's presence, at once pronounced a sentence of exile against De Blenau, as if the sovereign power had been entirely his own, without consulting Louis, or asking his approbation at all. Though, God knows, the king cares little enough about using his power, of course he does not like to be treated as a mere cipher before his own council; and accordingly he revoked the cardinal's sentence without hesitation, sending De Blenau, merely for form's sake, into Bourbon, and then rising, he broke up the council, treating Riche‚ lieu with as scanty consideration as he had shown himself. By Heaven! Fontrailles, when I heard it, I could have played the fool for joy. Richelieu was deeply touched, you may suppose; and what with his former ill health and this new blow, he has never been himself since; but I knew not that he was so far gone as you describe."

" It is so reported in Paris," replied Fontrailles," and he has become so humble that no one would know him.   But mark me, Cinq Mars. The cardinal is now upon the brink of a precipice, and we must urge him quickly down; for if he once again gain the ascendancy, we are not only lost forever, but his power will be far greater than it was before."

" He will never rise more in this world," answered Cinq Mars. " His day, I trust, is gone by : his health is broken; and the king, who always hated him, now begins to fear him no longer. I will do my best to strengthen Louis's resolution, and get him into a way of thinking for himself. And, now, Fontrailles, for the news from Spain."

" Why, my story might be made longer than yours, if I were to go through all that happened to me on the road. It was a long and barren journey, and I believe I should have been almost starved before I reached Madrid, if I had not half filled my bags with biscuits. However, I arrived at length, and not without some difficulty found a place to lodge, for these cold Spaniards are as fearful of admitting a stranger to their house, as if he were a man-tiger. My next step was to send for a tailor, and to hire me a lacquais or two, one of whom I sent instantly to Madame de Chevreuse, praying an audience of her, which was granted immediately."

" Why thou wert not mad enough to make a confidante of Madame de Chevreuse ! " exclaimed Cinq Mars ; " why, it is carrying water in a sieve. A thousand to one, she makes her peace with Richelieu, by telling him the whole story."

" Fear not, Cinq Mars," answered Fontrailles. " Have you yet to learn that a woman's first passion is revenge ? To such extent is the hatred of Madame de Chevreuse against the cardinal, that I believe, were she asked to sacrifice one of her beautiful hands, she would do it, if it would but conduce to his ruin."

Cinq Mars shook his head, still doubting the propriety of what had been done ; but Fontrailles proceeded.

" However, I told her nothing ; she knew it all, before I set foot in Spain. You must know, King Philip is a monarch no way insensible to female charms, and the duchess is too lovely to pass unnoticed anywhere. The consequences are natural—a lady of her rank having taken refuge in his dominions, of course the king must pay her every attention. He is always with her—has a friendship, a penchant, an affection for her—call it what you will, but it is that sort of feeling which makes a man tell a woman everything : and thus very naturally our whole correspondence has gone direct to Madame de Chevreuse. My object in first asking to see her, was only to gain an immediate audience of the king, which she can always command ; but when I found that she knew the whole business, of course, I made her believe that I came for the express purpose of consulting her upon it. Her vanity was flattered. She became more than ever convinced, that she was a person of infinite consequence,

and acknowledged discernment; entered heart and hand
into all our schemes; stuck out her pretty little foot, and
made me buckle her shoe; brought me speedily to the
king's presence, and made him consent to all I wished;
got the treaty signed and sealed, and sent me back to
France with my object accomplished, remaining herself
fully convinced that she is at the head of the most formidable conspiracy that ever was formed, and that future
ages will celebrate her talents for diplomacy and intrigue."

Cinq Mars, though not fully satisfied at the admission
of so light a being as Madame de Chevreuse into secrets
of such importance, could not help smiling at the account
his companion gave; and as it was in vain to regret what
was done, he turned to the present, asking what was to
be done next. "No time is now to be lost," said he.
"For the whole danger is now incurred, and we must not
allow it to be fruitless."

"Certainly not," answered Fontrailles. "You must
ply the king hard to procure his consent as far as possible.
In the next place, a counterpart of the treaty must be
signed by all the confederates, and sent into Spain, for
which I have pledged my word; and another, similarly
signed, must be sent to the Duke of Bouillon in Italy.
But who will carry it to the duke? that is the question.
I cannot absent myself again."

"I will provide a messenger," said Cinq Mars. "There
is an Italian attached to my service, named Villa Grand.
a sort of half-bred gentleman, who, lacking gold himself,
hangs upon any who will feed him. They laugh at him
here for his long moustaches, and his longer rapier; but
if he tell truth, his rapier has done good service; so, as
this will be an undertaking of danger, he shall have it,
as he says he seeks but to distinguish himself in my
service, and being an Italian, he knows the country to
which he is going."

"If you can trust him, be it so," replied Fontrailles.

"At present let us look to other considerations. We must seek to strengthen our party by all means; for though circumstances seem to combine to favor us, yet it is necessary to guard against any change. Do you think that the queen could be brought to join us?"

"Certainly not!" replied the master of the horse; "and if she would, to us it would be far more dangerous than advantageous. She has no power over the mind of the king—she has no separate authority; and besides, though Richelieu's avowed enemy, she is so cautious of giving offence to Louis, that she would consent to nothing that was not openly warranted by him."

"But suppose we are obliged to have recourse to arms," said Fontrailles, "would it not be everything in our favor to have in our hands the queen and the heir apparent to the throne?"

"True," answered Cinq Mars; "but if we are driven to such extremity, she will be obliged to declare for some party, and that of necessity must be ours; for she will never side with Richelieu. We can also have her well surrounded by our friends, and seize upon the dauphin should the case require it."

"What say you, then, to trying the Count de Blenau? He is your friend. He is brave, expert in war, and just such a man as leads the blind multitude. But more, he is wealthy and powerful, and has much credit in Languedoc."

"I do not know," said Cinq Mars thoughtfully, "I do not know.—De Blenau would never betray us, even if he refused to aid our scheme. But I much think his scruples would go farther than even De Thou's. I have often remarked, he has that sort of nicety in his ideas which will not suffer him to enter into anything which may, by even a remote chance, cast a shade upon his name."

"Well, we can try him at all events," said Fontrailles. "You, Cinq Mars, can ask him whether he will join the liberators of his country."

"No, Fontrailles," answered the master of the horse in a decided tone; "no, I will not do it. Claude de Blenau is a man by whom I should not like to be refused. Besides, I should hesitate to involve him, young and noble-hearted as he is, in a scheme which might draw down ruin on his head."

"In the name of heaven, Cinq Mars," cried Fontrailles, with real astonishment at a degree of generosity of which he could find no trace in his own bosom, "of what are you dreaming? Are you frenzied? Why, you have engaged life and fortune, hope and happiness, in this scheme yourself, and can you love another man better?"

"There is every difference, Fontrailles—every difference. If I cut my own throat, I am a fool and a madman, granted; but if I cut the throat of another man, I am a murderer, which is somewhat worse. But I will be plain with you. I have embarked in this with my eyes open, and it is my own fault. Therefore, whatever happens, I will go on and do my best for our success. But mark me, Fontrailles, if all were to come over again, I would rather lay down one of my hands and have it chopped off, than enter into any engagment of the kind."

A cloud came over the brow of Fontrailles for a moment, and a gleam of rage lighted up his dark gray eye, which soon, however, passed away from his features, though the rankling passion still lay at his heart, like a smoldering fire, which wants but a touch to blaze forth and destroy. But his look, as I have said, was soon cleared of all trace of anger; and he replied with that show of cheerfulness which he well knew how to assume, "Well, Cinq Mars, I do not look upon it in so gloomy a light as you do; though perhaps, were it now to begin, I might not be so ready in it either, for the chances we have run were great; but these, I trust, are over, and everything certainly looks prosperous at present. However, there is no use in thinking what either of us might do had we now our choice. We are both too far engaged to go

back at this time of day ; so let us think alone of insuring
success, and the glory of having attempted to free our
country will at least be ours, let the worst befall us."

The word glory was never without its effect on Cinq
Mars. It was his passion, and was but the more violent
from the restraint to which his constant attendance on the
king had subjected it, seldom having been enabled to display in their proper field those high qualities which he possessed as a soldier. "So far you are right, Fontrailles,"
replied he ; "the glory even of the attempt is great, and
we have but one course to pursue, which is straightforward to our object. You do everything to bind the fickle
goddess to our cause, and so will I ; but thinking as I do,
I cannot find it in my heart to involve De Blenau. Manage that as you like ; only do not ask me to do it."

"Oh that is easily done," answered Fontrailles, "without your bearing any part in it. Of course each of the
confederates has a right to invite whomsoever he may
think proper to join his party, and it would be highly
dishonorable of any other to dissuade the person so invited from aiding the scheme on which all our lives depend. The Count de Blenau, I think you say, is now
retired to Bourbon. There also is the Duke of Orleans,
and I will take care that he shall broach the subject to the
count without implicating you."

Cinq Mars started from his seat, and began pacing the
room with his eyes bent on the ground, feeling an undefined sensation of dissatisfaction at the plans of Fontrailles, yet hardly knowing how to oppose them. "Well,
well," said he at length ; "it is your business, not mine ;
and besides, I do not, in the least, think that De Blenau
will listen to you for a moment. He has other things
to think of. Mademoiselle de Beaumont is absent, no
one knows where ; and he must soon hear of it."

"Be that as it may," replied Fontrailles, "I will try.
And now, Cinq Mars, let me touch upon another point ; "
and the wily conspirator prepared all his power to work

upon the mind of his less cautious companion, and to urge him on to an attempt which had already been the object of more than one conspiracy in that day, but which, by some unaccountable means, had always failed without any apparent difficulty or obstacle. This was no other than the assassination of the Cardinal de Richelieu; and those who read the memoirs of the faction-breathing Gondi, or any other of the historical records of the time, will wonder how, without any precaution for his personal safety, Richelieu escaped the many hands that were armed for his destruction.

Princes and nobles, warriors and politicians, had thought it no crime to undertake the death of this tyrant minister; but yet there was something in the mind of Cinq Mars so opposite to everything base and treacherous, that Fontrailles feared to approach boldly the proposal he was about to make. "Let us suppose, my noble friend," said he, in that slow and energetic manner which often lends authority to bad argument, "that all our schemes succeed—that the tyrant is stripped of the power he has so abused—that the tiger is enveloped in our toils. What are we to do? Are we to content ourselves with having caught him? Are we only to hold him for a moment in our power, and then to set him loose again, once more to ravage France, and to destroy ourselves? And if we agree to hold him in captivity, where shall we find chains sufficient to bind him, or a cage in which we can confine him with security, when there are a thousand other tigers of his race ready to attack the hunters of their fellow?"

"I propose nothing of the kind," answered Cinq Mars; "once stripped of his authority, let him be arraigned for the crimes which he has committed, and suffer the death he has merited. The blood of thousands will cry out for justice, and his very creatures will spurn the monster that they served from fear."

"Then you think him worthy of death," said Fontrailles, in that kind of undecided manner which showed that he felt he was treading on dangerous ground.

" Worthy of death! " exclaimed Cinq Mars; " who can doubt it?—Fontrailles, what is it that you mean? You speak as if there was something in your mind that you know not how to discover. Speak, man. What is it you would say? "

" Who will deny that Brutus was a patriot? " said Fontrailles; " a brave, a noble, and a glorious man? And Brutus stabbed Cæsar in the Capitol!—Cinq Mars, when the freedom of our country is at stake, shall we wait tamely till we have preached a timid monarch into compliance, or drawn a foreign power to our aid, when one—single—hand could do the work of justice, and rid the world of a tyrant who has lived so much too long? "

" Ha! " exclaimed Cinq Mars, starting back, and laying his hand upon his sword; " dost thou suppose me an assassin? Art thou one thyself, that thou canst so well gloze over murder with a stale tale of antiquity?—Monsieur de Fontrailles," he continued more calmly, but still with stern indignation, " you have mistaken the person to whom you addressed yourself. Pardon me. We will speak no more upon this subject lest we end worse friends than we began."

Fontrailles was not a common hypocrite; he saw at once that on this point persuasion would be vain, and defence of his first proposal would but leave the worse impression on the mind of his companion; and therefore his determination was formed in a moment to take up the exact reverse position to that which he had just occupied, and if possible to force Cinq Mars into a belief that the proposal had only been made to try him. The first wild start of his companion had caused Fontrailles to draw back almost in fear; but instantly recovering himself, like a well-trained actor, every muscle of whose face is under command, he fixed his eyes on Cinq Mars, and instead of any sign of anger or disappointment. he threw into his countenance an expression of gratified admiration. " Cinq Mars, my noble friend ! " he exclaimed, opening his arms to embrace him as the other concluded; " you are the man I thought you ! Pardon me if I have sought to try you ! but when I heard you propose to affect the cardinal's life by our plans, I knew not how far that idea might lead you, and I wished to be sure of the man with whom I was so deeply engaged. I declare before heaven, that had I found that you proposed to do Richelieu to death by aught but legal means, I should have been deeply grieved, and would have fled from France where'er my fortune might lead, leaving you to follow your plans as best you might. But I am now satisfied, and demand your pardon for having ever doubted you."

Cinq Mars suffered the embrace which Fontrailles proffered, but returned it coldly. Acting is ever acting, however near it may approach to nature; and notwith-standing all the hypocritical art of which Fontrailles was a master, and which he took care to exert on the present occasion, the mind of Cinq Mars still retained its doubts as to the character of the man with whom he had so closely linked his fate. " If he is a villain," thought the master of the horse, " he is a most black and consummate villain ; " and though they parted apparently friends, the recollection of that morning's conversation still haunted the imagination of Cinq Mars like some ill vision.

CHAPTER XXII.

Which evinces the necessity of saying, no ; and shows what it is to hunt upon a wrong scent.

In journeying onward towards the Bourbonnois, the thoughts of De Blenau had full time to rest upon the late occurrences ; and though these had been of such a fearful nature, yet so rapidly had they passed, that dangers and sorrows, prisons and trials, floated before his remembrance like a confused and uncertain dream ; and it required an effort to fix all the particular circumstances in their correct position, for the purpose of investigating the motives of the principal actors in those events which had so deeply affected himself.

De Blenau first care, on arriving at Moulins, was to write to Pauline de Beaumont. As couriers and posts in those days were different from such things at present, De Blenau did not choose to trust his letter to the uncertain conveyance of the government carrier, or, as he was then called, the ordinaire ; but placing it in the hands of his trusty page, Henry de la Mothe, he sent him forth upon a journey to St. Germain, with orders to deliver many a kind greeting to Pauline in person, and to bring back an answer with all speed.

The boy set out, and De Blenau, flattering himself with the idea that his banishment from court would not be of any long continuance, took his residence for the time in the immediate neighborhood of Moulins, contenting himself with an old château, the proprietor of which was very willing—his fortune and his castle both being somewhat decayed—to sacrifice his pride of birth, in consideration of a handsome remuneration from the young count.

Here De Blenau had dwelt some time, waiting the return of his messenger, and in possession of that quiet solitude most consonant to his feelings, when he was disturbed by a billet left at his gate by a horseman, who waited not to be questioned, but rode away immediately after having delivered it. The note itself merely contained a request, that the Count de Blenau would ride in the direction of St. Amand on the following evening at the hour of four, when he would meet with one who had business of importance to communicate. The handwriting was unknown to him, and De Blenau at first hesitated whether to obey the summons or not; but curiosity has a thousand ways of strengthening itself, and at last he reasoned himself into a belief, that whatever it might be, no harm could accrue from his compliance.

Accordingly, on the following evening, as the hour drew near, he mounted his horse, and, accompanied by his usual attendants, proceeded towards St. Amand. Having ridden on for more than an hour without meeting any one above the rank of a peasant, he began to accuse himself for having been the dupe of what might prove some foolish joke. He had even reined in his horse with the purpose of returning, when he perceived a person approaching on horseback, who, notwithstanding a sort of carelessness,—even, perhaps, slovenliness of manner and carriage—had about him that undefinable air, which in all ages, and in every guise, denotes a gentleman, and a distinguished one. It was not, however, till he came near that De Blenau recognized Gaston, Duke of Orleans, whom he had not seen for some time. The moment he did remember him, he gave him the centre of the road, and saluting him respectfully, was passing on, never dreaming that the summons he had received could have proceeded from him.

" Good-day, Monsieur de Blenau. You are close upon the hour," said the duke, drawing up his horse, and at once allowing the count to understand that it was with him that the appointment had been made.

"I was not aware," replied De Blenau, "that the summons which I received last night was from so honorable a hand, or I should have had no hesitation in obeying."

"Why, that is right," said the duke. "The truth is, I wished much to see you, Monsieur le Comte, upon a business wherein you may not only be of much service to yourself and me; but also to your country. We will ride on, if you please; and as we go I will explain myself further."

De Blenau turned his horse and rode on with the duke; but the warning which Chavigni had given him came strongly into his mind; and Gaston of Orleans was too famous for the unfortunate conspiracies in which he had been engaged, for De Blenau to think with aught but horror, of acting in any way with a man, the weak versatility of whose disposition had already brought more than one of his friends to the scaffold. He therefore waited for the duke's communication, determined to cut it short as soon as propriety admitted; and even to deviate from the respect due to his rank, rather than become the confidant of a prince whose station was his sole title to reverence.

"You do not answer me, Monsieur de Blenau," said the duke, after having waited a moment or two for some reply. "Are you, sir, inclined to serve your country; or is the Cardinal de Richelieu your good friend?"

"That I am inclined to serve my country," replied De Blenau, "your highness need not doubt; and when my sword can avail that country against a foreign adversary, it shall always be ready at her call. In regard to his eminence of Richelieu, I hope that he is no more my enemy than I am his; and that he will no more attempt to injure me than I will to injure him."

"But has he not endeavored to injure you already?"

said the duke. "Listen to me, Sir Count. Suppose that
there were many men at this moment well inclined to free
France from the yoke under which she labors. Suppose
I were to tell you that——"

"Let me beseech your highness," interposed De Blenau,
"to tell me no more; for, if I understand you rightly, it
must be a confidence dangerous either to you or me—
dangerous to you, if I reveal it; and dangerous to me,
if I do not. Pardon me, my lord, for interrupting you;
but let my ears remain in their present innocence of what
you mean. What may be your wishes with me, I know
not: but before you proceed further, let me say that I
will enter into no scheme whatever against a government
to which his majesty has given his sanction, and which
it is always in his power to alter or remove at his pleasure,
without any one being entitled to question his authority
either in raising it or casting it down. And now, having
ventured to premise thus much, if I can serve your highness personally, in any way where my honor and my
allegiance are not at all implicated, I shall be most happy
in an opportunity of showing my attachment to your
royal person and family."

"Why, then, Monsieur de Blenau," replied the duke,
"I think the best thing we can do is, to turn our horses
different ways, and forget that we have met to-day at all.
Our conference has been short, but it has been to the
purpose. But of course, before we part, I expect your
promise, as a man of honor, that you will not betray
me."

"I have nothing to betray, my lord," replied De Blenau
with a smile. "We have met on the road to St. Amand.
We have not been five minutes in each other's company.
Your highness has told me nothing, whatever I may
have suspected; therefore you may rest perfectly secure
that I have nothing to betray, even if they put me to the
torture to-morrow. But as I think that for your highness's sake we had better be as little together as possible,
I will humbly take my leave."

22

So saying, De Blenau bowed low, and turned his horse towards Moulins, the Duke of Orleans preparing to take the other road; but suddenly the latter stopped, and turning his head, asked if De Blenau had gained any news of Mademoiselle de Beaumont.

"I am not aware of what your highness alludes to," replied De Blenau, quickly reining in his horse, and returning to the side of the duke.

"What, then you have not heard. When had you letters from St. Germain?"

"Heard what? In the name of God, speak, my lord!" cried De Blenau: "do not keep me in suspense."

"Nay, Monsieur de Blenau, I know but little," answered the duke. "All my news came yesterday in a letter from St. Germain, whereby I find that Mademoiselle de Beaumont has disappeared; and as no one knows whither she is gone, and no cause is apparent for her voluntary absence, it is conjectured that Richelieu, finding, as it is whispered, that she endeavored to convey intelligence to you in the Bastile, has caused her to be arrested and confined au secret."

"But when did she disappear?—Who saw her last?— Have no traces been discovered?—Why do they not apply to the king?" exclaimed De Blenau, with a degree of agitation that afforded amusement, rather than excited sympathy, in the frivolous mind of the Duke of Orleans.

"Really, Monsieur de Blenau, to none of all your questions can I at all reply," answered Gaston. "Very possibly the young lady may have gone off with some fair lover, in which case she will have taken care to leave no traces of her flight. What think you of the weather?—will it rain to-day?"

"Hell and fury!" cried De Blenau, incensed at the weak trifling of the prince at a moment when his feelings were so deeply interested; and turning his horse round without further adieu, he struck his spurs into the animal's sides, and, followed by his attendants, galloped off towards Moulins. Arrived at the château which he inhabited, his thoughts were still in such a troubled state as to forbid all calm consideration. "Prepare everything to set out. Saddle fresh horses. Send to Moulins for the propriétaire," were De Blenau's first commands, determined at all risks to set out for St. Germain and seek for Pauline himself. But while his orders were in train of execution, reflection came to his aid, and he began to think that the news which the duke had given him might not be true—that Gaston might either be deceived himself, or that he might have invented the story for the purpose of forcing him into a conspiracy against Richelieu's government. "At all events," thought he, "Henry de La Mothe cannot be longer absent than tomorrow. I may miss him on the road, and thus be four days without information instead of one." Accordingly, after some further hesitation, he determined to delay his journey one day, and counterordered the preparations which he had before commanded. Nevertheless, his mind was too much agitated to permit of his resting inactive; and quitting the château, he walked quickly on the road towards Paris; but he had not proceeded more than a quarter of a league, when from the top of a hill he perceived a horseman coming at full speed towards him. At first, while the distance rendered his form altogether indistinct, De Blenau decided that it was Henry de La Mothe—it must be—it could be nobody else. Then again he began to doubt—the horse did not look like his; and De Blenau had almost determined that it was not his page, when the fluttering scarf of blue and gold becoming apparent, decided the question, and he hurried forward, impatient even of the delay which must yet intervene.

The page rode on at full speed; and even from that circumstance De Blenau drew an unfavorable augury: he had something evidently to communicate which required haste. His horse, too, was not the same which had carried him away, and he must have changed him on the road: this too was a sign of that urgent despatch which could alone proceed from some painful cause. However, the page came rapidly forward, recognized his lord, and drawing in his horse, alighted to give relief to De Blenau's doubts, only by confirming his fears.

His first tidings were perfectly similar to the information which had been given by the Duke of Orleans; but the more minute details which he had obtained, forming part of the history which he gave De Blenau of all that had occurred to him on his journey, I shall take the liberty of abridging myself, instead of leaving them in the desultory and long-winded condition in which they proceeded from the mouth of Monsieur de La Mothe.

Setting out from Moulins on one of the Count de Blenau's strongest horses. Henry de La Mothe was not long in reaching St. Germain; and with all the promptitude of his age and nature, he hastened eagerly towards the palace, promising himself infinite pleasure in delivering a genuine love-letter into the fair hands of Mademoiselle Pauline. No small air of consequence, therefore, did he assume in inquiring for Mademoiselle de Beaumont, and announcing that he must speak with her himself: but the boyish vivacity of the page was soon changed into sorrowful anxiety, when the old servant of Anne of Austria, to whom his inquiries had been addressed, informed him that the young lady had disappeared, and was nowhere to be heard of. Now Henry de La Mothe, the noble Count de Blenau's gay page, was an universal favorite at St. Germain; so out of pure kindness, and without the least inclination in the world to gossip, the old servant took him into the palace, and after treating him to a cup of old St. Valier wine, told him all about the disappearance of Pauline, which formed a history occupying exactly one hour and ten minutes in delivering.

Amongst other interesting particulars, he described to

the page how he himself had accompanied Mademoiselle
de Hauteford and Mademoiselle de Beaumont from
Chantilly to Paris, for the purpose of conveying news to
Monsieur de Blenau, in the Bastile;—and how that night
he followed the two young ladies as far as the church
of St. Gervais, where they separated, and he remained
at the church door, while Mademoiselle de Hauteford
went in and prayed for the good succes of Pauline;—and
farther, how Mademoiselle de Hauteford said all the
prayers she knew, and composed a great many new ones
to pass the time, and yet no Pauline returned.

He then went on to describe their search for Pauline,
and their disappointment and distress at not finding her,
and the insolence of a lying innkeeper, who lived opposite the prison, and who assured him that the young
lady was safe, for that he himself had delivered her from
peril by the valor of his invincible arm. After this, he
took up the pathetic, and showed forth in moving terms
the agony and despair of Madame de Beaumont on first
hearing of the non-appearance of her daughter; and then
commented upon the extraordinary insensibility that she
had since shown. "For after two days," said he, "she
seemed to grow quite satisfied, and to forget it all, the
cold-hearted old————cat."

" 'Tis just like her," said Henry de La Mothe. "They
say, when her husband was killed, she never shed a tear.
But mark me, Monsieur Mathieu, she shall not have the
count's letter. As Mademoiselle is not here, I'll take it
back to him unopened; so have a care not to tell the
old marquise that I have been here. Before I go back,
however, I'll away to Paris, to gather what news I can.
That aubergiste meant something—I know him well. 'Tis
old Jacques Chatpilleur, the vivandier, who served with
the army in Rousillon, when I was there with the
count."

" Well, well, my good youth, go to Paris if you please,"
replied the old servant. "You'll gain no tidings more

than I have given you. Did not I make all sorts of inquiries myself? and they are not likely to deceive me, I wot. Young birds think they can fly before they can peck; but go, go,—you'll gain no more than what I have told you."

Henry de La Mothe did not feel very well assured of the truth of this last position; and therefore, though his back ached with a four days' ride as fast as he could go, he set out again for Paris, where he arrived before night-fall; and entering the city by the Port St. Antoine, directed his course to the house of our doughty friend, Jacques Chatpilleur, where he was instantly acknowledged as an old acquaintance by the worthy aubergiste, and treated with suitable distinction. Although every moment was precious, the page did not think fit to enter upon the business that brought him till the auberge was clear of intruders; and this being the hour at which many an honest burgess of the good city solaced his inward man with boudin blanc and Burgundy when the fatigues of the day began to cease, Henry de La Mothe thought he might as well follow the same agreeable calling, and while he was at Rome, do as Romans did.

More than an hour passed before the page had an opportunity of communicating fully with the good aubergiste; but when Jacques Chatpilleur heard that the lady he had delivered from the clutches of Letrames, was no less a person than Pauline, only daughter and heiress of the late celebrated Marquis de Beaumont, and that, notwithstanding his assistance, she had somehow been carried off on that identical night, his strange woodcock-shaped person became agitated with various extraordinary contortions, proceeding from an odd mixture of pleasure and grief, which at once took possession of him, and contended for the mastery.

"Mon Dieu!" cried he, "to think that it was Mademoiselle de Beaumont, and that she should be lost after all!" And the aubergiste set himself to think of how

it could all have happened. "I'll bet a million," cried
he at length, starting from his reverie, and clapping his
hands together with a concussion that echoed to the
Bastile itself—" I'll bet a million that it was that great
gluttonous Norman vagabond, who on that very night
ate me up a matelot d'anguille and a dinde piquée. He is
understrapping cut-throat to Master Chavigni, and he
has never been here since. He has carried her off, for
a million; and taken her away to some prison in the
provinces, all for trying to give a little news to the good
count. But I'll ferret out his route for you. On with
your beaver and come with me. Margueritte, look to
the doors while I am absent. I know where the scoundrel
lodged; so come along, and we'll soon hear more of
him."

So saying, the landlord of the Sanglier Gourmand led
Henry de La Mothe forth into the Rue St. Antoine, and
thence through the several turnings and windings by
which the Norman had carried Pauline to the late lodgings of Monsieur Marteville. Here Jacques Chatpilleur
summoned all persons in the house, male and female,
lodger and landlord, to give a full, true, and particular
account of all they knew, believed, or suspected concerning the tall Norman who usually dwelt there. And such
was the tone of authority which he used, and the fre-
quency of his reference to Henry de La Mothe, whom he
always specified as "this honorable youth," that the
good folks instantly transformed, in their own imagina-
tions, the page of the Count de Blenau into little less than
the valet de chambre of the prime minister, and consequently answered all questions with becoming deference.

The sum of the information which was thus obtained
amounted to this, that on the evening in question, Monsieur Marteville had brought thither a young lady—
whether by force or not, no one could specify; that she
was dressed as a Languedoc peasant, which Monsieur
Chatpilleur acknowledged to be the disguise Pauline had

assumed; and that the same evening he had carried her
away again on horseback, leading her steed by the bridle
rein. It further appeared that the Norman, while preparing to set out, had asked a great many questions about
Troyes in Champagne, and had inquired whether there
was not a wood extending over some leagues near Mesnil
St. Loup, which was reported to be infested by robbers.
From all this the inhabitants of the house had concluded
universally that his journey was destined to be towards
Troyes, and that he would take care to avoid the wood
of Mesnil St. Loup.

Henry de La Mothe now fancied that he had the clue
completely in his hands, and returning with Jacques
Chatpilleur to his auberge, he took one night's necessary
rest, and having exchanged his horse, which was knocked
up with its journey, he set out the next morning on his
return to Moulins.

After this recital, all considerations of personal safety,
the king's commands to remain in Bourbon, the enmity
of the cardinal, and the warnings of Chavigni, vanished
from the mind of De Blenau like smoke; and returning
to the château, he ordered his horses to be instantly
prepared, chose ten of his most resolute servants to accompany him, ordered Henry de La Mothe to remain till
he had recovered from his fatigues, and then to return
to St. Germain, and tell Madame de Beaumont that he
would send her news of her daughter, or lose his life in
the search; and having made all other necessary arrangements, he took his departure for Troyes without a consideration of the consequences.

CHAPTER XXIII.

The consequence of fishing in troubled water.

WE must now return to the two worthy personages whom we left jogging on towards the château of St. Loup, taking them up at the precise place where we set them down.

"Remember, Madame Louise, I take you with no good-will: you insist upon going; so now if you meet with anything disagreeable, it is your own fault—mark that, ma poule."

"I'm no more afraid of the devil than yourself," answered Louise, pertly; "and I suppose I shall meet with no one worse than he is."

"You may," replied the Norman; "but come on, it gets late, and we have no time to spare."

The tone of Marteville was not very encouraging; but Louise was resolved not to lose sight of her husband, and being by nature as bold as a lion, she followed on without fear. True it is, that she did not know the whole history of the Sorcerer's Grove, or perhaps she might have felt some of those imaginary terrors from which hardly a bosom in France was altogether free; although Louise, bred up by Madame de Beaumont, whose strong and masculine mind rejected most of the errors of that age, had perhaps less of the superstition of the day than any other person of her own class.

The first approach to the Sorcerer's Grove was anything but terrifying. The road, winding gently down the slope of the hill, entered the forest between some fine tall trees, which rising out of a tract of scanty underwood and open ground, with considerable spaces between each of the boughs, afforded plenty of room for the rich sun to pour his rays between, and to checker the green shadows of the wood with intervals of golden light. From this spot, however, the road, entering the deeper part of the wood, took a direction towards the old château of St. Loup; and here the trees, growing closer together, began to shut out the rays; gloom and darkness spread over the path, and the rocks rising up into high broken banks on each side, cut off even the scanty light which glided between the thick branches above. At the same time, the whole scenery assumed a wilder and more desolate character, and the windings of the road round the base of the hill prevented the eye from catching even a glimpse of the prospect beyond.

The deep solitude, the profound silence, the shadow of the overhanging woods, and the sombre gloom of every object around, began to have their effect on the mind of Louise, and notwithstanding her native boldness of heart, she set herself to conjure up more than one unpleasing vision. Her fears, however, were more of the living than the dead; and having now, against her nature, kept silence a long while, out of respect to the angry humor of her dearly beloved husband, she ventured to assert that it looked quite a place for robbers, and added a hope that they should not meet any.

"Pardie! I hope we shall!" replied the Norman. "Those you call robbers are merely gentlemen from the wars as I am myself: soldiers at free quarters, who have ever had a right prescriptive to levy their pay with their own hand. I beg that you will speak respectfully of them."

Louise looked at her husband with an inquiring glance, not very well knowing whether to take his speech seriously, or merely as a jest: but there was nothing mirthful in the countenance of Monsieur Marteville, who, out of humor with his fair lady for persisting to accompany him, was in no mood for jesting. At this moment a whistle was heard in the wood, so like the note of a bird,

that Louise was deceived, and would have taken no farther notice of the sound had not her companion applied
his hand to his lips and imitated it exactly.

" What is that?" demanded Louise, upon whose mind
a thousand undefined suspicions were crowding fast:
" what noise is that in the wood?"

" It's only a pivert," replied the Norman, with a grim
smile, in the effort of which the scar upon his lip drew
the corner of his mouth almost into his eye.

" A pivert!" replied Louise. " No, no, that is not the
cry of a woodpecker—you are cheating me."

" Well, you will see," replied Marteville; " I'll make
him come out." So saying, he repeated the same peculiar
whistle, and then drawing in his rein, shook himself in
the saddle, loosened his sword in the sheath, and laid his
hand on one of his holsters, as a man who prepares to an
encounter, of the event of which he is not quite certain
whether it will be for peace or war.

His whistle was again returned, and a moment after
the form of a man was seen protruding itself through the
tress that crowned the high bank under which they
stood. His rusty iron morion, his still rustier cuirass,
his weather-beaten countenance and dingy apparel, formed
altogether an appearance so similar to the trunks of the
trees amongst which he stood, that he would have been
scarcely distinguishable had it not been for the effort to
push his way through the lower branches, the rustling of
which, and a few falling stones forced over the edge of
the rock at his approach, drew the eye more particularly
to the spot where he appeared. In his hand he carried a
firelock, which, by a natural impulse, was pointed at the
Norman the moment he perceived a doublet of blue velvet
—as the fowling-piece of a sportsman is instinctively
carried to his shoulder, on the rising of a partridge or a
grouse. But Monsieur Marteville was prepared for all
such circumstances; and drawing the pistol which hung
at his saddlebow, and which, if one might judge by

length, would carry a mile at least, he pointed directly towards the rusty gentleman above described, crying out, "Eh bien, l'ami! Eh bien! Do you shoot your friends like woodcocks? or have you forgotten me?"

"Nom de Dieu!" cried the man above, "I'll come down to you directly. Christi! I had nearly given you a ball! But I'll come down!"

While the robber was putting this promise in execution, Marteville whispered a few words of consolation to Louise, bidding her not be afraid, that they were friends, et cetera; but seeing that his words produced no effect, and that the unfortunate girl, beginning to comprehend the nature of his character, had burst into tears of bitter regret, he muttered a curse or two, not loud, but deep; and without any farther effort to allay her fears, sat whistling on his horse, till the robber, half-sliding, half-running, managed to descend from the eminence on which he had first appeared.

"Eh bien, Callot," said Monsieur Marteville to his former companion, "how goes it with the troop?"

"But badly," replied Callot. "What with one devilry or another, we have but half a dozen left."

"And where is Pierrepont Le Blanc?" demanded the Norman. "Could not he keep you together?"

"Oh! we have sent him to the kingdom of moles," answered the robber, twisting his face into a most horrible grin. "First he quarrelled with one, and then he quarrelled with another, and then, as he was captain, and had the purse, he bethought him of taking himself off with all the treasure. But we caught him on the road; and so, as I have said, we sent the buccaneer on an embassy to the kingdom of moles. After that, there were two of us shot near Epernay, by a party of the guard; and then six more went to see what could be gathered upon the road to Perpignan, and one was taken and hanged at Troyes; so that there are but myself and five others of the old band left."

"And quite enough too, if you had a bold leader," replied the Norman. "But where do you roost, mes jolis oiseaux?"

"No, no; we do not perch now," answered the robber; "we go to earth. Under the old castle here are the most beautiful vaults in the world; and I defy Beelzebub himself to nose us, when we are hidden there."

"But why not take to the château itself? Is it so far decayed?"

"Nay," replied the other, "for that matter it is as good a nest as any one would wish to house in: but it is not quite so forsaken as folks think. We did put up there at first; but one night, while all of our party were out but three—being myself and two others who stayed—we heard suddenly the sound of horses, and looking out, we saw by the twilight five stout cavaliers dismount in the court; and up they marched to the very room where we were sitting, so that we had scarce time to bundle up our things and to cover. And there they sat for four good hours; while we were shut up in the little watch-tower next to them, with no way to get out, and no powder but what was in our carbines, or mayhap we should have given them a dose or two of leaden pills, for at first we thought they were on the look-out for our band. But presently after, up came another, and then they all set to to talk high treason. I could not well hear, for the door was so thick, and we dared not move; but I know they spoke of a treaty with Spain, and bringing in Spanish troops into France. Since then we have kept to the vaults, for fear of being nosed."

"Well, Louise," whispered the Norman, turning to the soubrette, "you see I did not come here for no purpose. It is this treaty with Spain I want to find out; and if I do our fortune is made forever, and you will eat off gold, and drink out of gold, and be as happy as a princess!"

The prospects which her husband held out, and which

might certainly be called golden, were not without their
effect on Louise; but still his evident familiarity with the
gentleman in the rusty steel coat did not at all suit her
ideas of propriety, nor were the matters which they
discussed in the least to her taste; but as remonstrance
was in vain, and she began to perceive that the influence
of her tears was not very great, she resigned herself to
her fate in silence.

Several more questions and replies passed between the
Norman and his ancient comrade, which, as they tend to
throw no light upon this history, shall not find a place
therein. At length Monsieur Callot, in as hospitable and
courtly a strain as he could assume, requested the pleasure
of Monsieur Marteville's company to spend the evening
in the vaults of the old château, if he had not grown too
fine, by living among the great, to associate with his old
friends. In return for this, the worthy Norman assured
him that he never was so happy as when he was in their
society, accepted the invitation with pleasure, and begged
to introduce his wife. Callot would fain have offered
his salute to the lips of the fair lady, and had mounted on
a huge stone beside her horse for that purpose; but
Louise repulsed him with the dignity of a duchess, and
Callot did not press the matter further, merely giving a
shrewd wink of the eye and screw of the under-jaw, as
much as to say, " She's nice, it seems," and then led the
way towards the present abode of Marteville's old band.

The road which he took wound through the very
depth of the wood towards that side of the hill which,
looking over the wide extent of forest-ground lying between the old castle and the high road to Troyes, seemed
to offer nothing but dark inaccessible precipices, from the
shallow stream that ran bubbling at its base to the walls
of the ruin above. Crossing the rivulet, however, which
did not rise higher than the horses' knees, the robber led
the way round a projecting mass of rock, that seemed to
have been forcibly riven from the rest, and which, though

it left space enough for the horses to turn, would have effectually concealed them from the sight of any one who might be in the wood.

The two sides of the hill next to the village of Mesnil, and the ridge of rising ground on which it was situated, sloped easily into the valleys around, and were covered with a rich and glowing vegetation; but on the northern as well as the western side, which the Norman and his companions now approached, the rock offered a very different character, and one, indeed, extremely rare in that part of the country.

Wherever the eye turned, nothing presented itself but flat surfaces of cold gray stone, with the deep markings of the rifts and hollows which separated them from each other.

Turning round the base of a large mass of rock, the robber uttered three loud whistles, to give notice that it was a friend who approached; and immediately after, from a cavern, the mouth of which was concealed in one of the fissures, came forth two figures, whose wild apparel corresponded very well with that of their companion.

"Morbleu! Monsieur Marteville!" cried one of them, the moment he recognized the Norman, "est-ce vous? Soyez le bien venu! Come at a lucky moment for some of the best wine of Bonne! The Gros St. Nicholas—you remember our old companion—has just returned from the Chemin de Troyes, where he met two charitable monks, who, out of pure benevolence, bestowed upon him three paniers of good wine and twelve broad pieces; though they threatened to excommunicate him, and the two who were with him, for holding steel poniards to their throats while they did their alms. However, you are heartily welcome, and the more so if you are come to stay with us."

"We will talk of that presently," said the Norman. "But in the first place, good friends, tell me, can one get up to the castle above, which, Callot says, is habitable yet? for here is my wife, who is not much used to dwell in vaults, and may like a lodging above ground better."

"Oh, certainly! Madame shall be accomodated," said the last speaker, who seemed to be more civilized than good Monsieur Callot. "Our own dwelling is well enough; but if she so please, I will show you up the staircase which leads from the vaults to the court above. However, I hope she will stay to partake of our supper, which is now before the fire, as you shall see."

"She shall come down again," said the Norman, dismounting, and lifting Louise out of the saddle, "and will thank you for your good cheer, for we have ridden far." So saying, he followed into the cave, which at first presented nothing but the natural ruggedness of the rock; but at that spot where the daylight began to lose its effect in the increasing darkness of the cavern, one might perceive, though with difficulty, that it assumed the form of a regular arch cased with masonry; and in a moment or two, as they proceeded groping their way after the robber, they were warned that there were steps: mounting these, and turning to the left, they discerned, at a little distance in advance, a bright red light streaming from behind a projecting angle, which itself remained in utter obscurity. The robber here went on first, and they heard him announce in a loud and jocular tone. "Le Sieur Marteville, et madame sa femme!" with as much ceremony as if he had been heralding them into the presence of royalty.

"Bah! vous plaisantez!" cried a thick merry voice seeming as if it issued from the midst of stewed prunes. But the Norman advancing, bore evidence of the truth of the other's annunciation, and was instantly caught in the arms of the Gros St. Nicholas, as he was called; who merited, at least, the appellation of gros, though with the sanctity he appeared to have but little to do. He was fat, short, and protuberant, with a face as round as the ful moon, and as rosy as a peony. In fact, he seemed much better fitted for a burgess or a priest, an innkeeper or an alderman, than for the thin and meagre trade of a cut-purse, which seldom leaves anything but bones to be hanged at last. However, he bore him jollily; and, when the party entered, was, with morion and breast-plate thrown aside, engaged in basting a large quarter of venison, which smoked before a stupendous fire, whose blaze illuminated all the wide vault, which formed their salle à manger and kitchen both in one.

"Est-il possible?" cried the Gros St. Nicholas, embracing our Norman, whose companion he had been for many years both in honorable and dishonorable trades. "Mon ami! Mon Capitaine! Mon Brave! Mon Prince! Enfin, mon Normand!"

Quitting the ecstasies of the Gros St. Nicholas at meeting once more with his friend, and the formalities of his introduction to Louise, we shall only say that, according to the request of the Norman, one of the freebooters led the way up the circular staircase in the rock, which soon brought them into the open air, through a small arch entering upon the court of the old castle. Here Marteville, having marked all the peculiar turns which they had taken, with the accuracy which his former life had taught, bade good-day to their guide, promising to rejoin the party below by the time the venison was roasted; and finding that more than an hour of daylight yet remained, he proceeded with Louise to explore the remains of the château.

The little attentions he had lately paid, had greatly conciliated his fair lady; and though still somewhat disposed to pout, she suffered him to explain his views with a tolerable degree of placability. "You must know, ma charmante Louise," said he, "that there is a tremendous plot going on against the government; and that Monsieur de Chavigni has intrusted me to discover it. You heard what Callot said, concerning a treaty with Spain. Now

23

I have always understood, that when these secret treaties are formed, a copy is deposited in some uninhabited place for greater security. You see, I have traced Fontrailles to this castle, and it is evident that here he met the other conspirators: now where, then, can they have secreted the treaty but somewhere about here? So now, Louise, help me to find this paper, if it is to be found; and then we will soon quit these men, of whom you seem so much afraid, and go and live like princes on the fortune that Chavigni has promised."

To this long speech of her husband, which he accompanied with sundry little caresses, Louise replied, in a tone still half sulky, that she was ready to seek the paper, but that she did not see how they could find it, with nothing to guide them in the search. But nevertheless, when they did seriously begin their perquisitions, she displayed all that sagacity in discovering a secret which women instinctively possess. Of course, the first place to which they particularly directed their inquiries was the chamber in which, according to the account of Callot, the meeting of the conspirators had been held.

Here they looked in every nook and corner, turned over every heap of rubbish, examined the chairs and the table of old Père Le Rouge, and having gone over every inch of the apartment, began anew and went over it all again. At length Louise, seemingly tired of her search in that chamber, left her husband to pursue it as he pleased, and sitting down in one of the settles, began to hum a Languedoc air, beating time with her fingers on the table.

"Pardie!" cried the Norman, after having hunted for some time in vain: "it is not here, that is certain!"

"Yes, it is!" said Louise, very quietly continuing to beat time on the table; "it is in this very room."

"Nom de Dieu! where is it then?" cried Monsieur Marteville.

"It is here, in the inside of this hollow piece of wood," answered Louise, tapping the table with her knuckles, which produced that sort of empty echoing sound that evinced it was not so solid as it appeared.

The Norman now approached, and soon convincing himself that Louise was right, he took her in his arms and gave her a kiss that made the ruin echo. The next thing was to get into the drawer, or whatsoever it was, that occupied the interior of the table; but this not proving very easy, the impatient Norman set it upright upon one end, and drawing his sword, soon contrived to cleave it through the middle; when, to the delight of the eyes that looked upon it, appeared a large cavity neatly wrought in the wood, containing a packet of vellum folded, and sealed at all corners in blue and yellow wax, with neat pieces of floss-silk to keep it all together. The Norman could have eaten it up: and Louise, with a degree of impatient curiosity, peculiarly her own, was already fingering one of the seals, about to break it open, when Marteville stopped her with a tremendous oath. "What are you going to do?" cried he: "you know little what it is to pry into state secrets. If you had opened that seal, instead of perhaps a reward of twenty thousand crowns, we should both have been sent to the Bastile for the rest of our lives." Louise dropped the packet in dismay; and the Norman continued, "Did you never hear of the Abbé de Langy, who happening to be left by Monsieur de Richelieu in his private cabinet only for five minutes, with some state papers on the table, was sent to the Bastile for twelve years, merely for fear he had read them? No, no; this must go to Monsieur Chavigni without so much as cracking the wax."

"Could not we just look in at the end?" demanded Louise, looking wistfully at the packet, which her husband had now picked up. But upon this he put a decided negative; and having now succeeded to his heart's content, the burly Norman, in the exuberance of his joy,

began singing and capering till the old pile both echoed
and shook with his gigantic gambols. "Ma Louise,"
cried he at length, "vous êtes fatiguée. Je vais vous
porter;" and catching her up in his arms, notwithstanding all remonstrance, he carried her like a feather into the
court-yard, through the narrow arch, and threading all
the intricacies of the vaults with the same sagacious
facility with which a ferret glides through the windings
of a warren, he bore her safely and in triumph into the
salle à manger of the honorable fraternity below. This
was not the mode of progression which Louise most
admired, nor was she very much gratified at being ex-
hibited to her husband's old friends in so ungraceful an
attitude; and the consequences, of course, were, that she
would willingly have torn his eyes out had she dared.

However, Monsieur Callot, Le Gros St. Nicholas, and
others, applied themselves successfully to soothe her ruf-
fled spirits; and the venison being ready, and a long
table laid, each person drew forth their knife, and soon
committed infinite havoc on the plump haunch which was
placed before them. The wine succeeded, and then that
water of life which very often ends in death. All was
hilarity and mirth, song, jest, and laughter. Gradually,
one barrier after another fell, as cup succeeded cup.
Each one told his own story, without regard to the rest;
each one sang his own song; each one cracked his own
joke. Louise had retired to a settle by the side of the
fire, but still mingled in the conversation, when it could
be called such; and Monsieur Callot, somewhat full of
wine, and a good deal smitten with her charms, plied
her with assiduities rather more perhaps than was necessary. In the meantime, the Gros St. Nicholas, running
over with brandy and good spirit, kept jesting the Norman upon some passages of his former life, which might
as well have been passed over and forgotten. "Madame!" cried he at length, turning round towards Louise,
with an overflowing goblet in his hand and his broad

face full of glee, " I have the honor of drinking to your health, as the fifth spouse of our good friend Monsieur de Marteville; and let me assure you, that of the three that are living and the two that are dead, you are the most beautiful beyond compare ! "

Up started Louise in an agony of indignation, and forth she poured upon the Gros St. Nicholas a torrent of vituperation for jesting upon such a subject. But on his part he only shrugged his shoulders, and declared that he did not jest at all. " Mon Dieu ! " said he, " it is very unreasonable to suppose that Monsieur Marteville, who is as big as five men, should be contented with one wife. Besides, it is très agréable to have a wife in every province; I always do so myself."

The thunder of Louise's ire now increased in a seven-fold degree, was turned instantly upon her dearly-beloved husband. Her eyes flashed, and her cheek flamed, and approaching him, where he sat laughing at the whole business, she demanded that he should exculpate himself from this charge of pentigamy, with a tone and manner that made the Norman, who had drunk quite enough, laugh still more. With an unheard-of exertion of self-command, Louise kept her fingers from his face ! but she burst forth into reproaches so bitter and stinging, that Marteville's mirth was soon converted into rage, and he looked at her with a glance which would quickly have taught those who knew him well not to urge him farther. But Louise went on, and wound up by declaring, that she would live with him no longer—that she would quit him that very moment, and finding her way to Monsieur Chavigni, would tell him all—adding, that she would soon send the guard to ferret out that nest of ruffians, and that she hoped to see him hanging at the head of them. With this expression of her intentions, Louise darted out of the vault; but the Norman, who, speechless with rage, had sat listening to her with his teeth clenched, and his nether lip quivering with suppressed passion, started suddenly up, cast the settle from him with such force that it was dashed to pieces against the wall, and strode after her with the awful cloud of determined wrath settled upon his brow.

The mirth of the robbers, who knew the ungovernable nature of their companion's passions, was now over, and each looked in the face of the other with silent expectation. After a space, there was the murmur of angry voices heard for a moment at the farther end of the passage; then a loud piercing shriek rang through the vault; and then all was silence. A momentary sensation of horror ran through the bosoms of even the ferocious men whose habits rendered them familiar with almost every species of bloodshed. But this was new and strange amongst them, and they waited the return of the Norman with feelings near akin to awe.

At length, after some time, he came with a firm step and unblenching brow, but with a haggard wildness in his eye, which seemed to tell that remorse was busy with his heart. However, he sat him down without any allusion to the past, and draining off a cup of wine, strove laboriously after merriment. But it was in vain; the mirth of the whole party was evidently forced; and Marteville soon took up another strain, which accorded better with the feelings of the moment. He spoke to them of the dispersion of the band, which had taken place since he left them; announced his intention of joining them again; and drawing forth a purse containing about a thousand livres, he poured them forth upon the table, declaring them to be his first offering to the treasury.

This magnificent donation, which came in aid of their finances at a moment when such a recruit was very necessary, called forth loud shouts of applause from the freemen of the forest; and the Gros. St. Nicholas, starting up, addressed the company to the following effect: " Messieurs—every one knows that I am St. Nicholas, and no one will deny that I am surrounded by a number of

goodly clerks. But although in my saintly character I
will give up my clerical superiority to nobody; yet it
appears to me, that our society requires some lay com-
mander; therefore I, your bishop, do propose to you to
elect and choose the Sieur Marteville, here present, to
be our king and captain in the wars, in room of the
Sieur Pierrepont Le Blanc, who, having abdicated without cause, was committed to the custody of the great
receiver-general—the earth, by warrant of cold iron and
pistol-balls. What say ye, messieurs, shall he be
elected?"

A shout of approbation was the reply; and Marteville,
having been duly elected, took the oaths, and received
the homage of his new subjects. He then entered into a
variety of plans for increasing the band, concentrating
its operations, and once more rendering it that formidable
body which it had been in former times. All this met
with the highest approbation; but the captain showing the
most marked dislike to remaining in the forest which
they at present tenanted, and producing a variety of
reasons for moving their quarters to Languedoc, where
the neighborhood of the court and the army, offered
greater facilities both for recruiting their numbers and
their purses, it was agreed that they should disperse the
next morning, and reassemble as soon as possible at a
certain spot well known to the whole party, about forty
leagues distant from Lyons.

This was happily effected; and the Norman, on presenting himself at the rendezvous, had the pleasure of in-
troducing to the band two new associates, whom he had
found the means of converting on the road.

Although abandoning himself heart and soul to the
pleasures of his resumed profession, our friend Marteville was not forgetful of the reward he expected from
Chavigni; and as his official duties prevented his being
himself the bearer of the paper he had obtained, he despatched it to Narbonne, where the statesman now was,

by his faithful subject Callot, with orders to demand
ten thousand crowns of Monsieur de Chavigni, as a reward for having discovered it, adding also an elaborate
epistle to the same effect.

The Norman never for a moment entertained a suspicion that the paper he sent was anything but the
identical treaty with Spain, which the conspirators had
been heard to mention; and he doubted not that the
statesman would willingly pay such a sum for so precious
a document. But the embassy of Monsieur Callot did
not prove so fortunate as had been anticipated. Presenting himself to Chavigni, with as much importance of
aspect as the ambassador from Siam, he tendered his
credentials, and demanded the reward at a moment
when the statesman was irritated by a thousand anxieties
and dangers.

Making no ceremony with the fine blue and yellow
wax, Chavigni, having read the Norman's epistle, soon
found his way into the inside of the other packet, and
beheld in the midst of a thousand signs and figures, un-
intelligible to any but a professed astrologer, a prophetic
scroll containing some doggrel verses, which may be thus
rendered into English :—

THE FATE OF RICHELIEU.

Born beneath two mighty stars,
   Mercury with Mars combined,
He shall prompt a thousand wars,
   Nor live the balm of peace to find.

Less than a king, yet kings shall fall
   And tremble at his fatal sway;
Yet at life's end he shall recall
   The memory of no happy day.

And the last year that he shall know,
   Shall see him fall, and see him rise;
Shall see him yield, yet slay his foe,
   And scarcely triumph ere he dies.

Begot in factions, nursed in strife,
  Till all his troubled years be past,
Cunning and care eat up his life—
  A slave and tyrant first and last.
                    PÈRE LE ROUGE.

Chavigni gazed at the paper in amazement, and then
at the face of Monsieur Callot, who, totally unconscious
of the contents, remained very nonchalantly expecting
the reward. "Ten thousand crowns!" cried the statesman, giving way to his passion. "Ho! without there!
take this fellow out and flog him with your hunting
whips out of Narbonne. Away with him, and curry him
well!"

The grooms instantly seized upon poor Callot, and executed Chavigni's commands with high glee. The robber,
however, though somewhat surprised, bore his flagella-
tion very patiently; for under the jerkin which he wore,
still lay the rusty iron corslet we have before described,
which saved him from appreciating the blows at their
full value.

The matter, however, was yet to be remembered, as
we shall see; for when Callot, on his return to the forest,
informed his captain what sort of reward he had received
for the packet, the Norman's gigantic limbs seemed to
swell to a still greater size with passion, and drawing
his sword, he put the blade to his lips, swearing that before twelve months were over, it should drink Chavigni's
blood; and promises of such sort he usually kept most
punctually.

CHAPTER XXIV.

Wherein De Blenau finds out that he has made a mistake, and what
follows.

DE BLENAU, blinded by anxiety for Pauline, took
the suspicions of his page for granted, without examination. He knew that Chavigni scrupled not at any
measures which might serve a political purpose; he knew
that the Norman was in the immediate employment of
the statesman, and was still less delicate in his notions
than his master; and he doubted not that Pauline, having
been discovered issuing from the Bastile, had been carried
off without ceremony, and sent from Paris under the
custody of the ci-devant robber. At all events, De
Blenau, as he rode along, composed a very plausible chain
of reasoning upon the subject; and far from supposing
that the Norman would avoid the wood in the neighborhood of Mesnil, he concluded, from his knowledge of
Marteville's former habits, that a forest filled with robbers would fulfil all his anticipations of paradise, and
be too strong an attraction to be resisted.

Thus cogitating, he rode on to Decize, and thence to
Corbigny, where day once more broke upon his path; and
having been obliged to allow the horses a few hours' rest,
he tried in vain for some repose himself. Auxerre was
his next halt, but here only granting his domestics one
hour to refresh, he passed the Yonne, and soon after
entered Champagne, which traversing without stopping,
except for a few minutes at Bar sur Seine, he reached
Troyes before midnight, with man and horse too wearied
to begin their search before the following morning.

It unluckily so happened that De Blenau did not alight at the hotel of the Grand Soleil, where he might have gained such information as would in all probability have prevented his farther proceedings; and as the keeper of the auberge where he stopped was at open war with the landlord of the Grand Soleil, to all the inquiries which were made the next morning, the only reply the aubergiste thought fit to give was that "indeed he could not tell; he had never seen such a person as De Blenau described the Norman to be, or such a lady as Pauline;"— though, be it remarked, everybody in the house, after having gazed at Marteville and Louise for a full hour on their arrival, had watched their motions every day, and had wondered themselves stiff at who they could be and what they could want. At length, however, De Blenau caught hold of an unsophisticated hostler, of whom he asked if within the last ten days he had seen a carriage stop or pass through the town containing two such persons as he described.

The hostler replied "No; that they seldom saw carriages there; that a tall gentleman, like the one he mentioned, had ridden out of the town just two days before with a lady on horseback; but devil a carriage had there been in Troyes for six years or more, except that of Monseigneur the Governor."

De Blenau, glad of the least intimation where news seemed so scanty, now described the Norman as particularly as he could from what he had seen of him while speaking to Chavigni in the park of St. Germain, dwelling upon his gigantic proportions, and the remarkable cut upon his cheek.

"Yes, yes!" replied the hostler, "that was the man; I saw him ride out with a jolie demoiselle on the road to Mesnil St. Loup; but devil a carriage has there been in Troyes for six years or more, except that of Monseigneur the Governor."

"Well, well," replied De Blenau, wishing if possible

to hear more, "perhaps they might not be in a carriage. But can you tell me where they lodged while in the city of Troyes?"

Even the obtuse faculties of the holster had been drilled into knowing nothing of any other auberge in the town but his own. "Can't tell," replied he. "Saw him and the lady ride out on horseback; but devil a carriage has there been in Troyes for six years or more, except that of Monseigneur the Governor."

It may have been remarked that a certain degree of impatience and hastiness of determination was one of the prevailing faults of De Blenau's disposition; and in this case, without waiting for farther examination, he set out in pursuit of the Norman as soon as his horses were ready, merely inquiring if there was any castle in the neighborhood of Mesnil which might serve for the confinement of state prisoners.

The landlord, to whom the question was addressed, immediately determined in his own mind that De Blenau was an agent of the government; and replied, "None, that he knew of, but the old château of St. Loup; but that monseigneur had better have it repaired before he confined any one there, for it was so ruinous they would get out, to a certainty, if they were placed there in its present state."

De Blenau smiled at the mistake, but prepossessed with the idea that the Norman was carrying Pauline to some place of secret imprisonment, he determined at once to proceed to the spot the aubergiste mentioned, and to traverse the wood from the high road to Troyes, as the most likely route on which to encounter the Norman, against whom he vowed the most summary vengeance, if fortune should afford him the opportunity.

As, from every report upon the subject, the forest had been for some time past the resort of banditti, De Blenau gave orders to his servants to hold themselves upon their guard, and took the precaution of throwing forward two of his shrewdest followers, as a sort of reconnoitring party, to give him intelligence of the least noise which could indicate the presence of any human being besides themselves. But all these measures seemed to be unnecessary; not a sound met the ear; and De Blenau's party soon began to catch glimpses of the old château of St. Loup, through the breaks in the wood; and gradually winding round towards the east, gained the slope which gave them a clear view of the whole building.

The whole appearance of the place was so desolate and delapidated, that the first glance convinced De Blenau that Chavigni would never dream of confining Pauline within such ruinous walls; as the mere consideration of her rank would prevent him from using any unnecessary severity, though her successful attempt to penetrate into the Bastile afforded a plausible excuse for removing her from Paris. However, in order not to leave the least doubt upon the subject, he mounted to the court-yard, and having ascertained that every part of the building was equally unfit for the purposes of a prison, and that it was actually uninhabited except by owls and ravens, he determined to cross to a town, the spire of whose church he saw rising on the opposite hill, and to pursue his search in some other direction.

Descending, therefore, by the same slope which he had previously mounted, he wound round the base of the hill much in the same path by which Callot had conducted the Norman and Louise. The stream, however, formed the boundary of his approach to the castle on that side; and passing the rocks, which we have already mentioned as strewed about at the foot of the precipices, he followed the course of the river, till, winding into the wood, the castle, and the hill on which it stood, were lost to the sight. Here as he rode slowly on, revolving various plans for more successfully pursuing the Norman, and reproaching himself for not having made more accurate inquiries at Troyes, his eye was suddenly attracted by the appearance of something floating on the river like the long black hair of a young woman.

De Blenau's heart sank within him; his courage failed, his whole strength seemed to give way, and he sat upon his horse like a statue, pointing with his hand towards the object that had thus affected him, but without the power of uttering any order concerning it.

In the meanwhile the hair moved slowly backwards and forwards upon the stream, and one of the servants perceiving it, dismounted from his horse, waded into the water, and catching it in his grasp, began dragging the body to which it was attracted towards the brink. As he did so, the part of a red serge dress, such as that in which Pauline had visited the Bastile, floated to the surface, and offered a horrible confirmation of De Blenau's fears. The first shock, however, was passed, and leaping from his horse with agony depicted in his straining eye, he sprang down the bank into the stream, and raising the face of the dead person above the water, beheld the countenance of Louise.

Perhaps the immoderate joy which De Blenau felt at this sight might be wrong, but it was natural; and sitting down on the bank, he covered his face with his hands, overcome by the violent revolution of feeling which so suddenly took place in his bosom.

In the meanwhile the servants drew the body of the unfortunate girl to the bank, and speedily discovered that the mode of her death had been of a more horrible description than even that which they had at first supposed; for in her bosom appeared a deep broad gash as if from the blow of a poniard, which had undoubtedly deprived her of life before her murderer committed the body to the stream.

According to the costume of her country, Louise had worn upon the day of her death two large white pockets above the jupe of red serge. These were still attached to the black velvet bodice which she displayed in honor

of her marriage with the Norman, and contained a
variety of miscellaneous articles, amongst which were
several epistles from her husband to herself in the days
of their courtship, which showed De Blenau that she had
been employed as a spy upon Pauline and Madame de
Beaumont ever since their arrival at St. Germain: added
to these was a certificate of marriage between Jean
Baptiste Marteville and Louise Thibault, celebrated in
the chapel of the Palais Cardinal, by François Giraud.
All this led De Blenau to conclude, that he had been
misled in regard to the cause of Pauline's absence from
St. Germain; and he accordingly proceeded to the little
bourg of Senecy on his return towards Troyes, making
his men bear thither the body of Louise with as much
decent solemnity as the circumstances admitted. Having
here entrusted to the good curé of the place the charge
of the funeral, and giving two sums for the very different
purposes of promoting the discovery of the murderer and
buying a hundred masses for the soul of the deceased,
De Blenau pursued his journey, and arrived at Troyes
before night.

Putting up this time at the hotel of the Grand Soleil,
De Blenau soon acquired sufficient information to confirm him in the opinion that the Norman had been accompanied by Louise alone; but, at the same time, the
accounts which the people of the house gave respecting
the kindness and affection that Marteville had shown his
bride, greatly shook the suspicions which had been entertained against him by De Blenau, who, unacquainted
with any such character as that of the Norman, knew not
that there are men who, like tigers when unurged by
hunger, will play with their victims before they destroy
them.

The next morning early, all was prepared for the
departure of De Blenau, on his return to Moulins, when
his further progress in that direction was arrested by the
arrival of Henry de La Mothe, his page, accompanied by

one of the king's couriers, who immediately presented
to the count two packets, of which he had been the
bearer from St. Germain. The first of these seemed, from
the superscription, to be a common official document; but
the second attracted all his attention, and made his heart
beat high by presenting to him the genuine handwriting
of Pauline de Beaumont. Without meaning any offence
to royalty, whose insignia were impressed upon the seal
of the other packet, De Blenau eagerly cut the silk which
fastened the billet from Pauline. It contained only a few
lines, but these were quite sufficient to give renewed
happiness to the heart of him who read it. She had just
heard, she said, that the king's messenger was about to set
out, and though they hardly gave her time to fold her
paper, yet she would not let any one be before her in
congratulating him on his freedom to direct his course
wheresoever he pleased. She could not divine, she continued, whether his choice would lead him to St. Germain,
but if it did, perhaps he might be treated to the history
of an errant demoiselle, who had suffered various adventures in endeavoring to liberate her true knight from
prison.

De Blenau read it over again, and then turned to the
other paper, which merely notified that the king, contented with his loyal and peaceable behavior while
relegué in Bourbon, had been graciously pleased to relieve him from the restrictions under which he had been
placed for his own benefit and the state's security; and
informed him, in short, that he had leave, liberty, and
licence to turn his steps whithersoever he listed.

"To St. Germain," cried De Blenau gaily. "To St.
Germain! You, Henry de La Mothe, stay here with
François and Clement. Take good care of Monsieur
l'Ordinaire, and see that he be rewarded." The messenger made him a reverence. "After you have reposed
yourself here for a day," continued the count, "return to
Moulins; pay notre propriétaire, and all that may be there

due. There is the key of the coffre fort. Use all speed that you well may and then join me at home. And now for St. Germain."

So saying, he sprang on his horse as light as air, gave a well-known signal with his heel, and in a moment was once more on the road to Paris.

Although I find a minute account of De Blenau's whole journey to St. Germain, with the towns and inns at which he stopped, marked with the precision of a road-book, I shall nevertheless take upon myself the responsibility of abridging it as far as well can be, by saying that it began and ended happily.

The aspect of St. Germain, however, had very much' changed since De Blenau left it. Louis had now fixed his residence there; his confidence in the queen seemed perfectly restored; every countenance glowed with that air of satisfaction, which such a renewal of good intelligence naturally produced; and the royal residence had once more assumed the appearance of a court.

The first welcome received by De Blenau was from his gallant friend Cinq Mars, at whose request his recall had been granted by the king, and who now, calculating the time of the exile's return, stood at the door of De Blenau's hotel, ready to meet him on his arrival.

"Welcome, welcome back! my long-lost friend, Claude de Blenau," exclaimed Cinq Mars, as the count sprang from his horse; "welcome from the midst of prisons and trials, perils and dangers!"

"And well met, gallant Cinq Mars, the noble and the true," replied De Blenau. "But tell me, in heaven's name, Cinq Mars, what makes all this change at St. Germain? Why, it looks as if the forest were a fair, and that the old town had put on its holiday suit to come and see it."

"Nay, nay! rather, like a true dame that dresses herself out for her lover's return, it has made itself fine to receive you back again," replied the master of the horse.

24

"But if you would really know the secret of all the change that you see now, and will see still more wonderfully as you look farther, it is this. Richelieu is ill at Tarascon, and his name is scarcely remembered at the court, though Chavigni, that bold rascal, and Mazarin, that subtle one, come prowling about to maintain, if possible, their master's sway. But the spell is broken, and Louis is beginning to be a king again: so we shall see bright days yet."

"I hope so; in truth I hope so, Cinq Mars," replied De Blenau. "But, at all events, we will enjoy the change so far as it has gone. And now, what news at the palace? How fare all the lovely ladies of the court?"

"Why well," answered Cinq Mars; "all well; though I know, De Blenau, that your question, in comprising a hundred, meant but one only. Well, what say you?—I have seen thy Pauline, and cannot but allow that thy taste is marvellous good. There is a wild grace about her, well worth all the formal dignity of a court. One gets tired of the stiff courtesy and the precise bow; the kissing of hands and the lisping of names; the monseigneurings and the madamings.—Fie! one little touch of nature is worth it all."

"But answer me one question, Monsieur le Grand," said De Blenau. "How came there a report about, that Pauline had been carried off by some of the cardinal's people, and that no one knew where she was? for such a tale reached me even in Bourbon."

"Is it possible that you are the last to hear that story?" exclaimed Cinq Mars. "Why, though the old marquise, and the rest at the palace, affect to keep it a secret, every one knows the adventures of your demoiselle errante."

De Blenau's cheek flushed to hear such a name applied to Pauline; but Cinq Mars continued, observing that his friend was hurt—"Nay, nay, every one admires her for the whole business, and no one more than I. But, as I was saying, all the world knows it. The queen herself

told it to Monsieur de Lomenie, and he to his cousin De
Thou, and De Thou to me: and so it goes on.   Well,
but I must take up the gossip's tale at the beginning.
The queen, wishing to communicate with you in prison,
could find no messenger, who, for either gold or fair
words, would venture his head into the rattrap, except
your fair Pauline; and she, it seems, attempted twice to
get into the Bastile, once by day and once at night, but
both times fruitlessly.   How it happened I hardly remember, but by some means Chavigni, through some of
his creatures, winded the whole affair: and posting from
Chantilly to Paris, catches my fair lady in the very effort,
disguised as a soubrette; down he pounces, like a falcon
on a partridge, and having secured the delinquent, places
her in a carriage, which, with the speed of light, conveys
her away to his castle in Maine, where Madame la
Comtesse de Chavigni—who, by-the-way, is an angel according to all accounts—receives the young lady and
entertains her with all kindness.   In the meanwhile, Monsieur le Comte de Blenau is examined by the king in
person, and instead of having his head cut off, is merely
relegué in Bourbon; upon which Chavigni finds he has
lost his labor, and is obliged to send for the pretty prisoner back again with all speed."

Although De Blenau was aware, from his own personal
experience, that Cinq Mars had mistaken several parts
of his history, he did not think fit to set him right; and
the master of the horse proceeded: "However, let us
into thy hotel.   Get thy dinner, wash the dust from thy
beard, array thyself in an unsullied doubtlet, and we will
hie to the dwelling of thy lady fair, to glad her eyes with
the sight of thy sweet person."

De Blenau smiled at his friend's raillery, and as the
proposal very well accorded with his wishes, every moment seeming mis-spent that detained him from Pauline,
he changed his dress as speedily as possible, and was
soon ready to accompany Cinq Mars to the palace.

As they proceeded on their way towards the gates of the park, a figure presented itself, which, from its singularity, was worthy of notice. It was that of a tall, thin, raw-boned man, who, naturally possessing a countenance of the ugliest cast of Italian ugliness, had rendered it still more disagreeable by the enormous length of his moustaches, which would have far overtopped his nose, had it been a nose of any ordinary proportion; but a more extensive, pear-shaped, ill-adapted organ never projected from a human countenance; and this, together with a pair of small, flaming black eyes, which it seemed to bear forward with it above the rest of the face, protruding from a mass of beard and hair, instantly reminding the beholder of a badger looking out of a hole. The chin, however, bore no proportion to the nose, and seemed rather to slink away from it in an oblique direction, apparently overawed by its more ambitious neighbor.

The dress of this delectable personage was a medley of the French and Flemish costumes. He wore a gray vest of silk, with sleeves slashed at the elbow, and the shirt, which was not conspicuously clean, buttoned at the wrist with agate studs. His haut de chausse, which was of deep crimson, and bore loops and ribbons of yellow, was fringed round the leg, near the knees, with a series of brazen tags or points but indifferently silvered; and as he walked along with huge steps, these aforesaid tags clattered together with a sort of important sound, which, put in combination with the rest of his appearance, drew many a laugh from the boys of St. Germain. Over his gray vest was drawn a straight-cut doublet of yellow silk, without sleeves; and a pair of long boots, of untanned leather, covered all defects which might otherwise have been apparent in his hose. His dress was completed by a tawdry bonnet with a high black plume: and a Toledo blade of immeasurable length, with a worked iron hilt and black scabbard, hung by his side, describing with its point various strange figures on the dust of the road.

" Here comes Villa Grande, the Italian luteplayer,"
exclaimed Cinq Mars the moment he saw him. " Do you
know him, De Blenau? "

" I have heard him play on his instrument and sing at
your house," replied De Blenau; " and from his language
that night, may say I know him through and through for
a boasting coxcomb, with as much courage as the sheath
of a rapier—which looks as good as a rapier itself till
it is touched, and then it proves all emptiness. Mind
you how he boasted of having routed whole squadrons
when he served in the Italian horse? and I dare say he
would run from a stuffed pikeman in an old hall."

" Nay, nay; you do him wrong, Claude," replied Cinq
Mars. " He has rather too much tongue, it is true; but
that is not always the sign of a bad hound. I must
speak to him, however, for he does me service. Well,
Signor Villa Grande," continued he, addressing the
Italian, who now approached, swinging an enormous cane
in his hand, and from time to time curling up the ends of
his moustaches; " you remember that you are to be ready
at a moment's notice. Be sure, also, that your mind be
made up; for I tell you fairly, the service which you
undertake is one of danger."

" Monsieur," replied the Italian with a strong foreign
accent, " I will be ready, when you call upon me, in
shorter time than you could draw your sword; and as
for my mind being made up, if there were an army drawn
out to oppose my progress, I would be bound to carry
the despatch to the Duke of Bouillon, or die in the
attempt. Fear not my yielding it to anybody; piutosto
morir vol' io, as the song has it," and he hummed a few
bars of one of his native airs. Oh, Dio! " continued he,
recognizing De Blenau, who had turned away on perceiving that Cinq Mars spoke to the Italian on some
business of a private nature. " Oh Dio! Monsieur le
Comte de Blenau, is it really you returned at last?

Benedetto quel giorno felice! Doubtless you are aware
of the glorious plans of your friend Monsieur le Grand."

"Good-day, signor," answered De Blenau; "I know
of no one's plans but my own, the most glorious of which,
within my apprenhension at present, is to get to the palace
as soon as possible. Come, Cinq Mars, are you at leisure?" and he took a step or two in advance, while the
master of the horse gave the Italian a warning to put a
bridle on his tongue, and not to let it run so loosely without any regard to necessary caution.

"For heaven's sake, take care what you are about,
Cinq Mars!" said De Blenau, when he was again joined
by his friend. "Of course you are the best judge of your
own plans; but unless you have a mind to ruin them all,
do not trust them to such a babbling idiot as that; and
beware that, in attempting to catch a lion, you do not
get torn yourself."

"Oh, no fear," replied the grand ecuyer; "that fellow
knows nothing more than it is absolutely necessary for
him to know; and as for the rest, I have plunged into a
wide sea, Claude, and must swim to land somehow."

They had by this time reached the gates of the palace,
and Cinq Mars, knowing that some meetings are better
in private, left his friend, and turned his steps towards
the apartments of the king.

In the meanwhile, De Blenau proceeded with a rapid
pace towards that part of the palace which had been
assigned to Madame de Beaumont; and his heart beat
with that wild uncontrollable emotion, which the meeting
with one dearly loved can alone produce. At that very
moment similar sensations were throbbing in the bosom
of Pauline de Beaumont, who from the window had seen
the approach of Cinq Mars and another; and long before
her eye could distinguish a feature, her heart had told
her who it was. A sort of irresistible impulse led her,
at first, to fly towards the door by which she expected
him to enter; but before she was half across the room,

some other feeling came over her mind. She returned
to her seat at the window, and a blush stole over her
cheek, though there was no other person present to
observe her emotion or pry into its cause.

The door was partially open, and more than once she
raised her eyes towards it, and thought that De Blenau
was long in coming so short a distance. But presently
she heard his step, and there was an impatient eagerness
even in the sound of his footfall that convinced her he
lost no time. Another moment and he entered the room.
Every feeling but one was at an end, and Pauline was in
his arms.

It is not at the moment when a lover has endured
many sorrows, and escaped from many dangers, that a
gentle heart can practise even the every-day affectations
which a great part of the world are pleased to mistake
for delicacy; and far less inclined to attempt it than any
other person in the world was Pauline de Beaumont.
The child of nature and simplicity, her delicacy was that
of an elegant mind and a pure heart. Of what she did
feel she concealed little, and affected nothing; and De
Blenau was happy.

Of course there was a great deal to be told, and De
Blenau was listening delighted to an account of the considerate kindness with which the Countess de Chavigni
had treated his Pauline, when the sound of voices approaching towards them stopped her in her history.

It is precisely at such moments as those when we wish
everybody but ourselves away, that the world is most
likely to intrude upon us; and Pauline and De Blenau had
not met more than five minutes, as it seemed to them,
when the queen and Madame de Beaumont entered the
apartment. How long they had been really together is
another question, for lovers' feelings are not always the
truest watches.

"Welcome, my faithful De Blenau," said the queen.
"We encountered the grand ecuyer but now, who told us

where we should find you. For my own part, I suppose I must in all justice forgive your paying your devoirs here before you came to visit even me. However, ere there be any one near to overhear, I must thank you for all you have done for me, and for all you have suffered on my account. Nor must I forget my little heroine here, who went through all sorts of peril and danger in conveying my message to you in the Bastile."

"Your majesty was very good in sending me such an angel of comfort," replied De Blenau. "And certainly, had it not been for the commands she brought me, I believe that his most Christian-like eminence of Richelieu would have doomed me to the torture for my obstinacy."

"Put it in other words, De Blenau," said Anne of Austria. "You mean that you would have endured the torture sooner than betray your queen. But truly, Pauline must have a stout heart to have carried through such an undertaking; and I think that the fidelity and attachment which you have both shown to me, offers a fair promise for your conduct towards each other. What say you, Madame de Beaumont?"

"I think, madame," replied the marchioness, "that Pauline has done her duty with more firmness than most girls could have commanded; and that De Blenau has done his as well as it could be done."

"Pauline merits more praise than her mother ventures to give," said the queen. "But I had forgot the king's summons; and probably he is even now waiting for us. Come, Pauline; come, De Blenau. Louis gives high commendation to your demeanor in prison; let us see how he greets you out of it."

A message had been conveyed to Anne of Austria just before the arrival of De Blenau, intimating that the king desired to see her; and she now led the way to the Salle Ronde, as it was then called, or the Salle des Muses, as it was afterwards named by Louis the Fourteenth, where the king waited her approach. Although the uncertain nature of Louis's temper always made her feel some degree of apprehension when summoned to his presence, the kindness he had lately shown her, and the presence of a large proportion of her friends, made her obey his call with more pleasure than she usually felt on similar occasions.

Louis's object, in the present instance, was to inform the queen of the journey he was about to make into the neighborhood of Perpignan, in order to confirm the inhabitants of Roussillon in their new allegiance to the crown of France; and Cinq Mars, who had always sincerely wished the welfare of Anne of Austria, took this opportunity of insinuating to the king, that to show publicly his restored confidence in the queen, so far from lessening his authority, even in appearance, would be in truth only asserting his own dignity, from which the proceedings of Richelieu had so greatly derogated.

De Blenau and Pauline followed a step or two behind the queen and Madame de Beaumont, and would willingly have lingered still longer by themselves; but as something must always be sacrificed to appearance, they quickened their pace as Anne of Austria approached the door of the Salle Ronde, and came up with her just as she entered the room in which the principal part of the French court was assembled. The moment she appeared, Louis advanced towards the queen from the brilliant circle in which he stood, and embraced her affectionately. "Welcome, my fair lady," said he. "I see you have brought the new returned exile with you. Monsieur de Blenau, I am glad to see you at court;—this is a pleasanter place than where we met last."

"I can assure you, sire," replied De Blenau, "that I will never be willingly in circumstances to meet your majesty there again."

"I do not doubt it, I do not doubt it," said the king. "You should thank Heaven that delivered you from such peril, Sir Count. Madam," he continued, turning to the queen, " I requested to see you, not only for the pleasure which your presence must always give, but to inform you, that affairs of state will shortly call me to Narbonne, in Languedoc, from whence I shall return with all convenient speed."

"Your majesty soon leaves St. Germain," replied the queen. "I do not think you love it for a sojourn, as in other days."

" Not so," answered Louis; " so well do I love it, that I had purposed to have worn out the rest of my days here, had not the duties of my station called me hence; but my return will be speedy if God give me life. What man can say how long he may remain? and I feel many a warning that my time will be but short in this world.—Ha! what mean those drops in your eyes?—I did not know, Anne, that such were your feelings." And he pressed the queen's hand, which he had continued to retain in his.

"Oh, Louis!" replied Anne of Austria, and by that simple exclamation conveyed a more delicate reproach to the heart of her husband than she could have done by any-other expression in the range of language. Louis felt it, and drawing her arm kindly through his own, he proposed aloud that the whole party should walk forth upon the terrace. It was the queen's favorite spot, and she easily understood that it was meant as some atonement for many a former slight. Those, too, who stood round and saw what had taken place, began to perceive that a new star was dawning in the horizon, and turned their eyes to watch its progress and court its influence.

The king and queen were followed by the greater part of the court; and during the walk Louis continued to manifest that kindness towards his wife, which had it been earlier shown, might have given him a life of happiness. "Let me beg you, madam," said he, as at length they turned to enter the palace, " not only to be careful of our children, for that I am sure you will be, but also to be careful of their mother, for my sake."

The queen's feelings were overpowering; the tears rolled rapidly down her cheeks, taking from her all power of utterance, and quitting the king, after pressing his hand to her lips, she retired to her own apartments, to indulge in solitude the new and delightful emotions which her husband's unexpected kindness had excited. The various preparations for the king's journey into Roussillon occupied no small space of time. Litters and carriages were to be provided; relays of horses to be stationed on the road; cooks and victuallers were to be sent forward; and a thousand other arrangements to be made, required either by the general difficulty of locomotion in those days, or by the failing health of the king.

One great object of Richelieu's policy had been to diminish the feudal influence of the nobility, and by forcing them to reside with the court, to break through their constant communication with their vassals. In pursuit of this, he had drawn the greater part of the nobles to Paris; and now that his absence and declining favor with the king dissolved the charm which seem to hold them in the capital, they congregated at St. Germain like a flock of bees, that, having lost their hive, flew in search of a new one. Many of these were bound by their various offices in the household to accompany the king in his present journey; others were particularly invited to do so either by Louis himself or by Cinq Mars and Fontrailles, who sought to surround the king with those who, on any sudden emergency, might support their party against the cardinal; and a crowd of others, from vanity or interest, curiosity or ambition, were glad to follow in the train of the monarch.

Thus the greater part of the nobles who had flocked to St. Germain, on Richelieu's departure from Paris, now again left it in order to take part in the journey to Narbonne. As all the horses, and every sort of accommodation on the direct road, were engaged for the service of the king and those immediately attendant upon him, the greater part of the court took the indirect roads by which they could always be near the royal party; and the rest followed a day or two after, taking advantage of whatever conveniences might be left unappropriated.

There were one or two, however, who departed before Louis, and of these the principal was Chavigni, who set out accompanied by a few servants, two or three days prior to that appointed for the king's expedition. His ostensible destination was, like that of the rest of the court, to Narbonne; but turning to the left, he directed his course towards Tarascon, and having travelled with the utmost rapidity, while Louis proceeded by easy stages, he had quite sufficient time to communicate fully with Richelieu, and proceed to Narbonne before the king's arrival.

The journey into Roussillon had been undertaken by the express advice of Richelieu; and though Cinq Mars ventured boldly to attack the conduct of the cardinal in every respect, to place all his measures in the worst point of view, and to encourage every sentiment in the king's mind which was in opposition to those of the minister, still no change, or even a proposal of change in the government had been mentioned, up to the time of the court reaching Narbonne. Richelieu was still prime minister, and the council remained composed of persons devoted to his interest, though the views of Cinq Mars were already spoken of in more than one circle, and the consent of the king was so far assumed as a matter decided, that the two parties were distinguished by the names of Royalist and Cardinalist.

While the court remained with the army near Perpignan, and after its removal to Narbonne, Richelieu still lay dangerously ill at Tarascon. His mind was deeply depressed, as well as his corporeal powers; and in the opinion of all, a few weeks were likely to terminate both his ministry and his existence, even if the eager hand of his enemies did not hurry him onward to more rapid destruction. But the fiery spirit of Cinq Mars brooked no delay: the lazy course of natural decay was too slow for his impatience; and though De Thou, who accompanied his friend to Narbonne, reiterated in his ears the maxims of caution and wisdom, on the other hand Fontrailles, fearful lest he should lose the merit and consequent influence he should acquire by the removal of Richelieu, never ceased to urge the favorite to hurry on the completion of their design.

In the meantime, everything seemed favorable to the conspirators; and Cinq Mars felt confident that the secret inclination of Louis would second all his views; but nevertheless, he wished for some more public and determinate expression of the king's opinion, before he asked his consent to the measures which had been concerted. After the arrival of the court at Narbonne, however, the monarch's conduct in respect to Richelieu became of so decisive a character, that no further delay appeared necessary. Within a few miles of the place where the cardinal lay ill, the king seemed entirely to have forgotten that such a man existed, or only to remember him with hatred. His name, if it was ever mentioned, instantly called into Louis's countenance an expression of uneasiness and disapprobation; and by no chance was the king ever heard to pronounce it himself. By all these circumstances, Cinq Mars was determined to communicate to Louis, as soon as possible, the schemes which had been formed for freeing the country from the yoke of Richelieu. He suffered, however, several days to elapse in waiting for a favorable opportunity, and at length, as often happens, growing impatient of delay, took perhaps the most inauspicious moment that could have been selected. It was on a morning when everything had gone wrong with Louis.

Notwithstanding his failing health, he still clung to his accustomed amusement, and very often rode forth to hunt when he was very unfit for any bodily exercise.

On these occasions, the distressing consciousness of his decaying powers always rendered him doubly irritable; and on the day which Cinq Mars unfortunately chose to broach the subject of the dismissal of Richelieu, a thousand trivial accidents had occurred to increase his ill humor to the highest pitch. His horse had fallen with him in the chase; they had beat the country for hours without finding any game worthy of pursuit, and when at length they did rouse a fine boar, and had brought him to bay, he broke out after killing two of the king's best hounds, and plunged into the deepest part of the forest. Louis was returning home from this unsuccessful chase, when Cinq Mars, turning his eyes towards the towers of Tarascon, which just then were seen rising above the trees in the distance, pointed to them with his hunting-whip, saying, " There lies the cardinal! "

" Well, sir," exclaimed Louis eagerly, catching at anything on which to vent his irritability—" do you wish me to go and see him? Doubtless he will be glad of the visit. Let us go." And he reined in his horse, as if with the intention of turning him toward Tarascon.

" Far be it from me to advise your majesty so to do," replied Cinq Mars, who clearly perceived that the king's answer proceeded only from casual irritation. " It was the sight of the old towers of the château, that called the cardinal to my mind. In truth, I had almost forgotten him."

" Forgotten him, Cinq Mars! " cried the king. " I think he has done enough to make himself remembered."

" He has, indeed, sire," replied Cinq Mars, " and his memory will long last coupled with curses in the heart of every true Frenchman. But there he lies; I trust, like the Tarasque, hideous but harmless, for the present."

" What do you mean by the Tarasque? " demanded Louis; " I never heard of it."

" It is merely a whimsical stone dragon, sire," replied Cinq Mars, " that lies carved in the church of St. Marthe,

at Tarascon on the Rhône—a thing of no more real use
than the Cardinal de Richelieu."

"Of no use, sire!" exclaimed the king, his eye flashing fire. "Do you think that we would repose such
trust, and confide our kingdom's weal to one who is of no
use? Silence, sir!" he continued, seeing Cinq Mars
about to reply. "No more of this subject—we have heard
too much of it."

Cinq Mars was too wise to add another word, and the
king rode on to Narbonne, maintaining a sullen silence
towards all around him.

Of the conversation which had passed not one word
had escaped the ears of Fontrailles; and the moment the
cortége had dismounted, he followed the master of the
horse towards a distant part of the grounds which lie
behind the château. Cinq Mars walked on as if he did
not see him, and at last finding that he persisted in following, he stopped abruptly, exclaiming, "Well, Fontrailles!
well! what now? What would you say? I can guess
it all, so spare yourself the trouble?"

"You mistake me, Cinq Mars," replied Fontrailles,
"if you think I would blame you. You did your best,
though the time was not the best chosen; but all I wish
to press upon you is, not to let this dispirit you. Let the
subject die away for the present and seem forgotten, till
the king is in a better mood. Every hour of his neglect
is death to Richelieu; and besides, the king's consent is
not absolutely necessary to us."

"To me, absolutely necessary," replied Cinq Mars, "for
I stir not one step without it."

"Nay, the king's private consent to you is of course
necessary," answered Fontrailles; "but you surely do not
think of informing him of the treaty with Spain. After
the affair is finished, and Richelieu's power at an end,
Louis will see the necessity of it; but such, you must
know, is his hatred towards Spain, that he would consider
the very proposal as little better than high treason."

" I am not yet determined in that respect," answered Cinq Mars; " my conduct will of course be decided by how I find the king inclined. I like no concealments, where they can be avoided. But in the first place, Villa Grande must carry the treaty to——"

Cinq Mars paused; for, as he spoke, Chavigni turned sharp round from an alley close by, and passed on. The statesman bowed, en passant, to the master of the horse, who but slightly returned his salutation, while, on the other hand, Fontrailles doffed his hat and inclined his head with a hypocritical smile, in which habitual servility was strongly blended with triumphant malice.

Chavigni spoke not, but there were two or three words had caught his ear as he passed, which at once turned his suspicions into the right channel, and stimulated him to know more. We have already said that it was a maxim with the statesman, that in politics nothing is mean; and he would have felt not the slightest hesitation in listening to the conversation of Cinq Mars, could he have done so without being observed. To effect this, it was necessary to take a large round in order to approach the alley in which the two conspirators walked without drawing their attention to himself; but as he turned to do so, he observed the master of the horse separate from his companion and come towards the spot where he stood, and not wishing to put Cinq Mars on his guard, by showing that he was watched, he turned away and directed his steps towards the château.

" Must carry the treaty—" thought Chavigni. " Who must carry the treaty? If I could but have heard that name, I should then have had the clue in my hands. However, Monsieur de Cinq Mars, you shall be well looked to, at least—take care that you trip not—for if you do, you fall." Thus thinking, he passed on to the stables, where his horses stood, intending, notwithstanding the lateness of the hour, and the failing light, to ride over to Tarascon and communicate with Richelieu, even if he should be obliged to become a borrower of the night for a dark hour or twain. His grooms, however, taking advantage of his absence, had dispersed themselves in various directions in search of amusement to pass the hours in the dull town of Narbonne; and consequently Chavigni could find no one to saddle his horse for the proposed journey.

Irritated at this impediment, he was about to quit the stable in search of some of the truant grooms, when he again perceived Cinq Mars approaching, accompanied by the Italian, Villa Grande. They were in earnest conversation, and Chavigni, knowing that Cinq Mars had horses lodged next to his own, drew back, and searching for a crevice in the wooden partition, which was as old and decayed as he could desire, he applied himself to listen to all that passed as soon as the master of the horse and his companion entered the adjoining stable. The first words he heard were from the Italian. " You know, monseigneur," said he, " that the utmost a man can do, is to die in defence of his charge; and that will I do, sooner than yield to any man that which you entrust to my hands."

" Well, well," replied Cinq Mars, " there is no need of so many professions, good sir. To-morrow morning then, at day-break, you set out. That is the horse—mind you use him well, but spare not his speed. Salute the noble duke on my part with all kindness and love. At nine you come for the treaty; but mark that you keep your time, for at ten I must be with the king."

" But, monseigneur, monseigneur ! " cried Villa Grande, as Cinq Mars turned to leave him; " perhaps your lackeys will not let me have the horse."

" Well then, when you come to-night," replied the grand ecuyer, " you shall have an order for him."

" Now then, your secret is in my power," thought Chavigni, as Cinq Mars and his companion left the spot. " Monsieur de Villa Grande, I will instantly make out an

25

order for your arrest to-morrow morning, and save you the trouble of your journey.—Salute the noble duke!" he continued, meditating on the words of Cinq Mars— "What duke?—It must be Gaston of Orleans.—But he is a royal duke. But we shall see." And as he walked on towards the château he bent his eyes upon the ground, revolving in his mind the various plans which suggested themselves for withdrawing his patron and himself from the brink of that political precipice on which they stood.

His thoughts, however, which for a moment wandered to every different circumstance of his situation, seeking amongst the many dangers that surrounded, some favorable point on which to found a hope, were all suddenly recalled to one object, by the approach of Cardinal Mazarin, who by his hurried step and anxious countenance appeared to be troubled by some unforeseen event.

Notwithstanding their being linked in one cause, notwithstanding their present interests drawing together, notwithstanding all the apparent friendship that existed between them, Chavigni looked upon the cardinal as one who with less zeal had rivalled him in the favor of Richelieu, and who with less talent had insinuated himself as much into the affairs of government; and Mazarin, although obliged to coalesce with Richelieu's favorite, looked forward to the day when the struggle for preeminence between them would come to a climax, and one would rise upon the ruin of the other: and he saw clearly that when that day did arrive, all his own subtlety would hardly qualify him to compete with the bold mind and vigorous talents of Chavigni, unless he could in the first instance gradually acquire for himself such a superiority of interest as to enable him to command rather than contend for the highest station.

The natural effect of these conflicting interests was a feeling of jealous suspicion in the mind of each, which in Mazarin only appeared by the care he took to strengthen his influence wherever it was most opposite to that of

Chavigni; while at the same time he showed his fellow-statesman an outward respect and deference almost amounting to servility. But on the other part, Chavigni's hasty disposition made his dislike more apparent, though he took no means of injuring his rival.

As they approached each other, the cardinal made a sign to the page who attended him to remain behind, and folding the train of his robe over his arm, he advanced quickly to Chavigni, embracing him with the greatest semblance of attachment. " My excellent friend," he exclaimed, " I have sought you everywhere: let me beg you to fly instantly to Tarascon, or all our hopes are ruined."

" In truth," replied Chavigni, not allowing Mazarin to explain the motives of his request; " your eminence requires what I can hardly comply with; as I have but now got business on my hands which needs some time to manage. But may I crave the object which would be gained by my going to Tarascon? I should think that he who could stay two hostile armies on the point of battle was fully sufficient to any stroke of policy."

There was a sarcastic smile on the lip of Chavigni as he alluded to the peace which Mazarin had procured at Cazal, at the moment when the French and Spanish armies were about to engage; but the cardinal would see only the compliment. " You are too kind," replied he; " but in this instance you only can succeed; you only, I feel assured—and that not without the exertion of all your influence—can prevent the cardinal prime minister from sending his resignation to the king."

" His resignation! " exclaimed Chavigni, starting back with unfeigned astonishment. " In the name of heaven, what do you mean? "

" I mean this, Chavigni," replied Mazarin, " that unless you reach Tarascon before daylight to-morrow morning, and use every argument in your power to produce, the courier who bears the official resignation of his eminence of Richelieu, will have set out for this place. I saw the paper signed to-day, with my own eyes, before I came away; and all that my utmost entreaties could gain was, that it should be delayed till to-morrow morning, in hopes of your arrival before that time. His eminence feels convinced that the king's favor and his own power are lost forever; and in truth I begin to think so too."

"Madness and folly!" exclaimed Chavigni, striking his hand against his forehead with vexation. "Madness and folly! Rascal, saddle me a horse," he continued to a groom, who now loitered into the court with that sort of slow indifferent air which would put an angel in a passion. "Where, in the name of all the devils, have you been lingering? Pardon me, your eminence—but I am vexed. I did not think his great mind was so over-thrown. Saddle me a horse, I say. Slave, must you stand eavesdropping. Better you had been born deaf than overhear my conversation. There are such things as oubliettes to cure listeners. Saddle me a horse I say."

"Will you not take some of my servants with you?" said Mazarin; "they are all in readiness."

"No, no," replied Chavigni, "I go alone. Do not let it get abroad that I am gone. I will be back betimes to-morrow."

"You had better take one servant, at least," said the cardinal. "The roads are not safe. It is dangerous."

"Dangerous!" exclaimed Chavigni. "Who thinks of danger when all is at stake? Your eminence has a great regard for human lives, I know—for mine more espe-cially. But depend upon it, I shall come home safe to-morrow, though I go alone to-night. Now, sir," he con-tinued to the groom, who led forth a strong black hunter for his service, "girth up the saddle a little tighter: un-buckle that cross from his poitral; I am neither going on a pilgrimage nor a procession."

And now, walking twice round the horse to see that all the caparisons were in right order, he sprang into the saddle, and dashing his rowels into the hunter's flank, galloped out of the court-yard, bowing with a smile as he passed by Mazarin, who started back a step, as the horse's feet, in the rapidity of its course, struck fire with the stones of the pavement.

CHAPTER XXV.

Which shows how a king made reparation, and what came of it.

WHILE, as we have seen, Chavigni galloped off towards Tarascon, forgetting in the agitation produced by
the tidings of Mazarin, to take those measures which he
had proposed in regard to Villa Grande, Cinq Mars returned directly towards the palace, or rather the house
which had been converted into a palace for the king's
use. It was one of those old buildings which at that time
were common in France, and which even now are often
to be met with in cities where the remains of ancient
splendor, left alone to the less destructive power of time,
have not been demolished by the violence of turbulent
times, or the still more inveterate enmity of modern
improvement. The whole front, with the two octagonal
towers at the sides, and the long corridors on the right
and left hand of the court, were ornamented with a multitude of beautiful arabesques and bas-reliefs. These last,
the bas-reliefs, entirely covered the principal façade of
the building, and offered a number of pictures in stone,
representing in some parts battles and triumphs, and in
others displaying the humbler and more peaceful subjects of pastoral life and religious ceremonies. Amongst
the rest was one medallion which caught the attention
of Cinq Mars; and as the failing light prevented him from
seeing it where he stood, he approached to observe it.
The chisel of the sculptor usurping the place of the pencil,
had there portrayed a landscape with a flock of sheep
pasturing quietly by the side of a brook, while a shep-
herd appeared sleeping under a hill, down which a wolf
was seen stealing upon the flock. Underneath was

written in old Gothic characters, " Eveillez vous, le loup
s'approche."

Cinq Mars smiled as he read it, applying the warning
to himself. " Let him come," said he, thinking of Richelieu ; " he will be caught himself." So saying, he turned,
and entering the palace, retired to his own apartments.
He had not remained there long, however, before he was
once more joined by Fontrailles.

" Follow me quick, Cinq Mars," cried the conspirator ;
" the king asks for you. Now is the moment to speak
to him. He thinks that his peevishness hurt you this
morning, and he is willing to make atonement."

It may be well supposed that Cinq Mars lost no time in
following his companion up the great staircase to the
king's apartments. It was, indeed, as Fontrailles had
said. Since his return, Louis had enjoyed an hour of
repose, which cleared from his mind the irritability induced by fatigue, and made him reproach himself for
the unkindness he had shown to one so devotedly attached to him as the master of the horse. The remembrance of it oppressed him, and he sent for his favorite,
not indeed to apologize, but to wipe away the impression
that his irritability had caused, by more than usual kindness and familiarity. The two conspirators found Louis
seated in a cabinet, which, being placed in one of the
towers, partook of its octangular form. The walls were
wainscoted with dark carved oak, and even the plafond
was all of the same gloomy-colored material, except a
massy gilt cornice and projecting rose in the centre, from
which hung a single silver lamp, the rays of which, falling on the figure of the king beneath, gave an additional
paleness to his worn but fine countenance, and slightly
touching upon his plain black velvet suit, shone full on
the richly illuminated book in which he had been reading.

Louis raised his eyes as Fontrailles entered, and then
turning them full on the noble countenance of Cinq Mars
who followed, a pleased smile beamed for a moment on

his lip, and he exclaimed, " Well, Cinq Mars, art thou Nimrod enough to hunt again to-morrow after our mis- fortunes of to-day?   Come in, Monsieur de Fontrailles," he continued, seeing that Fontrailles remained near the door, hesitating whether he should retire or not, now that he had done the king's bidding in summoning the grand ecuyer.   " Come in, I pray—sit you down, gentlemen— it is the king's request : you, Cinq Mars, here—Monsieur de Fontrailles, there is a seat.   Now," he continued, glancing his eye round as the light of the lamp gleamed faintly on the several countenances—" now we look like some secret triumvirate met to decide the fate of nations."

" And that might be too," replied Cinq Mars, " your majesty to command, and we to execute."

The king took no notice, but went on with what he had himself been saying : " There is Cinq Mars looks like a noble prince, and Fontrailles like a wily minister, and I———I believe," he continued laughing, " I have left myself no place but that of secretary."

" Alas ! " said Cinq Mars with a deep sigh, " alas ! that there should be any man in your majesty's dominions more a king than yourself."

Fontrailles and the king both started ; and the con- spirator internally pronounced, " All is lost," while Cinq Mars himself, who had spoken without thought, only felt the imprudence of his speech when it was beyond recall.

" Cinq Mars ! Cinq Mars ! " cried Louis, " that is a daring speech ;—but I know it proceeded from your love for me, and therefore I pardon it.   But I will tell you that no man is more a king in France than I am."

" I crave your majesty's gracious pardon," replied the master of the horse.   " If I have offended your majesty, it was from love for you alone that I spoke.   My words were bolder than my thoughts, and I only meant to say that I could wish to see my monarch show himself that great king which he naturally is.   I would fain see the staff of command withdrawn from one who abuses it."

" I pray sit you down gentlemen," said the king as Cinq Mars and
de Fontrailles entered the apartment.   Page 392.

Richelieu.

"Cinq Mars," answered the king, "that staff is in my own hand. It was but lent, my friend; and it is now resumed."

The master of the horse paused for a moment, not exactly certain how far he could rely upon the king's good humor, which he had already tried so incautiously, and turned his eyes towards Fontrailles, as if for counsel.

"Speak, Cinq Mars," said Louis, seeing his hesitation, "speak boldly, and fear not; for I fully believe that all your wishes are for my service, and I would fain hear the voice of those that regard me with affection, rather than for their own interest; and one of these do I hold you to be."

"Your majesty does me justice," replied Cinq Mars. "Let me not offend you then, when I say that the power you lent is scarcely resumed while the title under which it was enjoyed remains. The Cardinal Duke of Richelieu, my liege, is still prime minister of France. He has still all the power (though not exercised), the revenues, the offices. Our soldiers are fighting at his command, our provinces are governed by his creatures, our high posts are filled by his friends. He has an army for his servants, and more than the riches of a prince. Why not—oh, why not, sire, break the enchanter's wand that gave him so much sway, and sweep away the hordes that prey upon the state, like swarms of flies upon a slain deer? Why not direct the operations of your troops yourself and let the armies of France be the armies of the king, and not of Richelieu? Why not chase from your councils a man who has so often abused the generous confidence of his sovereign, and make him disgorge the ill-gotten wealth which he has wrung from the hearts of your people?"

As he spoke, Cinq Mars grew warm with his subject; his eye sparkled, his arm was extended with that wild and graceful energy for which he was conspicuous; his words flowed uninterrupted, with all the eloquence of enthusiasm, and his fine and princely features acquired a new and striking expression, while, animated in the cause of his country's liberty, he pleaded against the tyrant who had oppressed both king and people. Louis gazed on him at first as on one inspired; but as a host of consequences crowded on his mind, threatening him with a thousand vague and unsubstantial dangers, he placed his hands before his eyes, and remained for some moments in deep thought.

"My friend," said he at length, "what is it you would have me do? This man—this bad man if you will—but still this great man—is like an oak whose roots are deep in the earth; you may hew them asunder one by one, but it requires a giant's strength to pluck the tree up at once. Richelieu's power may be taken from him gradually; but to attempt what you propose, would instantly cause a rebellion amongst my subjects. He has so many who depend upon him; he has so many that are allied to him—"

"What!" exclaimed Cinq Mars, "shall it be said that King Louis was afraid to dismiss his own minister?"

"Not afraid for myself, sir," replied the king, somewhat sharply; "but afraid of bringing the miseries of civil war upon my people."

Perceiving that Cinq Mars was urging the king too impetuously, Fontrailles, who had hitherto remained silent, now joined in the conversation in a soft insinuating tone, calculated to remove any newly raised irritation from Louis's mind. "All danger, sire," said he, still laboring to quiet the king's fears without opposing his opinion, "all danger, which might otherwise be imminent, could easily be obviated, by commanding the noble Duke of Bouillon—"

At the name of the Duke of Bouillon Louis made an impatient motion with his hand. "He is Spanish at his heart," said he; "that Duke of Bouillon is Spanish, rank Spanish. But what of him, Monsieur de Fontrailles?"

"Believe me, my liege," replied Fontrailles, "the Duke of Bouillon, whom I know well, is not so much a friend to Spain as he is an enemy to Richelieu. Remember, sire, how he is linked with the Prince of Orange, the sworn adversary of Spain."

Louis shook his head doubtingly. "But what of him, Fontrailles? Come, to the point."

"Only this, sire," said Fontrailles. "The duke commands an army in Italy devoted to your majesty's service; but permit me or Cinq Mars to give him private orders in your name to march them into France, and who shall dare to murmur at your royal will?"

"Why, that might be done, it is true," answered Louis; "but I am afraid, mon grand," he continued, applying to Cinq Mars the term by which he distinguished him in his kindest and most familiar moments— "I am afraid, mon grand, that though thou art a keen huntsman and a good soldier, thou wouldst make but a sorry minister."

"I minister!" exclaimed the grand ecuyer: "God forbid! No, no, my lord! never did such a thought cross my imagination. Believe me, sire, I had no view of personal aggrandizement in the proposal I submitted to your majesty."

"But if you take from Richelieu his office, whom do you wish to substitute in his place?" demanded Louis; "some one must be minister."

"True, my liege; but are there not thousands well fitted for the post?" said Cinq Mars—"politicians as deep, but more humane than Richelieu—men who can govern yet not tyrannize? I will undertake to find such a one for your majesty, and yet remain myself fully satisfied with being the humble friend of my royal master, and the sincere well-wisher of my native country. But let me order, in your name, the Duke of Bouillon to march into France; and then, provided with sufficient forces to disarm this usurping minister, and overawe rebellion, your own royal will will be your only guide."

"At present," said Fontrailles, "the king's love for his people operates in two opposing directions, making him anxious to relieve them from the burden under which they groan, yet fearful of throwing a portion of them into rebellion. But by the presence of the duke's army, the minister might be removed without endangering the tranquillity of the realm."

"True," said Louis; "true. Monsieur de Fontrailles, you say right;" and placing his hand before his eyes, the king thought for a moment, struggling inwardly to exert the powers of his mind, and call up sufficient resolution to deliver himself from the thraldom in which he had so long been held. But dangers, and doubts, and difficulties swam before his mental vision like motes dancing in the sunbeam; and never destined in life to overcome his long-encouraged inactivity, he strove to cast the responsibility from himself. "Well, well," exclaimed he, "Cinq Mars, you shall decide it; I will leave the conduct of it all to you. But beware that you do not bring the miseries of civil war upon my kingdom; for be assured that if you do, I will require it of you deeply—it is your own seeking and the consequences be upon your own head."

"Let it be so, then, my liege," cried Cinq Mars, kissing the emaciated hand of the feeble monarch; "it shall not be my fault if France and my sovereign are not soon freed from the cloud that has so long overshadowed them both."

"Well, well," said Louis, "we will trust in God for the event. But beware of Bouillon; Cinq Mars, he is rank Spanish at his heart. And now, gentlemen, to bed, for we must rise in time for our sport. But, in truth, I fear I shall not hunt much longer—the body fails me, Cinq Mars, though I was once a thing of strength, as thou art."

CHAPTER XXVI.

How Chavigni rode fifty miles to ride back again.

WHILE these schemes for the downfall of his patron were going forward at Narbonne, Chavigni spurred on rapidly towards Tarascon, where the falling minister lay sick, both in body and in mind. Besides the personal attachment of the statesman to Richelieu, who had formed his fortunes, and led him in the way to greatness, every consideration of his own interest bade him oppose the resignation of the cardinal, which he clearly saw would bring inevitable destruction upon all persons connected with the existing ministry.

He had long perceived that a powerful party was forming against Richelieu, especially since his absence and illness gave facility to their operations. All Chavigni's talents and influence had been exerted to oppose them; but that the cardinal would resign his high office he had never suspected for a moment, and therefore the tidings brought by Mazarin came upon him like a thunder-stroke, taking from him all faculty of thought, but on that one thing. He was well aware, too, that it was no easy task to turn Richelieu from his purpose; and as he rode on, his mind was solely occupied by a thousand tumultuous and ill-digested plans for preventing the execution of what the cardinal designed.

Daylight set in the west, and night fell heavily over the earth, without exciting a thought in the bosom of Chavigni; for the irritation of his feelings took away all sensation of bodily fatigue, and almost all attention to external objects, till at length the failing pace of his horse showed him that he at least must have rest; and accordingly he paused for a short space at a little village a few leagues from Tarascon in order to refresh his beast. But even here the agitation of his mind prevented him from seeking any repose himself, and he continued walking up and down before the little auberge, for the time that he was thus compelled to remain.

It was considerably past midnight when Chavigni arrived at the residence of the minister. On entering the court-yard all was in darkness, except where, in one spot, a light was seen burning in the chamber of the invalid, and throwing dark across the window the bent shadow of a sleeping attendant. The statesman fastened his horse to one of the iron hooks in the court yard and advanced, intending to make himself heard by some one within, but he found that the grooms, grown negligent during their lord's sickness, had left the door unfastened, and pushing it with his hand, it readily gave way. "It is like his fate," thought Chavigni: "while he is ill and sleeping, the gate is left open, and any one may enter."

Passing onward through the hall, he now mounted the grand staircase, lighted by a lamp that had been left to die out as it might, and approached the room where the cardinal lay.

The door of the ante-chamber opened stiffly, but still the drowsy attendant did not awake; and Chavigni passed on into the bed-chamber of the cardinal, without any one being aware of his presence. "Were this but known," thought the statesman, "how many assassins' hands would now be armed for this one man's destruction!"

It was Richelieu alone, who, lying in feverish restlessness, caught the sound of approaching steps; and there was a sort of intensity in the glance which he fixed on the door communicating with the ante-room, which seemed to say that his judgment of the visitor's purpose

was not very favorable. However that might be, whether
from the recklessness of illness, or from the torpor of
one who regards the future as a blank, he took no further
notice of the sound he heard, than by fixing his eyes
sternly on the door. But the next moment, as the light
fell strongly on the face of his friend, the countenance
of Richelieu brightened with a smile; and perceiving
that Chavigni, who did not see he was awake, approached
silently towards the attendant to rouse him, the cardinal
pronounced his name in an under-tone, and beckoned him
towards his bedside.

"It is grateful," said Richelieu, as the statesman drew
near, "to find that even declining fortunes cannot alienate
some hearts. You have seen Mazarin, I suppose."

Chavigni was about to answer, but the sound of the
cardinal's voice had awakened the attendant, who was
now gazing about in no small alarm, on perceiving a
stranger standing by the minister's bedside. Richelieu,
however, without showing any anger at his negligence,
calmly commanded him to leave them; and as soon as
they were alone, Chavigni proceeded. "I have seen
Cardinal Mazarin, my lord, and from him I have learned
a piece of news which grieves me most deeply. I cannot
believe that illness can have so far depressed the spirits of
your eminence, as to make you entertain the thought of
casting from you all those high honors, which you have
so long enjoyed, and of leaving France, in a moment of
her greatest peril, to be governed by the hands of the
weak and the designing."

"It is not illness, Chavigni," replied the cardinal,
with a melancholy shake of the head. "No! but my day
is over. The power has passed from my hands, and it
only remains for me to yield the name of it, before that
too is taken from me by my enemies."

"Pardon me, your eminence," said Chavigni; "but
indeed the power is not gone from you. Under whose
orders are our armies fighting? Under whose command

is every city and fortress in France? Is it the character
of a great man—is it the character of a born man, to yield
all without a struggle?—to cast away the sword he has
so long wielded, and to give himself bound into the hands
of his adversaries?"

"Mark me, Chavigni," said Richelieu, raising himself
upon his elbow, "Louis is now within the distance of a
few leagues. He knows that I am ill—perhaps that I am
dying; and yet, by no sign of common courtesy does he
show that he remembers me. But that was not the beginning. I saw that my power was gone, when he dared,
in the face of all the council, to annul the sentence I had
passed on that arrogant, stiff-necked Count de Blenau,
who had the hardihood to defy the utmost extent of my
power." And the minister's eyes flashed with the
memory of his anger.

"Had your eminence followed my advice," replied
Chavigni, "that business would never have occurred,
There is that sort of gallant magnanimity about Claude
de Blenau which carries all before it; and I felt assured
that neither fear nor interest would ever induce him to
disclose anything intrusted to hi. honor. Depend upon
it, monseigneur, that it is better not to meddle with such
men, when we can avoid it."

"Well, well, sir," exclaimed the cardinal, impatiently,
"without doubt you were quite right and I was quite
wrong. But do not teach me to believe that you too,
Chavigni, lose your respect for my person when my
power is failing."

"Pardon me, your eminence," replied Chavigni, in a
tone of deep feeling, "you wrong me much. Your eminence has been more than a father to me. During the
continuance of your power you have always exerted it
in my favor; and whether it remains with you or not,
my respect and my affection will never fail to follow
you in every situation. Believe me, monseigneur, that
it is that respect and affection, which brings me here

even now, to petition that you will waive your intention
of——"

"Chavigni, it is useless," interposed the cardinal. "I
have only the choice left, to yield it of my own free will,
or to have it wrenched from my unwilling hand. Judge
which is the wisest—judge which is the best."

"Were that certainly the case," said Chavigni, thoughtfully.

"It is certainly the case," replied the minister. "There
are many, many combined against me: singly, they are
but reeds, and one by one I would break them like reeds;
but united together, and with the king at their head"—
and he shook his head despairingly—"they are far too
strong either for you or me!"

"But could no means be found to separate them? Be-
think you, monseigneur,—avarice, revenge, ambition,
might sow the seeds of discord amongst them, and give
them like sheep into our hands."

"It is too late my friend!" replied the cardinal; "it
is too late! Had I foreseen it, I might have prevented
their combining. I might have crushed some, and bribed
others; destroyed the powerful, and overawed the timid.
But it is now too late!"

"But whom does your eminence think particularly implicated?" demanded Chavigni.

"Oh, there are many—many—many!" replied Richelieu, withdrawing the thin pale hand he had stretched
over his face as he finished the last desponding words
"too late," probably desirous of hiding the emotion produced by the conviction that his power was irretrievably
gone. However, when that hand was removed, his countenance showed no traces of any remaining agitation.
"There are many, Chavigni," he said; "there are Ven-
dome, and Bouillon, and noisy Beaufort, and turbulent
Gaston of Orleans, and witty Marsillac, and cool, mor-
alizing De Thou who has so often dared to pry into my
actions and condemn them; then there is, above all, sly
Fontrailles, and Cinq Mars, whom I—"

26

" Ha ! " exclaimed Chavigni, as the cardinal's words recalled to his mind the conversation between Cinq Mars
and Fontrailles—" I had forgot—like an idiot, I had forgot ! " and he struck his clenched hand violently against
his brow, as if he sought to punish his own folly. " But
it is not yet too late," he cried—" it is not yet too late."

" Forgot what, Chavigni ? " demanded the cardinal,
seeing with astonishment the emotion which was called
up in his friend by the remembrance of so great an oversight. " Forgot what ? Too late for what ? What is it
moves you so deeply ? "

" Pardon me, your eminence," replied Chavigni, " I
have not time to explain ; only I have to ask two favors.
The first is, that you will let me take a stout horse from
your stables ; mine will go no farther. The next," he
added, in a tone of greater composure, but still one of
earnest entreaty—" the next is, if you had ever a regard
for me—if ever I served you well and faithfully, that you
will promise me to take no step in the business we have
spoken of, till my return ; which shall be before to-morrow evening."

" It can make but little difference waiting till that
time," answered the cardinal. " But what is the matter,
Chavigni ? What is it agitates you thus ? "

" Have I your promise, monseigneur ? " asked Chavigni, quickly.

" You have," said Richelieu. " Out of regard for you,
and solely because you ask, I will suspend my resolution
till you return."

" Well, then, God protect your eminence till we meet
again ! " exclaimed the statesman. " I go upon your service ; and if I do not succeed, I care not how soon my
head may be brought to the block, as a just punishment
for my mad forgetfulness." Thus saying, he quitted the
room, and descending to the stables, called up the grooms
whose sleepy movements ill accorded with the rapid
emotions of his bosom. Now the stirrups were not long

enough, then the girths had to be buckled tighter, then
the bit was mislaid, and then the crupper could not be
found. At length, however, the horse was fully prepared, and calling for a cup of wine Chavigni drained it
to the bottom, and galloping out of the court, was soon
once more on the road to Narbonne. But it was in vain
that he used whip and spur to arrive at that town before
the hour appointed for the Italian's departure. Ere he
had measured half the way, the day rose bright over the
hills before him, and clenching his hands, he exclaimed
in the bitterness of disappointment, " Too late! I am
too late! " Still, however, he went on at full speed,
hoping that by sending out couriers in every different
direction he might yet overtake the messenger.

Chavigni paused for a moment to make certain of the
course; and as he did so, his eye fell upon the figure of a
single horseman, descending into the valley from the
opposite hill.

" Whom have we here? " thought the statesman, not
without a faint hope that it might be the person he
sough. Spurring on his horse, however, he rode forward to meet him; but on reaching the bottom of the
descent, the figure he had seen from above became hidden by the windings of the road among the trees, and
Chavigni's heart fluttered lest the horseman, whoever he
was, might have taken the other road which turned
through the valley to the left.

At length, however, the sound of a horse's feet was
heard approaching quickly towards him, and, certain that
he must now pass that way, the statesman drew in his
rein, and stood with his eyes intently fixed on the spot
where the road verged into the forest. As there was still
a considerable descent from the spot Chavigni paused
to the bottom of the valley, the sound was heard for a long
time coming nearer and nearer before any one appeared.
At length, however, the horseman came in sight, presenting to the glad eyes of the statesman the identical figure

of the Italian, Villa Grande, with his long sword, extensive moustaches, and a pair of heavy pistols at his saddle-bow.

Chavigni doubted not that to possess himself of the papers which the Italian carried, would require a desperate struggle, but without a moment's hesitation he drew his sword, and galloped on to attack him. No sooner had Villa Grande perceived a stranger on the road before him, than he reined in his horse; but now, as Chavigni rode on full speed towards him with a menacing attitude and drawn sword, the Italian, in his terror, conceived at once that it was a robber, and throwing himself to the ground in mortal fear, he fell on his knees, exclaiming—" I will give it you all—every ducat, only spare my life!"

"Rise, rise! cowardly villain!" cried Chavigni, catching the bridle of the Italian's horse, which was starting away with a wild toss of the head, as the statesman rode up—" rise, Sir Poltroon! do you not know me?"

"Know you! know you!" exclaimed Villa Grande, gazing wildly at Chavigni. "Oh, monseigneur, is it you? How you frightened me!" But Villa Grande, who had trembled sufficiently when he thought it was a robber, trembled ten times more than ever as he recognized the statesman; and he could scarcely find strength in his knees to raise himself from the ground.

"Rise, sir!" exclaimed Chavigni, impatiently; "and instantly give me the treaty."

"Treaty!" cried Villa Grande, still trembling, but endeavoring to put on a look of astonishment. "What treaty does monseigneur mean? I know of no treaty."

"Lying slave!" exclaimed Chavigni, striking him with the flat side of the sword; "if you do not produce it within ten seconds of time, by Heaven I will cut it out of your base cowardly heart!"

"But if I do——" said the Italian, seeing there was no escape left.

"Come, sir," cried the statesman; "no buts for me. If you stand shuffling one minute more, I will run my sword through you, and search for it on your carcass myself."

"Well, well! monseigneur, I see you know it all, and therefore it will be no stain on my honor if I give it you."

"Honor!" cried Chavigni, with a scoff.—"Come, sir, the treaty."

Villa Grande approached his horse, and raising the flap of the saddle, with shaking hands, drew forth, from a pocket concealed in the padding, a large paper sealed in an envelope. Chavigni caught it easily from his grasp, and running his eye over the address, he read— "To Monseigneur the Duke de Bouillon, commander-in-chief of all the armies of France, warring in Italy."— "Ha!" continued the statesman, "this is not the road to Italy. What brings you here?" and he turned towards Villa Grande. But while the statesman's eyes were fixed upon the paper, the wily Italian had begun to creep towards the wood; Chavigni, however, perceiving his design, caught one of the pistols from the horse's saddle-bow, and pointing it towards the fugitive, soon brought him back again. "Stand you there, sir," said he. "Now tell me what makes you here, when this packet was intended for Italy?"

"Why, monseigneur—why—why—to tell the truth, there was another little despatch to be delivered on the frontiers of Spain; here it is;" and diving into a deep pocket in his doublet, he produced a packet smaller than the other, and gave it into Chavigni's hand. "And now, monseigneur, I have freely discovered all I know," continued Villa Grande, "I hope that you, monseigneur, will promise me your protection; for if the other party get hold of me, they will murder me to a certainty."

Chavigni made no answer, but without any ceremony broke the seals of the two packets, and passing his

horse's bridle over his arm while he read them, he opened
the treaty, and turned to the list of names by which it
was signed. In the meanwhile, Villa Grande kept his
eyes fixed upon him, watching for a favorable moment
to escape, if the statesman's attention should be sufficiently engaged to allow him so to do.

"Ah! here I have them fairly written," proceeded
Chavigni, speaking to himself. "Philip, the most
Catholic!—Olivarez!—then follow Gaston of Orleans;
Cinq Mars, grand ecuyer—Fontrailles; and a space—for
Bouillon of course. Now let us see the letter to the
noble duke;" and he opened the one which he found in
the same packet with the treaty. But as he read, his
eye fixed with painful earnestness upon the paper, and
the color fled from his cheek. "God of Heaven! what
is this?" said he, reading. "'Though I doubt not, my
noble friend, that after all which has lately passed, you
would put your forces in motion at my simple desire, the
king's command is yet higher authority; and that I now
send you, to march with all speed to the frontier, embarking five thousand foot at Porto Longone, to land at Mar-
seilles. All this in case the friends and adherents of
Richelieu should attempt to make head against the royal
authority——'"

"All is lost!" muttered Chavigni. "But let us see
the whole, at least, to provide for our own safety;" and
he again turned to the paper, which proceeded—"'I
send you the treaty with Spain for your signature, which
is especially necessary to the article relative to your
principality of Sedan. The troops of his catholic majesty
are on the frontier, ready to march at our command; but
I have been obliged to conceal from the king our Spanish
connection, as his hatred to that country is as great as
ever.'"

"I have you! I have you! Monsieur Cinq Mars," exclaimed Chavigni, clasping his hands with joy. "This
treaty is your death warrant, or I know not King Louis,

—Italian scoundrel!" he continued, turning to look for Villa Grande—"Ha! the slave has escaped—that must not be; he were the best witness in the world against them;" and springing from his horse, he tied him to a tree together with that of the Italian.

While Chavigni had been reading, with all his attention fixed upon the paper, and all his passions excited by its contents, Villa Grande, watching his moment, had crept gradually to the edge of the wood, and darted into a narrow path, half covered with branches. But though the way he had taken was thus, in a degree, concealed, it did not escape the quick eye of the statesman; and as the motions of the Italian, till he had got into the wood, had been necessarily cautions, in order not to call his attention, Chavigni following as fast as lightning, soon caught the sound of his retreating footsteps, reverberated from the rocks around. As he advanced, he called loudly to the Italian to stop, and that he should have a free pardon; but Villa Grande, trusting to the distance that was still between them, and hoping, if he could elude immediate pursuit, to be able to escape into Spain, continued running on, while Chavigni as perseveringly followed, threatening and promising by turns, but alike without effect.

At length the strength of the Italian, already diminished by fear, began to fail entirely; and Chavigni found that the distance between them was rapidly lessening, when in a moment the sound of footsteps, which had hitherto guided him, ceased entirely—a cry of agony reached his ear; and running still more quickly forward, he, too, had nearly been precipitated over the edge of a steep crag, which, in the hurry of his flight, the unhappy Italian had not noticed.

The statesman's first impulse was to start back, for he was on the very brink of the precipice before he was aware; but soon recovering himself, he approached the edge, and looking over, beheld the mangled form of Villa

Grande lying on some rough stony ground at the bottom
of the rock.

"God of Heaven!" cried Chavigni, "what a fall!
The poor wretch must surely be dead. However, he
must not lie there, for the wolves will soon be at him;"
and looking around, he sought for some way to descend
the rock. It was a considerable time before he could
accomplish his object, but at length he succeeded, and
on arriving at the spot where Villa Grande lay, he found
that the Italian, in his flight, had taken a diagonal path
through the forest, which cut off a large bend in the main
road, and joined it again by a zig-zag path down the
rock at some distance. Thus the spot where Villa
Grande was then lying, was about half a mile from the
place at which he had first been encountered by Chavigni,
if the high road was followed; but by the path through
the wood the distance could not be more than a few
hundred yards. Chavigni's first care was to examine the
body of the Italian, who was so entirely deprived of
sense, that at first the statesman believed him to be dead;
but in a moment or two some signs appeared which led
him to conclude that life was not completely extinct; and
taking him in his arms he carried him to the spot where
the horses stood. Here he placed him on the stout black
hunter which Cinq Mars had lent, and led him slowly to
a small town about a mile farther on the road.

It has been already stated, that hardly was there a
village so small in the whole extent of France as not to
be furnished with one or more of those agents of Richelieu's minute policy, whose principal duty consisted in
communicating everything that passed around them to
another class of superior agents, and also to facilitate all
the secret operations of government in the sphere as-
cribed to them. The actual pay received by these men
was but small; but the favor shown to them on all occasions, and the facilities afforded to them in their more
ordinary employments, put them above competition with
others in the same class, and amply rewarded their private

services: for it must always be remembered that their
connection with the government was held as a profound
secret, and consequently they always were seen to exercise some open trade, which, in most cases, prevented
their less ostensible employment from being even suspected by their neighbors.

It was to the house of one of these inferior agents
that Chavigni led the horse charged with the senseless
body of Villa Grande; and having commanded that he
should be taken in and placed in bed, he himself aided in
endeavoring to recall him to life, partly from the natural
humanity of his disposition, partly from those political
considerations which were ever paramount in his mind.
Villa Grande, if he could be restored, would prove, Chavigni knew, too excellent a witness against the conspirators whom he had served, to permit of his life being
lightly cast away; especially as it was evident, that either
fear or bribery would induce him to confess anything:
but even had it not been for this reflection, the statesman's
natural disposition would probably have led him to succor the unhappy man, in whose misfortune he had been
so greatly instrumental.

After many efforts, Villa Grande once more began to
evince that the vital spark was not yet extinguished; and
having so far succeeded, Chavigni, upon whose mind a
thousand subjects of deep import were pressing every
moment for attention, gave directions to the agent we
have already mentioned, to show every attention to the
wounded man, and to keep him for that day, at his own
house, which was situated a quarter of a league out of
Limoux; but as soon as night came, to have him privately
removed to Corneille, at which place a surgeon could be
more easily procured from Carcasonne; and having reiterated the most strict injunctions to keep the whole business profoundly secret, lest the conspirators should learn
the fate of their envoy, and take their measures accordingly, Chavigni once more turned his steps towards Tarascon, to recount to Richelieu the events of the day.

CHAPTER XXVII.

Which was written expressly to prove that there is many a slip between
the cup and the lip.

It was the small chapel of St. Catherine, otherwise
called the Queen's Chapel, attached to the palace-church
of St. Germain-en-Laye, to which Potier, Bishop of
Beauvais, proceeded with slow steps from the door of
private communication with the château, on a night in
October, one thousand six hundred and forty-two. He
was preceded by two young abbés, carrying lighted
tapers, and followed by a group, whose white garments
spoke that they came on some occasion of joy. The first
of these was Anne of Austria, with her eyes animated,
and her countenance glowing with the interest she took
in everything which bore the least appearance of secrecy
or romance. He right arm was passed through that of
the Marchioness de Beaumont, who moved on with a
calm, rather grave countenance; while on the queen's
left, walked a young lady in the first gay spring of life,
ever and anon turning a smiling, playful glance behind
to Pauline de Beaumont, who, leaning on the arm of
Claude de Blenau, followed, agitated, blushing and happy,
towards the altar at which they were to be united forever. Seguin, the queen's physician, and Henri de La
Mothe, the count's page, were admitted as witnesses to
the ceremony; and an attendant was stationed at the
door, to guard against any troublesome devotee entering
the church during the time it was thus occupied.

The idea of marrying Pauline de Beaumont privately
to the Count de Blenau, had entirely originated with the
queen, whose passion for anything romantic often threw
both herself and her friends into situations of great

danger. In the present instance, she represented to Madame de Beaumont that a thousand circumstances might occur in those unhappy times, to tear De Blenau again from her he loved; or that the cardinal might positively prohibit their marriage, and then, she asked, who would dare to oppose him? whereas their private union would obviate all difficulties, and incur no danger.

Madame de Beaumont made many objections, and her daughter hesitated; but the wishes of the queen overcame all the marchioness's scruples; and the entreaties of De Blenau were not less powerful with Pauline.

The appointed night being arrived, and all the arrangements having been made as privately as possible, Pauline, as we have said, followed her mother and the queen into the chapel of St. Catherine. But as she did so, there was a sort of despondency fell upon her that she could not account for. As she leaned upon De Blenau, she felt that she was most happy in being united to him. She was agitated, it was true, but still it was natural that she should be so, she thought. She had not, however, much time to analyze her feelings; for, by this time, the bishop had reached the altar, and waited their approach.

Potier, Bishop of Beauvais, had little of that gentleness of disposition, or suavity of manner, calculated to re-assure Pauline. He had undertaken the office which he came there to fulfil, merely at the desire of the queen, and that not without making considerable opposition. But, though Potier was obstinate, Anne of Austria was still more so. She had resolved that the ceremony should be performed, and that he should perform it, and she carried her point; but yet he made his dislike to the task very apparent, and regarded the innocent Pauline with no very friendly looks.

"Come, mademoiselle," said he, as Pauline seemed to linger for a moment, "you and Monsieur le Comte will have enough of each other's society after my office is over. Let us proceed with the ceremony."

The group arranged themselves round the altar, and
the bishop opening the book began to read. The promise,
which was to bind her to De Blenau forever, trembled
on Pauline's lips, when a confused noise at the private
door leading to the palace caught her ear, and she paused.

De Blenau, who had not heard it, turned towards her
in surprise; but imediately the voice of the attendant,
who had been stationed there as portgreve, was heard
exclaiming to some one, who apparently endeavored to
make his way into the church, "Stand back, I say. You
do not enter here! What is your authority?"

"My authority," replied another voice, "is a warrant
of council. Oppose it if you dare. Strike him down, if
he does not let you pass," and immediately the door bursting open, an officer of the cardinal's guard, with a file of
soldiers, entered the church.

"Guard the doors," cried the officer, "and let no one
quit the place." And giving his partisan to one of the
soldiers, he advanced towards the high gothic arch, forming the boundary between the main aisle and the chapel of
St. Catherine.

Pauline clung to De Blenau. "Oh, Claude!" cried
she, "they are going to tear you from me again. My
heart misgave me.—I was sure that something dreadful
would interpose between us."

De Blenau whispered a few words of comfort to her,
and Potier himself was moved by her agitation. "Do
not be afraid, young lady," said he; "we are on sacred
ground.—Stop, sir," he continued, advancing to the steps
of the chapel, which the officer had just reached: "what
seek you here? And how do you presume to bring
armed men into this church?"

"I come, sir," answered the officer, "with a warrant
from his majesty's council, to arrest Claude Count de
Blenau;" and he made a step towards the chapel.

"Hold!" exclaimed the bishop. "You arrest him
not here. This ground is sanctuary; and I command

you, in the name of God and our holy religion, to with-draw your men, and instantly to quit this church." And he waved his hand with an air of dignified authority.

The officer paused. " But, monseigneur," he replied, "the count is charged with high treason."

" With high treason!" exclaimed the queen.

" With high treason!" echoed Pauline, clinging still closer to De Blenau's arm, which she held encircled by both her own.

" He is charged with high treason," repeated the officer; "and I must fulfil my duty."

" Were he charged with all the crimes which disgrace humanity," replied the bishop, " here he is sanctuarized; and I command you, on pain of excommunication—you, Sir Officer, and your soldiers, to quit the church. I stand not here to see this altar violated, whatever be your authority."

The officer paused a moment, uncertain how to act. " Well, holy father," replied he at length, " I obey; but I shall take especial care to guard every door of the church; so that if there be any blame, it does not fall on me." And muttering between his teeth the discontent he did no dare to vent aloud, he slowly withdrew his men.

The eye of Anne of Austria watched them intently till the last soldier had passed through the door which communicated with the palace. Then turning quickly to the count, she exclaimed, " Fly quick, De Blenau, up that staircase, cross the jube, through the monks' gallery round the choir. You will find a door on the right that leads into the king's cabinet. Wait there till I send— Quick, fly—I desire—I command you."

" Oh fly, Claude, fly!" reiterated Pauline; "they will murder you surely this time, if you do not fly."

" Pardon me, your majesty—pardon me, dear Pauline," replied De Blenau; "it cannot be. There is no man in France more innocent, in deed, word, or even thought, of treason against his king and country than I am; and

Claude de Blenau flies from no one, so long as his honor and integrity remain by him: when these fail, then he may become a coward. But to these will I now trust, and instantly surrender myself to his majesty's warrant. I did not interfere while monseigneur defended the rights of the sanctuary, for he did but the duties of his high office; nor indeed was I willing to yield my sword to a servant of Cardinal Richelieu. Take it, Henry," he continued, unbuckling it from his side, and giving it to the page; " take it, and keep it for your master."

" De Blenau, you are an obstinate man," said the queen. " I will urge nothing; but look at this pale cheek, and fancy what the feelings of that sweet girl must be." And she pointed to Pauline, who stood by with the tears chasing each other down her face.

Notwithstanding the firmness with which he spoke, there had been many a bitter pang struggling in De Blenau's breast. The appeal of the queen, and the sight of Pauline's distress, overcame his calmness; and starting forward, he caught her in his arms and pressed an ardent kiss upon her lips. " Dear, dear Pauline," he exclaimed, " all will go well, be assured. My innocence will protect me."

Pauline shook her head mournfully, but her heart was too full to reply.

" Then you will not fly? " demanded the queen, with some degree of impatience.

" He is in the right, madam," said the bishop. " As a good subject, he is bound to obey the laws of his country; and in duty to himself, he ought not to give weight to the charge against him by seeming afraid to meet it."

Anne of Austria turned away with a look of angry disappointment. " Well, at all events," said she, " let us conclude the ceremony which has been thus interrupted, and afterwards the count can act as he pleases."

De Blenau hesitated. He felt that what the queen proposed, if carried into effect, would be the only con-

solation he could receive under the new misfortune that
had befallen him; but he felt also that it was a selfishness
to wish it, and he looked towards the bishop who had so
well supported his first resolution. But Potier bent his
eyes gravely on the ground, disapproving the proposal,
yet unwilling further to oppose the queen.

"It shall be as Pauline decides," said De Blenau,
taking her hand and raising it gently to his lips. "Pauline," he continued, "you know how deeply I love you;
you know how I have longed for the hour that should
give me your hand. But I fear that I should be cruelly
selfish were I to ask you to become the bride of one
whose fate is so uncertain. Speak, dear Pauline."

Mademoiselle de Beaumont spoke not, but she raised
her eyes to De Blenau with an expression which told that
every feeling of her heart was given to him. The
marchioness, however, interposed. "No!" said she:
"Claude, you are right; it is better to wait. The time
will come, I feel sure, when you will be able to claim
Pauline in the midst of smiles and happiness, instead of
tears and danger. Does not your majesty think this delay
advisable?"

"My opinion has been expressed already," replied
Anne of Austria, peevishly. "But it is not my affair—
act as you think fit. But were I Pauline, and my lover
gave me up so calmly, I would seek another in his absence to console me."

De Blenau, deeply hurt, bit his lip, and by a strong
effort forced himself to silence: but Pauline placed her
hand in his, and raising her eyes to his face: "Fear not,
Claude," she said; "in life and in death I am yours.
None other shall ever possess the hand of Pauline de
Beaumont."

"You are a noble girl, Pauline," exclaimed the queen.
"De Blenau, I was wrong; but it vexes me to see that
you will always be more in the right than I am. Do not
look so sad, Pauline. The more I think of it, the more I

feel sure that De Blenau's innocence will stand him in good stead yet, in spite of the meagre cardinal: and I begin to reckon also somewhat on my own influence with Louis; he is far kinder than in former days; and I will make it a point of earnest prayer that De Blenau be fairly used. Besides, they have now no plea against him. There are no secret letters to be discovered—no correspondence with the public enemy."

Pauline shook her head mournfully. A cloud had come over the sun of her days, and she fancied that he would never beam brightly again.

"If we could ascertain the reason of this arrest," said Madame de Beaumont, " it might in some degree satisfy our minds."

"That may be easily done," replied the bishop, " as Monsieur de Blenau is resolved to surrender himself. We can question the officer in regard to what occurred at the place from whence he comes; and by that means discover what circumstances have arisen to cast suspicion on the count."

What the bishop proposed was instantly agreed to; and De Blenau sent forward his page to inform the officer of his determination.

Anne of Austria then took a few steps along the nave, and turned to see if he still held his resolution. De Blenau bowed. "I follow your majesty," he said. "I feel that I have nothing to fear." And they passed on slowly and sadly to the other end of the church.

As they went, Pauline still clung to the arm of her lover, as if she feared that every moment they would tear him from her; and tear after tear rolled silently down her cheeks. The heart of De Blenau also was too full for words, so that silence hung upon the whole party.

At the door which communicated with the palace stood the cardinal's officer, with two or three of his men; and as she approached, the queen desired him to follow her to the saloon. The officer bowed low, and replied that he would obey her commands; but immediately advancing to De Blenau, he laid his hand upon the count's arm. "In the king's name, Monsieur le Comte de Blenau," said he, "I arrest you for high treason. Behold my warrant."

Pauline recoiled with a look of fear; and De Blenau calmly put the man's hand from off his sleeve. "Pass on, sir," he said, "I am your prisoner." The officer hesitated. "Pass on, sir," repeated the count; "you have my word. I am your prisoner."

The man passed on, but not before he had made a sign to the soldiers who were with him, who suffered the count and Pauline to pass, and then closing in, followed at a few paces' distance.

On reaching the saloon, the queen took her seat; and beckoning to Pauline, who, faint and terrified, was hardly able to support herself, she made her sit down on the footstool at her feet. "Now, Sir Officer," said Anne of Austria, "what news bring you from Narbonne? How fares his majesty the king?"

"May it please you, madam," he replied, "I come not from Narbonne, as your majesty supposes, but from Tarascon, where the king had just arrived when I departed."

"The king at Tarascon!" exclaimed Anne of Austria. "In the name of heaven, what does he at Tarascon?"

"That is beyond my knowledge," answered the officer. "All I can tell your majesty is, that for the last week there has been strange flying of couriers from one place to another. Monsieur de Chavigni has almost killed himself with riding between Tarascon and Narbonne. Everything is altered, evidently, but no one knows how or why; and just as Aleron, Monsieur de Brezé's maitre d'hotel, was about to give me the whole history, I received an order to set off for Paris instantly, and when I arrived there to take twenty troopers from the caserne,

27

and come on hither on the errand which I have the honor
to perform."

"But did you hear nothing?" demanded the queen,
earnestly. "Did this Aleron tell you nothing?"

"Nothing, madam," replied the officer. "He had just
made me promise inviolable secrecy, and we were interrupted before he began his tale; or I would have told
your majesty with pleasure."

"But from report?" said the queen. "Did you gain
no knowledge from rumor?"

"Oh, there were rumors enough, truly," answered the
man; "but as fast as one came, it was contradicted by
another. Some said that the troops at Perpignan had
revolted, and some that Monsieur le Grand had killed
Cardinal Mazarin. Others brought word that Monsieur
de Noyers had tried to poison the king; and others, that
the king had kicked Fontrailles for hunting in short
boots."

"Nonsense!" said the queen; "all nonsense. It is
unfortunate," she continued, musing, "that we can get
no information. But tell me, where are you ordered to
conduct Monsieur de Blenau?—to the Bastile?"

At the name of a place where both De Blenau and
herself had suffered so much, and which was associated
in her mind with every horrible idea, Pauline clasped her
hands over her eyes, as if to shut out the frightful visions
it recalled.

"No, madam," replied the officer, "I am commanded
to conduct Monsieur de Blenau, as quickly as possible, to
Tarascon; and allow me to remind your majesty that the
time is passing fast."

De Blenau made a sign to the officer, indicating that
he was ready. He saw that Pauline's hands still covered
her eyes, and, wishing to spare her the pain of such a
parting, he bowed profoundly to the queen, and moved
in silence to the door. The queen and Madame de Beaumont saw his intention, and remained silent; but as he

reached the door, he could not resist the desire to turn and
look once more upon her whom he was leaving perhaps
forever—who had so nearly been his bride—whom he
had loved so long—who had undergone so much for him.
It was excusable, but the delay defeated his purpose.
The sudden silence alarmed Pauline—she raised her eyes
—she saw De Blenau in the act of departing, and the last
fixed painful glance with which he regarded her. All
but her love was that moment forgotten; and starting
wildly forward, she threw herself into his arms, and
wept bitterly on his bosom. But Madame de Beaumont
advancing, gently disengaged her from his embrace.
Pauline hid her eyes upon her mother's shoulder; and
De Blenau, with a heart ready to break, fled quickly from
a scene that his fortitude could support no longer.

CHAPTER XXVIII.

Which shows that a man who has climbed a mountain may stumble at a pebble ; or the consequences of one oversight.

WE must once more go back to Narbonne, in order to explain the events which had there taken place since the day on which Chavigni possessed himself of the treaty with Spain. Cinq Mars, hearing nothing of his agent, of course concluded that he was quietly pursuing his way ; and willing to take every precaution to ensure the success of his plans, he spent the next day in riding over to the camp at Perpignan, and endeavoring to ingratiate himself with the officers and soldiers of that part of the army. The splendor of his train and equipages, the manly beauty of his person, his dexterity in all warlike exercises, and the courteous familiarity of his manners, attracted all eyes, and won all hearts ; and Cinq Mars, well contented with the day's success, did not return to Narbonne till very late at night.

The next morning had been appointed for hunting ; but that day the king was rather later than usual, and Cinq Mars, as he waited in the saloon till Louis should be ready, took up a romance which some of the pages had left behind, and stretching his tall elegant form at length in the window-seat, he began reading, to pass the time.

So much, indeed, was he occupied, that as some one passed to and from the king's chamber, he scarcely raised his eyes to notice who it was ; and when at last he did so, he found it was only a page.

The tale went on, and another step met his ear, whose firm, decided pace plainly told that it was not that of a domestic. Cinq Mars raised his eyes, and as he did so they encountered those of Chavigni, who was passing on to the apartments of the king. Chavigni bowed, with a peculiar smile. Cinq Mars returned his salutation, and again began reading his book. "It is all over with your power, Monsieur de Chavigni," thought the master of the horse; "I will but read out this adventure of the two lovers, and then I will come to disturb your tête-á-tête with his majesty."

Cinq Mars read on. Fontrailles entered the saloon and interrupted him. "In the name of heaven, Cinq Mars," exclaimed he, "what are you about?"

"I am waiting till the king is ready," answered the master of the horse, composedly, scarcely taking his eyes from the romance.

"And is it possible," asked Fontrailles, in a tone of angry astonishment, "that you have lain here reading that drivelling book, and suffered Chavigni to be again so long with the king?"

"Again!" said Cinq Mars, becoming more attentive; "he only passed once that I saw."

"And ought he to have been there once, if that were all?" asked Fontrailles. "But let me tell you, Cinq Mars, he was there last night for more than an hour. Oh, Cinq Mars! Cinq Mars! is this a time, when our lives, our fortunes, and our country's weal are at stake, to sit there dozing over a romance, and see our bitterest enemy have access to the king's ear, but too easy to be abused? Depend on it, something more will come of this."

"But why did you not let me know," demanded the master of the horse, "that he had seen the king last night?"

"I learned it but this moment," replied Fontrailles. "But here comes a page from the king's apartments. A message to you, Cinq Mars, on my life."

The page approached. "I am commanded by the king's majesty to acquaint you, monseigneur," said he, addressing the grand ecuyer, "that he feels himself too unwell to enjoy the pleasures of the chase to-day. But he

desires that his indisposition may not prevent you, and
the other gentlemen invited, from following your sport."
—And having delivered this message the attendant withdrew, without wating for any reply.

"Well, now you see, Fontrailles," exclaimed Cinq
Mars, "there is nothing wrong here. Nothing can be
more kind and considerate than, when ill himself, to wish
us to follow the sport without him."

An expression of heavy, deep-seated thought sat upon
the brow of the clear-sighted, suspicious Fontrailles.
He took two or three steps up and down the apartment,
and then, turning to Cinq Mars with a countenance in
which painful anxiety and bitter irony were strangely
mingled, he considered his companion with an attentive
glance, which ran rapidly over his tall elegant figure.
"Cinq Mars," said he, "you are more than six feet high,
and could spare a few inches of your height upon an
occasion—even were they to make you shorter by the
head, you would still be a tall man. As for me, I am
short already, and cannot afford to be cut down. A word
to the wise—I go to shelter myself from pruning-knives.
Do as you please. We shall meet in this world or the
next. Adieu!" And turning on his heel, he quitted the
saloon.

"The man is mad!" said Cinq Mars, aloud, as Fontrailles left him—"irretrievably cracked!" And jump-
ing up from the window-seat, he descended to the
court-yard, called the huntsmen together, mounted his
horse, and led the chase as merrily as if nothing had happened but the ordinary trifles of a day.

Had he known all, very different would have been his
feelings. The visit of Chavigni to the king was one on
which the fate of France depended; and the wily statesman had entered the apartments of the monarch, prepared equally to guard every word he uttered himself,
and to watch every turn of Louis's irritable and unsteady
mind.

The king was leaning on a table in his cabinet, dressed for the hunting expedition we have mentioned, and more than a usual degree of peevishness was expressed in his countenance. " Well, sir," exclaimed Louis as Chavigni entered, " what other bad news have you the pleasure of bringing me? What other friends have turned traitors? What other power is about to invade my dominions? By the Holy Trinity! I never see your face but it makes me melancholy."

Chavigni was not sorry to perceive the king's irritability. The night before he had conveyed to him, in general terms, the news of a private treaty existing between Spain and some that Louis supposed his friends, and had promised to bring him that morning the names of the different parties engaged. He now came to fulfil that promise, and he saw that the former information had been working upon Louis's mind, and raised in it a degree of impatience and anger that would fall heavily on the first object presented to his resentment. Nor did Chavigni doubt that he would easily be able to turn it in the direction that he wished.

" My liege," replied he, " when I find your majesty's confidence betrayed, your dominions threatened, and even your person in danger, it is my duty to give your majesty timely warning, although the news be as unpleasant for me to bear as for you to hear. To conceal treason is the part of a traitor, and as one of your majesty's council——"

" Well, well, sir," cried Louis, interrupting him, " spare your exculpation. The executioner is doubtless guiltless of the blood he sheds, but it is not a right honorable trade."

An angry flush came over Chavigni's countenance, but it quickly subsided; and he replied calmly, " I came here, as your majesty knows, to give you more minute particulars of the information I rendered you yesterday, and to prove to you that some whom you esteem your dearest friends, and some who are your nearest relations, are the veriest traitors in France. The affair for no one can be more unpleasant than for myself, for there are some to whom I wish well, that have in this merited their death; therefore, sire, if you find it too painful to hear, in the name of Heaven, let it rest in silence. I will hie me home and burn the papers I have brought here; and satisfied with having done my duty, only hold myself ready, when the misfortunes which must follow, do arrive, to serve your majesty with my hand and heart." And bowing profoundly, Chavigni took a step back, as if about to quit the presence.

"Hold, Monsieur de Chavigni," said the king, "you have done your duty, we do not doubt. But unpleasant tidings, sir, are not to be received pleasantly. Were it ourself alone that they aimed at, perhaps we might leave treason to overreach itself; but as the welfare of our kingdom is at stake, we must look the frowning truth in the face, and prepare to punish the guilty, be they who they may, that we may insure the safety of the innocent."

"Louis the Just," said Chavigni, advancing and using a term which had been bestowed upon the king by the astrologers of the day from his having been born under the sign "Libra"—"Louis the Just will not act otherwise than justly; and if I prove not to your majesty's satisfaction that a most dangerous conspiracy is on foot, let your royal indignation fall upon me."

"I know not what you call a conspiracy, sir," answered Louis, his mind reverting to the plans of Cinq Mars, to which, as we have seen, he had given his own sanction only a few nights before, and for the discovery of which he had felt as much alarm as if Richelieu possessed the power of punishing him also.

"The conspiracy I speak of, sire," rejoined the statesman, "is formed not only to oblige your majesty to change your ministers, but——"

"I can conceive no plan for obliging me to change my

ministers," interrupted the king. "You must have mistaken, Monsieur de Chavigni; perhaps the persons whom you style conspirators have only in view to make me dutiful petition and remonstrance, in which case I should give their arguments all due weight and consideration. Therefore, if this be the information you bring, I wish to hear no more."

Long accustomed to observe every particular point of weakness in the king's mind, Chavigni at once conceived the whole train of Louis's thoughts, and judged from the very alarm which he saw in the monarch's countenance, that if the cardinal's power could once be re-established, it would be more unbounded than ever; and as these ideas passed through his mind, they called a transient smile upon his lip.

"Why do you smile, sir?" demanded the king, sharply.

"Pardon me, sire," answered Chavigni. "But it was, that you should think me so weak as to trouble you upon such a subject. If leaguing with the enemies you have fought and conquered, be humble petition; if bringing foreign troops to invade your dominions, be dutiful remonstrance; if promising to deliver the strong places of France into the hands of Spain, be loyalty and faith,— then have I unnecessarily disturbed your repose."

Chavigni's speech worked upon the king, as he expected. "How say you!" exclaimed Louis, his eyes flashing fire. "Who has dared to conceive such a thought? Who has had the hardihood to unite himself to Spain—our sworn enemy—our mortal foe? Prove your assertion, sir—prove that such a traitor exists in our dominions; and were he our own brother, we would doom him to death."

Chavigni instantly caught at the idea. "Sorry I am to say, sire," he replied, "that your majesty has but too truly divined the person. The Duke of Orleans, unhappily, is the chief of this dangerous conspiracy. Behold, my liege, his name to this treaty with Spain;" and artfully contriving to conceal the greater part of the names with his hand in holding it before the king, he pointed out the great sprawling "Gaston," which stood the first on the list of signatures.

Louis instantly recognized his brother's handwriting. "Gaston of Orleans! Gaston of Orleans!" he exclaimed, "will nothing satisfy you? Must you betray your country to her enemies, as well as plot against your brother's life with magicians and astrologers?"

We have already had occasion to remark, that Louis, deeply imbued with all the superstitions of the age, put full faith in every part of astrology, and dreaded nothing more than the effects of enchantment. Nor could anything free his mind from the idea, that his brother had, in former times, conspired against his life, with certain magicians who were actually executed for the crime; one amongst others being the famous Père Le Rouge, whom we have more than once noticed in this sage history. The Duke of Orleans himself escaped with a temporary banishment, but the circumstance still rankled in the king's mind; and at present the anger which might perhaps have turned aside from Cinq Mars, had Chavigni at first suffered the favorite's name to appear, now burst with full force upon the less favored Gaston.

"Issue a warrant for his instant arrest," exclaimed the king. "By heaven, he shall not escape any more than another man."

"May it please your majesty," answered Chavigni, "to sign the warrant yourself. This is a case of no simple conspiracy, where the king's brother is at its head, and many of the first in the kingdom its supporters; and the warrants ought not to be simple letters de cachet of council, but ought to bear the royal signature."

"Well, sir," replied the king, "have the warrants prepared, and I will sign them. I am going now to hunt, and at my return we will examine these papers and speak farther."

"I have the warrants drawn out here," said the statesman, not choosing to let the first impression subside. "It
will not detain your majesty a moment; I felt convinced
that you would not allow justice to slumber, and therefore had them prepared. This is against the body of
Gaston of France, Duke of Orleans," he continued, looking at one of the papers.

"Well, give it to me!" exclaimed the king, taking up
a pen; "it shall be done at once."

Chavigni put the warrant in Louis's hand, and looked
at him with intense feeling, and a triumphant smile, and
he hastily wrote his signature to it. "Now," thought
Chavigni, "I have you one and all. Now, proud Cinq
Mars, and calculating Bouillon, you are in my power!
He signs the warrant against his own brother, and he
dare not let you escape;" and, countersigning the warrant, he put a second into the king's hand,—"That is
against the Duke of Bouillon, sire!" and he calmly took
up the first, and placed it in his portfolio.

"The Duke of Bouillon!" exclaimed Louis, with a
sudden start, remembering the orders he had sent him,
and terrified lest Richelieu should have discovered them.
"Is his name to that paper?"

"No, sire!" answered the statesman; "it is not. But
in the treaty itself, there is abundant proof of his con-
currence; and it was on its way to him in Italy when it
was discovered. The same messenger bore it that conveyed to him your orders to march his troops into
France:" and Chavigni fixed his keen penetrating glance
upon the king's countenance. Louis turned away his
head, and signed the warrant; while Chavigni proceeded
to place before him that against Fontrailles, and sub-
sequently one which authorized the arrest of Cinq Mars.

"How!" exclaimed the king, "here are the first and
most loyal men in my kingdom. Monsieur de Chavigni,
this is going too far!"

"Their names, my liege," answered Chavigni, "are
fixed to the treasonable treaty in my hand."

"It cannot be!" cried Louis, an expression of painful apprehension coming over his countenance: "it cannot be! My faithful, loyal Cinq Mars is no traitor. I will never believe it!" And he threw himself into a seat, and covered his eyes with his hands.

Chavigni opened the treaty calmly, and briefly recapitulated the principal articles. "The first item is, my liege," he proceeded, "that Spain shall instantly furnish ten thousand men to enter France by the way of Flanders; and for a security to his Catholic Majesty, a second item provides, that the Duke of Bouillon shall place in his hands, for the time being, the principality of Sedan. A third goes on to arrange, that five principal fortified towns of France shall be given into the hands of Spain; and the whole concludes, with a solemn alliance, offensive and defensive, between the conspirators and the Spanish king.—And to this treaty," added he, in a firm, deep tone of voice, "stand the names of Cinq Mars and Fontrailles."

"Cinq Mars has been deceived, misled, abused!" cried the king, with a degree of agitation almost amounting to agony.

"That will appear upon his trial, my liege," rejoined Chavigni; and then wishing rather to soften the hard task he called upon Louis to perform, he added, in a gentle manner, "Your majesty was born under the sign Libra, and have always merited the name of just. If anything in extenuation of his fault appear in the case of Monsieur le Grand Ecuyer, that can be taken into your merciful consideration after his arrest; but having calmly given an order for the imprisonment of your own royal brother, your majesty cannot—will not, show the manifest partiality of letting a person equally culpable escape. May I once more request your majesty to sign the warrant?"

"Well, well!" cried Louis, snatching up the pen. "But remember, Cinq Mars must be pardoned. He has been deceived by that treacherous Duke of Bouillon and that oily Fontrailles. Oh, he is all honor and loyalty; have I not experienced a thousand instances of his affection?—It is false! it is false!" And he dashed down the pen without using it.

Chavigni gazed on him for a moment with a feeling very nearly allied to contempt. "Well then, your majesty," he said at length, "is it your pleasure that I cause the arrest of the Dukes of Orleans and Bouillon, with Monsieur de Fontrailles, and others concerned in this conspiracy, and let Monsieur de Cinq Mars know that Louis the Just makes a distinction between him and other men?"

"No, no, Chavigni," replied Louis, mournfully; "give me the paper—I wil sign it.—But Cinq Mars must be saved. He has been deceived—I will sign it;" and turning away his head, he wrote his name with a trembling hand. But still he continued to hold the warrant, as if unwilling to part with it, repeating more than once in a tone rather of entreaty than command, "Indeed, indeed, Chavigni, he must be saved!"

"Will your majesty look at this part of the treaty to see that I have stated it correctly?" said the statesman, offering the papers to the king. Louis laid down the warrant to receive them; and Chavigni instantly raising the order for the arrest of Cinq Mars from the table, placed it in his portfolio with the rest. Louis saw that it was gone without recall; and dropping the treaty from his hands, hid his face in his cloak with feelings near akin to despair.

Chavigni's object was gained, and the power of Richelieu re-established. Not only all the conspirators were delivered bound into his hands, but the king himself was virtually in his power. Too weak, as the statesman well knew, to stand alone, or to choose new ministers for himself, Louis had no resource but to yield himself once more blindly to the guidance of the cardinal; and from the moment he had signed the warrant against Cinq

Mars, Chavigni looked upon him but as a royal tool to work out the designs of that great unshrinking politician, who had already so long used him for his own purposes.

The unfortunate monarch, also, was but too well aware of his own want of energy, and of the unsupported situation in which he had left himself; and yielding to his ancient dread of Richelieu, he charged Chavigni with a multitude of exculpatory messages to the minister, calling him his best friend and his cousin, and adding various civil speeches and professions, which both Chavigni and the cardinal knew how to estimate.

"There are many other persons, sire," said the statesman, as he was about to depart, "who are implicated more or less in this unhappy conspiracy; but as their guilt is either in a minor degree, or their rank less elevated, I will not trouble your majesty to put your personal signature to the warrants against them. In the meantime, allow me to hint that the king ought not to be seen hunting with traitors when they are known to be so."

"No, no," replied Louis, mournfully; "I am in no mood for hunting now. But where go you, Monsieur de Chavigni? You will not leave me for long," added the king, feeling that he must have some one to lean on, and little caring who, so that they yielded him support. "You will not leave me for long in this case of danger."

"I am about to proceed to Corneille," replied Chavigni, "to order up a body of the cardinal's guard. At present, I have no escort, but a few servants. We are surrounded by the retainers of the different conspirators, and, were I to attempt the execution of your majesty's warrants, we might meet with opposition. But I will soon set that at rest, and before to-morrow morning there shall be a thousand men in Narbonne, truly devoted to your majesty's service."

The king gave an involuntary shudder; and Chavigni, with a mockery of profound respect, which he felt but little, took leave and quitted the presence.

The moment he was gone, Louis called to one of the attendants, and carefully shutting the door when he had entered, " François," said he, " you are a silent, cautious man—I can trust you: Go to Monsieur le Grand Ecuyer, and, if he is alone, tell him, that France is a climate dangerous for his health, to betake himself elsewhere, and that speedily. But if there is any one with him, merely say, that the king feels himself too unwell to enjoy the pleasure of the chase to-day; but that he desires that his indisposition may not prevent the gentleman invited from following their sport. But, François, watch well Cinq Mars' return; find him out alone, and give him the first message. Only beware, that in it, the king's name is never mentioned. Do you understand? "

The page bowed profoundly but still maintained the same unbroken silence, and retired to fulfil the king's commands. The presence of Fontrailles, however, prevented him from delivering the warning, until the master of the horse returned from hunting, when he found an opportunity of speaking to him alone. Such a caution, delivered by the king's own page, alarmed the favorite; and though it was by this time late, he sent a servant to see if the city gates were shut. The servant scarcely gave himself the trouble to inquire, but returning immediately, informed his master that they were. Cinq Mars stayed—and before the next morning, every avenue from Narbonne was occupied by the cardinal's guard.

CHAPTER XXIX.

Containing a journey, a discovery, and a strange sight.

ALL Claude de Blenau's wishes had been nearly fulfilled; hope had almost grown into certainty; Pauline was almost his own; when he was snatched from the bosom of joy and security to new scenes of misery and danger.

When once he had torn himself from Pauline, the objects round him called forth little of De Blenau's attention; and the carriage in which he was placed rolled on for many leagues, before he had sufficiently recovered his tranquillity even to think of the minor points of his situation. Never before had he so completely abandoned himself to despondency; but as a second and a third day passed, he began to recover from the first bitterness of his feelings, and endeavored to draw from the officer the precise crime with which he was charged, and what circumstances of suspicion had arisen against him. But no further information was to be procured. The officer continued firm in the same story he had told the queen— that his orders were to conduct him to Tarascon, and that he was quite ignorant of the circumstances which led to his arrest. And with this De Blenau was obliged to be satisfied.

During the journey the officer showed much civility and attention to the prisoner, though he took good care to place a guard at the door of his chamber when they stopped for the night, which was always at the house of one of those private agents of the government, already mentioned, with whose dwellings the officers of the cardinal's guard were generally acquainted. After proceeding, however, for several days, he plainly perceived that nothing could be farther from De Blenau's thoughts than any plan for making his escape, and, in consequence, the watch he kept over his prisoner became far less strict, which afforded the count many opportunities of communicating freely with the persons at the various places where they stopped for horses or refreshment.

The arrest of Cinq Mars and several others, with the full restoration of the cardinal's power, was at that moment, in France, one of those topics of wonder and interest, which seem necessary from time to time to keep up the spirits of the gossiping classes of society; and though the good folks at inns and elsewhere found the appearance of a prisoner, escorted by a body of the cardinal's guard, to act as a great check upon their natural loquacity; yet, as the officer was somewhat of a bon vivant, and rather attached to his bottle, the awe inspired by his functions was not so strong as to prevent the news of the grand ecuyer's misfortune from reaching the ears of De Blenau, who easily concluded that, from their well-known intimacy, suspicion had fallen upon himself.

The prisoner and his conductors at length began to approach that part of the country where the re-established minister held his court, to which all his old retainers and friends were now flocking, together with many others, who, led by hope or impelled by fear, hastened to offer their servile adulation to a man they in general detested. The roads were thus thronged with people, and many a gay cavalcade passed by the carriage in which De Blenau was borne along, the horsemen looking for a moment into the vehicle out of curiosity, but quickly turning away their eyes again, least they should be obliged to acknowledge some acquaintance with a person who had fallen under the cardinal's displeasure.

It was night when they arrived at Montolieu, and De Blenau asked his conductor if he intended to stop there till morning.

"No, Monsieur le Comte," replied the officer; "we must proceed as speedily as possible to Mirepoix, where I expect orders for my further conduct."

28

"Then you go to Tarascon, in the Pyrenees," said De Blenau. "I thought his eminence was at the city of that name by the banks of the Rhône, opposite Beaucaire."

"He was there some time ago," replied the officer; "but he has since gone to the mountains, where, doctors say, there are waters which have great virtues in sickness like his. For my part, I always thought the springs there very bad, and neither fit for man nor beast. But, nevertheless, we must hasten on, sir."

The next place they stopped at was Corneille; and, according to his custom, the officer remained with De Blenau in the carriage, while the troopers arranged everything that was necessary for proceeding on their journey. There seemed, however, to be a considerable bustle amongst the men; and after waiting patiently for a few minutes, the officer drew back the curtain, and thrusting his head from the window, inquired the cause of delay? The answer he received imported that no fresh horses could be procured, and that those which had drawn them so far were incapable of proceeding even to the next town. "How happens it that there are no horses?" demanded he impatiently; "there ought always to be horses reserved for the use of the government." To this it was replied, that so many people had passed to the court at Tarascon, that every horse which could be hired, even at an exorbitant price, had been carried away.

The officer paused, as if doubting what course to pursue; but there being no remedy, he was obliged to alight, in order to pass the night at Corneille; taking care, however, to despatch one of the troopers to Mirepoix, to bring any orders which might be waiting for him in that town.

The moon was up, and as De Blenau descended from the carriage, he perceived a little stream dashing and glistening over the wheel of a mill, that stood dark and defined against the moonlit sky. It was to this they were apparently proceeding; and as they approached nearer,

there was seen an irregular part of the building projecting from the rest, which seemed appropriated to the
particular use of the miller. At the same time, on a
wooden staircase, which wound up the outside of the
house, appeared a man holding a light, and habited in
one of those dusty jackets, which have been the insignia
of flour-grinders from all generations. At the moment I
speak of, he was holding a conversation with one of the
troopers, and, by his quick articulation and busy gestures,
seemed engaged in making remonstrances, without any
great effect.

"What does he say?" exclaimed the officer, who
caught a few words of their conversation as he got out
of the carriage. "That we cannot stop here to-night?
Give him a cuff of the head, Joly, to teach him better
manners to the cardinal's guard. By heavens! he shall
find me horses to-night, or he shall lodge me till to-
morrow!"

"Stay, if you will, Sir Officer," rejoined the miller,
raising his voice—"but I tell you that you ought not to
stay; and as for laying a finger on me—you know I serve
the cardinal as well as you—and you dare not!"

"Dare not!" cried the officer, who was by this time
mounting the stairs, catching the miller by the collar, and
striking him a slight blow—"You are a refractory rascal,
sir—Open the door of your house, or I will throw you
over the staircase.—Come, Monsieur de Blenau, follow
me."

The miller offered no resistance, but threw wide the
door, and let the officer pass in. De Blenau came next,
having taken little notice of the altercation; but as he
went by the miller, who held the door open, he heard
him mutter to himself in an under voice, "He shall pay
for it with his blood," in a deep bitter tone of determined hatred, that made the count turn round, expecting to see the ferocious countenance of an assassin.
Nothing, however, could be more different from the ap-

pearance of the speaker, who was a smooth, pale-faced man, whose look expressed little beside peaceful tranquillity and patient resignation.

The room into which they entered was a large uncouth chamber, filled with various articles of household furniture, the unusual assemblage of which showed that it was used for most of the different purposes of life. There was a bed in one corner, with a large screen, or paravent, half drawn before it. Besides the fire hung a row of copper saucepans and cooking utensils; round about were several saddles, and other pieces of horse furniture; and in the centre was a large table, with two or three half-emptied bottles and some glasses, which bore marks of having been recently used; and at the same time a long bench was placed at one side of the table, with three single seats on the other.

On the opposite side of the apartment was a wooden partition, evidently new, which seemed to separate what had once been one large chamber into two, with a door of communication between them.

"Oh, ho! Monsieur Godefroy!" exclaimed the officer, looking at the table, and then turning a significant glance to the miller. "So, you have been carousing, and did not like to let us share in your good cheer. But come, we will not be sent away like a dog without his dinner. Let us taste your Burgundy: and if you were to lay three of those plump boudins upon the fire, they might savor the wine."

"You are very welcome, Sir Officer, to anything the house affords," replied the miller, neither civilly nor sulkily. "Help yourself to the boudins, while I go down for the wine."

"They say in my province, Monsieur de Blenau," said the officer, placing a seat for the prisoner near the fire, "Qui dort dine, et qui fait l'amour soupe. Now, as we have neither slept nor dined, and have no one to make love to, let us sup, at least."

De Blenau's only reply was, that he had no appetite; which seemed considerably to surprise the officer, who, as soon as the miller had brought in the wine, and his supper was ready, fell to with no small eagerness, and did not leave off till he had transferred the greater part of the trencher's contents to his stomach. The miller seemed more inclined to follow the officer's example than De Blenau; and his anger having apparently subsided, he pressed his guest to continue the meal in so sociable and friendly a manner, that De Blenau could scarcely conceive that the words he had heard as he entered, had been anything but the effect of momentary irritation. But shortly after he had again cause to alter his opinion; the eagerness with which the miller invited his companion to drink, producing bottle after bottle of different wines, generally denied by their price to persons in his station of life; and the subdued glance of triumph with which he viewed the various stages of intoxication at which the officer gradually arrived, caught De Blenau's attention, and excited his suspicion. However, the vengeance which the miller meditated was of a very different nature from that which the count imagined. Nothing which could, by any chance, recoil upon himself ever entered his thoughts, and his plan reached no farther than to render the man who had offended him, deeply culpable in the eyes of Richelieu, thus calling upon his head that relentless anger which would be much more effectual vengeance than any punishment he could himself inflict.

Two or three hours had passed in this manner, during which time the officer had made various efforts to resist the fascinations of the bottle, often pushing it away from him, as if resolved not to taste another drop, and then again, as he became heated in conversation, drawing it back and filling his glass with an almost unconscious hand, when the sound of a horse's feet was heard without, and starting up, he declared that it was news from Mirepoix, and staggered towards the door.

The moment he had quitted the room, the miller approached De Blenau, glanced his eyes round the chamber, and then addressed him in a whisper. "What a moment," said he, "for a prisoner to make his escape, while that drunkard's senses are confused with wine!"

De Blenau started at the suddenness of the proposal, and eyed his companion with an inquiring glance. "If you allude to me," he replied at length, "I thank you, but I have no thought of escaping."

"You have not!" said the miller, apparently surprised. He thought for a moment, and then added—"Oh, you reckon on your innocence. But let me tell you, Sir Count, that there is both danger and uncomfort in a long imprisonment."

"I know it," answered De Blenau; "but I would rather submit to both than cast a suspicion on my honor and my innocence by attempting to fly."

This was a sort of reasoning the other did not understand; and his lip curled with a slight expression of contempt, which would have shown itself more visibly, had not De Blenau's rank, though a prisoner, kept the bourgeoise in awe. He turned away, however, seemingly with the intention of quitting the room; but when he got to the other side, he paused, laid his hand upon his brow, and after thinking for a moment, again came back to De Blenau. "I advised you for your own good, Monsieur le Comte," he said; "and though you will not escape from the dangers of accusation, I will give you the means of proving your innocence. In that room," and he pointed to the small door in the partition, "you will discover two packets of papers exactly similar: take either of them, and in that you will find enough to disprove all that your enemies will say against you."

"But," said De Blenau, "what right have I to possess myself of papers belonging, probably, to another?"

"Pshaw!" cried the miller, "one would think that your neck itched for the axe! Are you not in my house?

Do not I bid you take them? Of course you will not betray me to the government; but take the papers, for I give them to you." And making a sign to De Blenau to use all speed, he went to the door which opened on the road. Before he passed it, however, he turned to the prisoner once more and cautioned him to make no noise, nor regard anything else in the room, but after having taken one of the packets from the table on which they were placed, to quit it as speedily as possible. The precaution, however, was useless; for before De Blenau had even time to determine upon any line of conduct, the officer again entered the room, and, balancing himself as well as he could, contrived to arrive at the table after many a zig-zag and many a halt. He had precisely reached that pitch of intoxication when a man, having for some time suspected that he is tipsy, finds out that such a supposition was entirely a mistake, and that he never was more sober, or more in his senses in his life: consequently he had not the slightest objection to drink a bottle of the vin de Saint Peret, which the miller set before him; although the Burgundy he had already imbibed had very considerbly dulled his perception, and detracted from his locomotive power. The wine, as it creamed and sparkled in his glass, was raised to his head with increased difficulty at every renewed draught; and at last, feeling something the matter with him he knew not what, he started from the table, made an effort to reach a chair by the fire, but receiving instantly internal conviction of the impossibility of the attempt, he cast himself upon the bed behind the screen which happened to be nearer at hand, and in a few minutes all his senses were steeped in oblivion. Immediately the miller raised his hand, pointed to the door in the partition, and left the apartment, as if unwilling to witness what was to follow.

De Blenau paused for a moment to reflect on this man's conduct; but however extraordinary it might be, he could

see nothing to prevent his possessing himself of papers
which, he was assured, would prove his innocence of the
crimes with which he was charged—a thing not always
easy to the most guiltless. Accordingly, rising from his
seat, he passed by the bed where the officer lay snoring
in the fulness of ebriety, and opened the door in the
partition to which he had been directed. The room with
which it communicated was small, and dimly lighted by
a lamp that stood flickering on a table, as if it scarcely
knew whether to go out or not. Near the lamp lay
various implements for writing, together with two papers,
one folded up and marked, the other open, and seemingly
hardly finished. Around were scattered various basnets
and vials, which appeared to contain the medicaments
for a sick man; and on one of the chairs was thrown a
long sword, together with a poniard and a brace of pistols.

De Blenau advanced to the table, and taking up the
open paper, ran his eye hastily over its contents. In
so doing, his own name met his sight; and forgetting the
caution 'he had received, to make speed and quit the
apartment as soon as he had possessed himself of it, he
could not refrain from reading on:—" With regard to
Monsieur the Count de Blenau," the paper proceeded,
" the prisoner feels perfectly convinced that he was always
ignorant of the treaty and the designs of the conspirators.
For, Monsieur de Cinq Mars particularly warned him
'(the prisoner) never to mention the circumstance before
the count, because that he was not to be made acquainted
therewith; and moreover——"

As De Blenau read, a deep groan came upon his ear,
evidently proceeding from some one in the same room
with himself, and, holding up the lamp, he endeavored to
discover who it. was that had uttered it; but in lifting
it suddenly, the feeble light was at once extinguished,
and the whole chamber remained in darkness, except
where a gleam came through the doorway of the other
room.

"Godefroy! Godefroy!" exclaimed a faint voice, "do
not put out the light; why have you left me so long?—I
am dying, I am sure I am dying."

"I will bring another light," said the count, "and
be with you instantly." And forgetting, in the hurry of
the moment, his peculiar situation, and the caution which
ought to have accompanied it, he hastened into the other
apartment, where the officer still lay undisturbed in his
drunken slumbers, and taking one of the rosin candles
from the table, returned to give what succor he could
to the person whose faint voice he had heard.

On re-entering the chamber with the stronger light
which he now brought, his eyes fell upon the drawn
curtains of an alcove bed at the farther extremity; and
approaching quickly, he pulled them back, shading the
candle as well as he could, to prevent its glare from
offending the eyes of the sick person.

But his precaution was in vain. Light and darkness
had become the same to the pale inanimate form before
him. De Blenau saw that, during the moment of his
absence, being had passed away; and holding the light
nearer to the bed, he could trace, in the disfigured countenance that lay in ashy paleness upon the pillow, the
features of the grand ecuyer's Italian lute-player, Villa
Grande.

He was engaged in examining them more attentively,
when some one silently laid their hand upon his arm,
and turning quickly round, he beheld Chavigni, while
the countenance of the miller appeared in the doorway,
very little less pale than that of the dead man. De
Blenau's first impulse was to point to the dead man, while
his eyes rested on the countenance of Chavigni, in which
a slight degree of agitation showed itself for a moment,
and then disappeared.

"So!" said the statesman, regarding the lifeless body
of Villa Grande, "he is dead, poor wretch!—Gone on
that uncertain journey which lies before us all, like a

land covered with a thick mist, whose paths, or whose temination, none of us can discover.—But to matters of life and moment," he continued. "What do you here, Monsieur de Blenau?"

"I should suppose, sir, that you are better acquainted with the object of my journey than I am myself," replied the count. "You must be well aware it was undertaken against my will."

"You have mistaken me, sir," said Chavigni. "The end of your journey hither, I am well aware of. But how came you in this chamber? What do you with that paper which is in your hand? I expect a straightforward answer."

"Did I give you any, sir," replied De Blenau, "my answer should be straightforward. But you ought to have known me better than so proudly to demand a reply, when you are unentitled to interrogate me. Being a prisoner, I must be guarded as such, though I tell you at once I have no intention of trying to escape; and being defenceless, you may take these papers from me, though they are material proof of my innocence. However, I will rely upon your justice—upon your honor—that whatever charges be brought against me, the confession of this man may be opposed to them in my justification."

"Monsieur de Blenau," replied Chavigni, "I wish you would sometimes give me an excuse for doubting your sincerity; for then I could see the fate which is like to betide you, without regret. When you were liberated from the Bastile, I told you that the eye of an angry man was upon you, and warned you as a friend to avoid all cause for suspicion. The minister has never forgotten you. You were the first who brought a shadow over his dominion—I hope, therefore, that your innocance can be proved beyond a doubt; for mercy or tenderness between you and the cardinal are out of the question. Nevertheless, I cannot let you keep this paper, which belongs to the council; but I will take care that anything which it contains in your favor shall not be lost. In the meanwhile I shall be obliged to send you to Lyons; and Heaven speed you as safely out of this scrape as out of the last."

" If perfect innocence of any crime towards the state can save me," said De Blenau, following Chavigni into the outer room, " I have nothing to fear."

" I hope it is so," replied the statesman. " And now," he continued, turning to the miller, " let me tell you, Master Godefroy, that you are highly culpable yourself, for leaving a state prisoner wholly without guard when you saw the officer, in whose custody he was, in such a state as this. Make no excuses, sir—it shall be remembered."

Chavigni now approached the drunken man, and tried to rouse him; but finding it in vain, he called in the sergeant, and writing a few words for his warranty, ordered him to conduct the officer, next morning, to Tarascon under arrest.

" Monsieur de Blenau," he continued, turning to the count, " you will do me the favor of accompanying me to Montolieu. The horses attached to my carriage are fresher than those which drew you."

The promptitude with which Chavigni's orders were given, brought all the preparations to a rapid conclusion. A few minutes sufficed him to issue the necessary commands for transferring the baggage which had been brought with De Blenau to the other carriage; and adding a few clear rapid directions to the miller concerning the body of Villa Grande, the statesman was ready to accompany De Blenau before he had been a quarter of an hour in the house.

At Montolieu, De Blenau was permitted to rest a day, and was then sent forward under a fresh escort to Lyons. The prisoner was now hurried rapidly on his journey, travelling the whole of the first night, and at last only stopping for a few hours to give him some repose at a village about eight leagues from the city to which he was proceeding. As soon as daylight dawned, they again began their journey; and taking the lower road by the banks of the Rhône, gradually approached the ancient town of Lyons.

The first pause they made was a compelled one, upon the wooden bridge, situated on the river just below the town. This entrance had been chosen to avoid the more populous suburbs; but the conductor of the escort had been mistaken in his calculation, for owing to some circumstances of general interest, which drew all the idle and the curious to that spot, the bridge and the alleys to it were entirely covered with dense masses of human beings, which completely obstructed the way. With difficulty the carriage was dragged half over the bridge; and then, notwithstanding the exertions of the guard, it was obliged to stop. De Blenau drew back the leather curtain which obstructed his view, and turning his eyes towards the river, a scene burst upon his sight which at once explained to him the cause of such an assemblage.

There was a small but magnificent galley making its way slowly to the landing-place. The rigging was adorned with streamers; the deck glittered with all the splendid apparel of a court, the rowers were clothed in rich uniform, scarcely different from that of the guards which flanked each bank of oars; gold, and jewels, and blazonry shone around. But the spot on which all eyes rested was a small canopy of rich embroidery, upheld above the deck on silver poles by four officers of the guard, in such a manner as to keep off the rays of the sun, but not impede the breeze of the river from playing round a pile of rich velvet cushions, on which, amidst the pomp and display of a sovereign prince, lay the emaciated form of the Cardinal de Richelieu. His countenance was calm and unmoved; indeed, he seemed hardly to regard the scene around, listening to the conversation of an abbé, who stood beside him for the sole purpose of amusing him by various tales and anecdotes during the voyage. Sometimes, however, he would raise his eyes, and appear to speak to some of those who stood by; and then his glance would rapidly turn towards a smaller boat, which, attached by two long ropes, was towed on at the stern of his own galley. In that boat, seated between two of the cardinal's guard, sat the imprudent and unfortunate Cinq Mars, and his companion in misfortune, De Thou. All the gay gallant spirit of the master of the horse, which once taught him to scoff at the very idea of adversity as at a bugbear of the imagination, was now quelled and lost, and with a bending head, and eyes cast down, he sat perfectly motionless, like a lifeless but elegant statue. De Thou, on the contrary, calmly surveyed the passing scene. He seemed to have forgot that he was there as a prisoner, borne, a part of that barbarous triumph which his enemy was enjoying; and, even when his glance met that of the cardinal, his countenance remained undisturbed by any emotion of anger, or any expression of reproach.

I have said that Richelieu would sometimes turn his look towards the boat in which his captives were borne along; and still when he did so, a momentary gleam would lighten in his eyes, and he would hastily glance them round the multitude that lined the shores and the bridge. But there was no sound of gratulation met his ear, no acclamation for his regained ascendency. The busy whisper of curiosity would stir amongst the people, or perhaps the murmur of compassion, as they gazed upon the victims about to be sacrificed to his vengeance. But there was no love to express; and fear changed their curses into the bitterness of silence.

Such was the scene in the midst of which De Blenau found himself, when the carriage stopped. He had just time to become aware of all its most painful circumstances, when the guards again opened a way through the people, and the vehicle passed on. The high round tower of Pierre-en-Scize, raising its dark mass above the rest of the prison, was the next thing that met his view, and he doubted not that the place of his imprisonment was before him; but the carriage rolled on into the great Place Terreaux, where it suddenly drew up.

"Then I am not to be taken to Pierre-en-Scize?" said De Blenau to the officer who had accompanied him from Montolieu.

"No, Monsieur le Comte," replied he. "Pierre-en-Scize will be sufficiently occupied with Messieurs Cinq Mars, De Thou, and others; and when Monsieur de Bouillon, and the Duke of Orleans——"

"Good God!" exclaimed De Blenau, "is the Duke of Orleans implicated in this unfortunate business?"

The officer smiled. "Why, they do say, sir, that the king himself is in the conspiracy. But as to the duke, you know more of his share in it than any one else—at least so we are told. But I must not beg you to descend."

"You are under a mistake, sir," replied De Blenau. "I know nothing of the duke, and as little of the conspiracy." And following the officer, he entered a house in the Place Terreaux, which had been changed for the time from one of the public offices of the city into a place of confinement, and offered all the security without the horrors of a prison. The windows were grated, it is true, but they looked out into the free world below, and the captive might sit there and forget that he was denied the power of joining the gay throng that passed along before his eyes in all the pride of libery.

De Blenau had not been long in his new abode, before he learned that the express orders of Chavigni had caused him to be carried thither, rather than to Pierre-en-Scize, where his confinement would have been more strict; and he felt grateful for this mark of the statesman's consideration. For the first few days, too, he experienced every kind of attention, and was permitted to enjoy all sort of liberty consistent with his safe custody.

But this was not destined to endure long; and his imprisonment gradually became more rigorous than that which he had undergone in the Bastile. The use of books and writing materials was denied him, and every means of employing his thoughts seemed studiously withheld. This mode of weakening the mind, by leaving it to prey upon himself, had its effect even on De Blenau. He became irritable and desponding; and as he received no intimation in regard to the charge against him, he began to conjure up a thousand vague unreal images, and to destroy them as soon as raised.

After this had continued for some days, he was surprised by the door of his apartment opening one night, at the moment he was about to retire to rest, giving admittance to the corrupt Judge Lafemas, and a person habited as one of the greffiers of the court. There are some who are cruel from fear, and some from motives of interest; but few, I trust, who from natural propensity rejoice in the sufferings of a fellow-creature. Such, however, was the character of Lafemas—at least if we may believe the histories of the time; and in the present instance he entered the chamber of De Blenau with a countenance which certainly expressed no great unwillingness in the performance of what is always painful when it is a duty.

In this place we shall but give a small part of the conversation between De Blenau and the judge; for the course of examination which the latter pursued towards the prisoner was so precisely similar in its nature to that which he followed on a former occasion in the Bastile, that its repetition is unnecessary, especially as our history is now hurrying rapidly to its awful and inevitable conclusion. A part of it, however may serve to illustrate the charges brought against De Blenau, and the circumstances on which they were founded.

" Good-night, Monsieur de Blenau," said Lafemas, approaching the table at which he sat. " I did not think to meet you again in prison: I had hoped that when last you escaped so well, you would have been careful to keep yourself free from anything of this kind."

"Good-night, Monsieur le Juge," replied De Blenau; "do me the favor of sitting down—for I suppose I may do the honors of my chamber, though it be but a prison. I am glad to see you, sir; for I trust you can inform me why I am here confined."

"Monsieur de Blenau," said the judge, seating himself, "we will be frank with one another. You are very well aware how deeply you are implicated in this conspiracy; and I will tell you that we have ample proofs of everything. But at the same time I know of a way by which you can save yourself; a way which one or two highly honorable men have embraced, having been misled at first by designing persons, but having returned to a sense of duty and honor, and confessed all they knew, together with the names of those they supposed to be amongst the guilty."

"I have no doubt, sir," replied the count, "that all and everything you say is correct and right. But there is one point on which I am in the dark. I am not aware of what conspiracy you mean.—I have it, it is true, conspired——" Lafemas turned an attentive ear, and De Blenau perceived that the greffier who had followed the judge was making a note of all that passed. "Stop, gentlemen," said he, nodding to the officer; "take the whole of my sentence, I beg. You shall have it in plain language—I have, it is true, conspired on more than one occasion, with sundry of his majesty's lieges, to kill a fat buck or a lusty boar, in various of the royal forests in this kingdom. But this is the only conspiracy of which I have been guilty; and for that I can plead his majesty's free permission and pardon."

"All this is very good, Monsieur le Comte," said Lafemas, his brows darkening; "but I must tell you that it will not serve the purpose you propose. I came here to you as a friend—"

"And as a friend," interrupted De Blenau, "you brought with you that gentleman in black to take down my words, in case I should be at a loss to remember what I had said."

" I must once more tell you, sir," said the judge, " that this will not answer your purpose, for a full confession has been made by Monsieur de Cinq Mars since his condemnation."

"Since his condemnation!" exclaimed De Blenau. " Good God! is it possible that he is condemned?"

Lafemas was little capable of understanding any of those finer feelings which brighten the dull void of human existence. He read from the black page of his own mind, and fancied that every other was written in the same dark character. All that he saw in the exclamation of De Blenau was fear for himself, not feeling for his friend; and he replied, " Yes, Monsieur le Comte, he is condemned to lose his head for the crimes of which he has been guilty: the question also formed part of his sentence, but this he has avoided by making a full confession, in which, as you may easily suppose, your name is very fully comprised."

" You may as well cease, sir," replied the count. " It may indeed be true that my unhappy friend is guilty and has confessed his guilt; but no language you can use will ever persuade me that, knowing my innocence, as he well does, he would say anything that could implicate me.—I will farther answer everything that can possibly be asked of me in a very few words. As to myself, I have nothing to confess, for I am perfectly guiltless towards the state: and as to others, I can give no information, for I am wholly ignorant of any plot, conspiracy, or treason whatsoever."

" I am sorry for your obstinacy, Monsieur de Blenau," said Lafemas rising; " for the cardinal has resolved that you shall confess, and we have the means of making the most stubborn answer. I am, in fact, commanded

29

this very night, to use measures which might not be very agreeable to you.   But I give you till to-morrow to consider, and so bid you farewell."

The plans of Cinq Mars had run into various ramifications, involving a multitude of persons in a greater or less degree; but all fell equally under the hatred of the cardinal, and he spared no means, legal or illegal, to discover the most remote windings of the conspiracy, and to force or induce the various parties to it to make confessions, which were afterwards used as evidence against themselves, as well as others.   As the proofs against De Blenau were, of course, very defective, the last command of Richelieu to Lafemas, before leaving Lyons, was to spare no power of intimidation, in order to make the prisoner criminate himself, before even granting him the form of a trial.   In pursuance of these directions, Lafemas ceased not for some days to torment De Blenau with continued interrogatories, mingled with menaces and irritation, ingeniously calculated either to frighten his victim into some confession of guilt, or to throw him off his guard by rousing his anger.   More than once he was carried into the chamber of the question, and once was even bound to the rack.   But though, in the secret halls of the Bastile, Lafemas would not have scrupled to proceed to any act of cruelty, yet at Lyons, amidst people upon whose silence he could not rely, he dared not put the prisoner to the question, without some appearance of legal authority.   At length, therefore, the day for his trial was fixed; but yet Lafemas prepared to make him previously undergo a species of refined torture, which none but a demon could have devised.

Denied all the privileges usually conceded to prisoners, unacquainted with the precise charges to be brought against him, refused all legal assistance, and debarred the use of pen and ink, De Blenau clearly saw that Richelieu had resolved on his destruction, and merely granted him the form of a trial to gloss over his tyranny, in the eyes of the people; nevertheless, he prepared to defend himself as far as possible, and at all events to establish his innocence, for the honor of his good name, though it might not even tend to save him from the injustice with which he was threatened. For this purpose he accurately examined his conduct since his liberation from the Bastile, and noted carefully every circumstance, that he might be enabled to prove the nature of all his operations so correctly, that the impossibility of his joining in any conspiracy would be made evident. He found, however, that to do this effectually, some aid besides that of mere memory would be necessary, and possessing no other means of committing his thoughts to writing, he had recourse to the expedient of pointing some pieces of wood, which he procured from the jailer, and then by charring them in the lamp, he was enabled to make notes upon some torn linen, preparatory to his trial. Being thus occupied the greater part of the night, his usual time of rest was from daybreak to mid-day; but one night, a few days previous to the time appointed for his trial, he was disturbed in his occupation by the dull heavy clang of hammers in the great square before his prison, and proceeding to the window, he endeavored to ascertain the cause. Through the bars he could perceive various lights, and people moving about in different directions, but could not discern in what they were employed; and quitting the casement, he returned to the slow and laborious operation of writing his notes, in the manner we have described. At length, wearied out, he threw himself upon his bed, without taking off his clothes, and soon fell into a profound sleep, which remained unbroken till late the next day. It is probable that he might have slept still longer, had he not been aroused by his tormentor, Lafemas, who, standing by his bedside with two of his inferior demons, roused him out of the happy forgetfulness into which he had fallen. " Rise, Monsieur De Blenau, rise!" said the judge, his eyes gleaming with malicious pleasure; " rise, here is something in the Place which it is necessary you should behold."

De Blenau, awoke suddenly from his sleep, suffered himself to be conducted to the window, where the judge and his two followers placed themselves behind him, so as to obstruct his retreat, and in a manner to force upon him the sight of what was passing in the Place.

The Square of Terreaux was filled with an immense multitude, and there was a deep awful silence reigned amongst them. All eyes were turned towards a spot exactly opposite the window at which De Blenau stood, where there appeared a high raised scaffold, covered with black cloth, and surrounded by a strong body of troops, who kept the multitude at a distance, without impeding their view of the dreadful scene which was acting before them. A large log of timber lay across the front of the scaffold, and beside it stood a tall brawny man, leaning on an immense axe, which seemed as if a giant's force would hardly wield it, so ponderous was its form. The Provost of Lyons, dressed in black, and bearing his staff of office, stood on the other side with several of the civil officers of the city; and a file of pikemen closed each flank of the scaffold, leaving the front open, as we have said, to the view of the spectators.

But it was the form of his unhappy friend, Cinq Mars, that first riveted De Blenau's attention; and he continued to gaze upon him with painful interest, while, standing beside the block on which he was to suffer, he calmly unloosed his collar, and made the executioner cut away the glossy curls of his hair, which otherwise, falling down his neck, might have impeded the blow of the axe. When this was over Cinq Mars raised the instrument of his death, and running his finger over the edge, seemed to ascertain that it was sharp; and then laying it down, he turned to the good De Thou, who stood beside him, a sharer in his punishment, though not a sharer in his fault. Cinq Mars appeared to entreat his pardon for

some offence; and it is probable that having implicated him at all in the conspiracy was the only circumstance that then weighed upon the mind of the
grand ecuyer. The only reply of De Thou was a warm
affectionate embrace; and then with the easy dignity of
a mind at rest, Cinq Mars withdrew himself from his
arms, and knelt down before the block—De Blenau
turned away his head.

"You had better observe, Monsieur de Blenau," said
Lafemas, "the fate which those two traitors undergo;
for such will be your own if you refuse the hand of
mercy held out to you, and persist in obstinate silence.
—Ah!—so much!" continued he, looking from the window, "so much for Monsieur de Cinq Mars! That
new fellow is expert—he has the head off at one blow!"

"Wretch!" exclaimed De Blenau, forcibly passing
him, and proceeding from the window, "unfeeling
wretch!—Monsieur Lafemas," he added, after pausing a
moment, "you were perhaps right in supposing that this
torture was superior to any other you could inflict. But
I have once more to tell you, sir, that by this or by any
other means you will wring from me nothing that can
betray my innocence or my honor."

"Then die as you deserve!" replied Lafemas; and
after once more looking from the window, and muttering
to himself a few words, whose import De Blenau did not
catch, he left the apartment with his two followers. De
Blenau cast himself on the bed, and hiding his face in
the clothes, endeavored to drive from his memory the
dreadful scene he had just beheld; but it still continued
for many an after-hour to hover before his eyes, and
deprive him of all rest or peace.

The hours of a prison are always slow, and they were
now doubly slow to De Blenau, having no other pastime
than painful reflections and anticipations equally bitter.

At length, however, the day of his trial arrived, and he
was conveyed in a carriage to Pierre-en-Scize, where,

in the hall of audience, sate three of the devoted creatures of Richelieu, presiding over a body equally governed by themselves, and all prepared to pronounce a sentence already dictated by the minister. Although the president of the parliament of Grenoble nominally directed the business of the court, Lafemas was not absent, and in his eyes De Blenau instantly discerned his fate.

The charge against the prisoner was read by one of of the clerks, declaring him to stand in danger of high treason, in having conspired with the Sieurs Cinq Mars, Fontrailles, De Thou, and others, to bring foreign troops into France, and for having treated and combined with a power at open war with the kingdom for various treasonable and disloyal purposes.

The evidence brought forward to establish this, was as frivolous as the accusation was unfounded. Even the very semblance of justice was nearly abandoned, the judges seeming to go through the trial as a useless and tiresome ceremony, which might very well be dispensed with.

It was proved, indeed, that the prisoner had often been seen in private with the unfortunate Cinq Mars; and it was also given in evidence by a servant of the Duke of Orleans, that he had carried a letter from that prince to De Blenau at Moulins; and that in consequence of that letter, as he conceived, the duke had gone, with a great air of secrecy, to a particular spot, where he was unaccustomed to ride upon ordinary occasions, and that there he was met by De Blenau. What conversation took place between them he could not tell; but after they had separated, the duke, he said, gave particular orders that their meeting should be mentioned to no man.

The next witness brought forward was the messenger who had carried to De Blenau the king's permission to return to court, and who proved that, instead of finding the count at Moulins, or anywhere in the Bourbonnois, to which, according to the king's command, he was bound

to confine himself, he had been conducted by the count's
page to Troyes in Champagne, where he found Monsieur
de Blenau himself ready to set off for some other place.
This witness also added, that he had learned in the town
of Troyes that Monsieur de Blenau had been absent one
whole day, during which time he had visited the old castle
of Mesnil St. Loup; and that at his return he did not go
to the same hotel from which he had proceeded in the
morning.

When the evidence was gone through, the President
of Grenoble signified to the prisoner that he might speak
in his own defence; and though well assured that on his
judges he could make no impression, De Blenau resolved
not to allow the accusation to remain unrepelled, and replied at some length to what had been urged against him.
He showed the impossibility of preparing any defence,
when the nature of the charge had never reached his ears
till that day. He pointed out that, though he had known
and loved the unhappy Cinq Mars, their friendship was
no proof that he was at all acquainted with the conspiracy
for which the other had suffered: and that though he had
met the duke of Orleans and received a letter from him,
that was not sufficient to show him concerned in any plot
against the state. He acknowledged that he had left the
Bourbonnois without the king's permission: but he stated
the powerful motives which had induced him to do so,
and gave a correct account, from the notes he had prepared, of every moment of his time since he had been
liberated from the Bastile. He further declared his innocence; he proved that he had been absent from all the
principal scenes of the conspiracy; and ended by demanding that the confession of the Italian Villa Grande should
be produced.

The President of Grenoble turned his eyes upon Lafemas; but that worthy judge assumed an air of perfect
unconsciousness, and demanded what Italian the prisoner
meant?

De Blenau now clearly and distinctly stated all he knew concerning him, and again demanded that his confession should be brought forward. But still Lafemas appeared in doubt. "Monsieur de Blenau," said he, "although this seems to me but a manœuvre to gain time, I have no objection that the papers of this court should be searched, if you can give us the baptismal name of this Italian, of whom at present we know nothing; and even this is a mere matter of grace and favor."

De Blenau declared his incapacity to do so, but protested against the unjust proceedings of the court, and showed that, if time and opportunity had been allowed for preparing his defence, he would have been enabled, by application to the Count de Chavigni, to bring forward the paper he mentioned, and to prove the truth of everything he had asserted, by the evidence of persons now at a distance. He was still speaking when Lafemas rose and interrupted him. "Perceiving," said the judge, with unblushing effrontery, "that the prisoner has concluded his defence, I will now occupy the court for a few moments, in order to explain the reasoning on which my own opinion is founded, although I see but one conclusion to which any one can come upon the merits of the case before us. It has been shown that the prisoner was the sworn—the bosom friend of the traitor who has already suffered for his crimes; that he was in constant communication with almost all the conspirators; and that the royal duke, who has unfortunately dyed his name with so black a spot, at the very same time that he was engaged in plotting the ruin of his country, was in secret correspondence with the individual before us. It has further been proved, that the prisoner, after having been relegué in Bourbon, quitted the place to which he was bound to confine himself, and went, upon what he cannot but own himself to be a wild romantic chase, into Champagne. This part of his story is a very strange one, according to his own showing: but when we come to compare it with the confession of the traitor Cinq Mars, the matter becomes more clear. It was in the old castle of St. Loup, near the city of Troyes, says the confession, that the principal meeting of the conspirators was held; and it was to this very castle of St. Loup that the prisoner direced his course from Moulins. Evidently for the purpose of concealment also, the prisoner, on his return to Troyes, instead of directing his course to the inn where he had formerly alighted, proceeded to another, at which, unfortunately for himself, he was overtaken by the king's messenger. I think it is unnecessary to say more upon these points. To my mind they are convincing. It is true, indeed, Monsieur de Blenau has shrewdly kept his handwriting from any paper which could prove him an active member of this conspiracy. But what man in his senses can doubt that he was criminally aware of its existence? This, then, is his crime: and I pronounce the concealment of treason to be as great a crime as treason itself. But if there was wanting a case in point to prove that the law considers it as such, I would cite the condemnation of De Thou, who, but two days ago, suffered with the traitor Cinq Mars. Let us now, my brethren," he added, " retire to consider of our sentence; for I have only spoken thus much, not to bias your opinion but simply that the prisoner himself, before he leaves this court, may know, at least, my sentiments."

The judges now withdrew to the cabinet appointed for their deliberations, and De Blenau was removed from the court to a small apartment hard by. He had not been there a moment when his page, Henri de La Mothe, burst into the room. " My dear, dear master ! " exclaimed the boy, throwing himself at his feet, " they tell me that you certainly will not be condemned, for that you have not been taken to what is called the dead man's dwelling : so the sentinel let me in to see you."

" Henry, how came you hither ! " exclaimed De Blenau,

hurriedly. "But we have no time to think of that—my fate is sealed—I have read it in the triumphant glance of that demon, Lafemas.—Mark me, my boy, and if ever you loved me, obey me well.—When I am dead, near my heart you will find a portrait. Take it, with this ring, to Mademoiselle de Beaumont. Tell her, that the one was the likeness of all I love on earth; and the other, the ring that was to have bound her to me forever. Say that De Blenau sends them to her in death, and that his last thought was of Pauline de Beaumont."

"Alas! Mademoiselle de Beaumont!" said the page. But as he spoke, the door opened and an officer of the court entered, followed by a priest. "Begone, boy!" said the officer, leading Henry to the door. "How came you in here? We have more serious matter in hand now."

"Remember!" said De Blenau, holding up his hand impressively, "remember!" And Henry, bursting into tears, was hurried from the apartment. "Now, father," continued De Blenau, turning to the priest, "let us to your business."

"It is a sad one, my son," replied he; "it is but to tell you, that you must prepare to leave a world of sorrow!"

"God's will be done!" said De Blenau.

CHAPTER XXX.

Which, if the reader can get through it, will bring him to the end of the history.

ALL delay in the execution of a sentence where there exists no hope of mercy, is but needless cruelty; yet De Blenau was suffered to linger fourteen weary nights and days between the day of his condemnation and that appointed for his death. It approached, however, at length. We are told, by those who have had the best opportunities of judging, that the last night of a condemned prisoner's existence is generally passed in slumber. It was so with De Blenau. Hope and fear were equally things gone by to him. The bitter sentence of death had rung in his ear. He had traced the last lines of affection to her he loved. He had paid the last duties of religion; and fatigued with the strong excitement which his mind had undergone, he threw himself on his couch and fell into that profound sleep which only despair can give, and which approaches near to annihilation.

He was yet buried in forgetfulness when the jailer came to announce that the fatal hour was come, and for a moment, even after his spirit had resumed her powers, memory still wandered far from the reality. He had not dreamed, but all thought of the last few months had been obliterated, and remembrance escaping from the painful present, lingered fondly over all he had left behind.

It lasted not long, and as all the truth came rushing on his mind, he thought alone of his approaching fate, and to meet it as it became him. His heart, indeed, was

sick of all the instability of this world's things, and for
an instant there was a feeling almost amounting to satisfaction, when he thought that the eternal balancing between hope and fear, between joy and disappointment,
was soon to be over, and that his soul, wearied of change
and doubt, would quickly have peace and certainty. But
then again the lingering ties of earth, the fond warm fel-
lowships of human existence, came strongly upon him,
with all the throng of kindly sympathies that bind us to
this world, and made him shrink from the thought of
breaking them all at once.

This also lasted but a moment—his fate was sealed,
and hurrying over all that might in any degree under-
mine his fortitude, he followed into the court-yard, where
the Prévôt de Lyons and several of the authorities of
the town, with a file of soldiers, waited his coming.

The distance was so short from the place of his confinement to the scaffold where he had beheld for the last
time his unhappy friend Cinq Mars, that the use of a
carriage was dispensed with; and the guard having
formed an avenue through the crowd, the gates having
thrown open to give him exit for the last time.

"Monsieur de Blenau, will you take my arm," said
the Provost of Lyons; "mine is a sad office, sir, but the
arm is not an unfriendly one."

De Blenau, however, declined it with thanks, saying
that he needed no support, and with a priest on one hand
and the provost on the other, he proceeded calmly towards the scaffold, and ascended the steps with a firm
unshaken footstep. The block, and the axe, and the
masked executioner were nothing in De Blenau's eyes
but the mere weak precursors of the one awful event on
which his thoughts were bent, and for which his mind
was now fully prepared. There was but one thought
which could at all shake his fortitude—there was but one
tie to be broken which wrung his heart to break. He
thought of Pauline de Beaumont—but he thought also

that he had merited a better fate; and proudly spurning the weakness that strove to grow upon his heart, he resolved to die as he had lived, worthy of her he loved. The very feeling gave new dignity to his air, and he stood erect and firm while the soldiers were disposed about the scaffold, and his sentence was read aloud by the provost.

A great multitude surrounded the place, and fixed their eyes upon the victim of arbitrary power, as he stood calm and unmoved before them, in the spring of youth and the dignity of conscious innocence. There were few who had not heard of the Count de Blenau, and all that they had heard was good. The heart of man, too, however fallen, has still one spot reserved for the dwelling of compassion, and its very weakness makes it soften to virtue in distress, and often even to forget faults in misfortunes. However that may be, there was a glistening in the eyes of many as they turned their looks towards De Blenau, who, according to the universal custom of the time, advanced to the front of the scaffold to address them. "Good friends," said he, "it is the will of heaven that here I should give back the spirit which has been lent me; and so help me that God into whose bright presence I now go, as I am innocent of any crime towards my king and country!" A murmur ran among the people. "This is my last asseveration," he continued; "and my last counsel to you is, to keep your hearts clear and guiltless, so that if misfortune should follow any one as it has followed me, he may be able to lay his head upon the block as fearlessly as I do now." And retiring a step, he unloosed his collar, and knelt for the stroke of the executioner.

"A horse! A horse! A council messenger! Pardon for the count! Pardon for the count!" cried a thousand voices from the crowd. De Blenau looked up. Headlong down the long narrow street that then led in a straight line from the square, his horse in foam, his hat

left far behind, and his long gray hair flying in the wind,
spurring as if for life, came a horseman, who ever and
anon held up a packet in his hand, and vociferated something that was lost in the distance. He wore the dress
of a lieutenant of the king's forests, and dashing like
lightning through the crowd, that reeled back on every
side as he approached, he paused not till he reached the
foot of the scaffold—threw himself from his horse—
passed unopposed through the guards—rushed up the
steps, and Philip the woodman of Mantes cast himself
at De Blenau's feet. " My noble, noble lord! " exclaimed
the woodman. It was all that he could utter, for his
breath was gone with the rapidity of his progress.

" What is all this? " cried the Provost of Lyons, coming forward. " And why do you stop the execution of
the prisoner, Sir Lieutenant?   What is all this——"

Philip started on his feet. " What is it? " he exclaimed, " why, that none of you blood-sucking wolves
dare put a fang to the count's throat: that's what it is!
There is his pardon, with the king's own signature; ay!
and the cardinal's to boot! At least, so Monsieur de
Chavigni tells me; for being no great clerk, I have not
read it myself."

The provost unfolded the paper and read, " ' Au-
jourd'hui,' etc. Ah! yes, all in form. ' The King having learned that the crimes of the Sieur Claude de Blenau,
Count de Blenau, and Seigneur de Blancford, are not so
heavy as at first appeared, and having investigated—etc.,
has ordained and does ordain—out of his great grace,
etc.—that the sentence of death be changed and com-
muted to perpetual banishment, etc. And if after sixteen
days from the date hereof he be found within the king-
doms of France and Navarre,' etc.—You understand,
Monsieur le Comte.—Well, sir, I congratulate you. Here
is the king's name; ' Louis,' et plus bas, ' Richelieu '—
Will you come and take some refreshment at my poor
lodgings? "

De Blenau was glad to accept the invitation, for his mind was too much confused to fix upon any plan of action at the moment. His resolution had borne him strongly up at the time when all hope seemed lost; but now the sudden change overpowered him; and amidst the acclamations of the multitude, he suffered himself to be conducted in silence to the house of the provost, where he was soon after discovered by his page, Henri de La Mothe.

We shall now pass quickly over the means which he took to procure money for the expenses of the journey before him, merely saying that, through the kindness of the provost, he was soon furnished with the necessary funds for proceeding; and accordingly set out from Lyons the second morning after that, the events of which we have described. Two powerful reasons induced De Blenau to turn his steps towards Spain; in the first place, it was much nearer than either Germany or Flanders, which were the only other countries where he could hope for perfect security; and, in the next place, his road to the frontier passed not only close to his own estates, but skirted the property of Madame de Beaumont, and he was not without hopes of meeting there some that were the dearest to him of the earth; for he learned from Henry de La Mothe, that the vengeance of the implacable Richelieu had extended to Pauline, and her mother, who had been ordered once more to quit the court of France, as a punishment for having conveyed information to him in the Bastile.

Philip the woodman was not forgotten in De Blenau's new arrangements; and under the pretence of charging him with a letter back to St. Germain, in case Madame de Beaumont should not be in Languedoc, the young count seduced him into a promise of accompanying him to Argentière. His real motive, however, was to recompense the woodman's services, on arriving at his own property, in a manner which the scanty state of his finances prevented him from doing at Lyons.

Notwithstanding all the joy he felt at his deliverance, there was a heaviness hung over De Blenau as he rode out of Lyons, which he could not account for, and a sensation of fatigue which he had never felt before. To shorten the road, he beckoned to the woodman, who, with Henri de La Mothe, had dropped a little behind, and made him relate the circumstances which led to his being despatched with the king's pardon to Lyons. Philip's story, which occupied a long while in telling, may be considerably shortened without disadvantage.

It must be remembered, that at the time of De Blenau's liberation from the Bastile, Chavigni had promised, as some compensation for all that Philip had suffered by his means, to have him appointed sous-lieutenant of the forest of Mantes; and he kept his word.

Philip was placed in the office, and exercised its functions, but the actual brevet containing his official appointment had been delayed by a multitude of other affairs pressing for attention, till the statesman's return from Narbonne. At length Philip heard that Chavigni had returned, and that the king, with all the ministers, were once more at St. Germain; and he ventured to wait upon his patron, as he had been desired, to remind him of expediting the brevet. There were several persons waiting, and in his turn he was shown into the statesman's cabinet.

Chavigni had forgotten his face, and asked the simple question, "Who are you?"

Such simple questions, however, often produce more important consequences. "I am the woodman," replied Philip, "who was in prison with the Count de Blenau."

"The Count de Blenau!" exclaimed Chavigni, while an expression of horror passed over his countenance. "By all the saints, I had forgot! Yet, let me see, to-day is Wednesday— there is yet time—stay here a moment!"

and he rushed out of the room, leaving the astonished woodman not knowing at all what he meant. In about a quarter of an hour the statesman returned, breathless with the expedition he had used—"There!" he exclaimed, putting a paper into Philip's hand—"there is his pardon, signed by both the king and the cardinal!—Away! take the swiftest horse in my stable!—lose not a moment, or you will be too late! Use the king's name for fresh horses, and show that signature.—Tell the count, Chavigni has kept his word."

"And where am I to go?" demanded Philip, quietly, still completely ignorant of the cause of Chavigni's agitation.

"To Lyons, to Lyons! you fool!" cried Chavigni. "If you use not all speed, the count's head will be off before you arrive with his pardon."

"The Count de Blenau?" demanded Philip.

"Yes, yes, I tell you!" reiterated the statesman, "your good old friend, the Count de Blenau! So lose no time, if you would save his life."

Philip lost no time, and arrived at Lyons, as we have seen, just at the critical moment of De Blenau's fate.

Though Philip's narrative served to interest De Blenau, and the chattering of Henri de La Mothe to amuse him on the way, nevertheless he could not conceal from himself that there was a lassitude gradually growing upon him, which seemed to announce the approach of some serious sickness. Naturally of a strong constitution, and an ardent temperament, he never yielded to indisposition, till unable to sustain it any longer; and though fatigue, anxiety, and distress had weakened him much, and his two attendants often hinted that he looked unwell, and required repose, De Blenau would not acknowledge that he was ill, until he arrived in the neighborhood of Tournon. There, however, the powers of nature failed him, and he felt that he could proceed no farther. Scarcely able to sit his horse, he entered the town, and looked

30

eagerly about for some place where he could repose,
when suddenly the eyes of Henri de La Mothe rested
upon the well-known sign of the Sanglier Gourmand,
which, as they afterwards found, was still kept by no
other person than the celebrated Jacques Chatpilleur, who
had at last been driven from the neighborhood of the
Bastile by the wrathful governor, for one of his drunken
achievements, very similar to the one recounted in a
former chapter, and had taken refuge in his native place,
Tournon.   Here De Blenau alighted, and was conveyed
to a bed-chamber, where he was soon attacked by a violent
fever, which rapidly increased.   Delirium followed; and
he quickly lost all remembrance of surrounding objects,
though the name of Pauline de Beaumont would often
tremble on his tongue, and he fancied that he saw a
thousand airy shapes hovering round his bed, and constantly reminding him of her he loved.

In about twenty days the disease had run its course,
and passed away, leaving him in a state of excessive
weakness; but, in the meantime, the fever, which had
nearly destroyed De Blenau, had entirely ruined the unhappy Jacques Chatpilleur.   The report spread through
Tournon, that the aubergiste had a malignant sickness
raging in his house; and instead of coming thither, as
usual, for the good things of this life, the citizens not
only passed his door without entering, but even crossed
over the way, as they went through the street, to be as
far as possible from the infected air.   For some days
after he discovered this defection, melancholy preyed upon
the unhappy aubergiste; but suddenly he seemed to have
taken a bold resolution; pulled down his sign; put by
his pots and pans; resumed his gaiety; and no sooner did
De Blenau talk of once more proceeding, than Jacques
Chatpilleur laid before him his sad condition, and prayed,
as an act of justice, that he would take him with him into
Spain, and suffer him to be his lordship's cook.

De Blenau had not the heart to deny him; but another

thing came now to be considered. The time which, according to the ordinance of the king, had been allowed him for the purpose of quitting the realm, had long expired, and he was now virtually an outlaw. Every one was called upon to deliver him up as an exile returned without grace, and by law his blood could be required at the hand of no one who shed it. These circumstances, though not very agreeable in themselves, would have given De Blenau but little concern, had not the Judge Lafemas been still in his immediate neighborhood. But from his vindictive spirit he had everything to fear if discovered within the precincts of France after the allotted time had expired; and in consequence he determined to travel by night, as soon as his strength was sufficiently restored, and to effect his escape into Spain with as little delay as possible.

Jacques Chatpilleur applied himself with all the vigor of an ancien vivandier to re-establish his new lord in his former robust health, and succeeded so well as to leave but little traces of all that fever and anxiety had done upon his frame. In the meantime, Henri de La Mothe took care to prepare secretly everything for their departure; and Philip the woodman, who was somewhat balanced between a wish to return to his family, and love for the good young count, determined to follow him to the frontier, as soon as he heard that his life was at the mercy of any one who chose to take it.

Under these circumstances, one clear autumn night, towards twelve o'clock, De Blenau sallied forth from the little town of Tournon, accompanied by the somewhat curious escort of the innkeeper, the woodman, and the page, and proceeding silently and cautiously, arrived safely in the neighborhood of La Voulte, where, betaking themselves to one of the large open fields of the country, the party reposed themselves under the mulberry-trees, which by this time had been long stripped both of their green leaves and their silken balls, but which still offered some degree of concealment, and something to which they could attach their horses.

At noon, Jacques Chatpilleur, as the most expert, was despatched to the town for some provisions, which commission he executed with great zeal and discretion, and returning, informed De Blenau that he had seen a gentleman in black pass through the town, accompanied by a considerable train, habited in the same sad color.

As De Blenau conjectured that this might be Lafemas, it was determined to take additional precautions, and rather to live upon scanty fare than send into any town again; and setting off as soon as it was dark, they passed by Privas, and reached the skirts of the thick wood that began about Aubenas, and sweeping round La Gorce extended almost to Viviers on the one side, and to L'Argentière on the other. Near to Viviers lay the estates of the Marchioness de Beaumont, and within a league of Argentière was the Château de Blenau; but it was towards the former that De Blenau bent his steps as soon as the second night had come. Before they had gone far, it began to rain hard, and though the wood afforded some covering, yet the lateness of the season had stripped it of all that could yield any efficient shelter, except at a spot where two evergreen oaks, growing together like twin-brothers, spread their still verdant branches over a considerable space of ground. De Blenau was inclined to proceed as quickly as possible; but Jacques Chatpilleur, who now acted as body physician as well as cook, so strongly cautioned his lord to avoid the wet, that the whole party betook themselves to the shelter of the oaks, in hopes of the rain passing away.

Before them lay a considerable tract of road, upon which, after about half an hour of heavy rain, the moon began to shine once more; and De Blenau was about to proceed, when the sound of horses was heard upon the very path which they had just passed. De Blenau and his party drew back as quietly as possible behind the

trees, and though the horses' feet still made some noise,
the water dropping from the branches of the forest was
enough to cover the sound. Scarcely, however, were
they themselves concealed, when a horseman appeared
upon the road in a sombre-colored suit, with some one
riding on his right hand, whom De Blenau judged to
be an inferior, from the bending position in which he
listened to what the other said. Six servants followed
at a little distance, and a straggler brought up the rear,
wringing the wet from the skirts of his doublet. One
by one, they passed slowly by; the uncertain light showing them to be well armed and mounted, but still not
shining sufficiently to allow De Blenau the opportunity
of considering their features, though he thought that the
form of the first rider was in some degree familiar to
him. It was not unlike that of Lafemas, yet as far as he
could judge, taller and more erect. The cavalcade
passed on, and were seen winding down the road in the
moonlight, till they came opposite to a spot where some
felled timber and blocks of stone embarrassed the ground.
Immediately that they arrived there, there was a bright
flash, the report of a carbine, and one of the horses fell
suddenly to the ground. In a moment, nine or ten
horsemen, and two or three on foot rushed forth from
the wood, and the clashing of steel, the report of pistols,
and various cries of wrath or agony come sweeping upon
the gale.

"Were it Lafemas himself," cried De Blenau, "this
must not be! En avant pour la France!" and dashing
his rowels into the horse's side, he galloped headlong
down the road, followed by the woodman, the page, and
the redoubtable Jacques Chatpilleur.

Two moments brought them to the scene of the combat, and the moon shining out seemed expressly to light
the fray. The one party was evidently to be distinguished
by their black habits, the other by their rusty cuirasses
and morions. Directly in the way of De Blenau was the

cavalier he had marked as he passed, contending with a man of almost gigantic strength; but, notwithstanding the superior force of the latter, his antagonist still foiled him by his skilful defence, when suddenly one of the robbers on foot attacked the cavalier also behind. Thus beset, he turned to strike him down, when the tremendous Norman (for it was no other) caught his bridle rein, and urging the horse back, threw him to the ground. The robber on foot shortened the pike he carried to plunge it in his body. But by this time De Blenau's party had come up; and the courageous aubergiste galloping on, bore the point of his long sword in a direct line forward, which catching the pikeman just below the cuirass, spitted him, to use Jacques Chatpilleur's own expression, just like a widgeon.

In the meanwhile, the Norman had turned upon De Blenau, and snapped a pistol at his head, which, however, missed fire. Enraged at his disappointment, he threw the weapon from him, and spurring on his horse aimed a tremendous blow at the count, which was instantly parried, and returned by a straightforward lunge that cut him above the eye, and deluged his face in blood. Mad with the pain, and half-blinded with the gore, Marteville attempted once more the feat by which he had overthrown his former antagonist; and, catching De Blenau's rein, urged his horse back with Herculean strength. In vain the count spurred him forward; he sank upon his haunches, and was floundering in the fall, when De Blenau, finding it inevitable, let go the rein, fixed his knees firm in the saddle, and, raising his sword with both hands, discharged it with all his force upon the head of the Norman. The true steel passed clear on, hewed through the iron morion, cleft through hair and skull, and sank deep into his brain. He reeled in the saddle; his hands let go their grasp, and he fell headlong to the ground, while the horse of De Blenau, suddenly released from the pressure, rose up, and plunging forward trod

The Norman catching De Blenau's rein, urged his horse back with
Herculean strength.   Page 470.

Richelieu.

him under its feet. De Blenau lost not his presence of mind for a moment, and while his horse was yet in the spring, he aimed a blow at the Gros St. Nicholas, who had been hurrying to the assistance of his captain, which disabled his shoulder, and threw him from his horse. " Sauve qui peut! " cried the robber, starting up on his feet and running for the wood, " Sauve qui peut! The captain is dead! "

" Sauve qui peut! Sauve qui peut! " rang among the robbers, and in a few minutes De Blenau and his party were left masters of the field. The count drew up his horse, exclaiming, " Do not follow! do not follow! Let us look to the wounded: " and dismounting he hurried to assist the fallen cavalier, who was struggling to disengage himself from his horse.

" Next to God, sir, I have to thank you," said the stranger, as soon as he had risen. " But—is it possible! Monsieur De Blenau! " he exclaimed as the moonlight gleamed on the countenance of the count. " God of heaven, I thought you were in Spain long ago! "

" Monsieur de Chavigni! or I am mistaken," said De Blenau. " But I know that I can trust to your honor, and therefore must say, that, though my late illness may have rendered me an outlaw, by detaining me in France after my sentence of exile, yet I will not regret it, as it has given me the opportunity of serving the man to whom I am indebted for my life.—There, sir, is my hand."

Chavigni embraced him warmly. " Let us look to the men who are wounded, Monsieur de Blenau," said he, " and then I will give you a piece of news, which, however painful to me, will be satisfactory to you.—Cannot some one strike a light, that we may examine more carefully what has occurred on this unhappy spot; for I see many on the earth? "

" It shall be done in the turning of a spit, monseigneur," said Jacques Chatpilleur, who had already collected some dry wood; and who now quickly produced a fire by means of the flint of a pistol.

The scene that presented itself was a sad one. On the earth lay two of Chavigni's servants dead, and one desperately wounded. To these was added Henri de La Mothe, who had received a severe cut on the head, and was stunned with the blow. Not far from the body of the Norman lay his companion Callot, who was the pikeman despatched by the bellicose aubergiste. In addition to these was a robber, whose head had been nearly severed from his body by the cutlass which was borne by Philip the woodman, in his capacity of lieutenant of the king's forests; and one so severely wounded by a pistol-ball from the hand of Chavigni, that his companions had been obliged to abandon him. From him they learned that the attack upon Chavigni had been preconcerted; that understanding he was bending his steps toward Montpellier, Marteville had obtained exact information of his course; and finding that he must pass through the forest by Viviers, had lain in wait for him, with the expectation both of revenge and plunder.

"And now, Monsieur de Blenau," said Chavigni, as soon as their investigation ended, "whither does your immediate path lay? You know you can trust me."

"I do," said De Blenau. "I go first towards Viviers, to the château of the late Marquis de Beaumont."

"And I go there, too," said Chavigni. "I am even now expected; for I sent forward a servant to announce my coming."

"Indeed!" exclaimed De Blenau. "May I ask your errand?"

A faint smile curled Chavigni's lip, which was uncommonly pale. "You will hear on my arrival," said he; "for I see you are ignorant of what has lately taken place, though the couriers must have arrived in all the towns three days ago.—But let us have our wounded brought along, and we will proceed to the château.—It cannot be far distant."

The preparations were soon made—the château was soon reached—and Pauline de Beaumont was soon once more clasped in the arms of her lover.—But let all that pass.

"Madame," said Chavigni, advancing to the marchioness, " you doubtless wonder as much as Monsieur de Blenau, what can have brought me hither. But as I came to Montpellier, I had the king's commands to inform you, that the fine which was imposed upon your estates is remitted in full. And to you, Monsieur De Blenau, I have to announce, that your banishment is at an end, for his majesty has given permission to all exiles to return to France, with a very few exceptions, amongst which you are not included.—I need not tell you from these circumstances, that—the Cardinal de Richelieu is dead!"

"Good God!" exclaimed De Blenau, "so soon!"

"Even so!" replied Chavigni. "Monsieur de Blenau, doubtless you are happy—for he was your enemy.—But he was to me a friend—he was nearly a father, and I mourn for him."

"May he rest in peace!" said De Blenau. "He was a great man. May he rest in peace!"

Little more remains to be said; for this long history draws towards its close. The sorrows, the dangers, and the difficulties which had so long surrounded De 'Blenau and Pauline, had now passed away, like the storms of a summer day, that overcloud the morning, but leave the evening calm and fair. They were united—in the beautiful valleys of Languedoc, and in the fair scenes where they had first met, they continued to live on in happiness and love, till the hand of time led them gently to the grave.

That generation and its events have passed away; but there still remains one record of the hero of this tale: for in a little village church, between Argentière and Viviers, stands a fine marble tomb, with the figure of a knight sculptured in a recumbent posture. Underneath is engraven the date—one thousand six hundred and eighty-five, with the simple inscription,

" Ci git Claude, Comte de Blenau."

THE END

www.ingramcontent.com/pod-product-compliance
Lightning Source LLC
Chambersburg PA
CBHW020919020726
47495CB00002B/255